NAIMISHA

GOD'S OWN STORY - THE END GAME

Check, Check & Mate

SESHA

INDIA • SINGAPORE • MALAYSIA

Narayanam Namaskritya Naram Chaiva Narottamam

Deveem Sarasvateem Vyaasam Tato Jayamudeerayet

Disclaimer

This book is a work of fiction superimposed on the epics of Mahabharat and Srimadbhagavatham with the intent to retell the story from a different angle. The fictional characters and their interactions with the epic characters are all created out of the author's imagination. The same holds good for the events and interactions between epic characters and the interpretation and deviations from the standard texts.

While the content has references to religion, beliefs and myths they are intended to present the story in an interesting way. The author makes no claim to the correctness of the historical, theological or mythological references implied in the story.

Any resemblance to actual persons, however remote, is not intented and inferences of such resemblances, if any, is only coincidental.

Contents

Contents

Prologue

Naimisha

"Would there be a truce? Could they arrive at some compromise? Could they call the game a draw?"

"Could they go on ruling two separate kingdoms after what all happened and co-exist peacefully?"

"Or would they prefer to settle the scores in a battle to end all battles?"

Animish did not doubt as to what would happen. The war between Kauravas and Pandavas was inevitable. All the earlier happenings and the deep-rooted ill feelings between Kauravas and Pandavas left no scope for a peaceful and permanent solution.

The epic end game was in the offing. Time was ticking, destiny was beckoning, and history was about to be created. In the end game of Chaturanga, the royals play, one of the kings ought to get checkmated.

Animish wished that there would be no war, though he knew it was inevitable. War might decide who is mightier but never who is righteous, and in a war between royals, it is the soldiers who die in large numbers, leaving their families as orphans. He would be one among the multiple witnesses to the historic war when it happened, Animish reflected.

Dwaraka

The arrival of a messenger from the Matsya kingdom was announced when Krishna and Balarama were in the court. The news of the successful completion of the Pandavas' Ajnatavasa, the period of exile in disguise, brought a surge of joy and relief to the royal family and, more particularly, to Subhadra, Krishna's sister and Abhimanyu's mother, who was eagerly counting the days anticipating the news for the past many days. They all knew that the period of thirteen-year exile had been completed and Pandavas would resurface any time, though nobody knew in which place.

Another news the messenger brought doubled their joy. Subhadra's son Abhimanyu's marriage to King Virata's daughter was to happen shortly, as Arjuna and Virata decided. They gathered from the messenger about the victories of Pandavas over the forces of Susharma of the Trigarta kingdom as well as that of Hastinapur. Arjuna's heroics were cheered on by the courtiers when the messenger narrated the sequence of events and the outcomes.

Soon, a large contingent of Dwarakites, their colourful attire and festive mood adding to the excitement, accompanied Subhadra and the groom Abhimanyu, carrying several gifts to present to the bride. Krishna and Balarama led the contingent, along with Satyaki and a retinue of trusted aides, and set out for the Matsya kingdom, where the wedding festivities were to take place.

On their way, a curious Balarama asked Krishna whether he anticipated that Pandavas would resurface in the Matsya kingdom. Krishna, his voice filled with a mix of admiration and intrigue, replied, 'I only started to think that it must be where they were hiding after we heard the news about Kichaka's death. Until then, there was no hint about their existence. I must say that they had perfectly maintained the secrecy.'

Balarama expressed, 'I, too, thought that way. I wonder how they remained unrecognised in the Matsya kingdom for one year. Kichaka's killing is a giveaway, and it was unwise for Pandavas to resort to that. I have a feeling that even Duryodhana thought along the same lines and knew that Pandavas were hiding in Matsya. That explains why he picked up a fight to capture the cows, a move that would bring Pandavas to the battlefront.'

'We have to learn the answers to these questions only through Pandavas, whom we will shortly be meeting. Anyway, don't say Duryodhana knew Pandavas were hiding in Matsya. At the best, he could have guessed. There is a big difference between guessing and knowing. Don't you agree?'

Balarama did not answer but asked another question. 'We heard that Arjuna spent a long period in Indra's kingdom. Is it not a breach of stated terms that prescribed Pandavas to spend twelve years in forests?'

'One might say that, but did Arjuna go there on his own volition? He was meditating in the forest; his purpose was to procure better weaponry. He had no desire to enjoy his time in Indra's place while his brothers and Draupadi were languishing in the forests. Indra took him to train and used him to get rid of his long-time rivals, Kalakeyas and Pulomas, as Gurudakshina, and then sent him back. There was no violation on Arjuna's part. Incidentally, that is where Arjuna perfected the art of single-handedly subduing large armies, which he displayed in the Virata war.'

Balarama thought and reflected, 'Even if he was capable of that feat, was it prudent of Arjuna to demonstrate that against his kinsmen? He should have announced himself and proposed a truce, more so if the period of Ajnatavasa was completed. Isn't it belligerent upon his part to take on his cousins, gurus and his grandfather?'

Krishna looked at his brother in surprise. *Was it not proper for Kauravas to release the cows and not fight with Arjuna? Why did they take on Arjuna in a fierce battle?*

'It was Kauravas who came all the way to fish out Pandavas. Arjuna was alone facing them and left them in no doubt about his identity, sporting his Gandiva. Was there a point in Kauravas battling for a few cows, having recognised Arjuna? That they preferred to attack Arjuna instead of honourably retreating reveals their true intentions. They are not going to return their kingdom to Pandavas. I think a bigger war is in the offing.'

'I also think the war is certain unless you intervene,' said Balarama.

Krishna did not respond. A thought cropped up in his mind, triggered by his brother's earlier question. Knowing him well, Krishna understood Arjuna's intention to demonstrate to Kauravas the taste of his abilities without a wish to kill any of his kinsmen and elders.

If a full-scale war unto death is to be fought with Kauravas, Krishna wondered, could Arjuna display a similar vigour to fight his grandfather, preceptor, and kinsmen and take their lives? Would he display the same nerve when it is a battle unto death?

Chapter 1

Looming War Clouds

Upaplavya

Upaplavya was a bustling town within the kingdom of Matsya, strategically close to the kingdom of Hastinapur. Following their period of exile, Pandavas made it their temporary home.

Virata was thoroughly surprised when the true identities of Pandavas and Draupadi, who had been in his service for the last one year, were revealed to him the day after the victorious Virata war. He was initially shocked to find them seated in his courtroom, fully dressed in royal attire, in the seats meant for royals. It was his son Uttar Kumara who told him about their true identities, stating that it was not him but Arjuna who had single-handedly defeated Kauravas and rescued the cows. Virata's surprise turned into a delight when he realised that Pandavas, and more so Yudhishthira, had considered him and his kingdom worthy enough for their Ajnatavasa. His gratitude towards Pandavas for saving him and his kingdom from the attacks multiplied once Pandavas' real identities were revealed. He offered to give his daughter Uttara to Arjuna in marriage to cement their relationship. Arjuna politely declined, saying he considered Uttara as his daughter, having been her preceptor for the past one year. However, he made a counteroffer that his son Abhimanyu, who was more suitable, would marry Uttara instead. Virata was glad to agree and decided to perform the marriage at Upaplavya, where Pandavas could stay till they finalised their further course of action.

Invitations were sent to friendly kings announcing the marriage of Abhimanyu and Uttara. Numerous allies and well-wishers of Pandavas flocked to Upaplavya to witness the wedding and greet Pandavas whom they had not seen for years.

Yadavas arrived in force, accompanying the bridegroom, Abhimanyu, and his mother, Subhadra. Arjuna beamed with pride seeing his son, Abhimanyu, now a skilled and handsome young man. Pradyumna told Arjuna that he had trained Abhimanyu and Upapandavas, and all of them would make their fathers proud. He playfully suggested that Abhimanyu was exceptional in all phases of warfare and would surpass his illustrious father on the battlefield, a remark that brought joy to Arjuna immensely. He thanked Pradyumna for his excellent support.

Drupada, accompanied by his sons Shikhandi and Dhrishtadyumna, came along with Upapandavas and a contingent of Srinjaya and Panchala warriors. The wedding was a joyous affair as the guests were happy to reunite with Pandavas. King Virata graciously hosted all the dignitaries who graced the occasion.

Once the formalities concluded, attention turned to strategic deliberations among Pandavas and their supporters. Except for Balarama, all others had taken a stand that Duryodhana would not respect the soft pleas and that the emissary being sent should talk firmly and demand the return of the empire as per the terms of the agreement. After detailed discussions, it was decided to send the scholarly purohit of Drupada to Dhritarashtra's court to stake Pandavas' claim based on the successful completion of the contractual terms.

Simultaneously, it was decided to send emissaries to different kingdoms requesting support, as they were sure that Duryodhana would not agree to a peaceful solution. Several neutral kings were close to both Kauravas and Pandavas, and hence, it was considered prudent to approach as many of them as possible before their counterparts made the overture.

Both Drupada and Virata busied themselves to send their emissaries to all the kings around.

Hastinapur

Duryodhana, flanked by Dusshasana, Karna and Shakuni, heard the report of the meeting of Upaplavya through the spies, who disclosed as much information as they could garner.

'My guess is correct. Pandavas are preparing to wage a full-scale war. They had sent their emissaries to all the places seeking support, even before they sent a word to Hastinapur claiming the return of Indraprastha.' Duryodhana continued, 'It only means that they were not sure of convincing my father that they had fully abided by the terms of the contract.'

Shakuni had a twinkle in his eyes and a twist in his tongue while saying, 'Or, they were sure that we would not allow him to get convinced.'

'We have information that Pandavas did not reveal their identities for one full day after the Virata war, which gives rise to suspicion that Yudhishthira was unsure that the one year of Ajnatavasa was completed when Arjuna faced us.'

Dusshasana continued, 'Even Draupadi was reported to have sought a few more days when Virata's queen asked her to leave them after the gruesome killing of Kichaka and his brothers, which shows that they are at least a few days short after killing Kichaka as per their calculations. Though they could have spent more than thirteen years in all, as suggested by Grand Sire, they might not have completed the exact one-year period of incognito existence as per the terms. Only they knew precisely when the period of exile commenced. Whatever extra time they spent in Aranyavasa is not to be reckoned.'

Duryodhana looked pleased with his brother's assured words and remarked, 'The point is that we found them before they presented themselves to the world as Pandavas. It is their mistake that they had not announced themselves as soon as the stipulated period expired and waited for us to find them.'

Karna joined the conversation. 'Had they completed the terms of the contract and approached Hastinapur, the Kingdom of Indraprastha could have been handed over to them. But their very mobilisation of armies and spreading the word about the possible war puts the question in a different light. It amounts to their asking Duryodhana to either return the kingdom or that they would gain it by force.'

'It is nothing but a threat, and we shall counter it with every means at our disposal. How about sending our emissaries afresh to all the places calling for support?' enquired Duryodhana.

'I am right on the job, Brother! We have already sounded many of them earlier and have been assured of their support. We will ask them again to mobilise their armies and meet us. I would personally monitor to ensure we contact all those who matter,' replied Dusshasana.

Shakuni suggested, 'My dear nephew, I suggest you need to visit one place yourself personally, and you know where!'

'Yes, of course. You mean Dwaraka. What would be the use of meeting Krishna, who turned out to be a complete champion of Pandavas' cause? Does it serve any purpose, I wonder!?

Shakuni gave his wisdom in reply to Duryodhana's question, 'It would count. It seems Balarama suggested that they should adopt a soft tone when dealing with this sensitive matter, particularly because Yudhishthira lost the kingdom entirely through his fault of being an inept dice player. He said that he was advising so in the best interest of both Pandavas and Kauravas. However, Satyaki went against this line and said that you would understand only the language of harshness and took a hard line that there need not be any appealing tone by the emissary being sent here, but he should be rather demanding. His line carried the day as Drupada and Virata, too, took the same line. Your visit to Dwaraka will help you understand the ground realities firsthand. If you could clinch Balarama on our side, the win would be assured even without war since Krishna would not dare face his elder brother. Even if Balarama remains neutral, it acts as a deterrent for others to join Krishna. However, do not bypass Krishna, whose word is a command in Dwaraka. You need to meet him first and seek his help. Let us attempt to sway the situation in our favour.'

'I will start tomorrow itself,' announced Duryodhana.

Chapter 2

War Yet to Come

Indraprastha and Hastinapur

The news of the impending conflict loomed over Indraprastha and Hastinapur, casting a shadow of fear and uncertainty. It became the topic of intense discussion among the subjects, as well as the sages and ashramites dwelling in nearby forests, including Naimisha.

'Are we going to get back our King Yudhishthira to rule us again?' A young wife had asked her soldier husband in Indraprastha. She heard whispers from neighbours that Pandavas had set up a camp near Upaplavya and would soon march forward to battle with Hastinapur.

'Who knows? Some discussions are surely underway, though we do not know how both groups settle between themselves. Anyway, I am being called for training to prepare myself for the war in case it happens.'

'You are fighting for Pandavas, aren't you?' pressed the wife, expecting her husband to reply, 'Yes'. She and her friends were quite agitated about the reported way Draupadi was treated thirteen years back. There was no dearth of different stories, each more harrowing than the previous, that had done rounds about what happened on that fateful day, though no one could say for sure what really had happened. Each believed the version they heard and were willing to accept. She vividly remembered the pall of gloom that had engulfed the twin cities of Hastinapur and Indraprastha in that period.

The young man shifted uncomfortably. 'Hope so! We are not sure about that at this stage. We work under a chief who would decide on his own, and then we would know to whom we would be fighting. On whichever side I will be asked to fight, it makes no difference to me. Whichever side I fight for, I only hope and pray I don't face familiar faces on the opposite side.'

The woman's initial excitement turned into deep-seated fear once she realised the gravity of the situation and the precarious position her family was put into. The potential loss and suffering that the war could bring to her family became a stark reality, overshadowing any initial enthusiasm.

The man held her hand to reassure her. 'I hope I will come back to you and tell you the stories of war.' 'Sure you will,' replied the woman, resting her hand on his shoulder as if to steady both their hearts.

Similar conversations took place in various households of Hastinapur and Indraprastha. The overall mood was gloomy, with the women folk's growing apprehensions about the war outcomes and the unintended personal sacrifices they were about to make. Amidst this grim mood, all the able men were readying themselves for the war and started reporting to their respective masters for training. They would be paid in gold in advance before going to war, which they could give to their families and kiss them goodbye. They would get something extra if they survived the war and ended up on the winning side. A soldier is safe if he is not drafted into the war, but why is he a soldier in the first place if he does not use the opportunity? The uncertainty of the war's outcome hung heavy in the air, adding to the prevailing sense of dread.

People's daily discussions revolved around past events, present developments, and future outcomes. Each new piece of information triggered fresh debates.

'Pandavas were the legitimate heirs of the entire Hastinapur kingdom, their father once ruled. However, they were given only a portion of the kingdom, and even that was taken away from them. Now it is not being given back.'

'It was entirely Yudhishthira's mistake. Why should Yudhishthira agree to such terms of wager? Why should he have played the game of dice itself? If he had placed himself at the mercy of Duryodhana, it is entirely his fault.'

'Some say the dice was loaded. The game was not fair, and it seems Yudhishthira was tricked.'

'It was much debated and a thing of the past. What if Yudhishthira had won? He would have got the entire kingdom, and perhaps he wished that it might happen like that. Only one can win, and the other will get blamed in a game of that sort.'

'The question now is not about the fairness of the game or the terms of wager. The question is whether Pandavas completed one year of incognito existence in the court of Virata or whether they were discovered at the last minute.'

'Only those who do not want to be on the side of dharma would say that. Even if it was breached technically by a few days, it should not matter. Dhritarashtra could condone that and invite Pandavas. The fact remains that they spent twelve long years in forests and served in positions unbecoming of their birth and past status in humiliating disguises in the last one year. It is only fair that the kingdom was given back honourably.'

'The emissary from Pandavas had come and gone but without any positive assurance. The king has told him that he would send an emissary from his side to Yudhishthira.'

'Whom did he send?'

'It was Sanjaya who was sent, and we do not know what happened afterwards. So far, there is no declaration of war either. We do not get the full information as to what exactly happened in those emissary meetings. Meanwhile, we can see the march of armies of various kingdoms passing through our village in support of either of them.'

Someone came running towards the chattering group.

'Latest news! Srikrishna is approaching Hastinapur to broker peace between the two sides. He will also be passing through a village next to us.'

There was a sudden change of mood in the group. All of them seemed excited upon hearing the news. Krishna was a close relative to both sides and well respected. One of his worthy sons, Samba, married the princess of Hastinapur, Lakshmana, the daughter of Duryodhana. Krishna was a cousin of Pandavas, and his sister Subhadra was married to Arjuna. Both the groups respect him as the upholder of justice, and nobody dares to cross his words. He had already acquired the status of a God and was widely recognised as such.

'This perhaps is the last hope for peace,' They agreed. *If there was one who could really prevent the war, it was Krishna.*

People started planning to move to nearby villages, which were on Krishna's expected route, *Hari-Yana,* from Upaplavya to Hastinapur, to wait for and have a glimpse of Srikrishna, who was to them nothing but an incarnation of Vishnu himself.

Naimisha

Ever since the Pandavas resurfaced, evening discussions in the ashrams of Naimisha grew longer and more fervent. Fast-changing political developments were the subject of intense debate. Hermitages like those of Vedavyasa and Little Master became hubs of lively discussions, where people speculated on war's inevitability and its potential outcomes.

The conversations were often polarised, driven by personal biases and conjectures. The discussions within groups of nameless multitude reflected their different perceptions and beliefs.

Person 1: When Pandavas completed the terms of the contract, where was the need for a war? Why can't they be given the throne of Indraprastha as agreed upon earlier?

Person 2: It is not that simple. There is a difference between Pandavas who played the dice game thinking it was friendly and those who returned now with bitter enmity. They had grouped no less than seven akshauhinis before sending their emissary to Hastinapur to claim their stake. The emissary, Drupada's Purohit, stated their strength and almost threatened dire consequences if the kingdom was not handed back. Duryodhana's camp took a stand that there was no point in parting with Indraprastha at this stage as Pandavas were sworn enemies now. Having them rule the neighbouring Indraprastha is more dangerous now than ever. Both groups can't be friends even if the kingdom is returned. A war will break out eventually. The game of dice has changed everything irrevocably.

Person 3: Whatever it might be, how can their claim be refuted?

Person 2: Karna openly declared that Duryodhana would give away anything for the sake of dharma but would not cede an inch on being threatened. Pandavas claimed their kingdom after mobilising armies. What do you say about that?

Person 3: You mean to say that Pandavas did not complete the contract terms thoroughly?

Person 2: Perhaps that was what Karna was alluding to. The time calculations of both camps differ. That could be one reason why Pandavas were making war preparations even before Dhritarashtra's mind was known.

Person 3: That is an unfair inference. Had Pandavas wanted to flout the terms and declare war, why would they wait till now? The fact is, Pandavas knew Duryodhana's mind better than others, and that was a good enough reason for them to mobilise support. They were sure that Duryodhana would not be amenable to gentle persuasion. That's why they gathered support from all over to put pressure on Duryodhana, though they had completed the terms of the contract.

Person 2: That was a false notion in itself. Would threats cow down Duryodhana? The moment he knew that Pandavas started mobilising support, he quickly sounded his supporters and raised as many as eleven Akshauhinis to fight on his side.

Person 3: Duryodhana did not wait for Pandavas to mobilise their armies before he acted. He had thirteen years to cultivate support for himself for the eventual war.

Person 1: Anyway, let us discuss the present. What was Dhritarashtra's reply to Pandavas' emissary?

Person 2: Dhritarashtra was too shrewd to say either 'yes' or 'no' in such a situation and sent back Pandavas' emissary with all honours, stating that his emissary would soon follow him to meet Yudhishthira with his message. Later, he sent Sanjaya with his message.

Person 1: Sanjaya was the right person. He knew the mind and the thought process of Dhritarashtra, as well as the psychology of Yudhishthira.

Person 4: Where is the need for another emissary? I do not fathom it. If the Kauravas wanted to honour the original agreement, they should simply accept parting with the Indraprastha kingdom. If they found any breach, they should point out and reject the claim. What might be the message Sanjaya is carrying? I am curious to know.

Person 2: We all are. We might know the message and also the reply soon.

These conversations took place before Sanjaya went to Yudhishthira carrying a message from Dhritarashtra. People in different places continued to discuss in groups, as the parleys between Pandavas and Kauravas progressed.

Person 1: Sanjaya had returned from Upaplavya, and he failed to persuade Yudhishthira to back out from the war. In fact, Sanjaya did not offer anything in return to Pandavas for not claiming the Indraprastha. We do not know how Dhritarashtra even thought such a proposition would be acceptable to Pandavas.

Person 2: Dhritarashtra is not naive enough to think that the Pandavas would agree. He knew Duryodhana would not listen to his advice. He hoped to appeal to Yudhishthira's sensitivities by pointing out the perils of war and the destruction of Kuru Vamsha. He has chosen Sanjaya because he is agreeable to Pandavas, and they would listen to his words.

Person 3: Wishful thinking! How can Pandavas withdraw from both their claim to the kingdom and war? They must have refused the proposal straight away.

Person 2: Yes, Sanjaya returned and conveyed Pandava's response to Dhritarashtra. It looks like the war is inevitable, except in the case of a miraculous change of Duryodhan's mind. The good news is that Krishna himself has proposed to visit Hastinapur to give his wise counsel!

Person 3: Yes, it is undoubtedly a great hope!

Person 4: Many sages are also visiting Hastinapur for the same purpose. They are all unanimous in their opinion that the war would be devastating and that no one would benefit from it.

At this stage, the group dispersed. Excitement and apprehension grew in equal measure as Krishna's mission became the focus of everyone's hopes. For many, he was the last beacon of hope in a time of looming chaos.

Chapter 3

Ajnatavasa Unravelled

Naimisha

While the discussions of war and alliances were underway, Naimishites could finally unveil the secret tales of Pandavas' year in hiding. Unbelievable, as it appeared in the first hearing, it satisfied the curiosity of many as it answered many lingering questions: How did Kichaka meet his end? What was the offence for which he was killed? How could Pandavas conceal their identities for an entire year? Most of the story emanated from Shamyaprasa through Vaishampayana's disciples, and it answered many questions pertaining to the mysterious existence of Pandavas during Ajnatavasa. Vaishampayana's reputation of being close to Vyasa lent credibility to this extraordinary tale.

After examining various options, Pandavas chose the kingdom of Matsya for their year of incognito exile. They entered the kingdom under assumed names one after another, not to raise suspicion. They duly disguised themselves in appropriate outfits, each adopting a unique role to mask their identities.

Yudhishthira, the first to enter the kingdom, disguised himself in Brahmin attire. He presented himself as a Dwija and claimed himself to be an expert dice player named Kanka, once entertained by Yudhishthira as a friend. He found immediate favour with the dice-loving Virata, who accepted him as a friend and took him into service.

Bhima came next to introduce himself as Vallava, an experienced cook in the royal kitchens of Indraprastha and a favourite cook of Yudhishthira. He also said wrestling was his hobby, and he could entertain the king wrestling with lions and tigers. Virata wondered at the bright lustre of his muscular body, uncommon for an ordinary cook, and immediately took him as the chef of the royal kitchen. All the existing kitchen staff were placed under him.

Soon after, Draupadi arrived in the city, her hair knotted and dressed in a soiled sari. Appearing as a sairandhri, a maid skilled in hairstyling and garland making, she walked on the main streets of the city. Her exceptional beauty and the attire of sairandhri attracted the attention of curious onlookers who stopped to ask her questions. Queen Sudeshna, meanwhile, noticed her from the balcony and called her in. Draupadi introduced herself as Malini and said that she had worked as sairandhri for Satyabhama of Dwaraka and Draupadi of Indraprastha. She further informed that it was Draupadi who named her Malini, having been pleased with her skill in making flower garlands. Sudeshna was tempted to employ someone like Malini, who has such high credentials, but also harboured doubts about hiring someone so beautiful. Malini's beauty might attract unwanted attention from men, even including her husband, who may be enamoured of Malini's beauty. Draupadi, realising Sudeshna's apprehensions, informed her that she was the wife of five Gandharvas, and they would protect her from anyone who dared approach her improperly. She is devoted to her husbands and would not flinch from dharma at any cost. Satisfied with this assurance, Sudeshna accepted Malini, aka Draupadi, into her household on honourable terms.

Soon, one day, Virata, on his visit to the goshala, found a bright man in gopalak's attire in conversation with other gopalaks. Upon enquiry, Virata found that the stranger had previously functioned as the chief of Yudhishthira's goshala, looking after his vast cow wealth, which numbered close to eight lakhs. He was now looking for a suitable employment. Impressed immensely, Virata employed the man as the chief of all the royal herds. Though he said that he was called Tantipala, he was none other than Nakula.

Thereafter arrived Arjuna, disguised as an eunuch named Brihannala. He sported long hair, adorned himself with bangles and earrings and dressed in women's attire. Though he had the mannerisms of an eunuch, his brightness and muscular body surprised everyone. He said that he was an expert in imparting dance and music, and he may be employed to train Princess Uttara and other girls. Virata could not believe that a person so bright and muscular was not masculine, but Arjuna confirmed that he was indeed such. Virata discussed with his ministers and got him examined by the women in dance and music. Having confirmed that he was telling the truth, Virata employed Brihannala, aka Arjuna, as the trainer for his daughter and her playmates.

Next, Virata saw Sahadeva examining his horses with a keen eye and enquired about his details. Sahadeva said that he was an expert on horses and knew how to cure their diseases and rein in the wildest horses. Yudhishthira earlier employed him to look after his prized stables. Yudhishthira named him Grandhika and looked after him well, satisfied with his services. He was now looking for employment. Virata was happy to entrust Sahadeva with his entire horse force.

Pandavas and Draupadi spent most of the Ajnatavasa period disguised in their new roles without giving room for complaint and without raising any suspicion as to their identities, bearing the indignity of servitude. Draupadi used to feel sad to see her powerful husbands working in servile positions, reverential to a lesser king like Virata. She used to curse at her fate sometimes for having to do jobs like making sandal pastes for Virata's bath, an act she had never performed before for herself or her husbands. Determined to complete the period of exile without any incidents, they bore the unpleasant stay with great fortitude.

With less than a month remaining, however, a new threat emerged in the form of Kichaka, the powerful general of Matsya, who returned after a long absence. He was the son of Kekaya, the king of Suta kingdom, and Queen Sudeshna was his step-sister. He had the loyal support of his brothers, numbering one hundred and five. Famed for his strength, which was said to rival that of ten thousand elephants, Kichaka was both respected and feared throughout the kingdom and in the royal palace due to his close contact with the royal couple. Rallying behind him, Virata and his brothers won many battles against Anga, Vanga, Kalinga, Kashi and Trigarta, to mention only a few. He used to shuttle between the Kekaya and the Matsya kingdoms to take part in wars and other affairs. A palace stood reserved for him close to his sister's. As Pandavas' luck would have it, Kichaka was absent from Matsya so far as the political affairs and wars in his native Kekaya held him back.

Upon spotting Draupadi, an ordinary Sairandhri in his view, Kichaka was surprised to find such a graceful woman in such a low position. He became enamoured with Draupadi's beauty and wanted to possess her even after knowing she was married. Sudeshna warned him about Malini's Gandharva protectors, but an undeterred Kichaka still pursued Malini, offering her wealth and proclaiming his desire. Draupadi, unyielding, refused his advances and made clear the impropriety of his passion. She reminded him of his royal status, advising him against pursuing a married woman, and even warned him of dire consequences from her Gandharva protectors.

Relentless, Kichaka demanded that his sister send Malini to his quarters under the pretext of fetching a special wine so that he could persuade Draupadi once again in private. Though unwilling initially, Sudeshna finally agreed to accede to her brother's demand, unable to resist any further. When Malini protested, fearing his intentions, Sudeshna downplayed her concerns, insisting Malini complete the assigned task. Reluctantly, Draupadi took an empty pot and entered Kichaka's palace, cursing her fate. Kichaka again started his pleas and demands, and when she refused his advances and was about to return, he seized her. Draupadi pushed him in an attempt to release herself and ran towards Virata's court. Kichaka got up and pursued her, his soft feelings turning into anger, and by the time she reached Virata's court, he caught up with her. In the full glare of the king and courtiers, including Yudhishthira and Bhima, Kichaka knocked her down and kicked her with his foot.

Outraged, Draupadi demanded justice. However, Virata hesitated, offering only mild rebukes to Kichaka, saying that he should not have behaved like that without any indication of punishment or attempting to restrain him from further offences. Malini, further enraged, accused the king and the court of their indifference when they witnessed an atrocity being committed in front of their eyes. Virata excused himself by stating that the court was not aware of what had transpired between the two persons in question in private and hence can not judge just based on her complaint without a full enquiry into the matter. While she still stood in the court, Kanka advised her to leave the court and leave the matter to her husbands, as she claimed they were powerful. He restrained Vallava-aka-Bhima, who was about to get up to punish Kichaka then and there, advising caution. Draupadi returned to her quarters, sorrow and shame writ large on her face, determined to take action into her own hands. Ashamed Sudeshna, who did not expect this turn of events, sought to placate Malini, stating that she would intervene and get Kichaka punished. However, Draupadi replied that there was no such need, as her husbands would now take stock, and Kichaka's days were numbered. She did not eat or drink that night in protest, despite pleas by the queen and other palace maids. When everybody slept, she visited Vallava in his kitchen unobserved. She demanded immediate retribution. Bhima had no problem in killing Kichaka, as it was his intention too, but he needed to act in such a way that his identity would not come out. Together, they hatched a plan to get rid of Kichaka the next night, and Draupadi returned, satisfied that her wish was going to be fulfilled.

The next day, when Kichaka approached her, she sweet-talked him into secretly meeting her in the dance hall that night, with the condition that he should not reveal their meeting to anybody. Flabbergasted, Kichaka agreed and visited the dancing hall at the appointed time, intoxicated with wine and the expectation to meet his desired target. The hall was semi-dark as there were no lights, but Kichaka could find a waiting personality, which he took to be Malini. He was shocked to see, instead, Bhima, whom he identified as Vallava, the royal cook and a wrestler. There ensued a bitter hand-to-hand fight, where both of them tried not to produce loud sounds, as each had a motive to keep that a secret. There was no one in the vicinity to hear any sounds either. After an equal fight for some time, Bhima's superior strength prevailed, and Kichaka breathed his last. Nobody knew whether he realised in his dying moments that his conqueror was the renowned Bhima and the lady he coveted was none other than Draupadi.

An upbeat Draupadi alerted the guards, stating that her Gandharva husbands killed Kichaka in the dancing hall. When the guards reached the place, they were astounded to find Kichaka's blood-soaked body, whose head, legs and hands were tucked into his torso. The signs of a brutal fight were evident all over the place. They believed this to be an act of Gandharvas, as averred by Draupadi, since an ordinary human can't deal so brutally with Kichaka.

As the news spread over the palace, everybody was frightened.

Kichaka's relatives and followers gathered around his dead body and cried aloud. Kichaka's brothers, known as Upakichakas collectively, arrived soon and were shocked to see their brother's state. They gathered from the guards that the cause of his death was a woman by the name of Malini, whom Kichaka coveted, and she declared that her Gandharva husbands had killed Kichaka. Upakichakas' sorrow turned into anger, and they wanted retribution. They sought permission from Virata to burn the lady who caused their brother's death, along with Kichaka's dead body. A frightened Virata meekly gave in, and Upakichakas forcibly took away Draupadi along with the funeral cart towards the cremation ground.

Draupadi shouted aloud to alert her Gandharva husbands with their code names, Jaya, Jayantha, Vijaya, Jayatsena and Jayadbala, the secret names they had given themselves for mutual use and to be used by Draupadi, in case of need. Jayantha-aka-Bhima jumped into action immediately and reached the cremation ground, even before the funeral procession reached there. Uprooting a big tree, he started rotating it with both his hands, waiting for the Upakichakas to appear. His very sight frightened the approaching Upakichakas, who took to their heels, fearing certain death in the hands of that ferocious Gandharva, leaving both the dead body and Draupadi then and there. Bhima chased them, pounding every one of them with the tree. None had survived to tell the story. Bhima then released Draupadi and went on his way to his place.

Soon, people gathered to find the one hundred and five Upakichakas scattered around like trees falling in a cyclone, and they ran towards the king to inform the news. A terrified Virata ordered the funeral of his dead relatives. Fearful, he urged Sudeshna to dismiss Malini from the palace to avert further danger from Gandharvas.

Meanwhile, Draupadi walked through the city streets towards the palace, and passers-by either ran away or closed their eyes for fear of Gandharvas. When she reached the palace, Sudeshna conveyed her king's apprehensions and pleaded with her to leave. Draupadi sought a further period of thirteen days, by which time her husbands would come to fetch her. Sudeshna, having no choice but to agree, requested Draupadi to protect the kingdom, especially her husband and children, from Gandharvas' wrath.

The news of Kichaka's death made the Kauravas suspect Pandava's existence in the Matsya kingdom, leading to war on both the southern and northern fronts. When Virata was preparing for the battle on the south front with Susharma's Trigarta armies, Yudhishthira, in the guise of Kanka, had volunteered to join the fight, which the king readily agreed. On Yudhishthira's further suggestion, Virata agreed to rope Bhima, Nakula, and Sahadeva in to join them. He left his son, Uttar Kumara, in charge of the palace. It was a prudent measure on his part as nobody is sure whether they would return or not when they embark on a battle.

The next day, when Kauravas attacked the northern front and seized the cows, there were none left in the city to confront them. Uttar Kumara boldly claimed, showing his bravado, that he was ready to face Kauravas but for the handicap of a suitable charioteer. On hearing this, Draupadi, among the audience, quietly suggested Brihannala's name to Uttara, Virata's daughter. She indicated that Brihannala was an expert charioteer, as she knew him in Indraprastha. He was the one who steered Arjuna's chariot during the famous Khandavaprastha burning episode. Uttara requested Brihannala, aka Arjuna, to steer her brother's chariot, to which he agreed. Uttar Kumara was now in a fix but gathered the courage to embark on the war.

After reaching the battlefield, when Uttar Kumara developed cold feet on witnessing the mammoth Kaurava army, Arjuna revealed his true identity to the prince. Exhilarated, the prince acted as Arjuna's charioteer as they retrieved that great bow 'Gandiva,' from Pandavas' hidden weapons. Arjuna waged a fierce battle against Kauravas and reclaimed Matsya's herds. While returning, Arjuna changed into his Brihannala attire and asked the prince not to reveal their true identities and to keep secret what had happened. Uttar Kumara agreed.

Meanwhile, on the southern front, Virata was victorious, thanks mainly to the valour shown by the Pandava brothers. When Susharma captured the king, Bhima overpowered Susharma and released Virata. Susharma's surrender signalled Matsya's victory. A grateful Virata expressed his heartfelt gratitude to his unlikely saviours and was ready to offer them whatever they wished. When they returned home, they heard that Kauravas attacked the northern front, and Uttar Kumara marched to confront them alone, taking Brihannala as charioteer.

Virata was terribly anxious about the safety of Uttar Kumar, who was unexposed to any war earlier, and Kauravas were renowned fighters. Yudhishthira assured him that Uttar Kumara was safe as the charioteer was none other than Brihannala. Resigned to fate, Virata wanted to divert his mind till further news and asked Yudhishthira to play the game of dice with him. While they were playing, news broke out that the battle was won, and the cows were recaptured. Virata was jubilant to hear the news and started repeatedly showing his elation at his son's achievement. Yudhishthira kept downplaying Uttar Kumar's victory, reminding Virata that he had already told him that the victory was expected as the prince was accompanied by Brihannala, much to the chagrin of Virata, who even threw the dice at Yudhishthira causing him to shed blood. Draupadi, who was nearby, immediately attended to him.

Around that time, Uttar Kumara arrived and confessed to his father that the war was not fought by him but by a divine person who suddenly appeared from nowhere. As cautioned by Arjuna, he did not disclose who that divine person was. Observing Yudhishthira's injury, Uttar Kumara chided his father for his impetuousness. Virata repented his act and sought apologies.

Virata's suspense was cleared only the next day when he attended the court to find Pandavas in their true identities. His initial shock turned into awe as the king and his courtiers realised that the legendary Pandavas had been in their midst. None could believe that the conquerors of the entire Bharatavarsha lived among them as commoners. They were happy to reminisce about their interactions with Pandavas and felt gladdened. Similar were the reactions of the maids of Sudeshna's palace, among whom Draupadi lived.

Queen Sudeshna felt ashamed and guilty for her past treatment of Draupadi, assuming her to be an ordinary sairandhri. However, she was happy and relieved to find that Draupadi was gracious in understanding her predicament and did not feel inimical toward her.

The secret of Malini's five Gandharva husbands has been unravelled, and this was an incredible story the people of Matsya would pass on to the generations.

Uttara, along with her playmates, was astonished to learn that her trainer for dance and music was none other than the famous Arjuna, her future father-in-law. Malini, whom she befriended, turned out to be the admirable Draupadi. Her friends had already started teasing her about her proposed marriage with Abhimanyu, about whom they had heard a lot.

Uttar Kumara was a transformed man after watching Arjuna fearlessly take on the multiple warriors while he faced the might of Kaurava warriors from close quarters, holding the charioteer's position. His self-confidence replaced his bravado, and the experience humbled him. He was confident to enter any battle now without fearing for his life. He was ready for a showdown with Kauravas fighting from Pandavas' side if such a war were to take place.

Thus ended the eventful period of Ajnatavasa for Pandavas and Draupadi.

When Naimishites discovered the entire story, they marvelled at the audacity of the Pandavas hiding in a kingdom so near to their rivals for a whole year. The tales of their remarkable courage and resilience were soon talked about throughout the ashrams of Naimisha, the cities of Indraprastha, Hastinapur and various other kingdoms. They became folklore in the Matsya kingdom and, in due course, everywhere else.

Chapter 4

Reminiscences of Animish And Asareer

Naimisha

During their private walks, Animish and Asareer often discussed the news they received from different sources. When Asareer heard Vyshampayana's discourse about the Pandavas' time in Virata's court, he was intrigued and wanted to share it with Animish. Asareer was particularly fascinated by the Pandavas' secret exile in Matsya and was even more enthralled when he heard Vyshampayana's narration of Yudhishthira's encounter with Yaksha.

The story of this strange encounter of Yudhishthira with Yaksha at the fag end of Aranyavasa unfolded as follows: During their exile in the forest, the Pandavas were approached by a group of Brahmins who had lost their 'arani' sticks—sacred tools used for igniting ritual fires. These sticks had become entangled in a deer's horns, and the startled animal had bolted into the woods. Yudhishthira and his brothers immediately set out to retrieve them, pursuing the elusive deer deep into the forest. After a long and exhausting chase, they grew thirsty, especially Yudhishthira, and found themselves in dire need of water.

Sahadeva climbed a tall tree nearby and spotted a lake in the distance. He reported the water source to his brothers and went on to fetch water for his elder brother. He was startled by an ominous voice warning him, "Beware! Do not touch the water before answering my questions."

Ignoring the caution, Sahadeva bent down to fetch the water, but the moment he touched the water, he fell lifeless to the ground.

One by one, Nakula, Arjuna, and Bhima followed, each ignoring the warning and meeting the same fate. When none of his brothers returned, Yudhishthira went in search of them and was horrified to find their motionless bodies by the lake. Then, the Yaksha revealed himself and reiterated his warning. Unlike his brothers, Yudhishthira listened and chose to answer the questions posed by the mystical being. Satisfied with Yudhishthira's wisdom in answering his many intricate questions, the Yaksha permitted him access to water and offered to revive one of his brothers.

To Yaksha's surprise, Yudhishthira chose Nakula. The Yaksha asked why he had not chosen Bhima or Arjuna, his biological brothers, who were mightier warriors and invaluable allies in battle. Yudhishthira replied with unwavering conviction that Nakula was his choice because he was the eldest son of Madri, and it was only fair that he be chosen as he, the eldest of Kunti's sons, alone survived. Pleased by this righteous and selfless response, the Yaksha, who was none other than Yama, the god of death, restored all his brothers to life. He also blessed them, ensuring that they would remain unrecognisable during their Ajnatavasa, their year of incognito exile.

Long after hearing this tale, Asareer found himself reflecting on Yaksha's questions and Yudhishthira's profound answers, many of which he considered deeply insightful. One answer stood out to him in particular: When asked what was the most astonishing thing in the world, a wonder, so to say, Yudhishthira replied, "Despite witnessing death all around, people live and act as if they are not going to die." Another question concerned the definitions of a 'Nastik' and a fool. Yudhishthira asserted that both words are synonymous, implying that one who does not believe in higher realms is a Nastik, and hence, he is a fool as he refuses to grasp the higher reality.

Eager to discuss these philosophical ideas, Asareer seized the opportunity during one of his walks with Animish. As he shared the story, Animish listened intently, giving careful thought to each question and answer.

While he acknowledged the wisdom in some responses, he remained sceptical about others.

'Asareer,' Animish said thoughtfully, 'this tale from Vyshampayana's ashram is indeed fascinating. I particularly agree with Yudhishthira's remark about people ignoring the certainty of death as a mysterious wonder. But I find many of his answers unoriginal—mere reflections of existing scholarship rather than profound insights of his own. Moreover, I find it difficult to believe the entire story and that Yaksha was truly Yama or that he granted the Pandavas the ability to remain unrecognisable. That interpretation seems to diminish the Pandavas' efforts in maintaining their disguises. To me, this story primarily serves to project Yudhishthira as the epitome of Dharma, and I am not sure it happened that way. On second thoughts, I might even say this narration is also useful to refute anybody suspecting Virata's inability to recognise the identity of Pandavas, whom he had earlier seen in close quarters.'

Asareer did not argue. He had anticipated that Animish would challenge some of Yudhishthira's answers, but he had not expected such intense animosity toward the Pandava prince. Their conversation drifted toward other topics of mutual interest.

A heavy gloom hung over the land, an eerie silence stretching like the calm before an impending storm. The war seemed inevitable. It was the only course left for the Pandavas after Dhritarashtra's message to Pandavas through Sanjaya. Neither side had declared the war yet. While peace negotiations continued on one front, armies assembled on the other. All signs pointed to Kurukshetra as the destined battlefield.

Nestled between the rivers Saraswati and Drishadwati, Kurukshetra carried a legacy rooted both in history and legend. It was named after King Kuru, the revered ancestor of the Kuru dynasty, who had ploughed its soil as part of a great yajna to uphold Dharma, by which this sacred land also came to be known as Dharmakshetra.

It also contained a famous kshetra known as Samantapanchaka, which was linked with the name of the legendary warrior sage Parashurama. It was here that Parashurama had filled five lakes with the blood of slain Kshatriyas and performed sacred rites to his father and brothers, who succumbed to the Kshatriya pride. For generations, warriors believed that to die on the holy grounds of Kurukshetra and Samantapanchaka would earn them a place in heaven.

During their conversations, Animish remarked to Asareer, indicating the inevitability of war, 'Samantapanchaka seems fated for yet another bloodbath of Kshatriyas.'

The name of Samantapanchaka stirred different memories in Asareer, drawing him back to a distant time when he and Animish had witnessed a great congregation at that very place. It was the time for a rare celestial event—a total solar eclipse, *the Sampurna Surya Grahanam*—an occasion deemed auspicious for performing ancestral rites. Samantapanchaka had drawn pilgrims from far and wide, coming to bathe in its holy waters and offer prayers.

Among the earliest arrivals was a grand delegation from Dwaraka, led by Ugrasena, Vasudeva, Balarama, and Krishna, accompanied by their wives. Soon after, Nanda, Yashoda, and a multitude of gopas and gopikas arrived from Brindavan—not merely as a pilgrimage but more for the chance to see Krishna once more. They had no occasion to meet Krishna and Balarama ever since the brothers left for Mathura at Kamsa's invitation.

The news of Krishna's presence spread swiftly, drawing sages from Naimisha and beyond. The Kauravas arrived in strength from Hastinapur, led by Bhishma, Dhritarashtra, Vidura, and Duryodhana, their wives accompanying them. Yudhishthira and his brothers came from Indraprastha with Draupadi, while kings like Drupada and Virata attended with large entourages. The entire event became a grand mela, attracting royals and commoners alike.

While Animish took the opportunity to strengthen his royal connections, Asareer was drawn to the Brindavan and Dwaraka camps, eager to observe Krishna more closely. There were many emotional reunions among the visitors.

Yashoda embraced her 'Kanna,' tears streaming freely, as she blessed Krishna and Balarama. Yashoda wondered at how her once little Kannaiah now sat in honour among kings, warriors, and sages. Vasudeva and Devaki felicitated Nanda and Yashoda. Devaki, with deep gratitude, thanked Yashoda for raising her son in his formative years and groomed him well while they were in Kamsa's captivity.

Wives of Krishna were excited to meet and get blessings from their husband's first mother, of whom they had heard a lot. Yashoda playfully remarked to Nanda, 'Count our daughters-in-law, if you may, Sage Garga's prophecy was not untrue.' Nanda remembered the prediction too well—that Krishna would grow to be a great statesman and philosopher and would marry sixteen thousand eight wives.

Another emotional reunion was between Kunti and her brother Vasudeva. Years had passed since their last meeting, and Kunti, overcome with emotion, wept as she lamented the absence of her brother in her times of suffering. Vasudeva, equally sorrowful, reminded her of their own years of torment under Kamsa's rule, which had left them powerless to aid others. The siblings embraced, and their grief eased by sharing the success stories of their sons.

Krishna, aware of Gopikas' longing for him, gathered them close and spoke from his heart. He explained why he could not return to Brindavan as promised and why duty had taken him far west to Dwaraka. Krishna reassured them, just as he had once done through Uddhava, that though he could not be with them physically, he was always with them in their hearts, and they all had a special place in his heart. The gopikas felt ecstatic that they had not lost their Krishna and were happy to share moments with him. They were detained for an extended stay, and they finally left carrying with them cherished memories of this reunion.

Another remarkable sight was the bonhomie among the women of Hastinapur and Dwaraka. The wives of the Kauravas, flanking Draupadi, visited Krishna's wives, eager to hear their stories. At Draupadi's request, each of Krishna's wives recounted the tales of how they had come to marry him, enthralling the audience with their narratives.

Amidst these moments of joy, rites were solemnly performed. Dhritarashtra, accompanied by both the Pandavas and Kauravas, paid homage to his ancestors—Vichitraveerya, Chitrangada, Shantanu, and others. It was a time of peace after the empire had been divided, and the relations between Indraprastha and Hastinapur were not yet strained.

The gathering was also an occasion for reverence. Dhritarashtra, Bhishma, and the Kauravas visited the Dwaraka camp to pay respects to Ugrasena and Vasudeva. They marvelled at the fortune of the Yadavas, for Vishnu himself had graced their clan in the form of Krishna. Sages from across the land flocked to the Dwaraka camp to meet Krishna and engage him in philosophical discussions.

Vasudeva, earnest in his devotion, sought guidance from the assembled sages on performing yajnas. Sages were amused to find that Vasudeva had not yet realised that he was a blessed soul for having a son like Krishna. When Vasudeva questioned Krishna about the sages' reverence, Krishna deflected with his characteristic charm, reminding his father that the divine resides within all beings.

The sages, however, satisfied Vasudeva by making him perform a suitable Yajna. Asareer heard this tale at Vyshampayana's ashram later and recounted it to Animish. Animish chuckled and said, 'Vasudeva was not as ignorant as sages surmised.' Asareer quipped, 'Maybe Vasudeva, being a father, is too humble to acknowledge his son's divinity.' Animish did not argue.

Asareer woke up from those memories of Samantapanchaka's celestial gathering, thinking that those echoes of past laughter and togetherness were about to sadly drown out in the brutal war that was about to happen soon.

Asareer asked Animish, 'Now that Krishna is going to Hastinapur for peace efforts, is it likely the war can be averted?' His voice was hopeful.

Animish replied, 'I do not doubt Krishna's abilities, but Duryodhana is very stubborn. Peace is unlikely at this stage. The story of cousins is reaching the final phase. I don't see any hope.'

While Kurukshetra, also known as Dharmakshetra, was bracing itself to host another battle, calling for another bloodbath, Krishna marched from Upaplavya to Hastinapur to negotiate peace.

Chapter 5

Peace Attempts Come to An End

Hastinapur

The news of Krishna's failed attempt to convince Dhritarashtra and avert war disappointed those who yearned for peace, though the royals, already prepared for battle, welcomed the outcome. People in Hastinapur and Indraprastha realised that the war they were talking about was in striking distance. They were agitated but kept on discussing the developments animatedly. So did the people in other kingdoms and Naimishites.

On the streets, the discussions about Krishna's visit to the court of Hastinapur were made in many hues. The events were recounted and analysed from different angles.

Person 1: The last hope for peace was shattered when Krishna was sent back without agreeing to the peace proposals of Yudhishthira. It is the most foolhardy action on the part of Dhritarashtra, and the entire royalty needs to pay the price for it.

Person 2: Don't blame Dhritarashtra alone. In fact, he and Gandhari advised their son to agree to peace but could not convince Duryodhana. Even Bhishma, Drona, and Vidura were against war with Pandavas, but Duryodhana would not listen.

Person 3: That's no excuse. Dhritarashtra is the king! He should have taken a stand instead of unthinkingly following his son, especially when the elders overwhelmingly opposed war. It is pathetic.

Person 4: Expecting Dhritarashtra to act decisively is asking too much. He has never been a real leader, though he ruled. Earlier, he followed the advice of Bhishma and Vidura, and now he toes the line of his son, who is under the influence of Karna, Dusshasana and Shakuni.

Person 5: In fact, these were perhaps the only four who thwarted the idea of peace despite the high pressure mounted on Duryodhana by the elders, who could not say 'no' to Krishna or gainsay his logic. Krishna warned them of total annihilation of the race and great destruction. He reminded them of their past misdeeds, which earned them the wrath of Pandavas, and he highlighted the matchless prowess of Pandavas—especially Bhima and Arjuna—but Duryodhana and his core supporters remained unmoved.

Person 1: For a moment, it seemed Dhritarashtra might side with the elders and disregard Duryodhana's faction. Dusshasana even expressed fear that their father might have them arrested, swayed by Krishna's compelling arguments. That's when the quartet contemplated capturing Krishna to prevent the peace process from progressing.

Person 2: Is it? Unthinkable! Arresting Krishna? Sheer madness!

Person 1: Yes, indeed. The ever-vigilant Satyaki sensed the mood and alerted Kritavarma, who was already in Hastinapur with an akshauhini of Narayanasena at his disposal, ready for action.

Person 3: Sorry for interrupting. Kritavarma and Narayanasena have already committed their allegiance to Duryodhana, so how can they go against him?

Person 1: That allegiance is for the war, not for treachery. The war has yet to start; when they would fight against Krishna, it is not now. Satyaki and Kritavarma were ready for action, though it was not needed. The moment Krishna knew what was cooking, he was angry at the foolishness of Duryodhana and his supporters. He challenged Kauravas to try to arrest him and find out who would arrest whom. The court witnessed Krishna's fierce reaction. Bhishma, Vidura and others warned Duryodhana against any such foolish attempts. Chastised, Duryodhana got cold feet and abandoned any such plan. But that also effectively ended the peace talks.

Person 3: I would say Krishna put God's fear in their hearts and was seen off with all due respect.

Person 1: Yes, Krishna walked gracefully out of the court holding the hands of Satyaki and Kritavarma. Dhritarashtra submitted that he was indeed favourable to peace but unable to accept it because of his son's steadfast refusal. Krishna declared to the elders that Dhritarashtra had admitted his helplessness and inability to follow the proper course. He said he would carry the message to Yudhishthira for further action.

There was no end to the different groups animatedly discussing the subject long after Krishna returned from Hastinapur, and here is another.

Person 1: Is it true that Krishna proposed that Yudhishthira had agreed to accept just five villages instead of the entire erstwhile kingdom, and even that was not agreed upon?

Person 2: Yes. Duryodhana declared he wouldn't concede even enough land to drive a needle through.

Person 3: Why did Yudhishthira offer such a drastic compromise? Was it not a significant climbdown for the Pandavas? And why did Duryodhana not accept?

Person 4: I think it was Yudhishthira's strategic move, not a retreat. It was not as if he asked for any random five villages or towns of Dhritarashtra's choice. Pandavas specified key locations—Indraprastha, Varanavata, Vrikasthala, Makandi, and one more, as chosen by Dhritarashtra. Duryodhana reckoned that he would have to face five fortified locations in future instead of one now. Pandavas were asking those places to set up their kingdoms, and Duryodhana probably perceived it as a future threat. That's why he refused outright.

Person 5: I have a feeling that Yudhishthira knew the outcome, that Duryodhana would refuse and wanted the blame to be firmly fixed on Duryodhana.

Person 4: Could be. That's why I told you it was a strategic move. However, Duryodhana is not the one conscious of a bad image and bluntly stated that there is no scope of conceding even an inch. What Pandavas asked seemed low, but the places have the potential to turn big and challenge Hastinapur under the able hands of Pandavas. If he were scared enough of Pandavas that he sent them to exile by indulging Yudhishthira in a dice game, he would be five times more scared now. He is not the one to tolerate strong kingdoms around him, more so if they were to be ruled by Pandavas. His policy was "either me or you" and never "two together." He was prepared to fight, whatever the cost. If Yudhishthira was then intoxicated to stake his all in a dice game, Duryodhana is now foolishly staking his all in an impending battle with cousins, unmindful of where he is leading himself and his supporters, in a fit of mindless fury.

Person 1: Well said! You summed up Duryodhana's mindset and the present predicament in precise terms.

There were discussions in groups of inmates in Naimisha ashrams, too.

'We hear that Krishna's peace talks failed, but it had a sobering effect on the Kauravas, particularly elders like Dhritarashtra, Bhishma and Drona. They tried their best to convince Duryodhana for a peace treaty, but failed.'

'Is it true that we hear from Vyasa's ashram that Krishna had shown his God-like divine appearance in the court of Hastinapur?'

'Yes, that is what we hear from sages. Though most of those present in the court could not bear the brightness and closed their eyes, a fortunate few like Bhishma, Drona, Vidura and sages who were bestowed with the divine vision could witness the supreme form.

'I wonder how the divine experience had failed to bring a change of heart on the part of Kauravas?'

'My information is Kauravas were not there in the court at that point in time, but I may be wrong. Even all those who were present were not blissful enough to have that divine experience, and it was limited to a few sages and elders. Another startling piece of news floating is that Dhritarashtra, though blind, could witness the grand appearance of Krishna as a supreme God.'

'Strange are the ways of God, whom he chooses to reveal his presence and whom he denies. When Sage Vyasa, who himself was one of those present in the court, attests to it, there is no reason to disbelieve it otherwise.'

There was no end to the conversations, discussions and debates concerning the happenings during Krishna's truce efforts till the war started, when all talks would be about war. However, for the present, it remained the sole talking point.

One unanswered question, however, lingered:

Being the Supreme God, why didn't Krishna prevent the war if he genuinely wished to?

Hastinapur, Dhritarashtra's Palace

The day after Krishna's departure, Dhritarashtra called for Sanjaya to learn more facts and assess the situation. Sanjaya, his trusted aide, could read one's thoughts and perceive distant events, thanks to the blessings of Vedavyasa; a rare skill that would prove crucial during the impending war when Sanjaya was expected to report to Dhritarashtra the war news.

Sanjaya narrated in detail what happened after Krishna left the court and till he drove away from Hastinapur. He informed Dhritarashtra that Krishna was accompanied by Bhishma, Drona, Karna and many other important people to see him off when he left Hastinapur's court. Krishna drove straight to Vidura's place, where Kunti resided and briefed her about the current developments.

Sanjaya went on narrating as Dhritarashtra keenly followed every word Sanjaya spoke.

'Separated from her sons and Draupadi for thirteen years, Kunti was eager to convey her mind to Yudhishthira. When Krishna visited her, Kunti opened up. She was apprehensive about Yudhishthira's mindset and his sensitivity to waging a war against his cousins. Kunti, hence, implored Krishna to remind Yudhishthira of his Kshatriya Dharma and invoked the story of Vidula—a queen who urged her hesitant son to reclaim his lost kingdom by waging war. Kunti further told Krishna that she wanted Yudhishthira to fight for his rights as enjoined by the Kshatriya code. Her message was very stern and straight. Krishna assured her that he would convey her sentiments to her sons and took leave of her.'

Dhritarashtra was engrossed in deep thought after hearing Kunti's advice, or rather an admonition, to her son. Dhritarashtra knew Vidula's story in detail. Vidula was a queen of Sindhu in ancient times whose son, Sanjaya, was spending time in the forests without making efforts to retrieve his lost kingdom by force. He was reluctant to fight on various pretexts, and Vidula provoked him in subtle ways to make him perform his duties as incumbent upon a Kshatriya. Inspired, the son shed his diffidence, fought with the rival, the Sindhu king, and emerged victorious. The conversation between Vidula and her son was a part of Kshatriya folklore. It is an inspiring story for any Kshatriya, and it should motivate Yudhishthira, who apparently was in a similar position.

Dhritarashtra still nurtured some outside hope that Yudhishthira, the pacifist ever, might back out from the war after the failed negotiations, disinterested in fighting for the kingdom and spilling a lot of blood. He had already planted the seed of such a course through the message he had sent through Sanjaya -the undesirability of fighting with relatives for a piece of land and shedding blood. However, Kunti's unambiguous message to Yudhishthira dispelled any such illusions he harboured. Dhritarashtra was convinced that the battle of cousins was inevitable now.

He motioned to Sanjaya to proceed with further narration.

'Krishna, after bidding farewell to all the accompanying elders at the city gates, had asked Karna to accompany him in his chariot.'

Dhritarashtra suddenly became alert upon hearing this unusual news. Without being able to wait further, he asked, 'What transpired between them? Brief me soon.'

Sanjaya continued, 'Krishna told Karna that the latter was a son of Kunti, born of Surya before she was even married to King Pandu, and Karna said he knew.'

Sanjaya checked for the shock of hearing such an astonishing revelation on the listener's countenance. However, it was his turn to be shocked, having found that no surprise was registered on Dhritarashtra's visage. *"He knew,"* Sanjaya thought and wondered, *"Since when?"*

Sanjaya continued, 'Krishna suggested that it was time that Karna came to his mother Kunti and Pandavas, and claimed his rightful place and that he would see to it that Karna was welcomed with due honours. Krishna said that, as per Dharmashastra, Karna is the eldest of Pandavas and deserves to be crowned. Karna can join the Pandava camp, lead his brothers, and become the king himself.'

'That was a tempting offer. What was Karna's response?'

'Karna replied that though he knew the secret of his birth and that Pandu was his father as per the law, it was too late in his life to think about reuniting with his mother and brothers. He was loved and accepted as a son of Adiratha and Radha, had been raised as a Suta's son, married into the Suta families, and performed all rituals as prescribed for a Suta. He had no desire to claim lineage or announce to the world that he was born a Kshatriya. He had developed a strong bond of friendship with Duryodhana, enjoyed his generosity for years, and could not desert his friend in the time of his need. Duryodhana chose him to fight with Arjuna, and he can not back out from that duty. He said he might die fighting Arjuna, but it would still be more honourable for him than switching sides and becoming a king.'

'Nothing less was expected of Karna; he fully deserves the confidence reposed in him by Duryodhana,' was all that Dhritarashtra commented.

'Karna finally requested Krishna to keep the matter a secret and not tell another soul. He was apprehensive that if Yudhishthira knew of this, he would abandon his claims to the throne and insist on Karna taking the kingdom, which, in turn, he would bequeath to Duryodhana. That would be a great injustice for Yudhishthira, who richly deserved to rule. Karna further said that he knew Pandavas were just, but he slighted them to please Duryodhana, and he knew that the war would see great destruction. He asked Krishna to ensure all the assembled kings, who willingly came to take part in war, attain the heavens reserved for warriors. He would certainly fight with Arjuna with all his might as expected of him and die if it was fated so.'

Dhritarashtra absorbed Sanjaya's narration and asked, 'What was Krishna's response?'

Sanjaya said,' Krishna commented that Karna was not heeding a beneficial piece of advice and was not able to distinguish what the right course was. Karna took leave of Krishna, expressing his fond hope to meet Krishna after the war, if he survived or in heaven later. With this, the meeting ended, and they both had a brief, friendly embrace before parting. Krishna proceeded to Upaplavya with Satyaki for his company.

Dhritarashtra had so many thoughts running in his mind. He knew he handled the entire situation wrong and squandered the last opportunity provided by Krishna. He knew he would be blamed for the impending war and bloodshed but consoled himself that if Krishna himself could not stop the war, how could he? Who could fight against destiny?

Duryodhana's Palace, Hastinapur

Duryodhana was exhilarated by his success in thwarting Krishna's peace mission and the subsequent pleas from the elders of the court and family. Even as his parents, Bhishma and Drona, individually and collectively urged him to reconsider, he remained stubborn. Eventually, he secured his compliant father's approval and assent from reluctant but duty-bound Bhishma to lead the armies into battle.

The certainty of war excited him and his associates. Though Yudhishthira had set up a war camp and assembled seven akshauhinis of forces, he had yet to declare war on Hastinapur formally. Duryodhana decided to send a provocatively worded war invitation to stoke the fires of anger in Krishna and Pandavas. Ulooka, Shakuni's son, was chosen for the task of delivering this incendiary message. Before dispatching it, Duryodhana wished that the message be read aloud for the information of his close associates who surrounded him.

Ulooka cleared his throat and began, addressing Yudhishthira as though he stood before him:

"O Yudhishthira! The long, protracted dispute over Hastinapur's throne has reached its final reckoning—only war shall decide the rightful heirs. The world watches eagerly. You spoke boldly when Sanjaya came with terms of peace that you were prepared for both peace and war; Krishna reiterated those words to us. It is time now to walk your talk and meet us on the battlefield.

You claim to be a champion of righteousness, yet you prepare to plunge countless lives of others into war for a piece of land which is not yours. Is this the Dharma you profess? Your devotion to the Vedas and your preachings of peace are nothing but a pretence—a mask to deceive the world. Cast aside that false cloak of righteousness and act as a true Kshatriya.

Your mother has suffered years of grief, watching your misfortunes unfold. If you have any courage, win this war and bring her peace. Remember the indignities you have endured—the carnage at Lakshagriha, your losing the kingdom over a game of dice, Draupadi's humiliation in open court, and the menial servitude you, your brothers and Draupadi bore in Virata's court. Let these wounds fuel your rage. Krishna declared you were ready for either peace or war. I rejected your shameless offer of taking five villages, only with the intention of drawing you into the war.

Let us meet on the battlefield and settle scores. Either you kill us all and claim the entire kingdom, or we destroy you on the battlefield."

Ulooka paused for breath. Duryodhana, relishing the moment, motioned for him to continue. The message now turned to Krishna.

"O Krishna! I summon you and Arjuna to the battlefield. Tricks, illusions, and threats hold no sway over true warriors. I beseech you to appear in the war in the same form you showed in the court of Hastinapur. We are not at all afraid. We, too, can soar to the skies, dry the rivers and march the armies thereupon, and alter our forms. Do you think we fear such magic? Now, we realise, Krishna, that you stumbled into great fame by accident, not by virtue. You are not even a king. Sanjaya tells me you sought to intimidate us with the prospect of facing Arjuna in your company. Come and fulfil your promise.

And you, Bhima! Recall the humiliation you suffered, living in disguise as a cook in Virata's court. It was I who reduced you to that fate. You swore to drink Dusshasana's blood, to kill all Kauravas—come and try if you dare! You are destined to fall before me and sleep on the battlefield. You revel in feasting and boasts, but neither will serve you in war. The arrogance and the antics you displayed in the dice hall will crumble when you face me on the battlefield. And you, Arjuna, may I need to remind you of your shameless disguise as Brihannala—"

Peals of derisive laughter floated in the air as the speech went on, as they imagined the reactions of the Pandava camp and, particularly, those of Krishna and each Pandava to those insinuations.

Duryodhana raised a hand, signalling Ulooka to stop. They all knew what was contained in the remaining portion. It called out not only each of Pandavas but also Drupada, Virata, Shikhandi, and Dhrishtadyumna. It reminded them of the near-impossible challenge before Pandavas of overcoming, among others, Bhishma, Drona, Karna, Shalya, and Bhurishravas.

While they revelled in their audacity, confident in their victory, Ulooka mounted his chariot and rode toward the Pandava camp with the incendiary message. Duryodhana burnt every last bridge to peace.

Dhritarashtra's palace

That evening, Duryodhana went to his parents and sought their blessings. Dhritarashtra sighed and blessed his son to be victorious. Gandhari affectionately hugged her son and ran her hand on his head and body, as if she was touching him for one last time, mindful of the unpredictability of war. She dreaded the consequences of her sons facing the rampaging Bhima on the battlefield. She tried her best to stop her son from pitching for war with Pandavas, but she couldn't stop him. She blessed her son, saying, 'Be blessed, my son, fight fairly with all your strength, let Dharma win.'

Chapter 6

Naimisha Braces Itself for the Battle

Naimisha, Shamyaprasa

Vedavyasa was presiding over the meeting of inmates after morning prayers. All his disciples gathered around him and were eager to hear what the sage would reveal. He had just the other evening returned from Hastinapur. Some people from other ashrams of Naimisha were also present in the gathering to listen to the latest news of Hastinapur from Vedavyasa.

Vedavyasa broke the confirmed news to the gathering. 'The war could not be averted, and even Srikrishna's persuasion did not work. Though the elders, including Dhritarashtra and Gandhari, were convinced, Duryodhana stood his word stubbornly. Krishna returned to Upaplavya, having talked to all persons publicly and addressed them in private as well. Duryodhana sent a final message to Yudhishthira to get ready for the battle. The battle is likely to take place in Kurukshetra shortly. Destiny is calling everybody for repayment of its debts.'

He looked at Vaishampayana, the learned disciple and said, 'We need to record the events for the benefit of posterity. It is no longer a war between factions of Kauravas and Pandavas, but the whole Bharatavarsha is involved. Royals from all corners assembled in Kurukshetra and are waiting for the beat of war drums. About eleven akshauhinis are fighting on the side of Kauravas, and seven akshauhinis are fighting for the sake of Pandavas.'

After saying so, he left the meeting, leaving the members to continue their deliberations.

Vaishampayana and other disciples were amazed to witness the calm composure of their revered teacher. The 'factions' he was referring to were none other than his grandchildren. Nobody knows who will survive the war. -'Eleven to seven in favour of Kauravas is a great advantage in an open war, but intrinsically, I feel the side on which Krishna showered his blessings should win.' averred Vaishampayana. 'We, too, believe the same,' echoed all other voices.

From then onwards, the only matter of interest in Shamyaprasa was war news.

Little Master's Ashram

Little Master's ashram was no exception. It, too, was fully engrossed with the news of war and the developments as they unfolded, like other ashrams of Naimisha. That they knew many participating kings, either as their one-time trainees or as present patrons, gave them additional interest.

Animish announced, 'The war is about to start, and the kings from all over are vying with each other to fight and die. At last, they had stopped the meaningless parleys as if each was interested in peace, but now they had cast aside their pretensions and decided to go to war. Ulooka, the son of Shakuni, went to Yudhishthira with an invitation to war, which was accepted. No more room was left for any negotiations. Any time the war will start, if not started already.'

The men who brought the news waited for further instructions. He looked at them and suggested, 'A few of you may cover the camp of Pandavas, and some others can cover Kauravas' camp. Your contacts are already in proper places, like food and wine supplies, cooking and medical services, and reserve charioteers on both sides who can feed you the information. You need not fear being spotted and punished because it is not any espionage but try not to be too conspicuous just to avoid unnecessary risk. There will be regular movement of food and wine stocks as long as the war lasts, and your positioning with those services will come in handy. People will be excited to talk about what they heard about war and would be willing to share with anybody who lends an ear. Hence, getting the news is not difficult. While some of you stay there, a few can come and report to us periodically.'

They nodded in excitement. It was the first time they were undertaking an assignment of this sort. People in the ashram, including the Little Master, would be looking forward to seeing them and hearing the news they brought.

Animish looked at the group and said, 'We need to know the true version of the war. We will be hearing so many false stories once the war is over. Our own Naimisha sages could sing songs of praise in honour of whoever wins. Truth, I am afraid, will be compromised. Hence, I would prefer to have firsthand information before it gets coloured.'

Animish signalled the end of the meeting, but the audience didn't move. There was a pin-drop silence. Finally, someone mustered the courage to ask the question uppermost on everybody's mind.

'Master, which side do you think would win the battle?'

Animish looked both amused and uncomfortable. It was a question he didn't want to answer. After a brief hesitation, he responded, 'Eleven akshauhinis of Kauravas is certainly an intimidating figure and certainly better than eight akshauhinis that Pandavas could muster. Contrary to original estimates, Pandavas' uncle Shalya was reported to have joined Kauravas. Most of the Yadava warriors, like Balarama, Pradyumna, Aniruddha and Samba, excused themselves from participating in the war of cousins. They all had embarked on a pilgrimage. Krishna parted with his personal army of 'Narayana Sena' to Duryodhana, and Kritavarma joined the ranks of Duryodhana. Even though Krishna joined Pandavas, he would not fight on their behalf.

Krishna publicly stated to Arjuna and Duryodhana that he would not wield a weapon, when they approached him simultaneously for help. Of course, I have my doubts about whether Krishna would respect his word when facing piercing arrows from all sides. Pandava camp mainly banks on Arjuna to neutralise the elders like Bhishma and Drona, but I very much doubt whether he could kill his elders and gurus, whom he respects a lot. Hence, the balance of favour is on the side of Kauravas.' He stopped for a moment, looked around, and added,' Except for one thing!'

He paused a little longer than necessary to continue, allowing the audience to guess what he was going to say.

Asareer had a smile on his lips. He was listening to what his longtime friend was saying with rapt attention. He thought he knew the answer. He framed the answer in his heart in his own words,' Except for Srikrishna, the eighth avatar of Vishnu, the upholder of Dharma.' He had that smile on his face because even his friend could not help but think of Krishna at that very moment. He waited for the breaking of silence by his friend.

Animish continued, 'Except for the glorious uncertainties of war. When equals fight, a single arrow can sometimes decide the result. Superior numbers are helpful, but that itself is not clinching. The big warriors are certainly great motivators, but in case they fall, the morale of the rank and file gets dented. Once the momentum slips and a side gets demoralised, anything can happen. Desertions of armies after the start of the war are not unknown. Moreover, there is no guarantee that the war will be fought on set rules, as both groups are fully determined to win at all costs. Hence, one can never be sure who will win the war.'

'Master, certainly you don't expect the seasoned warriors of either side to break the rules and resort to adharma?'

'Tell me about that after the war was finished.'

There was a sneer in his voice.

He dismissed the assembly and moved towards their cottages, with Asareer to follow closely. Animish slowed down after a while, and Asareer caught up with him. Despite their differences in beliefs, their friendship only grew stronger over the years.

'I think it is high time our Master visits us returning from the Himalayas,' suggested Asareer. Asareer knew how much their Master shaped Animish, and he felt that his friend needed the calm guidance of the Master at this stage.

Animish responded immediately in a positive tone as if he liked the idea. 'You are absolutely right about that. I hold the same opinion and sent him a message a few days ago requesting him to consider visiting us. Let's hope he will come.'

'What is worrying you?' asked Asareer, looking straight into his friend's eyes. They were just about to reach Animish's cottage.

'Nothing in particular and everything in general. We had cultivated friends all over in royal families of various kingdoms, and almost every one of them had entered the war. Most of them, if not all, would perish in this war. Maybe their impending news of death is weighing heavy on my heart. People in all the kingdoms are now feeling excited about the war and the glories attached to it. They all come and join in the fight between two groups who were nurturing bad blood between them. They are joining one side or the other and are excited about killing their opponents on the other side and are expecting to go to the heavens, which they say are reserved for those who die in war. But just visualise the scenario and how it would look after the war. Every kingdom would have lost so much, and none would gain anything except either Yudhishthira or Duryodhana, whoever wins and survives. And even those who win would have had to pay a heavy price for that victory. These thoughts make me feel sad as the war is about to start. Another reason is that after the war, most survivors become bitter as the memories of war would haunt them forever. People, in general, become weak and turn towards the unknown for fear of death and uncertainty in life. These are some of my apprehensions.'

Animish went inside his cottage, and as Asareer proceeded alone, he was joined by two other inmates who had been following the senior duo until then. They admired Asareer for his individuality; many like them liked Asareer's gentle manners. Asareer was different from the Little Master, different from many of them, and that, too, was a reason for their attraction towards him.

' May we ask you something?' One of those two asked Asareer.

'Pray, ask. What is bothering you?'

'We just wanted to know your opinion on who would win the war, Kauravas or Pandavas?'

Asareer was amused at the question. Animish explained in detail the uncertainties of war just a few minutes back, and these people started to collect opinions!

He thought for a while and said, 'Krishna would win.' Without giving the bewildered duo an opportunity to seek elaboration or ask further questions, he shut the conversation with his disarming smile and entered his cottage.

At that very instant, he got the answer to his earlier question as to what was really bothering Animish. Krishna, the emerging winner of the war, would be hailed as the upholder of dharma, and his credentials to be hailed as an avatar of Vishnu or Vishnu himself would be strengthened. Animish must have been bothered about that future scenario, whether or not he was consciously aware of it.

Asareer felt a wave of pity swelling in his bosom for his dear friend.

Chapter 7

Conversations Amidst Approaching War

Naimisha

There was no let-up in war conversations, which persisted and were further accentuated after Krishna's truce efforts failed. The war was imminent, with both sides gathering troops and preparing for battle upon summons. However, the exact date and battlefield were yet to be finalised. Once determined, war camps will be established.

Conversations among commoners in Indraprastha, Hastinapur, and the participating kingdoms, as well as in the ashrams of Naimisha, have intensified and reached new heights with daily developments unfolding.

Person 1: Who supported the Kauravas and Pandavas? How did the Kauravas mobilise eleven akshauhinis against the Pandavas' seven?

Person 2: Both Pandavas and Kauravas garnered support from their respective relatives. Duryodhana's rapport with many kings allowed him to amass more support. Karna's recent victories over these kings, coupled with the Pandavas' prolonged exile, consolidated Duryodhana's alliances. The Pandavas mainly relied on close relatives for support.

Person 3: Panchala and Virata kings committed their entire armies to Pandavas, each contributing one Akshauhini.

Person 4: Satyaki, Sahadeva of Magadha, and Dhrishtaketu of Chedi each brought an Akshauhini. Ghatotkacha and Pandya Raja's armies also pledged support. One set of Kekaya brothers, who always sided with Pandavas, joined, too. Then there are armies of some smaller kingdoms, too. Together, they exceed seven Akshauhinis.

Person 5: Pardon my ignorance. What is an Akshauhini, and how is it reckoned?

Person 4: It's a unit measuring military strength based on chariots, horses, elephants, and foot soldiers. It is a considerable figure.

Person 2: Let me explain from the base unit reckoning. One elephant, one chariot, three horses, and five foot-soldiers are taken as a group to reckon the basic unit of calculation. It is called 'Patti.' Three such patthis are called 'Senamukha'. Three Senamukhas are called 'Gulma.' Similarly, the higher measures like Gana, Vahini, Puthana, Chamu and Ankini are reckoned at three times the previous groupings. Finally, an akshauhini is reckoned to be equal to ten 'Ankinis, or 21870 times the basic unit 'Patti.'

Person 3: An akshauhini thus comprises 21,870 elephants, 21,870 chariots, 65,610 horses, and 1,09,350 foot soldiers.

Person 2: Multiply this by eighteen to envisage Kurukshetra's scale. It's mind-boggling!

Person 5: Indeed, yes! Lakhs of elephants and chariots, three times as many horses, and five times that many foot soldiers—it's overwhelming!

Person 1: Satyaki always sided with the Pandavas as Krishna's shadow and Arjuna's disciple and admirer. But why did Dhrishtaketu and Sahadeva join Pandavas' side, which Krishna supports?

Person 4: No doubt, their fathers, Shishupala and Jarasandha, harboured animosity towards Krishna all through their lives. The Chedi people were sour with Krishna when Krishna killed their king Shishupala in the open court, but they did not find fault with Pandavas, who were as much surprised at the killing of Shishupala as those of others. Shishupala was always friendly with Pandavas and even married his daughter, Karenumati, to Nakula.

Person 3: Dhrishtaketu understood the circumstances of his father's demise and saw no reason to oppose Pandavas. Remember, he was coronated as the king of Chedi immediately after his father's death, and he was in the camp of Pandavas all along. He was one of those kings who met Pandavas and pledged support at the very beginning of Pandavas' Aranyavasa.

Person 4: Sahadeva, the eldest son of Jarasandha, was grateful to Krishna and Pandavas for not occupying Magadha after his father's killing. Instead, they offered him a hand of friendship. Don't forget that both the incidents you mentioned were more than thirteen years ago, and time heals many wounds.

Person 3: With some exceptions! Sahadeva's younger brother, Jayatsena, however, had not reconciled and joined Duryodhana, taking with him an akshauhini, still nursing the old wounds.

Person 1: That's understandable; people have different perceptions. What about Ghatotkacha's danava army? I heard he, being Bhima's son, joined the Pandavas out of filial duty.

Person 3: Yes, Pandavas recognised him as a family member despite his danava mother. He helped them in their Aranyavasa period and associated with them during the Rajasuya wars earlier. Yudhishthira is said to have a great liking for this man. I don't know how much army he brought in, but it might be close to an Akshauhini. He was accompanied by his son Anjanaparva. Talking about Pandavas' sons, another son of Arjuna through Ulupi, his Naga wife, Iravan, is reported to have joined with a large contingent of Naga warriors.

Person 1: And how about Arjuna's other son, Babhruvahana, the son of Chitrangada and the future king of Manipura?

Person 3: Reports suggest he has not yet joined. As Manipura's only heir and young, his grandfather likely forbade his participation. Probably, the king of Manipura himself is joining Pandavas with his forces.

The conversation continued as more people joined, discussing, questioning, and answering based on their understanding.

Another day, another set of people in conversation about the Kaurava army and related matters.

Person 1: I heard that Duryodhana had mobilised more than eleven akshauhinis. Who supported him and came with their armies?

Person 2: He mustered support from various quarters in addition to his formidable troop strength. Jayadratha, the ruler of Sindhu, brought an Akshauhini. Bhagadatta, king of Pragjyotishpura and son of Narakasura, joined with another. From Dwaraka, an Akshauhini of Narayanasena joined Kauravas in fulfilling Krishna's promise to Duryodhana and Kritavarma, the chief of the Dwaraka army, came along. The Bahlikas, led by Bahlika, along with his son Somadatta and grandson Bhurishravas, and other clans sided with Duryodhana, contributing an Akshauhini. King Sudakshina of the Kambhoja kingdom and the Kekaya brothers each brought an Akshauhini. The Vinda and Anuvinda brothers of Avanti added two Akshauhinis.

Person 3: That accounts for eight Akshauhinis. Then, unexpectedly, Shalya, with one more Akshauhini from Madra, joined the Kaurava camp, which was, rather, a windfall gain to Kauravas. Additionally, there are armies from Gandhara under Shakuni, Mahishmati under Neela, the famed Samshaptakas of Trigarta under Susharma and his brothers, Jalasandha's army from Magadha, Brihadbala of Ayodhya, and the Kalinga army under Shrutayudha and his clan. These armies together total more than eleven akshauhinis. I haven't included the Rakshasa army under Alambusha yet.

Person 4: More might join once the battle starts. There are still armies making their way and aligning with each side.

Person 2: But could someone enlighten me on how Shalya, the maternal uncle of Nakula and Sahadeva, ended up joining the opposition camp?

Person 3: Initially, Shalya intended to join the Pandavas when he set out towards Hastinapur. He was delighted with the hospitality he received on the way, presuming his nephews had arranged it all. However, when Duryodhana, who actually made all the arrangements, pleaded for his support, Shalya was swayed despite his initial hesitation. He harboured jealousy towards Krishna and believed aligning with Duryodhana would earn him more respect. His long-standing cordial relations with Bhishma, Dhritarashtra, and Duryodhana's flattery played a role in his decision. He brought with him an akshauhini, widening the gap between the armies by two akshauhinis, as he would have otherwise joined the Pandavas.

Person 3: Shalya, it seems, visited Yudhishthira's camp to inform him of his decision to fight alongside Duryodhana and to bid his nephews farewell before they would meet again on the battlefield on opposite sides.

Person 4: Speaking of pride, no one surpasses Rukmi, the Bhoja king and brother of Krishna's wife, Rukmini. His pride was so hurt after Krishna defeated him and later pardoned him that he refused to return to his capital, Kundinapura. Instead, he established a new capital in the same place and named it Bhoja Kataka, where his parents, ministers, and court eventually relocated. Despite reconciling with his sister Rukmini much later and marrying his daughter Rukmavati to Pradyumna, Rukmi maintained a respectful distance from Krishna. He boasted about himself of being the greatest bowman alive, wielding the mighty bow called Vijaya.

Person 5: You're delving into history now, but isn't the Vijaya bow supposed to be possessed by Karna, received from his guru Parashurama? How did Rukmi come to have it?

Person 4: Regarding the Vijaya bow, Rukmi claimed he received it as a gift from Druma, the renowned Kimpurusha archer of earlier times with whom he trained. However, it is also perplexing to me how two mighty bows named Vijaya could exist simultaneously with different owners. Either one is a replica, or they share the same name for other reasons. Nonetheless, there was no record of Rukmi using this bow in any battle, despite his admirers believing him to be as skilled as Arjuna wielding Gandiva. Perhaps it was more about his boasting than actual prowess. Alas, it won't be tested since he wouldn't participate in the war on either side.

A few voices expressed surprise and asked him to explain further, and he went on.

Rukmi first went to the Pandavas' camp and met Arjuna. He had with him an army of one Akshauhini. He boastfully offered to join their side, stating that Arjuna need not get scared to face Kauravas and that he could take them on personally. This egoistic talk certainly touched a raw nerve in Arjuna, and Rukmi received a negative reply. Arjuna told him that he did not need any help from him to face Kauravas, as he could do it all by himself. He suggested that Rukmi could make his own decision on staying on the Pandavas' side or leaving. Rukmi was hurt that his offer was not valued by Arjuna and left immediately for Duryodhana's camp. However, Duryodhana himself declined Rukmi's help, feeling offended that Rukmi did not come to him as the first choice.

He was the only one refused by both sides and one of the very few kings who didn't join the war.

Person 2: Balarama also did not join the war. He met Yudhishthira along with other Vrishni warriors and confirmed that he was not joining either side. He told Yudhishthira that he advised Krishna not to take sides and to sincerely broker for peace, but Krishna's fondness for Arjuna had stood in the way. As far as he was concerned, he was bound by his brother's choice and hence decided to go on pilgrimage for the duration of the war. His parting advice to Yudhishthira was to conduct the war on dharmic lines.

Person 1: Though Balarama always says he is fond of both Bhima and Duryodhana as his favourite students, he always had a soft spot for Duryodhana. Sensing the difference of opinion among the brothers, the other Vrishni warriors, like Pradyumna, Samba, Aniruddha, etc., took a neutral stand and did not join either side and joined Balarama on the pilgrimage. Thus, only two known warriors from Dwaraka, Satyaki and Kritavarma, would be fighting in this war, albeit on opposite sides.

Another day, another meeting:

Person 1: Did any of you hear that Karna is not going to take part in the war?

Person 2: Surprise of surprises. But how come? He is the main person on whom Duryodhana rested his hopes for victory, and he is the chief of the Kaurava army. Why such a sudden decision?

Person 3: Surprising but true also. I also heard this news. There was a clash of words between Bhishma and Karna, which caused Karna to say that he would take part in the war only after Bhishma laid down his arms.

Person 1: What you heard is correct. Bhishma and Karna always held different views on the Pandavas. Even before the clash you mentioned, it seems, Bhishma had laid down a condition that he would accept being the chief of the army only if Karna was excluded from the team.

Person 2: But what is this latest clash about?

Person 1: Duryodhana asked Bhishma to appraise the relative strengths of warriors on both sides. Bhishma gave his frank assessment. He rated Karna as equal to half a Ratha, Ardharatha to be precise. He told Duryodhana point blank that Karna was foolish to part with his natural armour and earrings and had no chance in a fight with Arjuna. Karna, who considered himself the best man to take on Arjuna, felt this remark as a humiliation in an open meeting. He vented out his anger then and there and criticised Bhishma on various grounds, declaring his intention not to enter the war until or unless Bhishma retired.

Person 4: Didn't Duryodhana try to patch things up? Resting an ace warrior like Karna at the beginning of the war is certainly a disadvantage, isn't it?

Person 3: No doubt, it was humiliating and demotivating not only to Karna but to all who counted him as the best of warriors. But Duryodhana had no choice since Bhishma had declared that he would not like to have Karna on his team. Duryodhana probably thought keeping his grandfather, the best bet for him in this war, in a happy frame was important. Moreover, in case of Bhishma falling, he would have an immediate replacement in Karna, a strong and committed warrior. Duryodhana would have reconciled to

Karna entering the battlefield after a little delay might, in fact, prove to be a good strategy. Or, he had no choice and did not let that issue spoil the spirit of the warriors by making it an issue.

Person 2: Anyway, what are the ratings of other warriors? Do we have those details?

Person 1: There is a long list. Are you all really interested?

Persons 2, 3, 4, & 5: Yes, we are interested to know; may not be all, but a few that would matter.

Person 1: Then let us start with the ratings on the Kaurava side. Bhishma did not rate himself, probably thinking the scales did not fit him. Most have considered him equal or a shade better than Drona.

Drona was rated as Yudhapathi of Yudhapathis, meaning more than an Atiradha. He gave the same rating to Kripacharya and rated Kritavarma, Shalya, and Bhurishravas as Atiradhas.

Person A: Just a minute before you proceed. How about Ashwatthama?

Person 1: Bhishma lavished praise on Ashwatthama but said he could not rate him as Atiradha because Ashwatthama values his life very highly and may withdraw if he senses death.

Person 2: Looks like another unreasonable judgement to me. Ashwatthama values his father's life more than his own. He is soft towards Pandavas and respects them but considers Duryodhana as his friend. During the past thirteen years, he developed a strong bond with Duryodhana and is totally committed to fighting this war with his father and uncle.

Person 1: That may be the case. However, nobody raised an issue. He also rated Bahlika and Bhagadatta, the oldest warriors, as Atiradhas. He ranked Vrishasena, son of Karna, as Maharadhi, along with Alambusha, Satyavantha, Paurava, and others. He classified most of the others as Radhikas or Udara Radhikas, etc.

Person 3: Yes, he considered Duryodhana and all his brothers, as well as Susharma of Trigarta, as Udara Radhikas and Jayadratha, as equal to two Radhikas.

Person 5: How about the warriors on the Pandava side?

Person 1: I am coming to that. He did not rate Arjuna, as Duryodhana was well aware. Like him, Bhishma would have thought he was beyond rating. He rated Satyaki and Abhimanyu as "Yudhapathi of Yudhapathis," a very high grading akin to that of Drona. He rated Dhrishtadyumna as Atiradha. Other Atiradhas on the Pandava side are Satyajit, Vasudana, Purujit, son of Kuntibhoja, etc. Strangely, he put Bhima on par with eight Radhikas but not as an Atiradha or Maharadha. I doubt whether it was to please Duryodhana or if it was his genuine assessment. All others he rated as Maharadhis and Radhikas.

Person 3: I highly doubt some of his ratings. Anyway, when the war begins, those ratings will be meaningless. The vigour with which one fights, their alertness, and their coordination with other warriors on their side will count for a lot.

Person 2: When is the war going to start?

Person 1: Shortly, at any moment, or it may have already started while we are talking here. All hope of a truce had vanished when Krishna returned to Upaplavya with a 'No deal' from Hastinapur. Both sides are marching towards Kurukshetra, the chosen place, and work is underway to prepare the battleground: flattening the ups and filling up the pits. The ground should be strong enough to allow elephants, horses, and particularly chariots to move freely.

Person 2: We are all familiar with the skills of Bhishma, Drona, Karna, and Ashwatthama on the Kaurava side and the Pandavas on the Pandava side. Who are the others who might make a difference?

Person 1: There are many on both sides. On the Kaurava side, King Bhagadatta, son of Narakasura, is very strong. He held Arjuna at bay for a considerable period during the Rajasuya war. He had an elephant called 'Supratika', which is of the same breed as Indra's 'Airavat'. Susharma of Trigarta, with his brothers and a well-trained army, is a considerable force. Then their cousin, 'Bhurishravas', is a mighty warrior. They also have 'Shrutayudha', the son of Varuna, who wields an invincible mace. The king of Kambhoja, Sudakshina, is a great warrior. We all know about Shalya and Jayadratha. They also have the support of Neela, the renowned king from the south. There are many more; we will learn more details as the war progresses.

Person 3: You didn't mention the danava king "Alambusha", the brother of Baka.

Person 1: Yes, he joined Duryodhana immediately as he wanted to avenge the slaying of Baka, Hidimba, and Kimmira by killing Bhima and his son Ghatotkacha. There is another king by the same name 'Alambusha' who is also fighting for the Kauravas, so please don't get confused.

Person 4: How about Pandavas' side?

Person 3: Drupada and Virata are formidable warriors despite their age and have brought all their forces. Every son and every brother of those kings is taking part, and they are numerous. They are a significant force. Arjuna's Naga son Iravan and Bhima's danava son Ghatotkacha will neutralise Alambusha. Satyaki of the Vrishni race is eager to fight and torment the Kauravas' side. He, too, was a student of Drona along with Pandavas and Kauravas and improved further under Arjuna's guidance. He is battle-hardened, having fought many battles for Dwaraka. We may hear more about his skills as the war progresses. They also have strong warriors in Malayadhvaja, the Pandyan king, and Dhrishtaketu of Chedi. Every son of a Pandava is of great strength, especially Abhimanyu, who is rated to be equal to or even better than Arjuna on a given day.

Person 1: However, the numerical strength of the army is clearly on the Kaurava side. They also have great warriors. War is a strange sport. We cannot declare a side as the winner until the last head has rolled. Let us stop our analysis and wait for war news on a daily basis. We cannot predict how long the battle will last. Let us retire for the night.

And with that, they all got up to proceed to their respective places.

Hastinapur

Dhritarashtra was tense with expectation. He was both hopeful of winning and fearful of losing the battle at the same time. One moment, he would hear the thundering voice of his son, who was full of conviction.

"We have eleven akshauhinis on our side as against seven akshauhinis of the Pandavas. Our warriors Bhishma, Kripa, Karna, and Drona are formidable, as is Ashwatthama. The reputed Arjuna, who people consider invincible, will be subdued by Karna if Arjuna lasts until Karna enters the fray. Who can conquer Bhishma Pitamaha? None can defeat Drona, wielding a bow. You can be assured of that. I will pulverise that proud man Bhima, whom you fear so much, in a mace fight with one strong stroke of my powerful mace. You are overestimating the strengths of the enemy and are unnecessarily brooding. We are entering the war with the aim to win and make our kingdom strong."

Then, the very next moment, he would recall Vidura's words.

"It is impossible to find a man who can stop Arjuna. Now Krishna has joined them, and he will be Arjuna's charioteer. When Arjuna and Krishna come together in the same chariot, the battle is pre-decided in their favour."

Again, he remembers what Duryodhana had said in reaction to his suggestion to accept the peace treaty brought by Krishna.

"People would laugh at us if we accepted a truce now and ceded a part of the kingdom to them. They are not asking you; they are trying to force you by mobilising seven akshauhinis before sending their emissary. It was good that we mobilised a large army from our friends. Otherwise, they might have even attacked us by now. Agreeing to their proposal at this stage would amount to accepting defeat. None of the assembled kings on our side has shown an inclination towards peace. They are all raring to go. I am not a coward to stop

now. Kshatriyas are safe if they avoid wars, but they were not born to lead war-free lives. Kshatriyas are not meant to die in bed. The proper place for a Kshatriya to die is the battlefield. There cannot be any second opinion on this."

For most of his life, Dhritarashtra was guided by Bhishma, for whom he had great respect. He trusted the wisdom of his brother Vidura, who always gave impartial and straightforward advice. Dronacharya was considered the very incarnation of Brihaspati and always gave sound advice. His father, Vedavyasa, who is known to be aware of the past, future, and present, had asked him to be prepared for the worst if peace was not brokered. None of the old guards advised him to go to war. Vidura decided not to fight in the war. Bhishma and Drona would take part, but reluctantly.

Dhritarashtra called for Sanjaya and had a long dialogue with him. He asked him to be present on the battlefield and report important news to him. Sanjaya was provided with immunity from both sides, as suggested by Vedavyasa, who had picked Sanjaya for the mission. Dhritarashtra and Vidura would receive daily messages from the reporters, but it was for Sanjaya to convey any upsetting news to the king personally, as Vedavyasa advised.

Sanjaya asked for permission from Dhritarashtra to leave the palace and report to the war front, as the battle might start at any time. They had been discussing for the past two days, since Vyasa left, about the warriors that had come from various places and kingdoms in the world, the multiple ways people lived in different parts of the universe, and many other diverse things, to divert themselves from thinking about the impending war. Dhritarashtra had an inquisitive mind and a great memory. He always wanted to know things in minute detail. In Sanjaya, he found a great narrator. Sanjaya had a terrific memory and great perception. Son of Gavalgana, a Suta, he was the wisest of the youngsters. He was a contemporary of the Kauravas and Pandavas and trained along with them. He was a personal friend of Arjuna, an understudy of Vidura, and a confidant of Dhritarashtra. Vedavyasa personally picked him up for the present mission.

Vedavyasa knew that what Dhritarashtra needed was not just a carrier of war news but someone who could interpret events and answer his questions. The delivery of a series of sad news should be done in such a way that the shocks the king was going to receive would be as slow and gradual as possible. After a long silence, Dhritarashtra permitted Sanjaya to leave.

'Please go and stay safe. Though you have been given immunity from both sides of the war, accidents might happen on the war front. As my father Vedavyasa told me, now you are my eyes and ears to watch the war and convey to me whatever happens. Vidura will brief me on the highlights after he receives the news, but it is for your visits that I will be eagerly looking forward to. I have no doubt your narratives will cover the minutest details of what you see, hear, gather, and perceive. Give my blessings to Duryodhana and my other sons.'

Sanjaya bowed and walked with a heavy heart toward his chariot, which was to carry him straight to the Kauravas' camp at Kurukshetra.

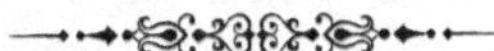

Chapter 8

War Camps and Warrior Ratings

Kurukshetra, Pandavas' Camp

All the warriors and soldiers from various kingdoms eagerly waited for the start of the war, making merry in the meantime in their respective camps. There was music and dancing around. The camps had huge dining halls and kitchens. Vast quantities of food and wine for the people and fodder for the animals were stockpiled. The doctors and medical staff were kept in readiness. It was the atmosphere of a great festival in both camps. People were moving across the camps, meeting their friends and relatives in the opposing camps. Once the war started, they would bitterly fight for their sides. They all knew they wouldn't be able to see most of the combatants from either side once the war was finished, even if one survived against heavy odds.

The countdown to the war reached the penultimate day, and everyone was waiting for the announcement of the generals who would be leading the army units. The leaders of the army, called 'Senapatis', were to be decided and announced. Yudhishthira had closeted himself with his brothers and Srikrishna to finalise the matter in Pandava's war tent.

Word was sent to Drupada to attend the meeting. The Panchalas and Srinjayas shouted aloud, in anticipation, as Drupada walked towards the war tent. Drupada was the central force around which all Panchala and

Srinjaya clans had pinned their hopes to settle scores with Hastinapur. Conquering the Kurus in the war was their long-cherished dream. Still, they could not dare to attack Hastinapur, which was under the protection of unconquerable Bhishma and had been strengthened by the additional support from Drona. Now that the Kurus were divided and fighting among themselves and with Arjuna, who could counter the formidable duo on their side, Panchalas and Srinjayas were euphoric about their victory.

The next name announced was that of Virata, who had come to support the Pandavas with his brothers, sons, and entire forces. Virata always had great respect for Yudhishthira, and he grew close to him during Ajnatavasa, where they two had spent considerable time together. He now had a personal stake in the future of Pandavas after marrying his daughter Uttara to Abhimanyu. He also felt indebted to the Pandavas, who took shelter in his kingdom and saved him from a certain death at the hands of Susharma. He came along with his brothers Suryadatta, Madiraksha, and Shatanika, as well as all his sons. He was accompanied by his sons, Shankha and Uttarakumara. They were all pleased that their supremo was considered a Senapati, and their camp welcomed the decision with loud sounds of horns and trumpets.

The next round of cheers was reserved for the camp of the Panchalas and Srinjayas again. Two more Panchalas, sons of Drupada, Shikhandi, and Dhrishtadyumna, who were expected to cause the downfall of Bhishma and Drona in that order, were announced as Senapatis to the loud cheers from the Panchalas and Srinjayas, the largest contingent of the Pandavas' army.

The remaining two slots were filled by Sahadeva of Magadha and Drishtaketu of Chedi. The eldest son of Jarasandha, Sahadeva, preferred the side of the Pandavas. Having been spared by them after the killing of their father, Sahadeva felt obliged to reciprocate the gesture by joining the Pandavas. However, his younger brother Jayatsena joined the side of Kauravas.

Drishtaketu had no such dilemma. Though Krishna killed his father Shishupala in the Rajasuya Yaga, he did not harbour any animosity towards Pandavas, who were his relatives from his grandmother's side and his sister Karenumati was married to Nakula. He was reconciled with the fact that Shishupala's destiny was pre-decided at the time of his birth itself, and Krishna was gracious enough to spare him a longer-than-deserved lifespan.

The sons of Jarasandha and Shishupala had each committed an army of one akshauhini, and it was fair that they were given command positions. Jubilant trumpeting was heard from the Magadha and Chedi camps.

Having settled six command positions, Yudhishthira anointed Dhrishtadyumna as the chief commander, the Sarva Sainyadhipati, after much deliberation. Arjuna, the foremost warrior of the Pandavas' side, was kept free from commanding the armies but was given the responsibility of directing all the Senapatis. A Senapati of Senapatis, so to speak.

Yudhishthira did not appoint any of his brothers, sons, and Satyaki as senapatis as a matter of strategy to allow them to concentrate on individual combats. Yudhishthira still had a masterstroke to deliver. He announced Srikrishna as Arjuna's commander and counsellor, which Krishna accepted, and Arjuna gladly welcomed. Though Krishna had initially said he would not take part in the war but only act as a charioteer to Arjuna, he had to accept the chief advisor's role and direct the efforts of the Pandavas' army towards the goal. Though Krishna's vow of not wielding any weapons remained sacrosanct, Yudhishthira was confident that, come what may, Krishna would lead them to victory.

There were boisterous shouts of celebration all around, and the joyous music was continuous and the loudest once the names of Krishna and Arjuna were announced. Bhima took out his conch, Poundraka, and blew it loudly. Taking that as a cue, all the Pandavas, Krishna, Satyaki, and other kings blew their conches in unison to raise the spirits of their army. Only the remaining part of the day and the night separated them from the much-awaited war.

⟶⟶⟶⟨⟩⟶⟶

Kauravas' Camp

Duryodhana decided that Bhishma would be the Sarva Sainyadhipati, the Supreme Commander, even before the armies marched to Kurukshetra. Dronacharya, Kripacharya, and Ashwatthama, the Acharya trio, were given the roles of Senapatis. All three were much-respected warriors, not only by the Kaurava camp but also by many in the Pandavas' camp. Many kings who had assembled to fight for either camp were, at one time or another, wards of Drona's gurukula. The Acharyas were pleased with the devotion shown to them by Duryodhana and accepted the roles.

Shalya, who brought an akshauhini of sena, was pleased to accept being one of the Senapatis. He had a long relationship with Bhishma ever since he gave his sister Madri to Panduraja at Bhishma's request. Though Duryodhana sort of tricked him into switching sides, Shalya wholeheartedly accepted serving the Kaurava army as a seasoned Kshatriya.

Jayadratha of Sindhu, who brought an akshauhini himself and who was also a formidable warrior trained under Drona, was another Senapati. Being Duryodhana's brother-in-law, he had a huge stake in their victory. He nursed a grudge against the Pandavas for the humiliation they had meted out to him during his failed attempt to abduct Draupadi.

The king of Kambhoja, Sudakshina, was another Senapati. Sudakshina had brought with him an akshauhini of sena comprising Yavanas and Sakas.

Kritavarma of the Bhoja race, a top-notch Yadava warrior who had joined the Kauravas with Krishna's permission, was made another Senapati. He had no qualms about fighting against the side of Krishna, being a true Kshatriya and would do all he could to fight for Duryodhana.

Karna was another Senapati, though he was not supposed to enter the battlefield as long as Bhishma was fighting in the battleground. Karna said if Bhishma could deliver victory to the Kauravas, he would congratulate him and leave for the woods for tapasya. He was sure Bhishma, being partial, could not and would not kill Arjuna, without which the win would not happen.

Shakuni, the king of Gandhara and Duryodhana's dearest uncle, was another Senapati. All of Shakuni's brothers and sons had rallied around him, ready to fight and die for Duryodhana.

Bahlika, the senior-most surviving member of the Bharata race and still active, was another Senapati, and his grandson Bhurishravas was another. They came with full force by themselves. Bahlika's son and father of Bhurishravas, Somadatta, had a personal interest in the war. He had a long-standing rivalry with the Sini family ever since Sini defeated him during Devaki's swayamvar. While Sini's grandson Satyaki was fighting on behalf of the Pandavas, Somadatta expected his son Bhurishravas to conquer Satyaki.

All lustily cheered Duryodhana's announcement of eleven Senapatis and Bhishma's anointing as the Sarva Sainyadhipati.

It had been a long time since they had seen Bhishma in serious action. The stories of his fights with Parashurama, Ugrayudha, and many other kings, as well as his audacious abduction of the princesses of Kashi, defeating multiple kings all alone, had become part of folklore. He was popularly remembered as the man who had not only withstood Parashurama but even had him concede defeat. His reputation and respect in the community of Kshatriyas had been high after he restored the Kshatriya pride by holding Parashurama, the man feared by all Kshatriyas until then. He has never tasted defeat in a war so far. He was an aged warrior, no doubt, but everyone believed that age had not withered his skills even to the slightest extent.

Bhishma had informed Duryodhana that the Pandavas were not his killing targets. However, he assured Duryodhana that he would kill a minimum of ten thousand foot soldiers and a thousand radhikas every day as his share as long as he was in battle. He also made it clear that he would not counter Shikhandi, the eldest son of Drupada, even if the latter attacked him because Shikhandi was born a woman first and later converted into a man, whom he referred to as 'Anganapoorv.'

Duryodhana respected his sentiment and counselled his brothers that as long as they ensured Shikhandi did not come face to face with the grandsire, they could expect Bhishma to destroy the Pandavas' forces. He specially assigned the duty of guarding Bhishma from Shikhandi to Dusshasana, who readily agreed.

With Bhishma and Drona on his side and Karna in reserve, Duryodhana was emboldened to inform his father that his forces were far superior to those of the Pandavas, not only in number but also in quality.

Chapter 9

The Mother of All Wars - The Beginning

Naimisha, Shamyaprasa

Vedavyasa was in deep meditation. He was receiving a stream of messengers from both the Kaurava and Pandava sides. Both camps wanted to keep their grandfather abreast of the news as well as their version of incidents. However, none was allowed to meet the sage, who wished to remain undisturbed. Perhaps he was praying for some good to happen or concentrating on visualising what was occurring on the battlefield. The messengers reported to Vaishampayana and his other disciples and answered their questions. They started early in the morning from the battlefield and returned at night. Another batch would arrive the next day.

The disciples discussed the news among themselves. Whenever Vedavyasa allowed them to speak after coming out of meditation, he would listen and nod. There would be no surprise on his face, no matter the news. He wouldn't ask any questions, as if he already knew what had happened.

The news deliberated in Vyasa's ashram would quickly spread through various ashrams in Naimisha. Some disciples relied on their memory to remember the news, and some others noted down the details to keep a proper record for the future. Survivors of the war or the successors of those who were killed would be interested in knowing how the war progressed.

The Little Master's Ashram

The Little Master's ashram also received news from the evening meetings at Vedavyasa's ashram, which were open to all. Besides, they were getting news through their ashramites who stationed themselves in the war camps and had no problem gathering information through their contacts.

As with all unfiltered information, sometimes there were erroneous reports. A warrior might fall from a horse, be injured, and be carried off the field, to be reported dead only to be corrected on his reappearance on the battleground the next day. There are also many warriors with the same or similar names, and the news can get corrupted during transmission through multiple people. However, they took maximum care to keep such possibilities low and double-checked the critical news.

On the seventh evening of the war, the Little Master presided over a meeting. The participants had received news of the first six days of the war and were discussing it.

Newsbearer: I will summarise the news received from various sources about the first six days of the battle. There are heavy casualties on both sides. Bhishma created havoc in the Pandavas' army and killed many foot soldiers and radhikas. His strategy is probably to create terror among the ranks and make them flee.

Uttara Kumara put up a great fight with none other than Shalya on the first day of the battle and seemed a fearless warrior. However, Shalya killed him, which enraged his elder brother, Shweta, who put up a spirited fight and challenged Bhishma. Surprisingly, this son of Virata could stretch Bhishma to his limits before finally succumbing. Other than these two notable names, there were no other killings of maharadhis on the opening day.

There were no notable Pandava casualties on the second day; Bhishma went on killing radhikas, and Drona was primarily engaged in fighting with the Srinjayas and Panchalas. However, Bhima showed his ferocious form from Pandava's side on the second day. He was particularly severe on the

Kalinga army led against him by Bhanumantha and killed Bhanumantha by cutting him in half with a swift sword manoeuvre. Bhima then destroyed Sakradeva by throwing a mace at him. He went on killing the Nishada king Ketumanta and the warriors Satya and Satyadeva, this time with arrows. Bhima's all-round display and ferocious form stunned those who had not seen him in action earlier. He left no one in doubt with this demonstration as to what they could expect from him in the remaining days of the war.

Again, on the third day, there were no killings of notable warriors on either side, though the carnage continued. Arjuna killed no less than ten thousand radhikas and five hundred elephants and was engaged in an even battle with Bhishma.

The fourth day was Bhima's day again, as he began to fulfil his vow of killing the hundred Kaurava brothers all by himself. He killed eight of Duryodhana's brothers, who attacked him together in a ferocious war. Nobody could protect them from Bhima's wrath. Besides Bhima, Abhimanyu, Dhrishtadyumna, and Ghatotkacha put up stiff fights from Pandavas' side. At the same time, Bhurishravas excelled on Kauravas' side and had a great battle with Satyaki's ten sons, killing them all and causing grief and rage in Satyaki's heart.

On the fifth and sixth days, the war continued to be tense, with many horses, elephants, and foot soldiers getting killed. However, all the prominent warriors survived to fight further.

This is the report up to the sixth day of the war. Except on the first day, the Kauravas have not been able to kill any notable warriors of the Pandavas. The Kauravas lost the Kalinga kings, and more importantly, Duryodhana lost eight of his brothers.

Little Master: Huge loss of human life, besides horses and elephants. Six days have passed. You said eight brothers of Duryodhana were killed. Do you have their names?

The newsbearer came nearer to the Little Master and handed him a piece of palm leaf where the eight names were written. "Senapati, Sushena, Jalasandha, Ugra, Virabahu, Bhima, Bhimaratha, Sulochana."

The Little Master read those names aloud and, coming to the end of the list, passed the piece to Asareer, who was sitting by.

Asareer looked at the names he had heard for the first time without much interest. Except for a few, Duryodhana's brothers were known only as Duryodhana's brothers and never by names. He passed the list to the next man for onward circulation for those interested. He then asked the reporting persons, 'How is Srikrishna? Is he confining himself to charioteering, or is he ever tempted to pick up a weapon?'

The Little Master looked at Asareer observingly. He knew his friend wanted to know whether Krishna was safe.

'Krishna has been keeping his word so far, though we are told that at one point, he found Arjuna fighting passively with Bhishma and told Arjuna that he would jump into the fray and kill Bhishma himself if Arjuna did not show aggression in his approach,' said one of them.

'We are told that this happened when Bhishma's arrows repeatedly hit Krishna. Arjuna had pleaded with Krishna not to break his vow and increased his tempo of fighting, another supplemented.

The man next to the Little Master, Anvesh, intervened, saying, 'Krishna might certainly break his vow anytime. He is a battle lover, and driving the chariot day after day must bore him, particularly if he finds Arjuna not being able to counter the Kuru elders; he might even plunge into the war.'

Little Master chuckled and said,' That must be one of the play acts of Krishna to pep up Arjuna and demotivate Bhishma without really intending to plunge into the act at this point. Let's see if he sticks to this stand to the last.'

The discussion then diverted to other aspects when somebody asked from the crowd, 'Who is Shweta, whom you were referring to as the son of Virata and who fought so valiantly against Bhima? We didn't hear of him before.'

Little Master answered, 'Shweta was the son of Virata from his first wife Suradha, the elder sister of Sudeshna. He was sore with his father and had parted ways, setting up a small kingdom of his own somewhere down the hills of Vindhya. However, he maintained good relations with Pandavas and came to help the Pandavas, thereby joining his father and relatives and setting aside all differences. Unfortunately, King Virata lost two sons on the very first day of the war! Anyway, it makes no difference whether it is on the first day or the last day when one is certain to die. All these warriors think that being Kshatriyas, they will reach the heavens reserved for war heroes who die fighting valiantly. That's why so many kings came to take part in the war as if it was a festival!'

He appreciated the newsbearers for their efforts. 'I hope the news you brought is accurate or as accurate as was possible under the circumstances. You stay back for a day or two before you travel to the war zone again. Others are already there to cover the further news. By the way, what are your sources?'

'We are staying with Vishoka's brother, who tends to horses, and gets the news from his brother and his other friends. Vishoka is the charioteer of Bhima.'

'We were also covering the Kaurava camp. I got the news from a young man who takes supplies to war tents and gets to know things from various people.'

'We cross-checked our information with each other while we were coming together and also had the company of official messengers sent to Vyasa ashram on the way. So, the information is more or less accurate.'

Little Master thanked them for their efforts and said, 'Glad to know you are doing a good job. However, war news can never be entirely accurate. We miss something or other as the battle is being fought in a large area, and no single person can watch everything that happens on various fronts. Meet me in the morning to brief me on more details.'

Little Master dismissed the meeting and walked towards his cottage along with Asareer and others.

Kurukshetra

The war was going on in Kurukshetra. Royal messengers of Hastinapur were travelling from the battleground to the capital and back with the day's dispatches. They would meet the ministers in Vidura's presence to report the news. The reports were mostly about heavy casualties on either side and the deaths of important warriors.

Similarly, messengers of various kingdoms gathered news of their kings and other warriors to be retold back to their countries. They had stationed themselves in the war camps to stay till the end of the war. Other messengers, like those reporting to the Naimishite ashrams, were busy travelling back and forth.

All the villages nearer to Hastinapur were busy replenishing the food supplies for both sides of the war kitchens. The work was mainly carried out by women and men who the armies could not recruit. They were all tense about what was happening in the war. Every family, whether from royal palaces or other houses, had at least one person presently engaged in the war. *"Would he return?"* That was the question uppermost in everyone's mind. They knew the answer could be mostly 'no,' but they were not prepared to accept it until the war was over.

Though the reporters carried the death news of important warriors, the commoners had no means to know what was happening to their dear ones. So, they felt it better to assume that their sons, brothers or husbands were still alive, fighting and would return at the end of the war. They would only know and accept the truth, sweet or bitter, only after the war ended.

Hastinapur, Dhritarashtra's palace

Dhritarashtra calls Vidura every day. He was increasingly restless. He even went to the war grounds for a few days to get a feel of the battlefield. He had a separate bed reserved for him in the tent of Somadatta, his cousin and a close friend. When he visited the camp, his sons and other close members would come to see him and seek his blessings. He used to hear the sounds of war cries, the beat of drums and conches during the day, and music from various tents at night. He would come back to the palace and share the news with Gandhari when he returned. He wouldn't retire to bed until the war bulletin was received every day.

'Why did Sanjaya not come to report?' he asked Vidura.

'My brother! He would visit us if anything important happened in the war, which would have the effect of tilting the results one way or the other. It is good that even though we are ten days into the war, he has not come. That means the war was on an even keel.'

'My twenty-five sons were killed by Bhima in the war so far as per the bulletins. I do not feel any status quo. I will never go back to the pre-war position. My son had brought this destruction without heeding the good advice.'

Dhritarashtra had no need to feel embarrassed, for he could not see Vidura's frown and irritated look in response to this comment.

Vidura kept his voice as normal as possible and suggested, 'Don't you think you still could ask your son to stop the war, as you are still holding the crown, and cut the losses?'

Dhritarashtra heaved a sigh and said, 'You know the answer very well. Too many horses had run away through the stable door, which I had allowed to be kept open. There is nothing I can do now, just as there was nothing I could have done then. When the war started, Duryodhana assumed the whole command, and he was the only person who could make decisions. I can only advise as you do, but you know what value your advice or mine carries with Duryodhana. What we heard so far makes me feel that the war hangs in the balance despite so much destruction as both sides had depleted proportionately.'

"The news of war was all Dhritarashtra wanted to discuss now," thought Vidura. Before he could answer, the doorman announced Sanjaya's arrival.

'Show him in immediately', said Dhritarashtra in an anxious voice.

Chapter 10

Fall of the Patriarch

Hastinapur, Dhritarashtra's Palace

The news Sanjaya brought had made Dhritarashtra crestfallen.

'Bhishma had fallen in the war after putting up a vigorous fight for ten days. The man who caused his fall was Shikhandi.'

Dhritarashtra could not bear the news of his father's fall. Vichitraveerya might have been his father, technically, but he never knew him. Vedavyasa was his biological father, but he was a sage and visited only occasionally. Bhishma was the one who took care of him and his brothers ever since their birth. Right from their naming ceremony, Upanayanam and fixing the marriages, Bhishma was the only father he and his brothers knew.

Though there was a possibility of Bhishma's death looming large once the war turned fierce, Dhritarashtra didn't expect Bhishma to fall. He knew his father to be the most formidable warrior on the earth. He never thought Pandavas would dare to harm their grandfather.

'Was Bhishma's fall due to Arjuna's valour, or was it because Shikhandi's arrows found their mark without being obstructed? And why could Dusshasana and others not stop Shikhandi, knowing that he was the nemesis of Bhishma and was specifically entrusted with that task?' Dhritarashtra posed.

'Dusshasana and others could not stop Shikhandi because he was in the same chariot as Arjuna and were effectively stalled by others. Arjuna fought brilliantly to shield Shikhandi from any attack and allowed him to release a barrage of arrows at Bhishma. Both Arjuna's and Shikhandi's arrows penetrated Bhishma's body, but Bhishma did not stop fighting till the moment he fell to the ground, unable to stand on his chariot. One can say Arjuna's arrows dug deeper to injure Bhishma and weakened him considerably.'

Dhritarashtra sighed and commented, 'Probably, it was how it was to happen, and there was no other way. Shikhandi was born out of a boon to Drupada to kill my father. He had to live up to the boon. Akashvani announced during Bhishma's fight with Parashurama that Bhishma would fall to a great warrior in a fierce war. That great warrior must be none other than Arjuna. Both these divine forebodings need to be fulfilled. It was pre-decided by destiny, and Arjuna and Shikhandi played their part. Sanjaya, I am deeply grieved by the loss of my father.'

Sanjaya continued, 'Though fallen, he is still alive. Arrangements were made to keep him rested on the battleground itself. The surroundings were cordoned off. He is practically lying on a bed of arrows, waiting for the final moment. He advised Duryodhana to make a truce with Pandavas even at this stage, but your son wouldn't listen.'

'My adamant and foolish son has brought this upon us. I had already lost my twenty-five sons and now my father. With him goes all hope of winning the war,' lamented Dhritarashtra.

Sanjaya was amazed to hear the words of his king, though it was not new to him, being in Dhritarashtra's inner circle for so long.

"Dhritarashtra is now throwing the entire blame on Duryodhana's doorstep and trying to extricate himself from the whole chain of decisions. He did not stop when he had to stop his son. Not that he was not advised. Elders like Bhishma, Vidura and even Gandhari cautioned him many times. Even sages and Krishna, whom he believed to be God incarnate, counselled him. But his love for his son outweighed all the advice in the world put together. Probably,

the ambitious attitude of his son to grab power by hook or crook had rubbed off on him at some stage and robbed him of his ability to look at the obvious," Sanjaya thought.

Sanjaya said, 'There is no point in blaming Duryodhana at this stage as you were the reason for this situation. All your sons are fighting in the war to the best of their abilities as fit for Kshatriyas.'

The king did not refute Sanjaya's statement. He took the comment stoically and said, 'All my sons who died in the war didn't display any fear. They all fought like heroic Kshatriyas. They had reserved their places in the higher worlds. My father Bhishma had done all he could in the war and paid his final debt to Hastinapur, though he did not owe anything to the empire in the first place. How is he now? Was he being attended to?'

'Bhishma Pitamaha had fallen, but he did not lose consciousness. Arrows pierced his whole body, and hence, his body didn't touch the ground when he fell from the chariot. He was floating in the air, so to say, on the bed of arrows. At his advice, Arjuna had shot a few arrows into the ground to support his neck so that your father could balance his head. He also shot an arrow so deep near to Bhishma's head that water emerged from the earth to quench Bhishma's thirst. Duryodhana had arranged for the doctors to remove the arrows and tend to his wounds. However, Bhishma refused all help and preferred to die on the bed of arrows on the battlefield itself. All Kauravas and Pandavas sat around him and heard him talk. He again advised Duryodhana to stop the war at this stage to avoid the gruesome future which he foresaw.'

Dhritarashtra was sad, visualising the picture of Bhishma on the bed of arrows, flanked on both sides by Pandavas and Kauravas in a sorrowful state, and kept silent for a while.

Vidura left the two alone after hearing the most important news of Bhishma's fall. He took the king's permission to go and attend the ministers' room to listen to what the messengers would say in their daily reporting. He, too, was a disturbed man after hearing the news, as Bhishma was like a father to him, too. In the fall of Bhishma, he lost his driving force and the elderly guidance, for which he regularly reported and consulted Bhishma. It would be a void that never can be filled.

Dhritarashtra continued his conversation with Sanjaya.

'Did Karna come to meet him?'

Sanjaya was surprised at the sudden question of the king. Not for nothing, Dhritarashtra was renowned as a man with eyes all around his brain.

'Yes, he privately met Bhishma after everybody left. Bhishma talked to him, dismissing the attendants. Karna was there for about half an hour and left. Obviously, both did not want their conversation to be heard or known to others.'

'However, nothing would escape you. Isn't it? Let me hear what they did not want the world to be aware of.'

Sanjaya recounted the scene to Dhritarashtra.

'Karna was let into the tent, and he announced himself to Bhishma in a sad voice with tears flowing down. Bhishma asked him to sit by his side and placed his hand affectionately on Karna's shoulders.

He said he knew Karna was the son of Kunti and Surya, as Narada and Vyasa told him. Bhishma further praised Karna for all his past heroic deeds and suggested he may now join with Pandavas for the greater good. Karna confirmed that he, too, knew he was a Pandava, but he valued his commitment to Duryodhana as sacrosanct.

Bhishma admitted that he purposely insulted Karna time and again, only to sow doubts in Duryodhana's mind about Karna's ability to counter Arjuna despite knowing that Karna was capable of facing Krishna and Arjuna in the war and stand up to them. He felt that Karna's influence on Duryodhana was emboldening Duryodhana to foster enmity with Pandavas. However, the ploy backfired, and Duryodhana's confidence in Karna only got stronger. In reality, he had no malice towards Karna, who, too, was his grandson.

A visibly moved Karna replied that he had the highest regard for Bhishma, and he visited Bhishma to apologise for all his past rude behaviour and seek blessings from his grandfather before he entered the battlefield the next day. Bhishma blessed Karna to put forth his best efforts in the war, face Krishna and Arjuna and test his tryst with destiny. Thus ended their meeting, after which Karna returned to his camp determined to plunge into the war the following morning.'

'Of course, both my father and Karna would behave like that only. Their fighting styles are similar, as both were groomed by the same preceptor. They always respected each other's warrior skills, but outwardly, they exhibited a mutual dislike. Good that they spoke heart to heart at last. Hope this meeting will soothe my father's heart and motivate Karna to take part in the war with greater composure.'

Sanjaya spent a good deal of time explaining the first ten days of the war in greater detail and answering all of Dhritarashtra's questions about the narrative. He then took leave and left the place. He needed to reach the camp fast, as it was almost early morning.

For Dhritarashtra, day and night make no difference. He doesn't sleep continuously at night. He keeps thinking a lot. He asked his attendants to call for Vidura. The attendants were not surprised. It was usual for Dhritarashtra to spend hours together with Vidura, particularly when he was tense. The king was tense to hear his father had fallen in the battle and was awaiting eventual death. It was natural he wanted to share sentiments with his brother, Vidura.

Chapter 11

The War Enters The Middle Phase

Naimisha, Little Master's Ashram

Twelve days had passed since the war started, and the messengers arrived late at night. They would report to the assembled members in the morning. Little Master was getting reports on a daily basis and selectively disclosed important news to members. However, ashramites yearned to hear the comprehensive report from the battlefield directly from the news bearers, getting clarifications and discussing. They all assembled to listen to the news as soon as the morning prayers were completed.

The news bearer has started narrating the detailed report.

'The battle was going unabated, and the major casualty was Bhishma, who had fallen on the tenth day of the war. He didn't die yet despite heavy loss of blood, but he would not survive. He was wounded at every place in his body. He had ignored Shikhandi, who aimed arrows at him and concentrated on fighting with Arjuna. Strangely, he would not fight with Shikhandi on the grounds that he was not born a male. He lost so much blood and is now literally on his deathbed. His role in the war was over. He killed many radhika warriors of the Chedi, Karusha, Panchala and Virata kingdoms, even on that final day as per his promise to Duryodhana, before he eventually fell.

Drona had taken over as the Chief Commander of forces after the fall of Bhishma, and then onwards, his ferocity had also increased. He had ideally replaced Bhishma, and Pandavas were finding it tough to break his defences. He opened his score against big names on the seventh day itself by killing Shankha, the son of Virata. His killing spree had gotten better each day after the fall of Bhishma. On the eleventh day, he killed Panchala warriors like Simhasena, Vyaghradatta, and Satyajit, the renowned son of Drupada. Drona then destroyed Panchala warriors like Dhridasena, Kshema Narapala, Vasudana and Shatanika, brother of Drupada, besides killing a number of foot soldiers.

Bhurishravas continued to fight relentlessly with force and killed Manimanta. He must be itching to fight Satyaki, and he knew Satyaki was also looking for the same.

Another warrior of note from Kauravas' side was Alambusha, the danava king who inflicted a significant blow on Pandavas by killing Arjuna's son Iravan. That was on the eighth day after Iravan killed five of Shakuni's brothers and showed a great promise. Alambusha was requisitioned for action by Duryodhana after finding Iravan to be irresistible to others, and after a ferocious duel between both warriors, Alambusha finally prevailed.

Bhagadatta was rampaging Pandava armies, mounting on his giant elephant called 'Supratika' and was at his fierce best on the twelfth day. Bhima tried his best to stop Bhagadatta and thought of killing the elephant first, which was causing great havoc by killing anybody who came near to it either by catching them by its trunk and throwing them afar or by smashing their horses and chariots trampling them under its feet. Bhima boldly faced the elephant on foot and encountered it physically by hitting it with his palms in sensitive places to tame the elephant by using his expert technique called 'anjalika vedhanam.' However, Supratika could not be subdued, and Bhima had to flee away, escape its wrath, and try to find another elephant on which he could mount and resume the fight.

Bhagadatta killed a king called Ruchi Parva, king of Dasarna and mounted a severe attack on Pandavas' army. Finally, on the twelfth day, when Bhagadatta encountered Arjuna, Arjuna killed both Bhagadatta and his mighty elephant after a great duel.

Gandhara princes Vishakha and Achala, brothers of Shakuni, put up a great fight against Arjuna, but both were killed. Karna encountered Arjuna, and they had a severe battle. Arjuna killed three brothers of Karna, including Shatanjaya.

For Kauravas, Ashwatthama put up a great fight to kill a mighty king called Neela. Dhrishtadyumna killed Chandravarma and Nishada king Brihatkshatra.

Somebody in the crowd wanted to know about the feud between the families of Satyaki and Bhurishravas. Little Master explained.

'You all are aware that Krishna's mother, Devaki, was married to Vasudeva in a swayamvar. It was not an incident-free celebration. Bhurishravas's father, Somadatta, challenged Vasudeva to a fight. However, instead of Vasudeva, his cousin Sini, a Vrishni king, fought with Somadatta and took him into his possession. He dragged him to the ground but did not execute him. The humiliated Somadatta came back and wanted to seek revenge at an appropriate time. Sini is the grandfather of Satyaki. Though Sini died long ago, the memories of that tussle are fresh in the minds of both families. The families did not get an opportunity to face each other in a battle earlier, which was now available. Before the war ended, I think this issue between the two families would be settled either way.

Another questioned. 'Who is this Danava king called Alambusha, and how could he kill powerful Iravan, the son of Arjuna?'

Little Master answered.

'This Alambusha was a brother of Baka who was killed by Bhima long years ago when Pandavas were in Ekachakrapura. Then Bhima killed Jatasura, who also happened to be another brother when the latter tried to abduct Draupadi during their pilgrimage. So, Alambusha volunteered himself to join the ranks of Duryodhana to avenge the killing of his brothers. Iravan had conducted a great fight and was tired when he was encountered by Alambusha, who was able to kill him after a bitter duel.'

'Arjuna must be upset at the killing of his son,' somebody commented.

'Why not? In fact, he was not the only father who would now be fighting to avenge the death of his son. He joined Virata, Drupada, and Satyaki as a father who lost at least one son. By the time the war ends. Whoever would survive would indeed have lost a son or two. As far as Arjuna was concerned, Abhimanyu was most dear to him, and he was very active in the war so far and had put up one of the best fights from the side of the Pandavas. Kauravas were thinking about how to counter Arjuna, but it looks like they are facing two Arjunas now, and they need to resolve this soon if they are to stand a chance to win the war.

'Bhagadatta was a known friend of Indra and even Pandavas. How come he was fighting for Kauravas and so severe on Bhima and Arjuna?'

'It is true that Bhagadatta put up an equal fight with Arjuna for seven days before they had a compromise during the Rajasuya war. It was almost fourteen years ago. It was also heard that Bhagadatta felt that he was not honoured adequately when he visited the Rajasuya ceremony of Yudhishthira, though I am not sure of its veracity. Whatever, Bhagadatta was won over by Duryodhana in the meantime, who, perhaps, had also harboured enmity with Srikrishna for killing his father, Naraka.'

'The best war elephant is now extinct. Supratika itself was a fighter on its own. It really gave a scare to all the stalwarts of the opposing army, including Bhima, before it was humbled.'

They kept on talking about various titbits about the war and disengaged themselves one after another.

Hastinapur, Dhritarashtra's Palace

Sanjaya revisited Dhritarashtra after the fifteenth day of war ended to announce Drona's death.

Dhritarashtra was deeply saddened to hear the news. Drona had been a longtime well-wisher of Hastinapur, and Dhritarashtra pinned his hopes on Drona's abilities to win the war for his son. Sanjaya briefed him on the series of events from the fall of Bhishma to the demise of Drona, account by account. He started the narration with Karna's entry into the war on the eleventh day after advising Duryodhana to make Drona the next Commander in Chief and Drona's acceptance of that position, considering it an honour.

Dhritarashtra was given a detailed day-by-day account of the last five days, during which both armies were greatly destroyed. Dhritarashtra, now and then, interrupted Sanjaya during the narration when he wanted more details or clarifications and got them answered.

'The focus of the war under Drona was quite different from when the reins were with Bhishma. Duryodhana, who felt emboldened by his preceptor's offer to do what he wished, requested Drona to capture Yudhishthira alive, which he never asked Bhishma. A pleasantly surprised Drona asked your son whether he intended to make an honourable truce with Pandavas by capturing Yudhishthira.

Duryodhana replied that he intended to play a game of dice again with Yudhishthira, defeat him, and send Pandavas into exile. Drona was shocked at this revelation but, nonetheless, agreed to try capturing Yudhishthira, stating that Arjuna should not be anywhere near Yudhishthira if this act were to be achieved. Drona's promise, when it was known by Pandavas' camp, was perceived as a challenge. As per Duryodhana's plan to divert Arjuna away from Yudhishthira, Susharma, the king of Trigarta, had converted his army into 'Samshaptakas' and challenged Arjuna for the fight.'

Sanjaya went on to explain the war on the thirteenth day in detail when Abhimanyu alone entered Chakravyuha and killed a number of Kaurava warriors. The very first was Brihadbala, a Maharadhi and king of Kosala, a descendant of the famous Ikshvaku lineage, and Abhimanyu continued his rampage by killing a brother of Shalya, a brother of Karna, a brother of Shakuni and Rukmaradha, a son of Shalya, among others and a number of foot soldiers. He was bravely encountered by your grandson, Lakshmana Kumara, the future crown prince of Hastinapur. After a vigorous fight by both youngsters, Abhimanyu prevailed and killed Lakshmana Kumara. He killed or gravely injured whoever challenged him, and warriors like Drona, Karna, Ashwatthama, or Duryodhana couldn't stop him.

Finally, they decided to disarm Abhimanyu, as he proved invincible as long as he was armed. They together proceeded to kill the horses and the charioteer and broke his bow, forcing him to fight on the ground. Abhimanyu, undeterred, had taken a mace and later a chariot wheel to continue his killing spree. He was finally involved in a duel with the son of Dusshasana. An already exhausted and badly injured Abhimanyu fought spiritedly but finally succumbed when he received a fatal mace blow on his head.'

Dhritarashtra sighed. He was happy that a son of Kurus had shown such great valour on the battlefield, but at the same time, the deaths of young princes pained him. The sons of Arjuna and Duryodhana, who both could have become kings one day but for this war, died on the same day. War changed certain things irreversibly.

'I can understand Arjuna was away fighting Samshaptakas, as he could not refuse a challenge, but how come Abhimanyu was not supported by other warriors from the Pandava side?' asked Dhritarashtra.

'Yudhishthira, Bhishma, Satyaki, and many others were just behind Abhimanyu when he breached the Chakravyuha and intended to enter it. But the moment Abhimanyu went inside, forcing a breach, the vyuha quickly regrouped again, and others could not breach it. On the side of Pandavas, there was none except Arjuna, barring Abhimanyu, who had the expertise to breach it. In the absence of Arjuna, who was dragged away to a war invited by Samshaptakas, Yudhishthira employed Abhimanyu to break the formation; Jayadratha spearheaded the resistance at the entry point and displayed great warrior skills in stopping others who attempted to enter the vyuha. Jayadratha fought like a man possessed, and none could stop him on that day,' replied Sanjaya.

'That was due to his spiritual power,' Dhritarashtra joined. I do not know whether you are aware that Jayadratha is a great devotee of lord Shiva, just like his father, Vriddhakshatra. He visualised Lord Shiva as if in a dream when he was deeply involved in meditation with an intent to defeat Pandavas. Jayadratha believed that the Lord assured him that he could beat everybody except Arjuna on a given day. Jayadratha was waiting for a day to face Pandavas without Arjuna and showed his full prowess without fear when he got that opportunity. He, too, was an ace student of Drona and could stop the Pandava warriors on a crucial day.'

Dhritarashtra was aware of his son-in-law's background.

Sanjaya continued the narration. 'Arjuna, on his return, was mad with furious anger on hearing the killing of his son when he was unaided. He was particularly sore with Jayadratha when he learnt that it was he who prevented Pandava warriors from entering. Arjuna took a vow that he would kill Jayadratha by the next day before sunset, failing which he would kill himself by committing suicide through self-immolation.'

Sanjaya paused to allow Dhritarashtra to recover his composure. He was now going to narrate the events of the fourteenth day of war.

'Your son-in-law was terrified on hearing the pledge taken by Arjuna. It baffled him as to why Arjuna should target him alone while the killing of Abhimanyu was the handiwork of other warriors. He had fulfilled his life's desire by holding the four Pandava brothers the whole day and was applauded by one and all, but now found himself in a quandary. Staying put in the war seemed like a certain death. He went to Duryodhana and Drona and indicated his intention to quit the war and proceed to Sindhu. Quitting the war would surely save him from certain death. However, such action would be a moral defeat for Kauravas, and it could not be afforded. Drona did not mince his words and said that while he would do his best to protect Jayadratha, Jayadratha should consider it as a matter of pride and honour to be killed in the war, and, after all, as nobody would live forever. He advised Jayadratha not to bother too much about such thoughts and fight like a true warrior.

Duryodhana was more sympathetic. He requested Drona to protect Jayadratha by all means. Drona suggested that they will form a complicated Vyuha, which is a combination of Sakata, Padma and Suchimukha Vyuhas, where Jayadratha will be kept protected, and to reach him, Arjuna need to face six formidable warriors, Karna, Bhurishravas, Ashwatthama, Vrishasena, Kripacharya and Shalya. Before reaching Jayadratha and the six warriors who would be protecting him, Arjuna needed to cross other obstacles like Drona, Kritavarma, etc. The strategy was to delay the progress of Arjuna's movement towards Jayadratha till sunset, forcing Arjuna to fail in his mission, leading to his self-immolation.

Duryodhana persuaded his brother-in-law not to leave the battle as Drona had come with a formidable formation, and all the warriors were determined to protect Jayadratha. Convinced, Jayadratha readied himself to stay on the battleground.'

Sanjaya paused for a while and continued. 'This day witnessed the maximum destruction for a single day. The fight continued at night also, for the first time, which I will describe later—in addition to Arjuna, who was the chief tormentor, Bhima and Satyaki also caused heavy destruction. The day started with Drona standing guard at the entrance of the vyuha to stop anyone from entering it. Pandavas took up the challenge, and Arjuna asked Bhima to protect Yudhishthira and embarked on entering the enemy formation. However, to save time, Arjuna avoided fighting with Drona, the first hurdle, offered him salutations, and bypassed him with a deft manoeuvring of the chariot by Krishna. Drona chased him but could not match his speed. He returned to his position at the entrance to stop further entries.

Arjuna faced resistance from Shrutayudha, a great warrior reputed to be the son of Lord Varuna, with a gifted mace. After a bitter fight, Shrutayudha employed his mighty mace, which was expected to hit Arjuna and return to him. However, he misdirected the mace towards Krishna, whom it could not hurt, and in return, it struck Shrutayudha himself, killing him on the spot. Arjuna killed many strong warriors like Sudakshina, the king of Kambhoja and his four sons, Shrutayu, Achyutayu, Niyatayu and Dheerghayuvu. He was then confronted by the Avanti princes Vinda and Anuvinda, who were consumed by his fury. Another king, Ambasta, who tried to stop him, was also killed. Arjuna destroyed many soldiers, horses and elephants and went on getting closer to Jayadratha.

After some time, Yudhishthira got restless as he had not heard the sound of Arjuna and Krishna's conches for a considerable time and asked Bhima to proceed to help Arjuna. Asking Satyaki to protect Yudhishthira, Bhima entered the formation by killing the horses of Drona. Sometime later, Yudhishthira asked Satyaki to proceed to join the other two. Satyaki entrusted Yudhishthira's protection to Dhrishtadyumna and entered the formation by managing to break in and join the fray.

Bhima killed twenty-three of your sons, my king, including able warriors Chitrasena and Vikarna. None in your army could stand up to Bhima.

Satyaki killed King Alambusha and proceeded further in his carnage by killing Jalasandha and Vyaghradatta of Magadha, as well as Sudarshana.

Satyaki was then stopped and challenged by Bhurishravas, who was looking for a duel with Satyaki. They had a bitter fight, and at one stage, both of them had exhausted all their weapons. They resorted to wrestling with each other. At one stage, Bhurishravas had Satyaki in his power, dragged him on the ground and was about to kill him with a sword. Satyaki was wriggling and moving his head sideways to avoid the sword falling on his neck, and we all thought it was the end of Satyaki. Just then, Arjuna hit Bhurishravas by severing his hand that held the sword.

Bhurishravas was shocked to the core by the unexpected offence from Arjuna. Accusing Arjuna of committing adharma that was not fit for a Bharatavamshi, Bhurishravas blamed Arjuna for resorting to adharma under the influence of Krishna. Bhurishravas squatted on the ground, having decided to breathe his last while sitting in Yoga. Arjuna justified his actions, saying that it was incumbent upon him to save his friends. Whether convinced or not, Bhurishravas, who was by then profusely bleeding, started to concentrate on yoga. Satyaki had meanwhile taken out his sword and chopped the head of Bhurishravas in one swift swish, ignoring the calls and cries from all the onlookers, including Krishna and Arjuna, not to indulge in that act.

Thereafter, Arjuna concentrated on reaching Jayadratha as the daylight was fading. He was encountered by the warriors who were given the special responsibility of protecting Jayadratha, but no one could match Arjuna that day. He was at his fierce best. The evening was fading, and there was only a short time left before sunset. Suddenly, it was dark, and the sun became invisible. There was jubilation in the Kauravas' camp, and Jayadratha felt euphoric that the sun had set and that he was saved. However, it was a false hope. The sun was not yet set and reappeared as if by magic. Nobody knew whether it was a solar eclipse or something else that caused a dawn-like darkness. Just at the time, Arjuna approached Jayadratha, and after a bitter fight, killed him by separating his head.'

Dhritarashtra signalled him to stop. He eagerly enquired, 'Sanjaya, where did the severed head of Jayadratha fall?' His voice had more excitement to know the outcome rather than a feeling of sadness at his son-in-law's death. Some others would have been surprised at this kind of reaction, but not Sanjaya, who knew why such a question was posed.

Dhritarashtra added as if to justify his enquiry, 'His father and my good friend Vriddhakshatra told me that as per divine foreboding, Jayadratha's head was to be severed in a war by a great warrior. Hence, Arjuna beheading Jayadratha was no surprise to me. He further told me that whosoever caused his head to fall would himself have his head broken into a hundred pieces.'

Sanjaya continued, 'This was what Krishna also said to Arjuna, and the head was driven in the direction of Vriddhakshatra's ashram near the battleground where the revered man was meditating. The head had fallen into his lap, which the sage immediately dropped to the ground involuntarily.'

Dhritarashtra did not have to wait for Sanjaya to inform him of Vriddhakshatra's fate. He commented, 'Sanjaya, destiny is so cruel that boons would turn to curses. This war has come to our terrible destruction.

My son had brought this on to us without hearing the good advice of elders, well-wishers and sages.'

It is not the only time Dhritarashtra would comment like this, and Sanjaya would give the same response.

'The blame can not be laid on Duryodhana alone. All your sons are struggling now in the war and putting in their best efforts. There was a time when you could have stopped and controlled him, but that was not to be.'

Dhritarashtra, as usual, did not choose to deny the charge. He knew the expected response; he knew it was a valid opinion from others' perspectives, and he was accustomed to hearing it often by now.

'Then what happened?'

'Both Pandavas and Kauravas were not in a mood to stop the war even after sunset. Drona himself felt guilty for not being able to save Jayadratha, and so did the other Kaurava warriors. Drona was also pained at Duryodhana's reaction to their collective failure to save Jayadratha and said that he would not rest unless he killed all the Panchalas and Srinjayas. Pandavas were on the offensive, and despite a hectic day of the war, they were eager to strike as the Kaurava warriors were thoroughly demoralised after the day's devastation caused by Arjuna, aided by Bhima and Satyaki. Drona proceeded towards the waiting Panchala army, and the battle resumed.

Drona put up a great fight against Srinjayas and Panchalas. Duryodhana himself entered the enemy camp and killed a number of people. He had indulged in a direct duel with Yudhishthira himself and had a great fight. He lost consciousness when Yudhishthira aimed a sharp arrow, causing alarm, but he recovered in time and rechallenged Yudhishthira. Meanwhile, Drona reached there to interfere and save your son and entered the Pandava army to annihilate multiple Panchala and Srinjaya forces.

The night war turned very violent, with Drona killing thousands of elephants, horses, warriors of repute, and foot soldiers. He killed all the sons of Dhrishtadyumna on that very night. He killed the king of Sibi, who is a Maharadha.

On another front, Bhima caused extensive damage to the Kaurava army and was furiously attacked by the Kalinga army, whose king he had killed earlier. However, the prince of Kalinga and other warriors like Dhruva and Jayaratha put up a great fight, only to be subdued and killed by Bhima's sheer physical strength.

Your sons Durmada and Dushkarna attacked Bhima, hitting him with arrows, but he overturned their chariots and hit them with his fists to kill them on the spot, to the horror of onlookers. While Bhima was hailed by the Pandavas' camp for his ferocious feats, more of your sons attacked Bhima in a rage along with their supporters, and a bitter group war ensued between both sides.

On another front, Somadatta encountered Satyaki. He aggressively rebuked Satyaki for his heinous act of killing his son, Bhurishravas, when the latter withdrew from the battle and squatted in a yoga posture. Satyaki replied as he deemed fit, and they had a bitter duel. At one stage, Somadatta lost consciousness and was taken away from the battleground, but some time later, he returned, and the fight resumed. Bhima joined Satyaki, and they killed Somadatta together. Furious at the fall of his son, the seasoned Bahlika attacked Satyaki and grievously injured him. He also injured Bhima with a mighty arrow, who was helping Satyaki. However, Bhima recovered and threw a heavy mace to hit Bahlika on his head, causing the mighty warrior to fall to the ground and die.'

Dhritarashtra heaved a deep sigh. *Bahlika and his sons would have been the inheritors of the Hastinapur kingdom after Vichitraveerya died without any children. However, Bahlika never objected to the wives of Vichitraveerya having sons through Niyoga to continue the lineage of his brother Shantanu. He had been a strong supporter of Hastinapur. Being the brother of Shantanu, he was elder to Bhishma and the oldest warrior of Bharatavamsha. With the deaths of Somadatta, Bhurishravas, and Shala, there were none left to perpetuate the lineage of Bahlika.*

Dhritarashtra asked Sanjaya to continue.

'As the night was deepening, danavas on both sides started to indulge in more aggressive fighting. As Ashwatthama attacked Satyaki, burning with rage to avenge the killing of Bhurishravas, Ghatotkacha intervened, and a great fight ensued between Ghatotkacha and Ashwatthama. Ashwatthama fought ferociously, accounted for an akshauhini of the danava army, and made Ghatotkacha unconscious. Dhrishtadyumna came to the rescue of Ghatotkacha and took him away. Angered by this, Ghatotkacha's son, Anjanaparva, waged severe aggression against Ashwatthama but was ultimately killed. Continuing the same form, Ashwatthama killed Drupada's sons Suradha, Shatrunjay, Balanika, Jayaneeka and Jayasva. He also killed other warriors like Shrutahyava, Hemamalini, Vrishadra and Chandrasena. He also killed ten sons of Kuntibhoja.

After Bhima killed Bahlika, ten of your sons attacked Bhima and perished, thus leaving the survivors in your sons to be thirty, including Duryodhana and Dusshasana.'

Sanjaya stopped the narration, sensing that Dhritarashtra wanted to ask something.

Dhritarashtra's voice was weak, 'Name those ten!'

Sanjaya recounted, 'They are Nagadatta, Dhridharatha, Mahabahu, Ayobhuja, Dhridha, Suhastha, Viraja, Pramadhi, Ugra and Anuyayi.'

Dhritarashtra slowly repeated those names to himself as if he were bidding farewell to the departed sons. Sanjaya resumed the narration.

'Bhima also killed six of your brothers-in-law, Shakuni's brothers, who pounced on Bhima after he killed your sons. Shatachandra, Gavaksha, Sarabha, Vibha, Subhaga, and Bhanudatta perished in no time, and he then took on Vrikaradha, the brother of Karna who encountered him.

The battle intensified with Yudhishthira, Satyaki, Drona, and Karna, each accounting for the massive destruction of the enemy's side. There were fierce duels between Karna and Arjuna, Karna and Satyaki, Ashwatthama and Dhrishtadyumna, Drona with Arjuna and Bhima, Dhrishtadyumna with Drona, and the fights continued all through the night even by lighting a large number of torches by both sides.

On another front, there was a big fight between Ghatotkacha and Alambusha. The duel between both these danavas was very ferocious. Still, in the end, Ghatotkacha killed Alambusha and the severed head was thrown to fall near Duryodhana, who was taken aback by the ferocity of Ghatotkacha.

Soon, Ghatotkacha was attacked by another danava warrior, Alayudha, who entered the war, having known that a battle was being fought at night and obtained Duryodhana's permission to take on Ghatotkacha. However, the rampaging Ghatotkacha killed Alayudha also after a long fight and again threw the severed head towards Duryodhana as if throwing a challenge.

As nobody was able to withstand Ghatotkacha at his best, Karna came forward to stem the rot and resisted his onslaught. However, Ghatotkacha went on from strength to strength and started harassing Karna. Karna had to employ the powerful Vasavi Shakti that he reserved for Arjuna on Ghatotkacha to save the day. Thus, Ghatotkacha was killed and fell on your army, killing a large number of soldiers.

There was a brief recess after this. Army rested on the battleground itself. As soon as Aruna appeared in the sky, signalling the advent of sunrise, all of them got up, offered Sandhya and recommenced the war.

Drona waged a fierce battle on the Panchala and Matsya armies and accounted for two Maharathis in the Pandava army, Drupada and Virata. Drona was particularly severe at Panchala army, the Chedi and Kekaya warriors and killed all those who crossed him, including three grandsons of Drupada.'

Dhritarashtra was absorbing the war news. Whatever he heard earlier was nothing before what he was hearing now. Many seniors like Bahlika and Somadatta, who were dear to him, died. He had so far lost seventy sons. Drupada and Virata were at last killed, but Dhrishtadyumna was still there. Satyaki had settled his family feud. Ghatotkacha died, but Shakti of

Karna was wasted. *Why hasn't Karna employed this on Arjuna so far? What prevented him from doing so?*

He stopped Sanjaya in the midst of narration and asked, 'Why did Karna not employ that Vasavi Shakti on Arjuna before it was wasted on Ghatotkacha? Why didn't any of you advise him to do so? It was Karna's best and perhaps his only chance to kill Arjuna, and how foolishly it was wasted? What was our war strategy? Where did he falter? How did we miss this?'

Sanjaya explained, 'It is very perplexing, but it is true that every evening, we were planning for Karna to use this Shakti on Arjuna the following day. Dusshasana, Shakuni, Jayadratha, me and everybody was advising Karna not to use Shakti on anybody other than Arjuna, and Karna also assured us that he would employ it on Arjuna only. Krishna was also aware that Karna had this Shakti and was avoiding a personal duel between Arjuna and Karna to assume serious proportions. He never allowed Arjuna to confront Karna seriously enough and always postponed their duel. In hindsight, we think that Srikrishna had planned to employ Ghatotkacha in the night war to challenge Karna, especially to rid Karna of that lethal weapon. When Ghatotkacha was killed, everybody was sad in Pandavas' camp, but Krishna appeared to be pleased that his strategy worked. He told Arjuna that bereft of Kavacha and Kundala earlier, and with the loss of Shakti now, Karna had been rendered an ordinary warrior, and Arjuna could kill him now. Krishna even appeared to be dancing with joy and was later seen sharing with Satyaki that his strategy had worked.'

Dhritarashtra heaved a sigh and said, 'The only hope to win the war was to kill Arjuna, and the only hope of killing Arjuna was to employ that Vaijayanti Shakti against him. Now that was wasted on Ghatotkacha, all my hopes of winning the war are lost. And it was Krishna who made this possible. Fate can not be changed!'

Sanjaya understood his king's mindset thoroughly. He was not surprised at Dhritarashtra's expression that he had lost all hope of winning the war, as a similar statement was made by Dhritarashtra when Bhishma's fall was announced. He would perhaps make the same statement again as if he retained some hope of winning the battle. Kings can't accept defeats in battles even while they are losing, Sanjaya reflected.

Dhritarashtra then signalled Sanjaya to proceed further.

Sanjaya continued. 'I will now narrate, in detail, how Dhrishtadyumna killed the great Dronacharya.'

Dhritarashtra readied himself to hear the saddest part of Sanjaya's narration of the day.

Chapter 12

The Death of Acharya

Hastinapur, Dhritarashtra's Palace

Sanjaya continued his narration.

'True to his word that Drona would not rest until he was killed. Drona was at his fiercest best after Jayadratha's death and went on causing heavy damage to Pandava forces. Pandavas realised that Drona, once determined, was unstoppable. The more time he fought, the greater would be their losses. Dhrishtadyumna, who was verily born to kill the Acharya, was unable to achieve the task despite struggling his best, as the seasoned preceptor had answers to every question posed by his one-time student. Drona's energy levels were astonishingly high, defying his age.

Krishna opined that, at this rate, Drona could not be killed as long as he held his bow in his hand, and it was necessary to make him so disinterested in the war that he would put his bow down. One way to make him realise that the war was futile was to make him believe that his dear son was dead.

Everybody knew that Drona loved his only son very dearly. If Drona was made to believe that his son Ashwatthama was killed, it was sure he would lose interest in war.

However, killing Ashwatthama was not an easy task. So, a plan was conceived by the Pandava camp, with active advice from Krishna. That plan had a high probability of success, but Yudhishthira was required to utter the necessary falsehood convincingly, as Drona would believe none else.'

Dhritarashtra enquired in haste, his voice betraying both incredulity and pain, 'Did Yudhishthira agree to be a part of such a nefarious idea?'

Sanjaya continued, 'It was not that easy to convince Yudhishthira to utter a blatant lie to kill their revered Acharya, but in the end, yes, he agreed to comply, though reluctantly. As far as Yudhishthira's acquiescence to this plan is concerned, he was forced to comply as he had no other alternative. He was made to see the point that unless stopped, Drona would annihilate Pandavas' army and all his supporters who came to fight on their side, and it was his bounden duty to save those supporters by agreeing to go with the plan.'

'There was an elephant belonging to the Malava king, Indravarma, bearing the name Ashwatthama. Bhima killed that elephant, went to Drona and loudly announced, *"Ashwatthama was killed."* However, Drona didn't believe his words as he was aware of the strength and near invincibility of his son and continued to fight without reducing the tempo by killing twenty thousand Panchala warriors, six thousand Srinjayas, and five thousand Matsyas besides an atiradha, Vasudana. However, Bhima's words slowly sank into his mind, creating doubt in him, and his concentration wavered. He looked for Ashwatthama but didn't find him, as he was fighting on the other wing with Panchalas and Srinjayas. Drona asked Yudhishthira, who came within his vicinity, to confirm whether Ashwatthama was killed. Yudhishthira replied, *"Ashwatthama hataha"*, feebly adding the word *"kunjaraha"* at the end of the sentence, clarifying that Ashwatthama was killed, but that was an elephant. The loud assertion that Ashwatthama was dead so shocked Drona that he wouldn't hear the later clarification that the killed Ashwatthama was an elephant, as muttered in a feeble voice by Yudhishthira.

Drona believed that his son was dead but continued to fight and warded off the belligerent Dhrishtadyumna, who thought he had an opportunity to get an upper hand in the war. However, Drona continued to foil his attempts.

Though Drona continued to fight, it was only defensive, and his fight lost its previous vigour. He suddenly realised the pointlessness of fighting. At this point, Bhima again came and reiterated that Ashwatthama was indeed killed and Drona was going against Brahmin Dharma by continuing his killing spree. He was indulging in the war to earn riches for his son, but the son himself was dead. What was the rationale for Acharya to continue his abhorrent act of sinful killing, which was not prescribed for Brahmins, was his straight question to Drona. Bhima reiterated the news of Ashwatthama's death again and even told him that he should not disbelieve Yudhishthira's words.

A totally frustrated Drona suddenly realised that he had indeed digressed from the path of his forefathers, and they were unhappy about his killing spree. He believed that his forefathers were asking him to stop the fight and join them in other worlds. Drona lost all interest in the war as well as life and decided to call it a day. He told Karna, Kripa, and Duryodhana that they could continue to fight their best without him. He also wished Pandavas to be good to them. He blessed one and all and sat in Yoga to die and leave this world.

Taking this as an opportunity, Dhrishtadyumna pounced on Drona's chariot and held his head by the hair with the intent to decapitate. Everybody shouted at Dhristadyumna not to indulge in that dastardly act, but he went ahead and did as he thought fit by severing Drona's head with a quick slash of his sword. However, it was a lifeless body by the time Dhrishtadyumna cut it. He threw the slain head of Drona into the Kaurava army and roared like a lion. He finally accomplished what he was born for.

Though Bhima congratulated Dhrishtadyumna, others in the Pandava camp did not digest the manner in which Acharya was killed. Arjuna lamented that Yudhishthira had to utter an untruth to kill Drona. He disapproved of Dhrishtadyumna's act of severing Drona's head when the latter was sitting in Yoga. Bhima chided Arjuna for blaming him and Yudhishthira for telling untruths and counselled him that such things were required in war. Dhrishtadyumna defended his act, stating that Drona was no Brahmin, having taken to arms. He reminded everyone that he was born to kill Drona, and he only did his duty, and it was divinely predestined. Satyaki entered into an altercation with Dhrishtadyumna for his comments on Arjuna.

There was a bitter exchange of words between Satyaki and Dhrishtadyumna, and finally, Bhima had to separate them from entering into a duel on the advice of Krishna. While Satyaki and Dhrishtadyumna were somehow thus pacified, the Pandava camp was surprised to see the Kaurava armies, which had retreated only minutes ago, advancing towards them, headed by none other than Ashwatthama.

The act of Dhrishtadyumna severing and throwing the head of revered Drona had unnerved the Kaurava army, and all the principal warriors were in a state of shock. The army started running back aimlessly. Karna, Kripa, Shalya, Shakuni, Duryodhana and all have begun retreating as if in a great shock. Ashwatthama, who just then emerged from his fight against Srinjaya and Panchala warriors on another front, was surprised to notice the retreating Kaurava armies in distress and enquired of Duryodhana the reason. He was then appraised by Kripacharya of the news and the manner in which Drona fought and was killed. Ashwatthama was full of rage to hear the manner of his father's death and the disrespectful way Dhrishtadyumna threw Drona's severed head unceremoniously. With an intent to punish the Pandava camp for their treacherous act, he led the armies back to the battlefield, followed by other warriors.

Pandavas saw the returning Kaurava army headed by Ashwatthama and readied themselves to counter it. Ashwatthama did an unusual thing by employing the fierce Narayanastra, which had no counter. This Astra started causing a great deal of damage to the Pandava army. Yudhishthira was so scared to see the destruction being caused by the astra that he began asking Satyaki and Dhrishtadyumna to retreat to their places. He announced his wish to withdraw from the war and immolate himself by entering fire, as Arjuna also blamed him for uttering untruth to Guru Drona.

Krishna took stock of the situation and asked everybody to drop their weapons and stand in reverence to Narayana. Whosoever stood fighting, defying the astra, was killed, and those who heeded Krishna's advice by dropping their weapons and stood on the ground duly alighting from their chariots were spared. Bhima, who defied the advice and stood his ground, was engulfed by the fires. He had to be forced by Arjuna and Krishna to alight from his chariot and made to drop his weapons so that he was saved from the fury of the astra.

Ashwatthama was disappointed to see that Krishna had foiled his attempt to destroy the Pandava army and resorted to normal fighting. A bitter fight occurred between him on one side and Satyaki, Dhrishtadyumna and Bhima on the other. Later, Ashwatthama killed Malava King Sudarshana and Paurava King Vriddhakshatra.

Arjuna had countered Ashwatthama, and after a bitter war of words, the beloved son and beloved disciple of Drona had a fierce battle. Ashwatthama employed Agneyastra with the intent to kill Arjuna and Krishna. Though the astra destroyed an akshauhini of the Pandava army, it could not harm Arjuna or Krishna. Ashwatthama got frustrated, having seen his astras becoming ineffective and retreated. Thus ended the fifteenth-day war, and the Kaurava camp was plunged into deep sorrow. I came back to report to you.'

Sanjaya rested his narration. Dhritarashtra was reflective. He heaved a deep sigh and said, 'Sanjaya! Are you aware that the trick played on Drona had a precedent, and it involved Krishna?'

Sanjaya thought for a while and did not recall any such precedent.

Dhritarashtra continued,' It was an old trick Yadavas employed earlier to get rid of redoubtable warriors Hamsa and Dimbhaka in one of their battles with Jarasandha. These two generals of Jarasandha were invincible and loved each other very dearly. Their bond was so strong that each could not live without the other. In one of their battles on Mathura, Balarama killed a king named Hamsa, and quickly, a rumour was spread on the battlefield that Balarama killed the general Hamsa, Dimbhaka's friend. When the rumour reached his ears, Dimbhaka was crestfallen and, on an impulse, killed himself by jumping into the nearby river Yamuna.

On knowing of this fact, Hamsa, too, killed himself by drowning in the same river. Jarasandha had to retreat from the war after that. Just as Balarama could find a king named Hamsa, so as not to lie, Bhima got an elephant named Ashwatthama, thus allowing the satisfaction of uttering only a half-truth and not a complete lie. Lie or half-truth, that statement served the desired purpose. However, Ashwatthama is no Hamsa to commit suicide after his father but would show his wrath on Dhrishtadyumna, as well as Pandavas; we had already witnessed his initial reaction.'

Sanjaya absorbed Dhritarashtra's story and marvelled at Dhritarashtra's capacity to store and recall information, the ability to find connections, and his comment about Ashwatthama.

He replied, 'It is an interesting story and certainly looks like how such an idea was generated. And as you rightly said, Ashwatthama might feel a personal stake in the war now.'

Dhritarashtra did not comment on Sanjaya's statement. He was still reflective and kept recalling his association with Drona. Finally, he said, 'Drona was a great man. Bhishma always appreciated him a lot. I am not sure whether you are aware of it, but Duryodhana relied so much on Drona's capabilities. When Pandavas were sent for exile, Duryodhana's initial joy turned into worry that Yudhishthira may launch a war on him. He had already decided that he was not going to cede the kingdom to Yudhishthira even after exile. He then went to Drona, along with Karna, Dusshasana. and Shakuni and prayed to him, stating that he was putting the entire kingdom in Drona's hands and sought his protection.

Drona prophetically told my sons thus. *"You have got your good days. The entire kingdom now belongs to you. Pandavas were sent to exile, and they would not return for the next thirteen years. Whatever you want to do, do it now. Whatever yagas you want to perform, perform now. Whatever enjoyments you have in mind, enjoy them in these thirteen years."* Drona knew that the Kuru clan was going to be decimated in this war.

Bhishma and Drona knew that they would be sacrificing themselves in the war, but they had put in their best efforts. Drona loved Arjuna just like his son or even more but chose to fight on our side as a matter of duty. Great man! Sanjaya! I have lost all my hopes about winning the war on Drona's death.'

Sanjaya took leave of Dhritarashtra and left. Dhritarashtra called for Vidura.

Chapter 13

The War in Final Days

Naimisha, Little Master's Ashram

It was on the morning of the sixteenth day of the war. The last time the ashram inmates had met for a detailed report was on the thirteenth morning. Drona's death on the fifteenth day of war had occasioned the morning meeting.

When everybody settled in their seats, the news bearers started the report.

'We are all aware of the happenings of war in detail up to the twelfth day, when giant warriors like Bhagadatta, along with his famous Supratika elephant, were killed. Now, let me briefly explain what happened on the thirteenth, fourteenth, and fifteenth days of war, when many important events took place. Significant destruction of armies on both sides occurred during this period.

At the end of the twelfth day, Duryodhana asked Drona to speed up the process of capturing Yudhishthira. Drona had a plan ready, and they worked out the field placements and other matters till the wee hours and were satisfied they had the perfect plan. Drona had formed Chakravyuha, which was not seen by either Kauravas or Pandavas till that date in any war. Of course, Drona knew that both Krishna and Arjuna were aware of the formation, but there was a way to drive them away to another front on the battlefield. Arjuna, as a matter of principle, never refuses to fight when challenged and taking advantage of this, Susharma's Samshaptakas would challenge Arjuna and drive him farther to the Vyuha. With nobody capable of breaking it, the vyuha would advance towards Yudhishthira and gobble him up to isolate his support. Once inside, Yudhishthira had to surrender, bereft of any assistance. Even if a few might manage to enter along with Yudhishthira, when it opens up, they would be tackled by the superiority of numbers.

The plan was executed, and Samshaptakas drew Arjuna away before he realised the trap laid by Kauravas. Bhima and Satyaki assured Arjuna that they would protect Yudhishthira at all costs.

Once Arjuna was away, Drona got the vyuha quickly formed, and the vyuha baffled the Pandava chiefs. Nobody had any clue as to how it could be countered. While the elderly were wondering what kind of counter-strategy may work against it, Abhimanyu informed them that he knew how to gain entry into the formation by breaking it, though not getting out. Yudhishthira was happy to know that there is at least one person who has that knowledge. They planned to rally behind Abhimanyu and enter as soon as Abhimanyu broke it. Coming out was not considered a problem as they could break it from inside wherever it was weak. They will find out the way once they are inside and together.

Drona and Duryodhana were waiting in the centre, satisfied that their formation was formidable. They stationed Jayadratha at the entrance to thwart any attempts of forced entry by opposing warriors. They were not expecting anybody to enter, as Arjuna was far away, and waited for the right moment to signal the formation to move and close in to capture Yudhishthira.

However, to their surprise, Abhimanyu entered, all of a sudden breaking the gaps like an expert. It looked like a child's play for him. He started killing whoever came in front of him without wasting time. He knew that the key to winning was to kill as many as possible to make the formation break and stop its advancement. He killed a number of warriors in double quick time. Some of his early victims were Aswakeswara, Sushena, Dhirgalochana, Kundabedhi, Vasatiya and others. By this time,

Drona's initial plan of advancing the vyuha had to be given a go-by, till Abhimanyu was killed, as allowing Yudhishthira and others inside with Abhimanyu rampaging would be counterproductive. So they thought of killing Abhimanyu first. Jayadratha, stationed at the entrance, continued to stall anyone from entering the vyuha.

'One minute, please!' somebody from the audience called for attention. Usually, the audience waited until the report was finished before asking questions, but sensing the mood of the audience, Little Master allowed the intruder to speak.

'Did other warriors like Pandavas, Satyaki, etc. also enter the formation as planned?'

The narrator continued, 'That is somewhat strange. The plans of either party were not working correctly that day. The breach was quickly filled up after Abhimanyu's entry, and nobody else could enter it as Pandavas had planned. Kauravas could stop further entries, but they only ended up capturing a rampaging Abhimanyu and not the targeted Yudhishthira. Yudhishthira, Bhima, Satyaki, and the twins were all trying to break in, but they could not find the breach as Abhimanyu did. They wanted to use brute force and break the formation, but to no avail. Their efforts were stalled by Jayadratha and his army, who had shown exceptional skills. Jayadratha, also once a star student of Drona, fought like a man possessed and encouraged his men to resist the Pandava army.

Hours passed, but the formation of Kauravas did not yield. Those who died were quickly replaced, and the resistance could not be broken. So Abhimanyu was left fighting all alone inside. He killed the brothers of both Karna and Shalya and then killed Rukmaradha, son of Shalya, who was himself no mean a fighter. He killed another Radhika by the name of Satyasrava. Inspired by the heat of war, Duryodhana's son Lakshman Kumar himself confronted Abhimanyu. The rampaging Abhimanyu did not give time to Lakshman and killed him in front of Duryodhana. He then killed a son of Kradha and accounted for Brihadbala, king of Kosala and a reputed warrior. There was no end to the killing spree as he went on killing warrior after warrior.

Ashwaketu, a prince of Magadha and Bhoja, the king of Murthikavata, were the next to fall. Shatrunjaya, Chandraketu, Meghavega, Suvarcha, Suryabhasa, and Kalakeya, brother of Shakuni, were added to the list. He had teased all big names like Drona, Kripa, Shalya, Karna, Ashwatthama, Vrishasena, and Duryodhana with his piercing arrows. Drona had decided to end the war and signalled for the destruction of his horses, suta, and bow, and the plan was executed. Even then, Abhimanyu took a mace and started killing those who came his way. Finally, the son of Dusshasana challenged him to a duel with mace, and the already exhausted Abhimanyu fought valiantly, and both the combatants fell to the ground. The son of Dusshasana, who recovered a bit early, could deliver a death blow on Abhimanyu while he was raising. Thus ended the fight of Abhimanyu after killing more than ten thousand men, including Radhika warriors and even an atiradha in Brihadbala, besides a large number of horses.'

The narrator stopped for a while, and the audience started talking to their companions nearby.

Asareer thought to himself, *'Krishna's nephew, who else can fight like this! The brave young man just didn't care for his life.'*

The narrator continued. 'Yudhishthira was shocked to see the incidents unfolding before him. He didn't expect Abhimanyu to die so helplessly. He thought they would fight together and win the day. They all waited for Arjuna's return, and Arjuna was angry and upset on hearing the news. He then took a public vow that he would kill Jayadratha before the next sunset, failing which he would immolate himself.'

The narrator continued as Animish temporarily shut himself off from the narration. He knew in detail what the narration would be. He heard it all in the last three days. His thoughts were wavering on the news about how Drona was tricked before being killed. What surprised him was Yudhishthira's hypocrisy. *The man who boasted or at least stated that he would not speak untruth had uttered a deadly lie to his guru. Why didn't they try to kill Ashwatthama first, in which case, they would not have to resort to a lie?*

Little Master recalled his last few meetings with Duryodhana. As he remembered, Duryodhana had a son and a daughter, and he saw Lakshmana Kumara, a young lad radiating with enthusiasm, in one of his meetings. Duryodhana told him that his son had no need to worry about his rights to the kingdom like he once faced, and Lakshmana Kumara would be the undisputed heir to Hastinapur. Duryodhana said in a lighter vein, 'Make friends with my son; you may need him one day in future'. The boy did not live to have a future. Then he remembered Duryodhana's reflection. 'What position would my son have had if I towed to Vidura's suggested course and did not stake my claim? Pandavas would have taken the entire empire, and my son would be, at best, one of the minor chiefs, junior in rank to all sons of Pandavas. Isn't it? I think what I did was right for my son, my brothers and their sons. I think Bhishma and Drona also started to understand the reasonableness of my stand, though Vidura wouldn't.'

What happened to that future heir? His body must be lying on the battlefield, uncared for like that of many others. Everybody was talking about how Arjuna would cope with the loss of Abhimanyu. Was Duryodhana's loss any less? How many fathers had lost their sons so far in this war? Virata was the first casualty. He lost both Uttara Kumara and Shweta on the very first day. Now, he lost his son-in-law. Satyaki lost ten of his sons. Even Drupada lost his son Satyajit. Now, Shalya and Duryodhana, too, lost their sons. Some of the fathers followed their sons, too. By the time the war ends, how many sons would be dying? And how many fathers to follow!

Animish came out of his reflections and began listening to the narration, which entered the fight of the fifteenth evening after the killing of Drona.

'Ashwatthama's late fury destroyed a sizable Pandava army, but Pandavas clearly showed an edge after killing Drona. However, with Karna still present, the Kauravas are now placing all their hopes in Karna and Ashwatthama. We think either of them will be made chief commandant of the war in place of Drona, which may have commenced today and is in progress while we are talking.'

The narration ended, and the session to answer the questions began.

'Ghatotkacha coming to fight for Pandavas is understandable since he was a son of Bhima. But how could Duryodhana mobilise the support of Alambusha and Alayudha?'

'Alambusha happens to be the brother of Bakasura, who was killed by Bhima when they were in Ekachakrapura. Alayudha was a friend of Hidimba and Kimmira, both of whom were killed by Bhima. So they joined the Kaurava army voluntarily to fight with Bhima and Ghatotkacha.'

'Does Ghatotkacha have sons?'

'Yes, he had. His son Anjanaparva, who joined in the war, was killed by Ashwatthama on that very day.'

'Who started the night war?'

'Drona was very upset that Jayadratha was killed despite a huge effort. Duryodhana had asked him how Bhima and Satyaki could enter the vyuha despite Drona guarding the entry point. This comment irked Drona, and he told Duryodhana that he was not going to rest until he killed all Panchalas. Even Dhrishtadyumna goaded his army to continue to fight. In a way, continuing the war beyond sunset looked like a mutual decision without mutual consultation.'

Little Master felt proud of the intelligence gathered by his people. They have gathered a lot of information.

'Did Yudhishthira really tell that Ashwatthama had been killed?'

'Yes. Yudhishthira spoke that very clearly. He might have said something else after that, as some claim, but that was not audible to anybody. He was talking to himself.'

'Ashwatthama would not leave Dhrishtadyumna unpunished for his heinous act,' someone from the audience said, which was greeted with assertions by many.

'Drupada died before witnessing his son execute his one-time friend and foe and his obsession. It was a dream for him,' someone else commented.

'Does it really matter? Anyway, Drupada saw Bhishma fall with the support of his son Shikhandi. He was, perhaps, destined to die in the hands of Drona, his one-time friend whom he wronged, even as he desired a son to kill Drona,' some other person who remembered the old history of bad blood between the two had quipped.

Questions stopped temporarily, and members proceeded to have intimate discussions. Little Master got up and made his way out, leaving the assembly to continue. Others on the dias followed him.

Hastinapur, Dhritarashtra's Palace

Sanjaya returned to report on the seventeenth day late in the evening. The arrival of Sanjaya in such a short interval in a serious mood indicated some big unfavourable news awaited all, and the palace got busy to hear the news. Dhritarashtra was heartbroken to hear about the deaths of Dusshasana and Karna. Unable to control his sorrow, he slumped from the chair and fell flat on the floor. Observing their king in such a sad state, some of the attending women went inside, themselves weeping, to inform Gandhari. Gandhari was escorted to Dhritarashtra, and the palace women gathered around them with deep sorrow. Word spread, and many of his sons' wives, too, gathered around. After a brief period of rest and contemplation, Dhritarashtra asked Sanjaya to proceed and give full details.

'On the sixteenth day morning, Karna entered the field as the Chief Commander of the Kaurava army, and there was renewed enthusiasm in the rank and file. They had immense faith in Karna's ability to lead them to victory. Karna formed Makara Vyuha and led from the front. Duryodhana enthused his army, stating that Karna would lead them to victory, and exhorted them to give their best. Karna soon launched an offensive and started killing the Pandava army at will.

From the side of Pandavas, Bhima opened the score for Pandavas by killing Kshemadhurti, king of Kulutha, after a bitter fight between the two warriors mounted on elephants. Satyaki accounted for Vinda and

Anuvinda, brothers of Kekaya. Shruta Karma, son of Draupadi, accounted for Chitrasena, the King of Abhisara, and another son, Prativindhya, killed Chitra, another king. Arjuna was involved in the war with Samshaptakas and later was drawn to fight with Ashwatthama. After putting up a great fight, Ashwatthama had to retreat when the injured horses dragged his chariot away from Arjuna.

Later, Arjuna killed the warrior brothers of Magadha, namely Dandadhara and Danda. Later, he was again involved in the war with Samshaptakas, accounted for a number of Samshaptakas as well as a large number of their horses and elephants, and killed the son of Ugrayudha.

From the Kaurava side, Karna and Ashwatthama continued the offensive and caused significant damage to Pandava forces. Ashwatthama killed Malayadhvaja, the king of Pandya, who killed a sizable Kaurava army and put up a stiff fight till the end. Karna, too, had killed a lot of enemy forces.

On Pandavas' side, Satyaki killed the king of Vanga, and Nakula killed the son of Angaraja. Samshaptakas had again regrouped and engaged Arjuna in a fierce fight, and Susharma's brothers coordinated their efforts to attack Arjuna. Arjuna killed Shrutanjaya, Sausruti, Chandradeva, Chitrasena, Satyasena, Mitra Varma, and Mitradeva, all brothers of Susharma. These are the notable casualties, though there were lots of duels and group fights involving various people.

Karna had Nakula in his power once but left him unharmed for the reasons best known to you.

While Arjuna was harsh on Samshaptakas, Karna killed many in the Srinjaya and Panchala armies. Yudhishthira, Nakula, Sahadeva, Shikhandi, Yuyutsu and others tried to stop Karna's offensive but could not. Karna expertly parried all their threats and killed a big chunk of their army, including many horses and elephants, at will. Frustrated by Karna's offensive, the Pandava army almost retreated before Arjuna led them to counter Karna and mount an attack on the Kaurava army. Then, it was the turn of the Kaurava army to retreat. It was about the time the sun was to set, and the battlefield became dark. Unable and unwilling to continue the war in the darkness, both armies retreated.

Thus, the war of the sixteenth day ended at sunset, and both parties had returned to camps to strategise the seventeenth day of the war.'

After a brief pause, Sanjaya resumed the narration of the seventeenth day of the war in which the two crucial and dear warriors died, making Duryodhana the saddest man in the war.

'Karna suggested to Duryodhana a crucial change in war strategy for the next day. He said he would take on Arjuna the following morning, fully prepared to fight to the finish, and appraised his friend on their relative strengths based on his assessment. Karna indicated that he did not fear Arjuna's Gandiva as his own bow, Vijaya, given to him by Parashurama, was equally effective. Neither did he fear Arjuna's archery skills or his astras; he had his own astras for defending himself and for counter-attack. Arjuna, however, had an edge over him because of Arjuna's superior mobility, which was due to Krishna's skills as his charioteer. If Shalya were to be his charioteer the next day, Karna said, that advantage would be neutralised to a large extent, and he could give his best performance. He assured Duryodhana that he would kill Arjuna with such an arrangement.

Duryodhana agreed to this idea and persuaded Shalya, playing to his ego, and convinced Shalya to take up this job. Shalya, though initially peeved at the request to act as a charioteer to Karna, who was a non-Kshatriya, felt proud that he was considered equal to Krishna as a charioteer. Shalya accepted Duryodhana's request, and he also remembered Yudhishthira's request to demotivate Karna when Shalya was to act as Karna's charioteer.

Shalya wondered at Yudhishthira's wisdom and foresight in predicting Karna's need to have him as the charioteer much before the war had started. He was determined to play his role and fulfil the hopes placed on him by both the rival kings who were fighting a bitter battle.

The seventeenth day of war started, and Karna, being charioted by Shalya, wanted to face Arjuna as soon as possible. There was a prolonged verbal duel, exchanging carping criticism, between Shalya and Karna as Shalya proceeded to fulfil the promise he had given to Yudhishthira. Karna could not understand why Shalya was behaving in that manner but gave appropriate answers. Duryodhana needed to intervene and request both of them to calm down and concentrate on the crucial battle ahead.

However, towards the later part of the day, Shalya refrained from talking in that manner, having satisfactorily fulfilled the promise he had made to Yudhishthira. After that, he entirely became involved in the war.

Karna started the day by killing five Panchala warriors, namely Bhanudeva, Chitrasena, Senabindu, Tapana and Surasena. He went on a rampage and entered the Pandava army, destroying the opposing forces at will. Later, he killed other Panchala warriors, including Chandradeva and Dandadhara, while fighting with Yudhishthira. Yudhishthira put up a great fight and made Karna swoon out of pain but did not proceed to kill him. Karna got up, resumed the war, defeated Yudhishthira's supporters, killed his horses and made him withdraw from the field, badly injured and with a heavy heart. Karna wanted to touch him but was cautioned by Shalya not to do so, as it can be considered a dishonourable act. Karna heeded the advice and let Yudhishthira go after sarcastically advising him to seek the shelter of Krishna and Arjuna.'

'Yes, we know that he gave the word to his mother, and he would not flinch from that under any circumstances,' intervened Dhritarashtra in a low voice to be heard only by Sanjaya, who paused for a minute and resumed.

'Arjuna was at that time engaged in battling with Samshaptakas on a different front, and then Ashwatthama invited Arjuna and engaged him in a fierce duel. The battle saw the employment of different astras, and finally, Arjuna made the horses of Ashwatthama run without direction by killing his charioteer. Ashwatthama was thus drawn away from the field by his horses. Arjuna then destroyed a large part of the rival army.

Looking at the Kuru armies retreating, Karna employed his famous Bhargava Astra, and it started destroying the Pandava army like fire.

While Arjuna was wondering about the incredible power of Bhargavastra, he was told that Yudhishthira was severely injured in his duel with Karna and retired to his tent, leaving the field. Arjuna felt anxious and asked Bhima to go and enquire about the welfare of their elder brother. Bhima suggested that Arjuna may better go himself and visit Yudhishthira while he continued to fight. Krishna also advised that the badly exhausted Arjuna may take on Karna a little later, and meanwhile, they may visit Yudhishthira and enquire about his welfare. Both Arjuna and Krishna went to Yudhishthira and returned to the field after some time.'

'Karna continued to put in his best performance and killed a number of Chedi and Srinjaya warriors, besides destroying a vast number of horses, elephants and warriors. The warriors he killed included Jishnu, Jishnukarma, Devapini, Bhadra, Dandu, Chitra, Chitrayudha, Hari, Simhaketu, Rochamana, Salabha, Kekaya king Vishoka, Ugrakarma and a son of Dhrishtadyumna and Surasena. On the other side, Bhima was on a rampage, killing Karna's son Bhanusena and then fifteen of your sons in two batches and added Dusshasana to the list, who fought valiantly till his death. Oh, King! You have lost eighty-seven sons so far, including Dusshasana.

Kripacharya killed Suketha, a son of Chitraketu and a son of Kulinda. Uttamouja killed another son of Karna by the name of Suseshana. Shakuni killed Kulinda's brother, and Parvatiya killed Kulinda's Kradha. After Arjuna killed Vrishasena, there was a great duel between Arjuna and Karna, and in a long, absorbing battle, Arjuna killed Karna by severing his head.'

Sanjaya paused, and then Dhritarashtra asked him, 'Please give me the details of how the invincible Karna was killed. Was his chariot broken? Or did he forget the astras? Was he not given support? By losing Karna, I think Duryodhana lost all his hope of winning. And how did he cope with the killing of Karna and his dear brother Dusshasana? How was Dusshasana killed?'

Sanjaya continued. 'Dusshasana encountered Bhima and hit him with sharp arrows. He had broken Bhima's bow and injured his charioteer.

He fought bravely and probed Bhima with a number of arrows. While your son threw a Shakti towards Bhima, Bhima threw his heavy mace with such great force that it hit Dusshasana on the head, neutralising the Shakti on the way. Dusshasana had fallen to the ground from the broken chariot and was in great pain. Bhima pounced on Dusshasana and derisively asked him to show the hand with which he had pulled Draupadi to court. Your son was facing certain death but proudly displayed his hand and announced that he had made thousands of go-danas with the same hand and also dragged Draupadi to the court with the same hand. Bhima, who was in a state of great anger and a vengeful mood, had cut Dusshasana's proffered hand. Dusshasana became unconscious as the blood sprang up like a fountain, but Bhima was still not finished. He pierced with his sword Dusshasana's chest and finally cut his throat to kill him. It was a ghastly act, and people ran far away from the scene, unable to witness it. Bhima had taken Dusshasana's blood into both his hands and was seen drinking and dancing with great joy. He displayed his jubilation about what he had just done and loudly declared to Krishna and Arjuna his intention to kill Duryodhana soon. It was at this time that ten of your sons pounced on Bhima with arrows but were quickly killed by Bhima.'

Dhritarashtra was unhappy to hear the gory details of Dusshasana's death, and he also felt sad for Gandhari, who had been listening too! Which mother can bear the death of her sons, that too being brutally killed in a war field!

Sanjaya was aware of Dhritarashtra's mood, but he had to do his duty, no matter how unpleasant it may be. He continued his narration about the killing of Karna, of which he was asked.

'Before killing Dusshasana, Bhima challenged the Kuru warriors Karna, Duryodhana, Kripa, Ashwatthama, and Kritavarma to try to save Dusshasana if they could. Before anyone could even react and reach to rescue Dusshasana, Bhima had pierced the chest of Dusshasana and soon killed him, as I said before. Karna was in great shock to see Dusshasana thus being brutally killed before his eyes, and feeling bad about not being able to prevent that.

Finding his father in such a shocked state, Vrishasena took it upon himself to raise the tempo of his battle with Nakula. Nakula stopped battling with bow and arrows, got down from the chariot, and marched towards Vrishasena with a sword and shield. However, he had to be rescued by Bhima when Vrishasena broke both Nakula's sword and shield midway. Vrishasena, unrelenting, continued to pursue Nakula and Bhima, who were then fighting from a single chariot. When Arjuna approached them, Nakula asked him to kill Vrishasena, who tormented them. Arjuna remembered his vow that he would kill Vrishasena in front of his father, Karna, and just proceeded to do that. Vrishasena put up a valiant fight but was no match for Arjuna and was soon beheaded. Looking at his dearest son falling to the ground thus, Karna was sad and shed tears. He decided that the time had come for him to avenge and have his final battle with Arjuna.'

'Karna knew that it would be a do-or-die battle for him, and Duryodhana's fortunes depended upon the outcome of the fight between him and Arjuna. He pepped himself up by recalling his conversation with Bhishma on the day Bhishma fell and rested on the bed of arrows when Bhishma asserted his confidence in Karna's capabilities to counter Krishna and Arjuna. He remembered his repeated promises to Duryodhana, that he would kill Arjuna, which were more strongly believed by his friend than himself. The time has come for him to redeem his debts to Duryodhana and Hastinapur by putting his best performance to counter Krishna and Arjuna.

He asked Shalya to steer the chariot to face Arjuna.'

Chapter 14

The Last Battle of Karna

Hastinapur, Dhritarashtra's Palace

Sanjaya continued the narration to describe Karna's final battle with Arjuna.

'Karna asked Shalya while he was manoeuvring the chariot towards Arjuna what he would do if Arjuna killed him, and Shalya boldly replied that he would then take on Krishna and Arjuna and kill both of them. Even Arjuna asked Krishna a similar question to elicit his reaction. Krishna assured Arjuna that it wouldn't happen, but in case it happened, he would have no hesitation to take up arms and kill both Karna and Shalya. The chariots came face to face, and the warriors looked at each other. Soon, the long-awaited Arjuna-Karna duel started.

Once the duel had started, all the others were reduced to spectators. The battle went on for a long time. Initially, Karna was supported by Kaurava warriors, including your son, Kripa and Kritavarma, but Arjuna beat them all. Arjuna destroyed the army surrounding Karna's chariot, and the Kaurava army went back beyond a point, out of range for Arjuna's arrows and stood watching Karna fight alone. Karna similarly accounted for a number of Panchala and Srinjaya armies who were surrounding Arjuna.

Karna was in ascendancy from the beginning and injured both Krishna and Arjuna heavily. Bhima and Krishna observed this and asked Arjuna to speed up the tempo and quickly kill Karna. Bhima even said he would kill Karna with his mace if Arjuna did not increase the tempo. Krishna even proposed to offer Arjuna his own Chakra to deploy against Karna. Arjuna rejected both offers, stepped up the tempo of his fight, and started using Divya astras to mount pressure on Karna. However, Karna had effectively countered them and aimed his serpent-faced astra, which he was preserving for the occasion.

Unknown to even Karna, the serpent Ashwasena, the son of Takshaka, had hidden himself in the chest of arrows and got attached to this particular astra. Ashwasena knew that Karna would employ this particular arrow against Arjuna and wanted to take revenge on Arjuna for the Khandava fire years ago. Shalya had cautioned Karna that he was aiming higher than necessary. Karna preferred to keep the aim the same, relied on his judgement and released the arrow. At the same time, Krishna, noticing the lethal dart being aimed at Arjuna's neck, had made the horses bend a little so that the height of the chariot was lowered by a few inches. Instead of hitting Arjuna's face, the arrow hit his crown. The crown fell on the ground, burning, and turned into a molten mass, making people wonder what Arjuna's fate would have been had the arrow touched its target.

When Ashwasena returned to Karna's bow and asked him to re-release the arrow again, Karna declined, saying he did not need others' help to kill Arjuna and refused his offer. Ashwasena, who could not control his anger, proceeded towards Arjuna on his own. Arjuna, who was prepared this time, cut the flying serpent into three pieces by his deft placement of arrows, thus killing Ashwasena.'

Dhritarashtra asked Sanjaya to stop and questioned, 'Who is this Ashwasena, and why he wanted to kill Arjuna?'

Sanjaya explained, 'Ashwasena is the son of Takshaka. When Arjuna caused the Khandava to be consumed by fire, Ashwasena was lucky to escape, but his mother was killed. He was waiting for a chance to seek vengeance against Arjuna and entered Karna's favourite serpent-faced arrow, which Karna had reserved to use against Arjuna.'

Having received a go-ahead nod from the listener, Sanjaya proceeded with the rest of his narration.

'They continued to fight this way, and suddenly, Karna's chariot wheel stuck into the ground. Karna got down from the chariot and tried to lift it by extracting the wheel, but he could not. He again parried Arjuna's arrows and made Arjuna lose his senses temporarily through a very sharp draft. He again started to try to lift the chariot wheel but in vain.'

Dhritarashtra released a deep sigh, ' The chariot wheel would not come out. The curses are working on Karna. I remember that he was cursed by a Brahmin that his chariot wheel would get stuck in the ground when he was fighting his final war. That it happened meant Karna was doomed to get killed soon.'

Sanjaya continued, 'Arjuna regained his senses and was ready for the duel. Karna appealed to Arjuna to wait till he got the wheel lifted, but Krishna advised Arjuna not to procrastinate and finish the job. A sharp arrow from Arjuna cut Karna's neck, and that ended the glorious life of Karna.'

Dhritarashtra commented, 'Krishna knew no effort from Karna could reverse the Brahmin's curse, and the wheel could not be extricated. He, perhaps, did not want to prolong Karna's ordeal. It was how it was to happen. I deeply mourn for Karna's death.'

After hearing the full details and absorbing Karna's death news, both Dhritarashtra and Gandhari underwent a great shock, lost their energy, and fell to the floor. Vidura had spoken to Gandhari, and the maids had lifted her and escorted her to her chambers. Both Vidura and Sanjaya had spoken to Dhritarashtra, comforting him. Dhritarashtra looked like a man in deep shock and sat motionless and silent for a long time.

Sanjaya waited till Dhritarashtra was fit enough to listen and narrated to him the proceedings after Karna's death.

'Yudhishthira energetically came out of his rest to visit Karna's dead body, and the Pandava camp rejoiced as if they had won the battle itself. Your son, despite his grief, put up a great fight and killed a sizable Pandava army to boost the spirit of his army. But still, the morale of the army was so badly dented by Karna's death that they preferred to retreat. Shalya, who returned from the field with the empty chariot, consoled Duryodhana and advised him to call off the war for the day. The sun was also about to set, and Kauravas retreated with heavy hearts upon Karna's loss, whereas Pandava's camp witnessed great jubilation and blew conches and trumpets.'

Dhritarashtra, deeply upset with Karna's death, asked Sanjaya, 'Who are the important warriors left on our side, and what are the relative strengths of armies?'

Sanjaya gave the details as asked for and also filled in many details of the battle that he omitted in his narration to answer Dhritarashtra's questions.

Finally, the king permitted Sanjaya to leave, expressing his deep-felt sadness. 'I lost all hope of winning the war with Karna's death, and have a feeling that the war had come to an end with his death. Vidura's words are coming true. You may go now.'

Unlike Dhritarashtra's similar statements made on hearing the deaths of Bhishma and Drona, Sanjaya felt there was a ring of truth and sincerity in his confession this time. It was a king's statement conceding the defeat.

Then Vidura, too, took Dhritarashtra's permission and retired.

Dhritarashtra was escorted to his bed chambers. Dhritarashtra heard Gandhari sobbing and muttering some words about Karna's death.

She heard her husband's approaching footsteps and addressed him, 'Did Sanjaya go back?'

Dhritarashtra answered in the affirmative. 'I wish he would not come too soon', he added.

Gandhari agreed and supplemented her husband's wish and said,' I wish he would not come at all.'

Both knew, through insight, that Sanjaya's next visit would bring the saddest news of all, and Sanjaya would be returning soon to break that. They held each other's hands and silently suffered.

⟶⬦⟶

Naimisha

Little Master felt uneasy hearing the war report that night.

The deaths of Karna and Dusshasana had given him a clear signal that the war would not last for many more days. He knew how much Duryodhana depended on Karna to win the war and how much he loved Dusshasana, his brother. Coping with the loss of two most important people from his support group would be tough for him.

He asked the reporter, 'What are the relative strengths of Pandava's army now compared to Kaurava's army?'

'The huge difference of four akshauhinis between the two sides at the beginning kept on changing at the end of every day, and now the difference is meagre. Even now, elephants, horses, chariots and foot soldiers seem to be more for Kauravas, but their morale is rock bottom with the death of Karna.'

Animish signalled the reporter to leave and turned to Asareer, who was sitting in the same room. He suggested that they go for a walk, and they proceeded.

After walking a few yards, the Little Master asked Asareer, 'What is the latest news of our Master's return to Ashram? I haven't yet met the man whom we sent to meet him.'

Asareer told. 'The messenger had just returned in the afternoon. He conveyed that the Master had planned for his return soon. He may come here anytime.'

'I plan to visit Kurukshetra once. Duryodhana's days are now numbered as Karna has passed away. I think I should meet Duryodhana once before he departs.'

'What purpose would it serve? Would it be safe for you to visit the war site under the present circumstances?'

Animish didn't answer the first question and only said, 'I hope to meet him in the war camp, and there should not be any problem. I will be returning soon anyway.'

Asareer knew his friend had a fondness for Karna and Duryodhana for many years. Duryodhana particularly admired Little Master's vast knowledge and always enjoyed his talks. It was no surprise that his friend wanted to meet him when Duryodhana was in great sorrow and might feel comforted by the visit from his friend. There was no stopping Animish when he decided once.

'When do you start?' asked Asareer.

'I should reach there by evening tomorrow, by which time he will have returned from the battlefield. So, I will start early in the morning.'

They parted ways. Somehow, Asareer felt a little odd. It was as if his friend was saying, '*If he comes back from the battlefield.*' Asareer dismissed the idea and proceeded to his cottage.

Chapter 15

The Final Day's War

Hastinapur, Dhritarashtra's Palace

Sanjaya entered Hastinapur in a terrible state on the morning of the nineteenth day of war. His grief was uncontrollable. The people who saw him knew instinctively that the worst had happened and started weeping for their dead prince, Duryodhana. Sanjaya entered the palace of Dhritarashtra to break the bad news.

Dhritarashtra and Gandhari were present in the room and were talking to Vidura for comfort. They were waiting for Sanjaya to arrive. It is as if they knew what had happened and were waiting for Sanjaya to fill in the details. Sanjaya came in, touched Dhritarashtra's feet, and cried. Vidura got down from the chair and sat near Dhritarashtra, holding his hand. The palace maids had taken Gandhari's hands into their hands. Some of the wives of Kauravas were present, too, and there was a collective sobbing. There was no need to announce the news. They all knew it instinctively, but Sanjaya needed to tell.

'The war was over, and after great destruction, only seven warriors from the Pandava side and three warriors from our side survived. Shalya, Shakuni, Ulooka, Trigartas, Dhrishtadyumna, Shikhandi, Upapandavas, Panchala, Chedi, and Srinjaya warriors all had died. Whoever had come to take part in this war had all died except the ten survivors.'

'Your son Duryodhana fought like a lion with Bhima without any fear and displayed great skills worthy of a disciple of Balarama in front of his guru, who made it a point to be present there. In a blatant disregard to the rules of fair play, Duryodhana was hit on his thighs and was fatally wounded and died by early morning today. King Dhritarashtra! We had been defeated in the war despite putting in all our efforts for eighteen days.'

The collective sobbing increased to a higher pitch as the women became louder and more joined the group.

All three senior members of the royal family, Dhritarashtra, Gandhari, and Vidura, lost consciousness of their senses, and their bodies were cold and sweaty. Dhritarashtra was shown Gandhari's hand, which he was searching for, after gaining consciousness. The couple cried together aloud.

A little later, Dhritarashtra gained composure and asked the palace maids to escort Gandhari and the other queens into the inner chambers. As the room was cleared except for Vidura, Dhritarashtra asked Sanjaya to give a detailed report.

Sanjaya started to narrate. 'The Kaurava camp held discussions on the seventeenth night, after Karna's death, as to how they should proceed for the eighteenth day. Duryodhana had appointed, at the advice of Ashwatthama, king of Madra, Shalya, as the chief commander of the army. Shalya was pleased with this honour and promised Duryodhana that he would do his best the next day and would either kill the enemies or die fighting them. Still, the numbers were positive on Kauravas' side. Shalya led the troops the next day to the war, and the army had actively followed him.'

'Shalya put up a great fight, as never before, and none from the Pandava side were able to resist his onslaught. Shalya killed a number of Panchala and Chedi warriors and had a great duel with Bhima, where they fought with maces till both fell to the ground and were rescued by their teams. Shalya was attacked by Yudhishthira, Nakula, Sahadeva, Satyaki and Dhrishtadyumna, but he resisted them all, displaying excellent skills. Arjuna was drawn to fight Samshaptakas led by Susharma and his brothers, and Bhima concentrated on taking on your remaining sons. Nakula, Sahadeva acted as protectors to Yudhishthira. Satyaki and Dhrishtadyumna had also joined the attack on Shalya. From your side, Ashwatthama, Kripacharya, and Kritavarma were on the offensive along with Duryodhana.

Nakula accounted for the balance of three Karnaputras who fought fiercely, determined to avenge their father's death. All three, Chitrasena, Suseshana and Satyasena, were killed by Nakula.

Your son Duryodhana had killed the Vrishni warrior 'Chekitana' after a brief fight. Ashwatthama continued his offensive on Panchalas and killed a Panchala king, Suradha.

Yudhishthira had chosen to fight with Shalya as per Krishna's advice. Having killed the protectors of Shlya's chariot, Drumasena and Chandrasena, Yudhishthira went on the offensive against Shalya. Shalya, who had beaten many other Pandava warriors with his arrows and looked in irresistible form, had finally met his match in Yudhishthira. Yudhishthira looked menacing and showed no mercy in killing Shalya's supporting army and taking an aggressive stand. Finally, Yudhishthira killed Shalya with a sharp 'shakti', and Shalya fell from his chariot and died instantly.

Madra warriors were infuriated by their king's death and increased their offence. However, Yudhishthira killed Shalya's brother, and the Madra army was ambushed by the Pandava army before Duryodhana and Shakuni could come to their rescue.

The Mleccha king of Salva did put up a good fight for Kauravas on his mighty elephant, but Satyaki eventually killed him. Satyaki also accounted for Kshemadhurti.

Meanwhile, your sons had put up a great fight with Bhima and died in his hands, thus taking the tally of killed to ninety-eight, leaving just Sudarshana and Duryodhana. Bhima accounted for Sudarshana also sometime later.

Arjuna had annihilated the remaining Samshaptakas, along with their leaders, the brothers of Trigarta, Satyakarma, Satyeshu and finally Susharma. Though they were no match for Arjuna, Susharma and his brothers put up a brave fight with Arjuna. The entire Samshaptaka army and its leaders, who took an oath to kill or be killed, were eventually destroyed after busily engaging Arjuna to fight with them throughout the war.

Duryodhana had joined Shakuni, who was busy leading the cavalry. Shakuni told Duryodhana that he had accounted for most of Pandavas' cavalry and that they may proceed to destroy the chariots and foot soldiers. Duryodhana mounted a horse and surveyed what was happening.

Bhima and Sahadeva had taken on the Gandhara army. Sahadeva had duelled fiercely with Ulooka, son of Shakuni and killed him before the eyes of his father. Shakuni fought with Sahadeva but could not face him and retreated. Later, he returned to the battlefield, reinforcing himself, but could not stand up to Sahadeva and was killed. Thus, Sahadeva fulfilled his vow to kill Shakuni.

Having witnessed the killing of all his brothers and Shakuni and the almost total decimation of his army, Duryodhana lost all interest in war. Heavily wounded, he dismounted his horse and walked away alone from the battleground with just his massive mace for company. He didn't even notice that three more capable warriors still survived on the other front of the battlefield. Meanwhile, Kripa, Kritavarma and Kripacharya started searching for Duryodhana in the battleground full of dead horses, elephants, corpses and broken chariots. Unable to find him on the battlefield. They began to search him outside.'

'As for me, I fought to my maximum ability but was caught by Satyaki and Dhrishtadyumna, who thought of killing me. But just at that moment, Ved Vyasa had appeared and told them not to do so, and I was left free.

While I was coming back, I saw Duryodhana standing alone near "Dwaipayana Hrada," a little distance away from the battlefield. He told me that he would freeze the pond and rest there for a while. He told me that he had lost all desire to live, having lost all his brothers, sons and friends. He wanted me to tell you all that happened and that he was entering that lake with heavy injuries without any desire to live.'

'I took his leave and proceeded while he entered the waters and made them still. I came across Ashwatthama and others who were searching for

Duryodhana. I told them his whereabouts, and I was sent to the base camp on Kripa's chariot, where I waited for them.

When they reached your son, Ashwatthama asked him to come out, stating that the three of them were still available and willing to fight. Duryodhana told them that he was in no mood to fight in his present state and badly needed to rest. He suggested they may resume the fight the next day. As they heard the Pandava army coming in their direction, the trio retreated to a safer place, and Duryodhana had again made the waters of the lake still.

Pandavas invited Duryodhana to fight at once. Your son told them he was not in the mood to fight, and Yudhishthira may take the entire kingdom and leave him to spend the rest of his life in forests. Yudhishthira counselled Duryodhana that it would be improper for a Kshatriya like him to take the kingdom as a gift, and it does not behove well for Duryodhana to quit the battle and live in forests, after shedding so much blood on both sides. He made a counteroffer to Duryodhana to choose to fight any one of them with a weapon of his choice.

Duryodhana came out of the water with a mace in his hand, agreeing on the proposal. He, in turn, offered that any of them may come to duel with him with maces. Bhima stepped in and challenged Duryodhana.

They wore their armours and were readying to fight, and just then, Balarama approached them. He was appraised of the current situation leading to the duel between Bhima and Duryodhana, who both were trained under him. Balarama, who had just returned from his pilgrimage, was pleased with the request to witness the battle. He suggested that they fight in the nearby Samantapanchaka, which was not only a suitable place for a mace fight but was also divine. The belief was whoever died there would attain heavenly worlds. All of them walked to the suggested place, and the fight commenced. They started fighting like two tigers.'

'Tell me whether the fight was fair?' Asked Dhritarashtra.

Sanjaya replied, 'It was as fair as the entire Mahabharata war and the events leading to it, I would say,' there was a trace of sarcasm in his voice.

Then he continued, 'The final act was the consequence of all prior acts, and it matched all the prophecies that said Bhima would avenge the humiliation of Dyuta sabha by a hard blow on the thighs of Duryodhana. Maharaja, the final ending of the duel, was due to the blow by Bhima on the thighs of Duryodhana when he was in the air trying to land a blow on Bhima's head.

Balarama said it was unfair and that the rules of the mace fight wouldn't permit hitting below the navel. He was so furious that he marched menacingly towards Bhima with his plough as if to teach him a lesson. The onlookers were stunned at the fury of Balarama, but Bhima stood his ground unperturbed, holding his mace prepared for any consequence. However, Krishna ran behind his brother and held him tight before he reached Bhima and pacified him. Convinced or not, Balarama did not proceed further and left the scene in disgust. He did not want to be a part of further ongoings there.'

Dhritarashtra stopped him again. 'What justification Krishna would give to such a major indiscretion?'

Sanjaya explained, 'Krishna said that Bhima had publicly announced the mode of killing as far back as the time of dice hall, and everybody knew it. Sage Maitreya reiterated it when he advised Duryodhana to go for peace. Hence, it was Duryodhana's fault for leaving his thighs unprotected. Moreover, Duryodhana's feet were not on the ground to apply that rule because Duryodhana jumped high in the air. Bhima had stuck his blow before Duryodhana's feet touched the ground.'

Sanjaya stopped for a while to hear Dhritarashtra's comment, but the king was silent. Whatever his reaction, he did not share it.

Sanjaya continued, 'The fight, in fact, was on an evil keel for most of the time, and they had exhibited all kinds of variations in mace fight. Duryodhana was more agile on his feet, but Bhima could absorb the hard blows on his body and did not lose his concentration. At one stage, Bhima appeared to be so tired and clueless in the duel that Satyaki and Sahadeva came forward, offering Bhima rest and announcing their interest in fighting with Duryodhana in Bhima's place. However, Bhima asked them to refrain and refocused himself to put up a great fight.

Duryodhana had parried all the threats posed by Bhima and struck him so hard that Bhima's armour was broken, and he suffered great pain. Duryodhana leapt high into the air and was about to land a decisive and perhaps fatal blow on Bhima's head. In that process, his thighs were available to Bhima to deliver a deadly blow on your son. It was touch and go between the blow Duryodhana aimed against Bhima's head and the blow that Bhima aimed at Duryodhana's thighs. Bhima was the first to find the target, and Duryodhana had fallen to the ground with no chance to get up and stand again. He was severely injured, with bones broken, and bled profusely. Bhima jumped in joy, placed his left foot on Duryodhana's head, and declared that he had finished his job.'

'What did Yudhishthira say about Bhima's conduct?

'He did not like Bhima's conduct, but having understood the rationale of Bhima's action, Yudhishthira approved it after mildly admonishing him. Bhima was jubilant and announced that all the enemies had been dealt with, and Yudhishthira had secured the kingdom that was legitimately his.

Panchalas and Srinjayas hailed Bhima's feat, praised him a lot and talked ill of your son. Srikrishna then prevented everyone from talking ill of Duryodhana, saying that it would be unfair to speak like that before a dying man. He advised them that, having finished the job, they should all leave the place and let Duryodhana suffer the fate of all the adharmas he had done towards Pandavas.

At this stage, your son raised his body with difficulty, showed his anger at Krishna, and said as much.

"Krishna, you are the son of a servant of Kamsa. You had conspired to kill me by suggesting Bhima hit me on the thighs. I had seen you suggesting Arjuna, who then signalled to Bhima to do that heinous act. Not only me, you have contrived to kill everybody from our side only by deceit. Bhishma was killed by using Shikhandi as a shield. Drona was told a lie and was killed when he was in yoga. Dhrishtadyumna killed him, and you didn't say a word to him. You had planned to get Ghatotkacha killed by Karna with Shakti, thus saving Arjuna. You did not allow Arjuna to duel with Karna as long as he had Shakti at his disposal. I very much suspect you had tricked Jayadratha into believing that the sun had set and come out of protection, offering his neck to Arjuna, though we couldn't fathom how. You have got Bhurishravas killed unfairly. And finally, you got Karna killed when his chariot wheel got stuck in the mud without giving him time to get into another chariot. You could not have killed any of us if you fought righteously like an Arya. You are an anarya. You have got all of us killed while we were fighting righteously like Kshatriyas for our swadharma!'

'What was Krishna's reply to it?' Dhritarashtra asked.

Sanjaya continued. Krishna addressed Duryodhana like this.

"Duryodhana! All the indiscretions are on your side. You were the one who had started this process of adharma by trying to kill Kunti and Pandavas in Varanavata. It was you who called Yudhishthira for a dice game, won by cheating, and dragged Draupadi to the court. Your brother-in-law Jayadratha had tried to abduct Draupadi when she was in Aranyavasa. He should have been killed then and there but was spared by Yudhishthira. You killed Abhimanyu by flouting all the rules when he was alone and without support. Bhishma, who was killing many people every day, was confronted by Arjuna, supported by Shikhandi, who had done what was expected of him. He was born for that, and Bhishma knew that. Arjuna cut Bhurishravas's hand to protect Satyaki, who was fighting on his side. Satyaki killed him to fulfil his promise. Drona was killed as he had deviated from swadharma and killed many people by use of divyastras. Dhrishtadyumna, who was born for that purpose, killed him. Arjuna gave Karna a fair fight and won because of his skills. Pandavas won the war because they were the better side. You have not heard the good words of elders. You have reaped the consequences of your misdemeanours. You did things which ought not to be done. Now, you have to pay the price for it."

Duryodhana replied, "I did whatever was expected of me. I had learnt all shastras, satisfied brahmins, and ruled the earth from end to end as none did. I was loved by my friends and feared by my enemies. I subjugated whoever opposed me. What more can I expect? I'm getting the death, which is worthy of a Kshatriya who followed swadharma. Who would get a better life than me? I am going to meet my relatives and friends who laid their lives in the war for my sake.'

Pandavas felt ashamed as Duryodhana recited how they killed the Kaurava stalwarts and felt sad. Krishna consoled them and stated that there was nothing wrong with what they had done, as the enemy was strong, and without these methods, the win would have been difficult.

Then they had reconciled and gladly blew their conches to declare victory and left the place.'

'They went straight to the Kaurava camp, took possession of the gold and other valuables, and took charge of the camp. Yuyutsu had already transported the women and other people to Hastinapur the same evening after obtaining permission from Pandavas. The attending servants of the camp surrendered and joined Pandavas' service.

Krishna, Satyaki, and Pandavas decided to camp on the banks of the Oghavati River for rest and recuperation. Shikhandi, Dhrishtadyumna, and Upapandavas led the rest to the Pandavas camp, their regular resting place. While Pandavas were thus resting on the banks of Oghavati outside the camp, Yudhishthira requested Krishna to proceed to Hastinapur to convey the news to you personally and console you without loss of time. Krishna agreed to that and moved immediately.'

'Yes, Krishna came to us yesterday and briefly reported the unpleasant happenings. Before Krishna's coming, Vedavyasa had already told us the sad news. Krishna reiterated the circumstances leading to the war without Pandavas' fault and asked us to show goodwill to Pandavas. He said Yudhishthira was feeling sad for me and Gandhari and that we should forget everything and be prepared for a peaceful co-existence with them. Krishna reminded us that they are our only sons now for all purposes. He also consoled Gandhari and reminded her that she had blessed Duryodhana, saying that "the righteous would win," and that was exactly what had happened and that she should reconcile with the circumstances. Then suddenly, he showed urgency and said that Ashwatthama might attempt an attack on Pandavas, and he needed to leave at once and alert Pandavas.'

'Sanjaya nodded and said, 'Yes, Krishna was correct. But I don't think Krishna was in time to have alerted Pandavas, who were resting on the banks of Oghavati, thinking they had finished the war. Before they realised, Ashwatthama had already done what he had contemplated.'

Dhritarashtra asked him for more details about his son when Pandavas left him alone to bleed and die.

'After Krishna and Pandavas left, Duryodhana was surrounded by many people, including the news bearers who were anxiously looking at him to hear what he would say in his final moments. I was there, too. He looked at me and told me this.

"Time is the Master of all, and nobody can escape what time decides. A few days back, I was a possessor of eleven akshauhini in the army. I had the best of warriors like Bhishma pitamaha, Karna, Drona, Kripa, Shalya, Ashwatthama, Kripa, and many others, but now, I have reached this sorry state.

Tell everybody who is still alive that Bhima hit me against all propriety of rules. Pandavas won the war with their unseemly acts, which were responsible for the fall of Bhishma, Drona, Karna, and Bhurishravas. They have to repent for their misdeeds, and no wise man will praise them for this.

Sanjaya! Please tell my parents, who are aware of all the rules of war, that their son fought like a Kshatriya throughout. I did not back out of the war and did not seek compromise at any stage. I completed all my duties, enjoyed the kingdom, and helped those whom I liked. I will leave the kingdom only after my death.

Sanjaya! Tell Ashwatthama, Kripa, and Kritavarma never to trust Pandavas. They have flouted all the rules of war many times."

Sanjaya said, 'Your son had then turned towards news bearers and said, "Bhima had dealt his fatal blow exceeding the rules of war. Now, I will be going to the place where all my slain warriors have gone, and I will meet all of them."

Maharaja! Then, your son had lamented about his sister Dusshala, who had lost her hundred brothers and her husband. Then he felt sorry for you and Gandhari, who are left with the widows of sons and grandsons. Then he expressed sorrow for his wife, who had lost both her son and now her husband. Then he remembered Charvaka, the man of sweet words and hoped that he would surely take revenge on his behalf if and when he came to know about his death. Then, he declared that he was going to attain heavenly worlds by dying in the holy place, Samantapanchaka. After that, he fell silent and closed his eyes. All the surrounding people wept aloud and dispersed in all directions with heavy hearts and tearful eyes.'

Sanjaya paused for a while, and Dhritarashtra asked him what had happened afterwards, as he said earlier that Ashwatthama had resorted to night carnage. Sanjaya then narrated the incidents of the night of the eighteenth day of war. In fact, it was not a war in the conventional sense. It was an ambush that had never happened in the past, and nobody had any clue until it happened like that.

Chapter 16

The Mahabharata War - Not Yet Finished

Hastinapur, Dhritarashtra's Palace

Sanjaya continued his narration of the events that unfolded on the darkest night of the Kurukshetra war.

'Ashwatthama, Kripa and Kritavarma heard about the fall of Duryodhana through the news bearers and went on swift horses to see Duryodhana. They were shocked to see Duryodhana lying down on the bare earth and shifting restlessly from one side to the other, in extreme discomfort. They had lamented a lot, finding him in such a position. However, Duryodhana talked bravely to them and said he was happy to see the three of them alive and asked them not to lament for him as he would be reaching the heavens, reserved for the brave soon, as he had fought like a Kshatriya.

Ashwatthama could not bear to see the agony of your son and could not digest the manner in which he was beaten. His grief turned into anger. He took the hand of your son into his hands, and with tears rolling down his cheeks, he declared that Pandavas had committed untold war crimes and they shall pay for it. He said that he was more upset and pained to witness the manner of deceiving Duryodhana in the mace fight, more heinous than the unmanly act of Dhrishtadyumna beheading his father, Drona. He sought Duryodhana's permission to continue the war, vowing to kill the enemies who now believed that they had become victorious and were celebrating.

Duryodhana was pleased with Ashwatthama's offer and asked Kripa to anoint him as the Supreme Commander and to take actions as Ashwatthama may deem fit. The brief ceremony was duly done. Ashwatthama embraced Duryodhana for a moment and roared like a lion, pepping himself up for the task ahead, and marched forward with a firm determination to fulfil his word given to Duryodhana, followed by Kripa and Kritavarma. They went to the Kaurava camp, which had just been vacated by Pandavas after securing the valuables. Apprehending the return of Pandavas, the trio left the place and went to nearby forests far from the sounds of the victorious camps of Pandavas. I stayed in the camp for the night.

Though Kripacharya and Kritavarma had fallen asleep under the trees, the restless Ashwatthama was immersed in deep thinking about the mission he had undertaken. He had no resources except the company of Kripa and Kritavarma. He suddenly sighted a night owl, killing the unsuspecting sleeping birds in their nest. He took it as divine guidance, suggesting to him the right course of action. Within minutes, he made his resolve and decided to finish things in the night itself, taking advantage of the surprise factor. He knew Dhrishtadyumna, his chief nemesis, could not be killed with weapons, and he needed to be killed with bare hands only.

He woke up the other two and briefed them on his plan. The three discussed the propriety of the action extensively.

Despite Kripa and Kritavarma's advice that fighting in the morning would be fair and reasonable, Ashwatthama did not budge from his stand. He started to prepare his chariot to march ahead with his plan, all alone, whether the other two would join him or not.

Sensing that their commandant was totally convinced of his idea and was assuming full responsibility, the two maharathis gave in and assured Ashwatthama of their support and followed him.

Ashwatthama asked the two to remain at the entrance of the Pandava war camp to ensure that they would deal with the people who escaped him. He then invoked for himself the blessings of Mahadeva and boldly entered the camp alone. He searched for the cottages of the Panchala camp to confront the Chief Commandant, Dhrishtadyumna, the slayer of his father.

Soon, he spotted a sleeping Dhrishtadyumna, woke him up and physically overpowered him before the latter realised what was happening. Dhrishtadyumna had no chance at all to wriggle out from Ashwatthama's iron grip. Dhrishtadyumna pleaded for an honourable death by the sword, but Ashwatthama refused and stated that he did not deserve any such privilege, having heinously killed his Guru. He then brutally killed him by physical blows on sensitive parts. Dhrishtadyumna, who commanded the army of Pandavas for eighteen days and brought them to victory, had thus become the hapless first victim of Ashwatthama's unusual fury.

Ashwatthama then proceeded to kill Uttamouja, who was sleeping nearby in a similar way, and Yudhamanyu, who tried to resist Ashwatthama by using his mace, was next to be killed. After this initial adventure in the Panchala contingent, Ashwatthama unsheathed his sword and started his terrific and indiscriminate killing spree.

The loud cries of Dhrishtadyumna's wives and others who woke up alerted the whole camp, and the warriors quickly surfaced to engage Ashwatthama in battle. However, none could stand before Ashwatthama, and they fell one after the other. He went on killing Shikhandi and Upapandavas and then marched into the camp, holding his sword and killing everyone without exceptions. He was particularly harsh on the remaining sons of Drupada. None of the Panchalas and Virata warriors, including ordinary soldiers, were spared. In his rage, he even took on elephants and horses, cutting them to pieces.

Kripa and Kritavarma set fire to the camp in a few places and killed whoever was trying to escape from Ashwatthama. Within hours, except for the women and kids, all others who were camping there were totally butchered.

Then, congratulating one another on their deeds, the three went on to meet Duryodhana, intending to inform him of the good news, if he was still alive by providence.

By the time they reached Duryodhana, he was still alive and was delighted to see them. Ashwatthama conveyed to him that barring the seven persons, Krishna, Satyaki and five Pandavas, who were not available in the camp, all others were killed without exception. Duryodhana was highly pleased to hear the news and praised Ashwatthama, "Whatever you have done today, along with Kritavarma and Kripacharya, is remarkable. Nobody, including Bhishma, Karna, and your father, had done this much of a great favour for me. I am content and consider myself a victor. I will meet you again in the other worlds. May everything good happen to you."

With these final words, Maharaja, your son breathed his last. Before he died, he embraced all the three warriors fondly, and they, too, embraced him. After Duryodhana had thus fallen lifeless, they had gone to their chariots and left. I proceeded immediately to convey the news to you and am now here.'

Dhritarashtra was deeply engrossed in his thoughts. The excitement of the eighteen days of war had vanished after his last hopes had been shattered, and reality started staring at him. His whole world had collapsed in front of him. He had no kingdom, no sons and no friends. He would now live at the mercy of Pandavas.

He particularly dreaded Bhima's attitude towards him. Bhima was the one who always made his sons restless. Bhima was the one who killed all his sons. And now Bhima would be the one to whom he shall look for favours. Then, his mind started to think about the fate of his sons. What a glorious life they were leading! Why didn't his son heed the advice of elders and well-wishers? Why did he pitch for the war? And now he was lying dead on the grounds of Samantapanchaka. He sobbed aloud. He continued sobbing.

Sanjaya put a hand on his shoulder and started consoling. 'Oh! King! This is not the time for brooding. You have to control yourself and perform the prescribed rituals for the departed. We also need to arrange for the cremation of innumerable kings and princes who came from far-off places and died for you.'

'Where is Vidura?' Sanjaya heard Dhritarashtra speak thus in between sobs, and Vidura quickly came forward to hold his brother's hand. Sanjaya asked the housemaids to alert all the women folk to assemble to visit the Kurukshetra to have the last glance of their slain beloved. Vidura kept on consoling Dhritarashtra with appropriate words.

Kurukshetra, Pandava's camp

Pandavas got up to meet the charioteer of Dhrishtadyumna, who came running on foot to break the sad news. He was the lone survivor who somehow managed to escape. He narrated the gory devastation caused by Ashwatthama, who had ambushed the whole camp with the help of Kripacharya and Kritavarma and didn't spare a single man, elephant or horse.

Grief-stricken and deeply shocked, they hurried to the camp and were filled with anguish to witness the dead bodies and severed limbs of men, elephants and horses scattered all over the ground. Nakula immediately rushed to Upaplavya to fetch Draupadi and the other women who were still camping there.

Draupadi, who was already mourning for her dead father and other relatives, was crestfallen to hear the news. She lamented the deaths of her dear brothers, including her twin brother, Dhrishtadyumna, and all her five sons. She was inconsolable when she saw the slain bodies of her dear ones. She fell unconscious, unable to control her grief.

Her grief turned into anger, and it demanded action and retribution. She asked that the main perpetrator of the incident, Ashwatthama, should be brought to book. He should be searched and killed wherever he might have hidden. Unable to see Draupadi lamenting like that and on account of his anger, Bhima rushed to take quick action. Without waiting for a minute, he took Nakula as the charioteer to pursue Ashwatthama. Just in time, they got information that Ashwatthama had been seen going towards Vedavyasa's nearby ashram.

Krishna alerted Yudhishthira that Bhima was exposing himself to grave danger. A desperate Ashwatthama might employ superior astras, which can be countered only by Arjuna. While saying so, Krishna took Yudhishthira and Arjuna into his chariot and drove fast to stop Bhima.

Bhima's chariot reached Vyasa's Ashram in no time, and Bhima spotted Ashwatthama sitting by the side of Vyasa in meditation. He rushed towards Ashwatthama, shouting in anger. Ashwatthama looked at the angry Bhima advancing towards him menacingly, flanked by Nakula. He also spotted the three others who were alighting from their chariot. Ashwatthama had no time to think about how to defend himself, as Bhima might pounce on him at any moment. The only idea that struck him was the employment of deadly Brahmashira astra, which was not employed even at the height of the Kurukshetra war. It was the only weapon meant to save him. He had taken a blade of grass and invoked it, intending to destroy all Pandavas.

Before it could destroy Bhima, Arjuna countered it with the same astra, as Krishna advised. As both astras were of equal power, no one gained advantage, and the sages, including Narada and Vyasa, urged them to withdraw the astras, as they would only cause damage to the environment and harm to others without killing either Pandavas or Ashwatthama, the intended targets.

Both had to accede to the wisdom of the advice. Ashwatthama said he was unable to withdraw it totally but would dilute its impact by acting on the wombs of pregnant women carrying the Pandava lineage clan instead of on Pandavas.

Vedavyasa said, 'So be it and withdraw your Astra.'

Ashwatthama intended that the astra would destroy the baby in Uttara's womb, the only pregnant woman in the Pandava clan carrying Abhimanyu's child. With Ashwatthama's consent, Arjuna withdrew both the astras.

The sages advised Pandavas not to pursue the dispute and to drop the idea of killing Ashwatthama. Ashwatthama was, in turn, advised to part with the diamond on his head as a token of surrender, as Pandavas demanded. Ashwatthama had to accede to that command and surrender the diamond, which he had since birth and which gave him immense power and strength.

Krishna was unhappy with Ashwatthama for his wish to kill an unborn infant who had no connection with the war at all. He challenged Ashwatthama and said that the child in Uttara's womb would not only survive but would be a worthy successor to Pandavas. He cursed Ashwatthama to stay alive for long, but without any contact or companionship with fellow humans, tending to the unhealed wound on his head caused by plucking the natural diamond, which would never heal.

Ashwatthama, having surrendered the diamond to the Pandavas, left the ashram of Vedavyasa, resigning himself to his fate. His departure to the forests effectively signalled the end of the Mahabharata war.

Bhima gave the diamond to Draupadi, and she was told that Ashwatthama's life was spared, but his fame had been dented, and he would be powerless with the diamond being cut off from his head. Draupadi, too, felt that the action was in order regarding the son of their preceptor. On her request, Yudhishthira adorned it on his crown, treating it as a gift from Guru.

Naimisha

The messengers of various kingdoms returned to their respective places to give their final reports after the death of Duryodhana. Vyasa stationed himself in Hastinapur to be on the side of his son, Dhritarashtra. Naimisha's contingent of newsbearers returned, too. They need not go again to Kurukshetra for this purpose.

The inmates of Little Master's Ashram assembled that late evening to hear the final bulletins of newsbearers. The top chair was empty for two days, as Little Master had left and did not return. Anvesh, who had been acting as the deputy to Little Master, presided in his place. He always sat on the other side of Little Master as an observer, mostly silent and would occasionally provide clarifications.

The news of the series of deaths was received in hushed silence. The war was over, the destruction was complete, and there was nothing to cheer about. However, there were questions nonetheless, and they were all an inquisitive bunch.

'Why did Yudhishthira attack Shalya and put himself in danger? Would it not have been better to allow Arjuna, Bhima, or Satyaki to do it?'

Anvesh answered, 'Yudhishthira, for all general impressions, appears to be a man of peace but not a man of war. Though he was well trained and adept at the art of warfare, he generally depended on his capable brothers, not that he couldn't do. However, deep inside, Yudhishthira probably wished to prove that he was a warrior in his own right. He had held himself well in his earlier fights with Drona, Duryodhana and Karna, too, though Karna defeated him once. He knew all astras, and he knew the fighting style of Shalya, whom he had keenly observed. Yudhishthira had used Nakula and Sahadeva as his chariot protectors, and was ably assisted by other warriors. He had given a true fight to Shalya that perhaps surprised his opponent. Yudhishthira had shown that he could be as merciless to foes as others.'

Another senior inmate commented. 'Bhima took on Shalya with his mace and wanted to finish him, but Shalya was equal to him, and neither could beat the other, so they were exhausted. Shalya has the propensity to excel himself when he is possessed by anger. He had immense respect for Yudhishthira and could not summon any anger in fighting with Yudhishthira. It seems Krishna especially asked Yudhishthira to take on Shalya for that very reason. However, full credit be given to Yudhishthira who fought gustily and employed a very special shakti to end the life of Shalya.'

'In fact, it was an honour for the rampaging Shalya to be killed by none other than Yudhishthira, whom he respected a lot,' someone said, and another from the audience commented, 'Perhaps Shalya was the only Kaurava general who had a heroic death.'

The topic then turned to the killing of Duryodhana.

'Was it not a gamble to offer Duryodhana a choice to fight any of them with mace? What if he had chosen anyone other than Bhima to fight with maces?'

'Yudhishthira knew Duryodhana would choose only Bhima, as Duryodhana's only desire at that time was to prove himself. He could achieve that only by fighting with Bhima. Though it seemed as if he wanted to give Duryodhana a fair chance and, showing his confidence in himself and his brothers to take on Duryodhana with any kind of weapon, he, perhaps, knew intuitively that Duryodhana would pick Bhima only. You may say it was a gambler's instinct,' Anvesh answered.

A senior member supplemented. 'We also hear that Krishna chastised him for giving that offer, which would have negated all their earlier efforts to bring the battle to this final stage. However, much to the relief of everybody, Duryodhana himself counteroffered that he would fight with whoever wanted to fight with him, and Bhima came forward to accept the challenge.'

'Then, we should agree with Yudhishthira's instinct. His gambler's instinct had finally paid off,' someone quipped in mild humour.

There were a few laughs in the audience as if to appreciate the comment.

Anvesh elaborated further, 'Duryodhana always publicly said, even to his father, that he could kill Bhima in the mace fight. He perhaps wanted to prove a point that he was superior to Bhima in the mace fight. Duryodhana wanted to kill Bhima first and, given a chance, take on others one by one. He must have determined to fight with all five and kill them all. He no longer desired any kingdom. Death stopped worrying him any more. If one is not worried about death, one can put up a fierce fight even against a better man.'

Asareer found that the answers mostly satisfied the audience, who were nodding in agreement. Some of the answers and the reactions they elicited surprised Asareer. *Why can't they believe in the fairness of Yudhishthira's offer? Why do they interpret Yudhishthira's fair thinking as a gambler's instinct?* He mused.

Asareer thought about his Animish, who had yet to come back. He felt sorry for him, as Duryodhana would have fallen to the ground and breathed his last or been unconscious by the time his friend reached Kaurava camp and waited for his return. *"My friend would not have met Duryodhana while he was alive,"* thought Asareer.

He was brought into the conference again by the voice of the deputy.

'True, Ashwatthama did not show that much spirit on other days. He was a capable warrior and held even Arjuna at bay for a considerable time in the war. He was burning with rage against Panchalas ever since Dhrishtadyumna severed Drona's head and threw it unceremoniously. His rage further increased when he witnessed Duryodhana languishing agonisingly on the bare earth in Kurukshetra. Ashwatthama showed his brute force and accounted for everybody who came his way. Moreover, the Pandavas' absence had helped him. If they had been there, the story could have been different.'

'But why were they not there?'

'It is gathered that they stayed overnight on the banks of the River Oghavati, resting and reminiscing about the events of the past eighteen days of war.'

"What a costly rest it turned out! Where is Ashwatthama now?'

'We do not know yet. The trio had met with Duryodhana, and after his death, they left towards Hastinapur after the carnage to dutifully pay respects to their King, Dhritarashtra. They met him while he was on his way to the war field to pay homage to the departed. After informing him,

Kripacharya left for his home in Hastinapur, and Kritavarma took the way to Dwaraka. We do not know where Ashwatthama had gone, but Pandavas were already on his trail and would have found him by now.'

The meeting ended. Asareer went back to his cottage, thinking about his friend, and was happy to find Animish returning in the late evening. He looked tired from his journey and was obviously unhappy at the fall of Duryodhana. He did not talk much but quickly retired to his cottage. Asareer had just time to say a few words to his friend. Asareer remarked to his friend that he did not expect the war to end this soon and this way, more as a matter of consolation and to draw his friend into a conversation.

Animish nodded and said, 'By the time I reached the place, the war was over. I stayed in our Kurukshetra Ashram for the night and started in the morning. Yes, I, too, agree the war should not have ended this way. Duryodhana was killed by unfair means and in the presence of his guru, Balarama. You must have heard all those details.' Asareer answered that they did.

'Did you hear that Duryodhana offered to quit the kingdom and wanted to retire to the forests? But Yudhishthira, whom you all consider to be a personification of virtues and a peace-loving man, did not allow this. He insisted that Duryodhana should fight and die or win and retain the kingdom if he escaped death. Duryodhana had no choice but to fight. And the fight was not fair either! Anyway, I am too tired for the day, and we should talk more about this some other time. There is so much to tell.'

Asareer returned to his cottage, bidding goodbye to his friend and had his bedtime prayers. He looked at the small statue of Srikrishna and thought about what his friend commented. Why did the Lord have to let it happen this way? Had he willed, couldn't he make Duryodhana fall for a proper stroke by Bhima? Why did he give scope to people to think that Bhima could not have won against Duryodhana but for following Krishna's advice? Asareer retired to his bed, but sleep eluded him. He started thinking about other aspects as well. Why should he ask Arjuna to kill Karna when Karna's chariot wheel is stuck and Karna is fighting without a chariot? Can't Arjuna kill Karna while Karna was fighting from his chariot? Similarly, the deaths of Drona and Bhishma were not achieved by the skills of Pandavas alone. Everywhere Krishna's hand was to be seen, Asareer went through a process of deep thinking.

All of a sudden, a thought struck him, and his face brightened. He rose from his bed and squatted. It was as if he discovered some explanation for the mystery that had been vexing him all along. *The answer was always there, but he failed to see; the invisible is visible now.*

God's Hand! The invisible hand! Asareer repeated aloud the thought that flashed in his mind. Krishna wanted to prove to the whole world how God's Hand is absolutely necessary for success in any work, and to whom that hand will be offered. A man's competence is not sufficient to achieve success. Even the most competent man needs God's support to achieve success in his purpose. God's support is given to people who uphold Dharma.

Duryodhana may be competent. Karna may also be worthy. But they did not take the outstretched hand of God when offered. They would have followed Dharma had they accepted his advice and would have lived with peace and purpose. On the other hand, Pandavas grabbed Krishna's hand with both hands. Krishna was the difference between victory and defeat. The war of Mahabharata clearly demonstrated that.

Duryodhana was accusing Krishna of helping Pandavas win the war by dubious means. His friend, Animish, was echoing the same thought process. What they were clearly missing was that they did not realise that Krishna was God. The moment one realises that Krishna was indeed God, his actions would make sense. His actions can not be reproached. Had he wanted, he could have made everything look fair. He did not. He wanted to show that God would go to any extent to save 'Dharma'. He encouraged and emboldened Pandavas to commit things which apparently looked like 'Adharma', but at a higher level, they were justified as 'Dharma' as the acts were in pursuance of Dharma. It was a subtle message on the true purpose of Dharma.

Asareer's mind became peaceful, and he gradually slipped into blissful sleep.

The next day, Little Master was chairing the morning meeting. The news bearers narrated more details.

Duryodhana's message to news-bearers was well received by the inmates.

Some of them were seen commenting openly, 'A worthy Kshatriya' 'and Died fighting like a Hero'. There was some sympathy for Ashwatthama. 'They should have killed him instead of taking the diamond from his head. Without that diamond, Ashwatthama can never be his previous self.'

Some said that Ashwatthama should have respected Kripacharya's advice and refrained from that night's ambush. 'He should have waited for the next morning,' they asserted.

Many did not accept this. 'Ashwatthama did the right thing. If killing was not wrong in itself, what was the impropriety in killing in the night? By morning, Duryodhana would have been dead, and the revenge would be meaningless.'

'Ultimately, he was the sufferer. He had to surrender to Pandavas, though not defeated, on the stern advice of sages. He lost his respect and was reduced to living like a wandering hermit without friends.'

The meeting was about to conclude, and the excitement of war, which had gripped them all these days, had given way to grief over the great destruction. Some of them had lost a friend or a relative or knew someone who had. The war had caused enormous human loss, and every family in Hastinapur and Indraprastha had lost more than one man. The people who cheered either Yudhishthira or Duryodhana before the war had nothing to cheer about now. The atmosphere of gloom that pervaded the twin cities had crept into Naimisha as well, and the inmates, too, were caught in that mood.

Just then, a new batch of news bearers appeared who were carrying the news from the erstwhile war field, now a field of dead bodies, corpses of humans and animals.

The news they brought shook the audience like nothing before.

'While Yudhishthira and others were about to offer the final rites to the departed relatives, Kunti asked Yudhishthira to perform the same for Karna as well, in the capacity of a brother. She revealed that unknown to anybody, Karna was her eldest son, born years before Yudhishthira, when she was yet to be married.'

The audience was shocked to receive the astounding news, which was simply unbelievable.

The narrator continued, 'She told a shocked Yudhishthira that the boon she had received from the sage Durvasa, as a girl, was tested by her in all innocence invoking Lord Surya. She was shocked when the deity appeared and wanted to withdraw. However, she was told that even a deity was bound by the power of mantra, and once invoked, there was no going back. She feared the consequences and later abandoned the child born thus, who was later raised by Adiratha, and that child was none other than Karna.

There was a huge commotion. The audience started passing remarks on the absurdity and even the timing of the revelation, as they thought fit. Somebody raised his voice and said, 'It is absurd! How can that be? Then why didn't she reveal it so far? How could she allow the brothers to hate each other, even to the extent of swearing to kill the other? Which mother can do that?'

The questions echoed in everybody's mind, reflecting the general sentiment as a first reaction. The conservatives who never approved of Kunti invoking her boon three times had a tough time digesting that she invoked her boon even before marriage and kept it a secret from her husband.

Little Master looked unfazed. His face did not reveal any surprise. Asareer thought that his friend might have been aware of this news and crossed the first stage of disbelief.

Little Master answered, 'Yes, it is true that he was a son of Kunti. She had given birth to Karna as an unwed mother and left the boy in a river to seek his own fate. It was not unknown to many that Karna was found by Adiratha, his adopted father, as a days' baby in a box floating in the river. That the baby was a Queen's secret should not surprise anyone; it was long suspected, and now we know who that queen was. If at all, there is something to be surprised about, it is why she revealed it now after his death. I think she was overcome with feelings of guilt and remorse, and it was her last chance to reveal the fact burning within her heart. We may not find fault with her.'

There were many questions relating to the new revelation, and the inmates came up with a plethora of them. They discussed the issue from various angles. *"Who else knew about this secret?" "Did Bhishma try to avoid a showdown between the brothers and hence insist that Karna should not fight?" "Was Duryodhana aware of the fact, and that was why he respected Karna's friendship so highly?" "Was Kunti under pressure to reveal the secret since she suspected that many others knew it too?" "Did Karna's performance suffer on account of his awareness that he was fighting with his own brothers?" "How come Yudhishthira did not know it till the end of the war? Wouldn't Krishna, Ved Vyasa or his mother tell him this much before?"* were some of those questions. They could not come to any conclusions as the issues were primarily matters of conjecture and personal opinion.

Someone commented, 'Pandavas must be repenting for killing Karna, after knowing that he was their brother, especially Arjuna, who nurtured a lifelong enmity with Karna and finally killed him.'

Another added, 'Yudhishthira's remorse would be no less either since he is the beneficiary of war.'

Finally, someone declared in a loud voice, 'Karna was not a Sutaputra as he was mostly addressed but was, in fact, a Surya Putra.' The assembly was suddenly silenced by this loud assertion for a little while, after which the boisterousness continued.

Little Master did not take part in those discussions, leaving the hotheads to debate on various scenarios themselves and expressing different opinions.

Asareer was surprised to see the overwhelming sympathy generated towards Karna by this revelation, which obliterated his past misdeeds and his role in pitching for the war. Karna had, in fact, more responsibility to stop the destructive war, if he knew Pandavas were his brothers, but all his actions seemed to be counter-intuitive. Now, some of the inmates even went to the extent of suspecting Yudhishthira knew that Karna was his elder brother, and that was the reason for his undue fear about him! Strange are the ways the human minds love to fabricate and tend to believe in conspiracies rather than plain truths, Asareer reflected.

The meeting went on for an hour or so when they received a message that gladdened their hearts. 'Master is on his way back and is now very near. He would reach us soon.' The assembly went into raptures.

Most of the new inmates had not seen him, though they had heard a lot about him. They were eager to see him. Some who had known him were happy at the prospect of a reunion.

Asareer was happy, too. It had been a long time since he saw his mentor. He looked at Animish, who obviously looked pleased and relieved, and was seen instructing some of the inmates about the arrangements to be made. The cottage that was occupied by the Master earlier was still kept unoccupied and was regularly serviced. The inmates had grown in number, and the Ashram was flourishing. Master would really be impressed by the progress achieved in his absence, Asareer thought.

Chapter 17

The Post-War Gloom

Hastinapur

The formalities of paying the last tributes to the departed took about thirty days. Until then, Pandavas, Dhritarashtra, and their families camped on the bank of the Ganga.

Though they had won the war, Pandavas were not happy in their hearts. They had lost their children, close relatives, and friends. It was taking them time to reconcile to the new realities and get back to the task of ruling the kingdom. Vidura, with the help of Yuyutsu, took care of the administration during the interim period.

Yudhishthira was crestfallen with grief as the enormity of destruction was now crystal clear in front of his eyes.

'How many people had died in all? You might have estimated it by now!' Dhritarashtra asked in one of their meetings after the war. Yudhishthira remembered his reply- *"One crore sixty-six lakhs and twenty-six thousand. And then an enormous number of horses and elephants."*

'To hell with being a Kshatriya! This wretched Kshatriya dharma made me cause this destruction! Is there any way I can escape from the sin of causing this death spree!' Yudhishthira had been thinking along the same lines ever since the war was over.

His misery was compounded upon learning that Karna was his elder brother. He recalled his observation that Karna's feet looked almost like Kunti's. *'Why didn't my mother tell me this earlier?'* Yudhishthira cried aloud.

"May the women not be able to keep secrets!" It was a curse statement he addressed for all the women in general. Kunti explained to him that she had asked Karna to reconcile with his brothers, but he refused. She knew there was no way she could stop the eventual confrontation resulting in the death of one of her sons, but she was resigned to the fact as a royal woman. Yudhishthira was not satisfied with her logic. He thought he sinned, and the blood of his brother was on his hands.

He thought about Bhishma; he thought about Drona; he thought about Abhimanyu and Upa Pandavas repeatedly and mourned their deaths.

He continued self-introspecting his conduct and started brooding.

'Was he not aware of the risks that were at stake before the war? He certainly knew. He tried his best to avoid war, but Duryodhana forced the war on him. But how would the people perceive it? Would they blame him for the destruction of royal families of various kingdoms? Whom did he earn the kingdom for, and whom would he bequeath it?'

The last words Duryodhana spoke to them were still reverberating in his ears. *"Krishna! You are the son of a slave of Kamsa. You had advised Bhima to hit me on the thighs, fully knowing it was adharma. You are not ashamed of this. You got the great warrior Bhishma killed by placing Shikhandi before Arjuna! You made the fall of Drona possible by resorting to an untruth! You had sacrificed Ghatotkacha to save Arjuna from Karna's Shakti! You had advised Arjuna to sever the hand of Bhurishravas while he was fighting with Satyaki and then encouraged Satyaki to kill Bhurishravas, who withdrew from fighting! I very much suspect you had tricked Jayadratha into believing that the sun had set and come out of protection, offering his neck to Arjuna. You incited Arjuna to kill Karna while Karna's chariot wheel got stuck in the battlefield. You are Anarya! Had Pandavas fought the war in a dharmic way, you could not have defeated any of us! Shame on you!"*

Yudhishthira still remembered what Duryodhana finally said to all of them. "*I performed all my duties. I enjoyed all the pleasures. I had ruled the world for the last thirteen years without any defeats. Who can live better than that? I have fought a brave war and am dying on the battlefield like a Kshatriya. I will meet my friends in the heavens. Who can have a better death? You survived the war, but will you be happy after killing all of us and getting all your friends and relatives killed in the war for your sake? I am going to heaven, and you will live a miserable life!*"

Yudhishthira never got over the grief caused from that moment on. The words of Duryodhana had a profound impact on him. *'He is correct,'* Yudhishthira thought.

'Duryodhana was the cause for this total decimation caused by the war, but he died. People would only blame me for this—me, who never aspired for riches and kingdoms. I fought the war to redeem my honour and for the sake of my brothers, who suffered on my account. Let my brothers enjoy the benefit of war. As far as I am concerned, I will take to Tapasya and redeem myself from the sins of war committed by me.' Yudhishthira decided to relinquish the kingdom and informed his brothers and Draupadi of his decision, who were utterly shocked to hear the same.

Naimisha

Asareer accompanied Animish and others to receive Master at the river bank and brought him to their ashram. There was not much change in the Master—the way he looked and walked. The passing years did not show much effect on him. His face looked as radiant as ever and more peaceful. He brought with him two disciples from the Himalayan ashram who were visiting Naimisha for the first time.

Master greeted one and all, and while the old inmates queued up to pay their respects, the new inmates were introduced to him, one by one. Master had spent the evening with the inmates, chatting with them, and also engaged the other guests, who had come to see him from nearby ashrams, in conversations. Mostly, he had told them about the forests, rivers, mountains, kingdoms and kings on the way from Naimisha to the Himalayas. He answered their questions patiently, and his associates from the Himalayas also answered some of the questions relating to their place and culture.

Master enquired with the audience about the recent war happenings, of which he was partly aware. After a briefing of what had happened and eliciting specific responses, he said that on the way to Naimisha, he had been to Kurukshetra and camped with the Brahmins on the banks of the Ganga, where all the Pandavas were camping. He informed the audience that Yudhishthira had firmly expressed his decision not to take up the kingship and proposed to take up an early Vanaprastha. His brothers were trying to convince him to change his decision, but Yudhishthira stood his ground. Vedavyasa and other sages were also there, trying to reason with Yudhishthira. That was the position when he left their company and came to Naimisha.

This new angle stirred the interest of the inmates, who started discussing it. Master left them to brood over the matter and proceeded to his quarters, accompanied by Little Master, Asareer, and a few others.

Naimisha

Master was sitting in his room surrounded by his close associates later in the evening. They were discussing various things one after the other. Master was happy to learn about the developments during his long absence and prided himself on his choice of successor. Animish had undoubtedly improved the number of ashrams and inmates. He was able to maintain close contact with royal families and was able to improve patronage.

'I could not have done this much myself,' the Master complimented. He was happy to find that his favourite student was doing better than him and still maintaining the fervour of youth. Later, Master permitted all others to leave and was left with Little Master, Asareer, Anvesh, the two disciples he had brought with him from the Himalayas, and a few senior inmates. He then briefed them about the conversations between Yudhishthira and his brothers.

'Yudhishthira was speaking about the virtues of Vanaprastha, whereas his brothers wondered why he intended to deviate from the path of elders and leave the path of Karma. They suggested that having fought the war and won, it was incumbent upon him to rule the kingdom and perform Yajnas and please the gods and Brahmins. They even accused him at one stage of talking like a Nastik, renouncing the path of Karma. In turn, Yudhishthira said that he knew the shastra better; the lure for money was the root cause of misery. He said 'karma' should be relinquished at some stage, and both options were postulated in the Vedas. He accused many learned pundits of not realising the existence of 'atma' and becoming 'nastiks' and spreading false knowledge in the world. He said that a man should control his desires, forsake his ego and perform tapasya with detachment. He said he was on that path, and he had no interest in the kingdom. At this stage, I had slipped away from the crowd, not to be too late to catch the boat waiting for me. What surprised me was the conviction with which Yudhishthira was maintaining his stand. Another point that interested me was his observation about learned pundits spreading false knowledge, and I thought it might have something to do with our Ashram.'

The listeners could not suppress their similes. The Master had not forgotten his unique art of entertaining speech, which had endeared him to all in the first place.

Little Master was the first to speak, 'I hardly believe in Yudhishthira's intentions to relinquish the empire for which he waged a war that resulted in large-scale destruction. He was talking, maybe, out of temporary grief owing to the loss of his sons and feeling guilty of killing many relatives. A few days later, he would get back to his senses.'

'Quite the same way I think too!' said Master, 'but for the present, the uncertainty continues.'

Later, Master broached about two associates who had accompanied him from the Himalayas. 'These two young persons are experts in the philosophy of Sankhya and had a direct association with the disciples of Asuri, who had been closely associated with sage Kapila, the propounder of Sankhya Philosophy. I thought we may impart their knowledge to our inmates.'

Little Master asked in surprise. "But, Master, doesn't Sankhya go against our core philosophy and beliefs? They believe in abstract concepts like Purusha and Prakriti, which can not be proved. Moreover, they believe in five elements, including Akash, as opposed to our belief in four elements, which we have difficulty accepting. Though the real philosophy of Sankhya espouses Nireeshwarvad, some new offshoots are changing the original tenets.'

Master was surprised at the sharpness of Little Master's reaction and his boldness in expressing his views instantly without a moment's hesitation.

'But don't you think the students should be exposed to all the prevailing philosophical systems? Irrespective of whether we accept it or not, Sankhya philosophy is becoming popular. Even if one wants to refute it, one should understand its tenets if one is to refute it logically.'

'Master, you are always correct. And these two scholars are most welcome in our ashram. The inmates need to know the subject, but care should be taken to ensure that these experts do not convert our students into Sankhites, and that is my worry. We may first scan what they propose to teach and modulate the course.'

'Whatever you think best. I leave it to you; you are in charge of the well-being of inmates. And let me share another thing with you. I have heard from the sages in the Himalayas that Krishna had discussed the concepts of Sankhya with Sankhite sages when he came to the Himalayas for Tapasya. They were surprised by his deep knowledge of the subject. And again, I heard from sages whom I met in Kurukshetra just before coming here that Krishna was floating ideas of Sankhya as well as Yoga in Pandava camp.'

'Kapila was a great intellectual, and though we differ from Sankhya's philosophy in certain aspects, it is closer to our method of emphasising reason and intellect over blind faith. It also doesn't base its tenets only on Vedas, though inspired by it.'

'Yes, it gives the monotheists and Nireeshwaravadis a theoretical basis of conceptual understanding. One good thing is that it doesn't support the Karma system of performing Yagas as the ultimate. We will give it a try.'

Then, they had a long discussion on the theories, refutations, and counterarguments of various issues pertaining to Brahman, elements, tatva, Karma, Yoga, Sankhya, and many others. The night was turning cold, and they had already overstepped their usual bedtime routine by more than an hour or two.

Kurukshetra

Yudhishthira's brothers and Draupadi again persuaded him to take up the crown. Sages Vedavyasa, Narada, Devasthana, and Srikrishna joined them in convincing Yudhishthira to change his mind.

Devasthana had advised him that being a Kshatriya, he needed to rule the kingdom in a dharmic way till such time he had strength, and then only relinquish and go to the woods to perform tapasya. A king would get the higher worlds not by doing penance but by establishing a just rule.

Vedavyasa endorsed what all the previous speakers had said and advised Yudhishthira to first perform his duties as a king before taking up Vanaprastha. He suggested performing Yagas like Sarvamedha and Ashwamedha in that process.

Even then, Yudhishthira did not relent. He again recalled how stalwarts like Bhishma and Drona were killed and how he considered himself to blame for Abhimanyu's death. Vyasa again preached to him about the philosophy of the inevitability of death and told him he should not blame himself for the destruction. Krishna, too, joined and told him the stories of kings who ruled and died before him to create in him a realisation that he was not responsible for the deaths of others. With all his well-wishers urging him to change his decision and take up the crown, Yudhishthira's earlier resolve has softened.

The final advice, along with the action plan, came from Vedavyasa.

'Yudhishthira, you are a man of pure heart. You have been drawn into war by the others, though your nature did not permit wars. You are repenting now because of the people who died in the war. There is one remedy which I would suggest to you in this regard, and that is to do 'Ashwamedha Yaga'. You have won the war because of your strength. You and your brothers may visit the kingdoms where the kings died and ensure that their brothers, sons or grandsons are properly coronated. If there are no sons, you may coronate the daughters. You need not, for a moment, think about the kings who died in this war, as all of them have already reached the worlds they deserved on account of their karmas. Now is the time for you to perform your 'Dharma' and look after the people with care and concern.'

Yudhishthira relented and was pleased with the idea of 'Ashwamedha', which he was convinced would be an ideal remedy for whatever omissions and commissions he performed during the war.

When Yudhishthira asked him more questions about 'dharma', Vedavyasa suggested that Bhishma, who was still resting on his bed of arrows, was the best person to clear all his doubts about 'raja dharma'. Bhishma was still alive and counting the days until the arrival of 'Uttarayana,' as the death in Uttarayana was considered auspicious.

'Meet him before he breathes his last, and learn whatever you want. He learned everything through great people like Sanatkumara and the sages Markandeya, Parashurama, Chyavana, and Vashishta. He would tell you all the minute dharma,' Vyasa advised.

Krishna seconded the proposal and gave his final advice to Yudhishthira.

'This is not the time for grief. Follow the advice of all the sages, including your grandfather Vedavyasa, treating that as an order. You need to do this to please all the kings, your brothers, Draupadi, Vedavyasa, and well-wishers like me. The people of the kingdom are looking towards you to assume the kingship. Make up your mind and please all the people.'

Yudhishthira, who had already mellowed by this time with the advice of all sages and well-wishers, had responded positively to Krishna's suggestion.

Pandava camp was happy to hear the news. Dhritarashtra, too, was informed about Yudhishthira's decision. The preparations for proceeding to Hastinapur for Yudhishthira's coronation gained momentum.

Chapter 18

Yudhishthira's Coronation

Naimisha

The Little Master had called for Asareer to meet him in his cottage. Asareer was surprised at the unusual call and presented himself in his friend's room.

'Asareer, I am going to Hastinapur in a couple of hours. Would you like to join the contingent? There are indications that Yudhishthira will be proceeding to Hastinapur after the final rites at Kurukshetra, which are about to be finished. He will soon assume the crown. Many people from Naimisha are going to attend the function to greet him. I wish to be one of them.'

Asareer was surprised for two reasons. *How did Yudhishthira change his mind? And how did his friend so quickly reconcile to the change of guard and be eager to greet the new king? The Ashram was apprehensive about the discontinuation of liberal royal patronage under the new regime. Did Animish want to build bridges with the new administration, as there is no other alternative?*

'Sure, I will be on your side whenever you call. But how come Yudhishthira agreed to take up +the crown after his seemingly steadfast denial, and why did you propose to meet him so early?'

'That Yudhishthira would take up the crown was never doubted by me. I know the sages would come up with one face-saving way or the other to allow him to backtrack on his earlier stand. Any crime committed by people in power can be condoned by performing an appropriate yaga. As far as my urgency to proceed to meet Yudhishthira, I would talk about that on the way, where we would find plenty of time. So will you get ready?'

'I am already ready,' Asareer declared.

'How about Master then?'

'We can not expect him to join at this short interval, as he travelled miles and miles to reach here, and he needs to rest.'

Soon, they were ready to proceed. The carts were made ready. They were taking a road route for speedy travel, avoiding travelling by boat. Little Master went to see Master in his cottage before leaving with his contingent, informed him about the trip, and sought his blessings.

A little surprised at the haste with which Animish planned the trip, Master enquired, 'Are you sure why you are going, Anaimish?'

Master looked straight into Animish's eyes as if searching for some answers. Little Master could see his Master's concern for him in those large, fully opened eyes that were surveying him.

'Yes, Master! It is the right time to go. I came to take your blessings.'

'You always have my blessings,' replied Master.

Little Master bent and touched his feet. Then, without looking back, he proceeded towards the carts waiting for him. Asareer, who was standing behind him, had to run a little to catch up with him.

The two friends were seated in a separate cart. The contingent proceeded on its way. Master came out to look at the departing convoy. By the time he reached the front door, the convoy had already started moving. Master stood there until he could see the last cart disappear from his viewpoint, and then he went inside.

On the journey to Hastinapur

Asareer observed that his friend was in a state of excitement. They were the only two in that carriage. He was surprised that the deputy was asked to join others in a separate cart. He thought his friend had meant to tell him something in private. They had to make a long journey from Naimisha to Hastinapur. Ashram's horses are not used for long-distance travel, and they need to stop at least four to five times to allow the horses to feed on grass, take water and rest. A few minutes after they started, Asareer broke the silence and initiated the conversation.

'It has been a long time since we travelled together on a long journey.'

'Yes. Somehow, I remember our first long journey through the forest to the city of Mathura, long, long years ago. We were both so young then and walked all the way.'

Asareer did not relish Animish's reminiscence. *'Why would Animish remember that journey now, after all these years?'* Asareer wondered. *In fact, he no longer relished his part in that whole incident. It was an utterly foolish and unnecessary exercise in his ignorant adolescence, egged on by a senior inmate, who later left the ashram for good. "Kamsa! The man who is destined to kill you would be born through the womb of your sister Devaki."*

The haunted words he had practised had flashed in his mind. Words he didn't speak when the time for performance was due. His friend did not believe he did not speak.

Akashvani delivered it, adding additional information. *"It is the eighth born that would be your nemesis."*

His friend didn't believe it was Akashvani then; he opined that somebody else with the same idea had executed it successfully. Does he now believe?

Asareer remembered the years that followed: his state of utter shock and bewilderment, loss of speech, lack of purpose in life and those lost years.

Suddenly, on his second visit to Mathura, he got his speech back, and a new life flowed into his body. Asareer attributed his recovery of speech and revival of spirit to his looking at Krishna and being noticed by him—or at least that's what he thought and believed. His life had changed forever after that. That whole exercise now seemed totally meaningless to Asareer, though it brought him close to Srikrishna and the truth.

Asareer was brought back to the present when he heard Animish say, 'I wanted you alone to be here with me in this journey as I wanted to tell you something.'

'That's what I thought, too, though I have the least idea what you wanted to talk about,' thought Asareer. He looked at Animish askingly, and Animish started to speak.

'Ever since I returned from Kurukshetra, I wanted to have a detailed talk with you. However, the time did not suit me enough to speak to you privately. Now, let me begin at the beginning. As you are aware, I was planning to meet Duryodhana on the eighteenth day and reached there before evening. The camp of Kauravas was in a pell-mell condition. The message reached them that Shalya, Shakuni, and all the other warriors had fought a last-day war and were killed. All the remaining brothers of Duryodhana were dead, too, and Duryodhana was not found to be anywhere on the battlefield.

The whole lot of women folks were crying inconsolably. The war was lost for Kauravas. They were crying for their dead sons and dead husbands. They were crying about their future plight. They were cursing Yudhishthira, Bhima, Krishna, and you name anybody. They were scared of the harm that might befall them if they stayed there. They needed to be transported back to Hastinapur to the care of Dhritarashtra and Gandhari as they felt scared and unsafe there.'

'We know that Duryodhana had gone and taken shelter in that lake!' Asareer interjected.

'We knew that later. At that point in time, nobody knew. Pandavas were reported to be searching. Then I saw the three warriors of Kripa, Ashwatthama and Kritavarma briefly coming to the camp and making a quick exit. I heard that Yuyutsu was arranging for the women folk to be safely transported back to Hastinapur. There was no point in waiting in the camp to meet Duryodhana, so I came out. I stationed two of my associates near the camp to report to me if anything happened, and I proceeded to our local ashram, which was nearby, to rest for a while.

On the way, I met some of our newsbearers and learnt that Duryodhana was lying fatally injured at Samantapanchaka. They told me blow by blow an account of the fight, which was fresh in their memory. They said Balarama was so furious when Bhima landed that fatal blow on Duryodhana's thigh that he surged forward to punish Bhima by himself but was stopped by Krishna.'

He paused for a moment, sipped some water and then continued.

'I was told that Duryodhana found energy and conveyed his final message to those news bearers. He expressed no regret for his decisions and was proud that he had done his duty and was dying on the battlefield. He told them to tell his father that they fought well, though luck was not on their side. He said that he had spent his life the way a king should live and had no regrets about joining his brothers and friends in the outer world.'

'Yes, we had heard that too,' Asareer said. He wondered why Animish was repeating the whole story, as the inmates had discussed these details extensively, and they were fresh in everyone's minds.

'Now, I will tell you what you didn't hear. I am told that Duryodhana said this: *How nice it would be if the sage Charvaka, the "Vagvisharada," were present here! He would surely find a way to retaliate for the injury caused to me.*"

'Really?' Asareer was shocked at this startling disclosure. 'But our reporters didn't say this, such important news when they arrived the next day!' Asareer exclaimed.

'I told them not to. There was no point. The inmates have no business to know that. I was moved to my bone on hearing that. Duryodhana was always reverential towards me, but I didn't expect that he trusted me to this extent, that he remembered me in his final moments. It was harrowing to know that I was not, and would not be, able to do anything concrete despite such huge expectations. My immediate impulse was the thought that the least I could do was to meet him immediately if he was still alive.'

'You wanted to meet him when he was lying alone in that Samantapanchaka, waiting for death and keeping the company of vultures? In that dead of the night?' Asareer's voice did not hide his heightened fears.

'Yes. My associates asked me to rest and wait until sunrise, as it was close to midnight by then, but how would I? I had a premonition that Duryodhana might not live until the next morning as he was reported to be bleeding for hours. It was pitch dark by then. My two associates followed me with lamps, and we proceeded towards Samantapanchaka.'

'As we kept going, I saw huge red flames at a distance, and my interest aroused, and I asked one of my associates to proceed towards the fire and find out. He came back to report that the camp of Pandavas was in flames, and he was stunned to see that Kripacharya and Kritavarma were standing at the entrance of the camp and shooting arrows towards whoever was coming towards the entrance door to escape from the fire. I surmised that Ashwatthama, the third survivor, must be the one to be causing great damage to those inside the camp. I proceeded towards Samantapanchaka.'

'And you found Duryodhana alive and able to speak?' Asareer could not resist his anxiety.

'I am coming to that. By the time I located Duryodhana, he was unconscious. The loss of blood, trauma and the cold weather must have speeded up the deterioration. Anybody else would have died within an hour after receiving such a blow and loss of blood. I sat by his side and whispered continuously into his ears that I had come. My touch and my voice must have brought him back to his senses again, and I found his body getting warmer. I spent close to an hour or more with him alone. Didn't I tell you that I would meet him alone?'

'Yes, you told me. But you didn't mean like this.'

'Yes, you are right. I was expecting to see Duryodhana in his camp, readying for the next day's battle. But there I was, finding him preparing to exit from all the battles of the world. Duryodhana just did not believe that it was me when his sight fell upon me, but his face brightened on recognising me. He started to talk about various things, such as how Pandavas resorted to unethical practices in killing certain warriors. Those were the same accusations that he made towards Krishna and Pandavas, which we all heard from the reporters.

Duryodhana was in and out of being awake while we were thus conversing. He told me that the war was not over as he had anointed Ashwatthama as the commandant, and they might wage a war the following day. He said that though he might not live to hear the outcome, he was happy about Ashwatthama's determination and hopeful that he would torment his enemies.

I told Duryodhana that Ashwatthama and his associates did not wait for the day to break but were already on the job and that he should hold himself alive for a few more hours to know the outcome. He was pleasantly surprised to hear that and asked me if I was sure. I assured him so. He was highly pleased to have me on his side in his final hours and confessed to me that he did whatever he thought was his Dharma, had ruled the earth for the past thirteen years without any challenge and was dying like a Kshatriya. He said that he would be happily meeting all his brothers and friends in the outer worlds and again drifted into unconsciousness.'

'Didn't you tell him that there are no outer worlds to go to, and whatever is here is only here? Your strong belief?' Despite his intent not to disturb his friend in his current mood, Asareer's voice was a little mocking.

'I understand why you said that. However, the deathbed is not an ideal place to learn new ideas and for debates. A man should better die with the beliefs with which he lived all those years. Anyway, that is beyond the scope of our present conversation.' Asareer nodded and waited for the continuation.

'When he woke up again, I asked him what he expected of me now that everything was over. He asked me to tell the people how he was defeated by unjust means. He wanted me to tell Yudhishthira that what he had done was not right. While we were thus talking, we heard the sounds of approaching carts.

Ashwatthama and his associates were returning from their mission. I gave Duryodhana a last hug and bid him goodbye. I told him, "Wait for the good news Ashwatthama is bringing to you. The fact that they are returning alive shows that they had finished the fight successfully." His eyes were hopeful. He bade me goodbye.

I waited for some time in the shadows without being noticed and saw the three warriors sitting near Duryodhana, talking and hugging him in turns. Then they saw their king breathe his last, and they proceeded to their carts. They didn't notice me. I returned to our local ashram, and the following noon, I returned to Naimisha.' Animish heaved a long sigh, having finished his narration.

'All stories come to an end, and that was how Duryodhana spent his last hours. Anyway, it was good for him that you comforted him at a time when he needed it most. Would you now plan to find new friends in the Pandavas, as there was no point in blaming them, particularly since Duryodhana was no longer there? Even his parents must have reconciled to live under the protection of Pandavas, however painful it might be for them. Isn't it?' Asareer asked.

'Quite the contrary! I am not happy with Pandavas for what they did, which was so opposite to what they professed. I don't think I would ever reconcile.

'In which way would it be useful to hate Pandavas? You are looking from one side only, whereas Duryodhana himself committed so many improprieties both in the war and the events leading to it, and there is no need to list them again; is there?'

'I don't say Duryodhana had done all the right things. All his negative reactions and actions were primarily on account of his enmity with his cousins, whom he always considered usurpers of the Hastinapur kingdom, which rightfully belonged to him. Mind you, he was given the impression that he would inherit his father's crown till Kunti surfaced with Pandavas when he was fifteen years of age. All his clan accepted his aspirations and his claim to the throne of Hastinapur, though they tried to accommodate the sons of Pandu and foster unity in the clan. The old guards Bahlika and Bhishma fought for Duryodhana, which shows that they approved Duryodhana's claim. They may be unhappy about fighting against Pandavas, but they fought on Duryodhana's behalf. Overall, Duryodhana acted like a typical Kshatriya. Many Kshatriyas rallied around him. However, Yudhishthira, who always kept the company of sages and relished discussing various philosophical topics with them, indulged in the massive killing. Even the way he engaged himself in trickery to win over the key warriors, particularly Drona, is loathsome to me. Even Arjuna did not approve of the manner in which Drona was killed. Krishna, a man who is called and hailed as the God, supporting them to do such things, citing Sukshma Dharma, is really distasteful.'

'He is not just being called God, but he is God; when will you realise, my friend?' Asareer felt instantly. He didn't say a word to Animish, though. He understood his friend's agony and the enormous moral burden Duryodhana placed upon Animish in his dying moments. He was disturbed by his friend's aggressiveness towards Yudhishthira. He could understand his friend's fondness for Duryodhana due to a long-term cordial relationship but was surprised that his friend could not see the grave injustice Duryodhana had committed and foolishly triggered a war that killed one or two generations of royals all over Aryavarta, besides a vast number of Kshstriyas, foot soldiers, horses and elephants.

Having said whatever he wanted to say, Animish dropped into silence. Both of them were deeply immersed in their thoughts before they slept and did not converse further for the rest of the journey.

⟶•⟶❖❖❖•⟵•⟵

Hastinapur

After days of grief, Hastinapur was getting ready to welcome its new king.

Yudhishthira had requested that Dhritarashtra, the present king, lead the convoy to Hastinapur. As per tradition, Dhritarashtra and Gandhari sat on the first chariot at the forefront of the procession drawn by humans. People were sympathetic towards their old king and queen who had lost their hundred sons in the war and cheered them all the way.

Next to follow them were the five Pandavas in a separate chariot drawn by sixteen white oxen as per the custom. Bhima had donned the charioteer's role, and Arjuna held the white royal umbrella for Yudhishthira. The twins Nakula and Sahadeva stood on either side of Yudhishthira with fans in their hands. The presence of their new king, Yudhishthira, along with his famous four brothers, was lustily greeted by one and all with loud cheers and claps. Yuyutsu followed them in another chariot.

Krishna, along with Satyaki, followed them on another chariot. He was lustily cheered all along the way, and the people vied with each other to watch him for as long as possible. Behind Krishna's chariot followed the carts and chariots carrying women like Kunti, Draupadi, and others, keeping Vidura in the lead chariot.

Many groups of people, including women folk, the troops of bards, musicians, and contingents of Brahmins and other groups of citizens, followed these chariots. Animish and his followers mingled in those contingents.

Behind them were the army troops, chariots, cavalry, and elephant forces. It was a full-scale royal procession by the new ruling family. The roads were decorated with flowers and flags. Music was played along the way, and dances expressed the joy of the occasion.

The schedule of events was precisely drawn. The procession would culminate when it reaches the royal palace, and Yudhishthira would descend from the chariot and be taken inside the palace along with Dhritarashtra,

Gandhari, Kunti, Draupadi, his brothers, Srikrishna, Satyaki and all others who were accompanying him. There, he would be received by Brahmins who would bless him with Vedic chants, and after that, he would go inside chambers for prayers. After an hour or so, he would come out along with Dhritarashtra and meet the assembly of Brahmins, felicitate them with gifts, and receive their blessings. After these formalities, the coronation would take place in the court hall.

The procession was proceeding slowly towards the royal palace. Animish told Asareer, 'We will meet Yudhishthira when he comes out to meet the Brahmin contingent as no permissions need be required at that time. The next stage of his coronation would be too crowded, and we would not get near access to find his ears.'

Asareer felt uneasy. *'Why should he be a part of this unpleasant mission?'*

Whether Animish sensed his friend's uneasiness or not, he addressed the contingent, 'You all would stand a few rows behind me; nobody needed to know that you all had come with me. I don't want any of you to suffer the consequences of royal anger. Is this understood?'

'Why should Animish indulge in this dangerous and unpleasant mission?' was the thought that flashed uppermost in Asareer's mind.

Turning again towards Asareer, he whispered, 'I want you to report to Master whatever I told you about my meeting with Duryodhana in case I am not in a position to meet him again.'

Asareer could not find the right words to respond and just held his friend's hand. *'What is this man up to? Was he apprehending a danger to his life?'*

Their conversation broke as they needed to walk faster as the convoy stopped at the entrance of the royal palace. Animish gently released his hand from that of his friend and moved faster into the crowd, and the team hurried behind him.

——◆◈◈◈◆——

Naimisha

Master had seen off Little Master and waited till the last cart was out of sight. He walked inside, but something bothered him. The manner in which Animish had taken his blessings and scurried away triggered his thoughts. Master started feeling that his favourite student- cum- his successor was bent on doing something adventurous. The way he suddenly told him that he proposed to go to Hastinapur looked unusual. He did not reveal why he needed to go urgently. He did not seek any permission. He just informed him as a matter of fact and did not enquire whether he, too, would like to come. The behaviour and body language appeared odd. *'Was he up to some misadventure, which he knew that I would not approve, and proceeded to carry the same while he was resting here in the Ashram?'*

Master cursed himself for not stopping Animish and not indulging in dialogue with him to enquire deeper. He decided to follow them on the same route and catch up with Animish. Master decided to find out what Animish was planning and to stop him if it was a hasty act. He had a premonition that Animish was set on some misadventure, though he was not sure what it could be. If everything went well, Master thought, he could catch them in one of the regular stops midway.

He called the ashram caretaker and asked him to arrange a cart for himself and his associates with the swiftest available horses. Soon, the carriage was ready, and he embarked on the journey to Hastinapur, escorted by two of his trusted inmates.

Master was determined to find out what Animish wanted to do without being late. He hoped he would meet Animish in time as he started only a little less than an hour behind Animish, and on a long journey, he could make up the time to join them. The chariot started moving swiftly.

After the prayers in the palace, Yudhishthira left for the area where the Brahmins assembled. He was accompanied by Dhritarashtra and others, including his purohit, Dhaumya.

Yudhishthira proceeded to felicitate the Brahmins with flowers and sandalwood cream, asking each of them what they wished to fulfil their wishes. Gold, diamonds, cows, cloth—whatever was asked for—were given.

His associates went to the rows of the Brahmins to enquire repeatedly, 'What do you want?' and they arranged for that to be given by Yudhishthira and Dhritarashtra and the other dignitaries. The whole atmosphere wore a festive look, aided by the music, followed by the Brahmins' Vedic chants and the praise of the victors by the bards of the court.

Krishna and Satyaki were among those watching the proceedings from the balcony. They were happy to see Yudhishthira and his brothers in a peaceful frame after years of uncertainty. Gandhari, Kunti, Draupadi and other women were also watching the entire proceedings from the balcony. Despite the grief inside their hearts over losing their dear ones in the battle, they were happy that Yudhishthira had at last agreed to crown himself, and the festivities were on.

Little Master had seated himself in the middle rows and positioned himself at the centre of the hall, directly facing the stage where Yudhishthira and others were placed. He was waiting for the right moment to address the audience and Yudhishthira. He was waiting for the Vedic chants to conclude.

His deputy, other associates, and Asareer had stationed themselves scattered amongst the crowd. Asareer chose a far corner from where he could watch Animish from a distance and also have uninterrupted access to look at Srikrishna stationed on the balcony. It had been a long time since he had seen him last, and he was immersed in such joy that he even forgot where he was standing.

Asareer awoke from his trance when he was firmly tapped on the shoulder and turned to look at the person who caused it. He was startled to find Master standing behind him. Master had no time to lose. He asked Asareer in a whisper, 'What is your friend up to? Where is he? Be brief and tell me the essence.'

Asareer said, 'I don't know what he is up to, but it has something to do with his meeting Duryodhana before Duryodhana died. Duryodhana requested him to expose the misdeeds of Yudhishthira to the world, and Animish thinks this is the best opportunity to speak to Yudhishthira before the coronation.'

Master said, his voice quavering, 'Dangerous! It is a very, very dangerous idea and serves no purpose. Go, tell him to come to me announcing that I had come. Better lead the way, and I follow you.'

Just then, the music had stopped, and melodious conches and slogans praising Yudhishthira filled the air. Then there was silence, and Yudhishthira was about to be ushered out of the stage and proceed to the inner chambers.

Asareer realised the urgency in his Master's voice and tried to find their way towards the middle row at the centre of the hall. Master followed Asareer, along with his associates, using the way Asareer created it in between the dense crowd. Asareer, while moving, kept his eyes fixed on Animish, and to his horror, he saw Animish standing. The inmates in the audience, too, were surprised to find their Little Master rising among Brahmins.

Then, all of them heard a loud voice from one of the middle rows addressed to Yudhishthira.

'O! Yudhishthira, the king to be incarnated, the son of Pandu, the victorious, we are all here to celebrate your victory, and I want to speak on behalf of all the assembled Brahmins here!'

The opening remarks were well received and lustily cheered by the Brahmins all around. Seniors among them wondered who this man taking up the stage to represent the whole contingent of the Brahmins in attendance was.

Asareer had to slow down and stop a few rows behind before his friend continued his speech. He could not push his way any faster.

The loud but clear voice of the speaker attracted the attention of the crowd as well as those on the stage and the entire audience.

'Yudhishthira! All the learned brahmins had followed the course of events that took place in the war of eighteen days, which was bitterly fought. You were the victorious party, and the vast army of Duryodhana was vanquished. Your achievements were by no means small. The opponents whom you faced were no mean ones that could easily be defeated. Your grandfather Bhishma was the greatest archer on the earth, and your preceptor Dronacharya was invincible as long as he held a bow in his hand.'

The speaker paused for a while and seemed to enjoy the claps around. Master exchanged looks with Asareer.

The speech was not provocative. Whatever Animish's inner feelings might be, Asareer thought the speech was going well. Everybody looked pleased with it.

The speech continued, 'You could vanquish the fiercest warrior Karna, whom we now know to be your elder brother, Shalya, the maternal uncle of twins and the ferocious Prince Duryodhana, your cousin, who led his army till he and all his brothers breathed their last.'

People's glances searched for the feelings in the face of Dhritarashtra, who looked visibly moved by these words. There was no stopping the speech. It continued. Asareer and Master stopped, still a few rows away from the speaker. They could not push further.

'What a great victory you had! Bhishma could be killed by using Shikhandi, who himself was later killed. Acharya Drona was killed by Dhrishtadyumna when he laid down his weapons, falsely believing his son to be dead, on believing your words. Even Dhrishtadyumna didn't survive any longer. Karna was killed when he was unable to retrieve the chariot wheel, and Duryodhana was conquered by resorting to an illegal strike during the mace fight. The war saw you lose all your sons, Ghatotkacha, Abhimanyu, Iravan, Upapandavas, everybody. You sacrificed the entire clan of your father-in-law, Drupada. Many Kshatriya clans were wiped out. This mass destruction of Kshatriyas is the biggest blow to the Kshatriya race after Parashurama killed Kshatriyas with a vengeance.'

Master uttered in a disappointed tone, 'I am late by a few minutes,' as the speaker's voice continued to fill the room. Asareer observed that his Master's face was drenched in perspiration.

There were murmurs and protests all over, but nobody expected the remainder of the speech that followed. The dignitaries on the stage were assimilating the message. Yudhishthira's face looked colourless for the first time in the day's proceedings.

'All the Brahmins feel that a lot of injustice took place in the war, which was not fought on the correct lines. They all wanted me to tell you this. Oh, Yudhishthira! You have committed the greatest crime, and you are not fit to rule the kingdom. The man who killed his guru, brother, and grandfather and was responsible for the decimation of the Kshatriya race is not fit to sit on the throne of Hastinapur. The only way you can redeem yourself is to sacrifice yourself to the God of death, whose son you are reputed to be.'

Blood drained out of Master's face, and Asareer was in a daze. The speech had sent shock waves amongst the contingent of Brahmins who least expected such a bitter speech from one amongst them. It was certainly not their opinion. *Who is this man to represent them all?*

The audience was momentarily speechless; their hearts felt fear, shame and pain together. Yudhishthira, too, was shocked to the core and felt ashamed to hear the accusations made. It was this very assessment he dreaded, which initially prompted his hesitation to take up the crown. It is as if Duryodhana, rising from the ashes, stood before him and accused him. His face was pale, and all the blood drained out of his face. He got up and pleaded in a voice full of sadness.

'My salutations to all the Brahmins. You all know the circumstances that forced me to embark on this war, where there was great destruction, but I am not the cause of it. I, myself, have no pleasure in this coronation, and I am ready to abdicate if it is your collective wish. I had accepted this responsibility only for the sake of the people. The war was taken up only to protect Dharma as understood and respected by sages and learned Brahmins. I most respectfully seek your permission and blessings to take up the crown.'

Yudhishthira stopped with this short speech and waited as if to hear the verdict of the court of Brahmins. The crowd cried out loud, praising Yudhishthira.

Little Master was still standing, staring towards the stage, having accomplished what he intended.

"It was not Ashwatthama who fought the last battle for Duryodhana, but it was me. I had fulfilled my promise. I uncovered the facade of Yudhishthira for all to see and leave it to their wisdom." He told himself.

As he looked around, he found angry Brahmins moving menacingly towards him from all directions with hateful looks, cursing his imprudent speech.

The senior Brahmins collected themselves and came to the front of the crowd. They had identified the Little Master and wanted to clarify their position so that they could set the record straight. They addressed a visibly shaken Yudhishthira thus.

'Yudhishthira! Hear us well. This man is not one of us. His opinion is not ours. In fact, we suspect he is not even a Brahmin, his parentage unknown, and we doubt he must be a Rakshasa for sure, which suits the way he just now spoke. We know him to be called "Charvaka", which means a man with a pleasant speech, but his speech does no justice to his name.

He is known to be argumentative and defies tradition. Every word he had spoken was meant to demotivate you on the auspicious moment of your coronation. We know him to be a man who held views against Vedas, but he had the royal patronage of Duryodhana. He calls himself a friend of Duryodhana, and he talks this way to please the followers of Duryodhana who still exist. We do not support a single word of what he said.

None of us endorse whatever he said. On the contrary, you are the only person we accept as the king of Hastinapur. You should not mind his speech, and we implore you to remove any feeling of guilt from your heart.

Let the blessings of the gods be showered on you and your brothers. Leave all your fears and guilt behind and rule the kingdom with your great kindness and wisdom. Let the villains that come in your way perish and go to hell.'

The Brahmins resorted to veda chanting to restore Yudhishthira's confidence.

All the while, an angry crowd of Brahmins gathered around the Little Master so that he could not escape and were cursing him.

Animish knew about the repercussions of what he did. He was sure he would not be spared. He thought of his Master and the associates. *What would the Master and the inmates of Ashram think of him? Did he put the Ashram and the inmates in any danger? No, it is never wrong to express what one believes to be right or wrong. Let the ashramites take courage from his boldness of expression and spread the truths they learnt in the ashram...*

He did not have much time to think. His thoughts came to an abrupt end as the angry crowd surrounded him. He waited for the verdict to be pronounced and executed.

Asareer looked aghast at the scene that followed in utter shock. Master held his head in both hands. The ashram inmates, who had all come there, flocked around Master as if to ask for directions or just for comfort. Suddenly, they saw that the body of Little Master was in flames. Nobody knew how it was ignited. It must have been the collective anger of the Brahmins, and their looks were enough to ignite the fire. Most of them always held the means to generate fire any time to perform the daily prayers to the God of Fire. Whatever may have been the cause of the fire, nobody tried to stop it. The palace guards didn't move in his direction for a lack of orders. The crowd distanced themselves from the burning body in all directions.

Meanwhile, Yudhishthira was ushered away from the stage to take part in the coronation ceremony, and many started moving to the coronation room to witness the proceedings.

Master and his group found themselves in the forefront of the circle that formed around the burning body. In one quick, long glance, the Little Master seemed to have seen them all, including his Master. Asareer thought that he had found a smile on the face of Animish, and there was a waving of his hand in their direction - *Like it was a burning flag!*

Soon, it all ended, and there was only ash and bones. The room was almost empty except for Master's group, which remained waiting there, transfixed and immersed in its thoughts. The only sounds audible were those of the celebration of Yudhishthira's coronation from the next room.

When the palace staff came to clear the remains, the ashram inmates volunteered to do the job, which was not objected to. They silently gathered the remains and slipped out of the palace to join the Master, who had stepped out a little before and was standing awhile outside looking distraught and forlorn. They needed to show the inmates back at the ashram what had remained of their Little Master. Their convoy proceeded towards Naimisha. Theirs was the only group that looked unhappy amidst the joyful Brahmins, who were happy having done what was necessary in the interest of preserving order.

Master and Asareer took the same coach, which carried Asareer and the Little Master to Hastinapur, followed by others. It gave Asareer time enough to narrate to his Master whatever his friend asked him to convey.

The convoy proceeded towards Naimisha at its own pace. Thus ended the story of Little Master, alias Animish, who was identified by the name Charvaka, the name that Master fondly gave him once for his pleasant way of presenting the arguments.

Asareer was in a pensive mood throughout the return journey, and so were the others. A thought has flashed in his mind. *Animish was no more, but he will be remembered as Charvaka, a friend of Duryodhana who attempted to disrupt the joyful proceedings of Yudhishthira's coronation by an unholy speech but was promptly destroyed by the powerful glances of angry, disapproving and righteous Brahmins, as a footnote to the history of Mahabharata.*

Hastinapur

The coronation of Yudhishthira went on smoothly. Yudhishthira was soon restored to his usual cheer. He was assured that Charvaka did not represent Brahmins. In fact, he was not even a Brahmin. He was a Rakshasa known to be against Vedas, and deserved the death he had met. The Brahmins had spared Yudhishthira the trouble of conducting a trial and executing him. Justice was delivered instantly.

Yudhishthira had his equilibrium restored, accepted the coronation formalities performed by Dhoumya, and was anointed the king by Krishna, Dhritarashtra, and others. Later, Yudhishthira gave his thanksgiving lecture to the assembly and publicly declared that Dhritarashtra, his father, was his ultimate guide and that he would serve him faithfully till the end. Though he accepted the kingdom, the entire kingdom belonged to Dhritarashtra only.

Yudhishthira then declared Bhima the crown prince and decided the portfolios for the rest of his brothers. He continued Vidura in his previous position of strategic consultations and appointed Sanjaya as treasurer. Yuyutsu was specially asked to take care of Dhritarashtra, in addition to other responsibilities. Yudhishthira then expressed his profuse gratitude to Krishna for all he had done for them, and in turn, Krishna returned the compliments and wished him well.

After the coronation was over, Krishna accompanied Yudhishthira and others to Bhishma, where he was lying on the bed of arrows. At the request of Yudhishthira, Bhishma cleared various doubts raised by Yudhishthira regarding the conduct of the empire, morals, and ethics. Bhishma had interwoven his narration with multiple illustrations of the past to drive home the point. No question of Yudhishthira was left unanswered by all-knowing Bhishma.

Bhishma extolled the virtues of Krishna and lauded him, chanting the various names of Lord Vishnu through which he was known. He then advised Yudhishthira to return to him after the Uttarayana set in, by when he would be ready to depart.

Fifty days later, Yudhishthira returned at the appointed time indicated by Bhishma. Bhishma was given a grand farewell by the assembly of sages and royalty who were in total attendance. Bhishma gave his parting advice and blessings to Dhritarashtra and Pandavas and took leave of them and that of Krishna. Having satisfied that the auspicious time had arrived, he took the yogic stance, released life from various limbs, and drew his final breath.

The funeral rites were performed, and Yudhishthira was saddened at the departure of the senior most Kuru. He again started repenting about the destruction caused by war and started talking about abdicating the kingdom and going to the woods. Dhritarashtra, Krishna, and Vedavyasa reasoned with him again, and Vyasa reminded Yudhishthira to perform Ashwamedha Yaga to get rid of his guilt.

Vedavyasa advised Yudhishthira that he could procure the necessary resources by possessing the treasures once owned by King Maruttu of the Ikshvaku dynasty in a bygone era, which were lying idle in the Himalayas. Vedavyasa narrated to them the fascinating story of the treasure as to how Samvarta, the wise brother of Brihaspati, had helped King Maruttu to perform a great yaga, defying both Indra and Brihaspati. A vast quantity of gold and diamonds were procured from the gold mines of Kubera. Vast reserves of gold, silver, ornaments, and precious stones so procured for that yaga were left over despite giving fabulous gifts to all the assembled brahmins, and those were kept preserved in the Himalayas, securely in a treasure. The treasure was located near Mount Munjunatha, behind the Himalayas. That treasure now rightfully belonged to Yudhishthira, the lord of Bharata Varsha, and it was for Yudhishthira to take that and use it for Yaga.

Yudhishthira was pleased with this idea and braced himself to procure those treasures and perform Ashwamedha Yaga.

Chapter 19

The Successor Was Born

Hastinapur

When Yudhishthira resolved to perform Ashwamedha Yaga, his heart lightened, and he started to indulge himself in the affairs of the kingdom with a calm mind bereft of guilt. He performed all the necessary rituals for the departed relatives and gave huge compensations to families that lost men in the Mahabharata war.

Krishna was happy to watch Yudhishthira come out of his sorrow and regain his confidence. He visited Indraprastha with Arjuna to spend time. They wandered in forests, trekked mountains, and swam in rivers together to rejuvenate. They also discussed various matters of interest. Krishna took considerable time to spend with Arjuna to help him get over his grief about the dear and near ones, including Abhimanyu. Arjuna wanted to hear Krishna's message again, which he heard at the start of the Kurukshetra war, which propelled him to shed despondency and motivated him to plunge into action.

Unknown to many, before the war began, Arjuna wanted Krishna to drive the chariot into the middle of both warring sides, who all readied themselves to fight. And, when Arjuna looked at all of them, he realised that he was going to fight against his friends and relatives, and he needed to kill them to win the war. Arjuna entertained second thoughts and doubted the very rationale for indulging in the war with Kauravas for a piece of the kingdom that required heavy bloodshed. Krishna then made him realise, after a prolonged debate, that he needed to perform the duty enjoined on him, unmindful of consequences, as only the actions are under his control and not the results. Arjuna, being a Kshatriya, needed to fight the war to protect Dharma, and he should not back out from his duty. Though Arjuna might think he was killing somebody, the death was only for the physical body and not for the 'jiva' inside. Krishna also preached to him about different yogas and methods available to a man on the spiritual path. Arjuna realised the Godhood of Krishna and the profound wisdom of his message, shed all his doubts and fought the war like a man possessed and earned victory for his brother.

Arjuna now requested Krishna to tell him that Gita again, as he could get benefitted hearing it with a calm mind now, unlike at the time of Gita, when he was in an agitated mood and a fierce battle was on the cards. Arjuna said that though he remembered the salient points, he had forgotten the finer aspects and, hence, would like to hear from Krishna again.

Krishna mildly chided Arjuna for saying that he had forgotten Gita and expressed that he couldn't recite the same message verbatim again. However, honouring Arjuna's request, Krishna explained the summary of the Gita, including multiple subjects and answered all of Arjuna's questions. Unlike Bhagavadgita, which was a wartime discourse to motivate Arjuna to perform his bounden duty, this second discourse in peacetime was meant to guide people on the spiritual path. This discourse later became famous and is known as 'Anu Gita,' which means it is a continuation of Gita. Arjuna, who still nurtured some sadness about his killing so many people in the battle and for losing dear ones, had felt relieved after hearing Krishna's detailed discourse. He felt rejuvenated, shed his diffidence, and readied himself for his new role as the protector of Hastinapur, a role previously performed by Bhishma.

Krishna and Arjuna returned to Hastinapur, and having taken Yudhishthira's permission, Krishna bade goodbye to Pandavas. He stated that he would return in time before they returned from their Himalayan expedition, bringing treasures to commence the Ashwamedha function.

After Krishna left for Dwaraka with Subhadra, Pandavas proceeded to the Himalayas with a considerable army to locate and fetch the hidden treasures of King Maruttu, as suggested by Vedavyasa. Vedavyasa told them where to look for the treasure.

After reaching Dwaraka, Krishna reported the details of the Kurukshetra war to his father, Vasudeva and others. The death of Abhimanyu broke their hearts, as Abhimanyu had spent almost thirteen years in Dwaraka during Pandavas' exile and was admired by the Yadavas as if he were their son.

Krishna returned to Hastinapur along with Balarama and Subhadra from Dwaraka just when Uttara was supposed to deliver the baby. Pandavas were yet to return from the Himalayan quest. The women were all in great fear as they remembered the curse of Ashwatthama. Finally, on the appointed day, Uttara delivered a baby boy who looked like a stillborn and had no hope of revival, as per the attending doctors. While Uttara was stricken with grief, Subhadra placed the baby in the outstretched hands of her brother, Krishna, who had just then entered. As Krishna had taken the baby boy into his hands, the boy started to cry as if by a miracle. All the women folk were ecstatic and praised Krishna for breathing life into the boy. The baby was Kuru Vamsha's only hope. Krishna named him Parikshit, which meant 'the one born when the race is about to become extinct.'

When Pandavas arrived a month later, they were happy that Krishna's very presence had repulsed the curse of Ashwatthama and that their clan was now represented by a boy child, a grandson of Arjuna and Subhadra to take their lineage and glory forward.

Now that they had brought enormous gold, silver, and precious stones from the hidden treasures, they embarked on performing Ashwamedha Yaga under the guidance of Vedavyasa.

The birth of Parikshit brought cheer to the women of the royal palace and great relief to Pandavas. The entire kingdom celebrated the arrival of its future king, and the people were happy with the knowledge that the suspense had ended. The succession of the Kuru Vamsha's reign was ensured, marking a significant moment in the glorious history of the Kuru dynasty.

Chapter 20

The Ashwamedha Yaga

Hastinapur

Arjuna, the valiant hero of the Kurukshetra battle, assumed a pivotal role in the wars preceding the Ashwamedha Yaga. His bravery and leadership were unparalleled, and he was chosen to lead the army that followed the ceremonial horse. His brothers remained in Hastinapur to look after the kingdom's affairs.

The Ashwamedha Yaga process involved the demonstration of an emperor's authority and power. A horse is declared as the Yagashwa after necessary rituals, and it would be left free to move across territories of its own volition. It would be hopping the length and breadth of Bharatavarsha on its own. The emperor's representatives, along with the army, would follow Yagashwa wherever it treads. The kings, whose kingdoms the Yagashwa would pass, are expected to let the horse pass, indicating that they accept the sovereignty of the emperor. Stopping the horse on its course would be construed as a challenge to the rule and an invitation to fight.

Yudhishthira's counsel to Arjuna was to use minimal force and to avoid unnecessary bloodshed, as most of the kingdoms took part in the recent Kurukshetra war and bled heavily. The sole objective of the Ashwamedha was to establish the supremacy of Hastinapur over the entire Bharatavarsha and to ensure peace. The whole exercise was expected to take close to one year to enable the horse to travel far and wide. The Yaga would start around Chaitra Pournami after the triumphant return of Arjuna with the victorious Yagashwa.

Arjuna embarked on his mission on the appointed day following the Yagashwa after taking the elders' blessings to the tumultuous cheers of the Hastinapur crowds.

The journey was not without its challenges. The first test arose when the horse was captured by Trigarta warriors, whose kin had perished in the Mahabharata war at the hands of Arjuna. Their then king, Susharma, had converted his army into 'Samshaptakas', engaged Arjuna in the battle for most of the time, and died in his hands. All Susharma's brothers and sons who took part in that war were vanquished by Arjuna. Trigartas, hence, harboured enmity against Arjuna and desired a battle. Despite Arjuna's peaceful intentions, the Trigartas, led by Surya Varma and his brothers, were set on revenge. A fierce battle ensued, but eventually, Trigarta surrendered.

The next kingdom that attempted to capture the Yagashwa was Pragjyotishpura, which was ruled by Vajradatta, son of Bhagadatta. He, too, ignored Arjuna's peaceful words and wanted to take vengeance for his father's death at Arjuna's hands. He resisted Arjuna bravely for three days. He, too, was an adept fighter mounting on a ferocious elephant like his father. Arjuna killed the elephant but spared Vajradatta and invited him to attend the Yaga, which the latter agreed to.

Another notable experience Arjuna faced was in the kingdom of Sindhu, which was under the rule of Suratha, Jayadratha's son. The moment Suratha heard about Arjuna's arrival, he died heartbroken with fear. However, the other Sindhu kings and warriors engaged Arjuna in a fierce battle intending to avenge the death of their king, Jayadratha. While Arjuna was involved in the fight with Sindhu warriors who were fighting a losing war, Dusshala, the queen of Sindhu, arrived on the battlefield, bringing her grandson along with her. She requested Arjuna to bless the child, informing him that her frightened son, Suratha, died heartbroken hearing about Arjuna's arrival in their kingdom. A shocked Arjuna cursed himself for the Kshatriya ways of living, stopped the war, consoled his sister and blessed the grandson.

A similar experience happened in Gandhara, too. Shakuni's wife entered the battlefield to request Arjuna spare her son, who was clearly losing the battle but was not surrendering out of pride. Arjuna respected her words, spared Shakuni's son, and invited him to attend the Ashwamedha function.

Arjuna had also visited Manipura, the kingdom of his wife Chitrangada, now being ruled by their son Babhruvahana. Babhruvahana wanted to surrender and invite his father. However, Arjuna goaded him to fight and show his prowess befitting a Kshatriya. They had a great contest, and Arjuna was happy to find his son capable of not only standing against him but even making him swoon. Both Chitrangada and Ulupi, wives of Arjuna, arrived at the battlefield knowing a war was going on between their husband and their son. A truce was agreed upon, and Babhruvahana sought his father's blessings. Arjuna had a happy reunion with his family, Ulupi, Chitrangada and Babhruvahana. He was proud of his son's valour. Arjuna invited all of them to the Ashwamedha function.

Even before Arjuna reached Hastinapur, his feats and even folk stories reached the people of Hastinapur. People were surprised as to how Babhruvahana, even though he was Arjuna's son, could fight equally with his father and even make him swoon. They then heard that it was not just a swoon, but his son actually killed Arjuna, and Arjuna's Naga wife, Ulupi, came to the battlefield along with Chitrangada and miraculously revived Arjuna with her 'Nagamani'. Ulupi is then said to have unravelled the mystery by revealing to all that unknown to Arjuna he was cursed by Ganga to die in the hands of his son, in view of his mercilessly pounding arrows in Bhishma's body, keeping Shikhandi as a front, that led to his death. Hence, Ulupi, who knew this curse through her father, was ready for the situation and presented herself to rescue Arjuna with the antidote she possessed. The story was believed by many as it was next to impossible for anyone to kill Arjuna in a war unless, of course, a curse worked on him.

Arjuna mostly avoided killing the warriors to the greatest extent possible, as Yudhishthira advised him not to destroy the kings who were already in grief, having lost their dear ones in the Kurukshetra war. Arjuna personally invited all the kings whom he met on his course to take part in the ensuing Ashwamedha Yaga at Hastinapur, showing respect even to those who had opposed him. It was time enmity was buried, and friendship prevailed.

He returned to Hastinapur in time, and the people cheered their greatest hero all the way when he entered the city and celebrated his arrival. Krishna and Balarama had already arrived by then, and everything was set for the conduct of Ashwamedha Yaga.

The yaga was completed successfully, and many kings participated. Enormous quantities of gold and innumerable cows were given as gifts to Brahmins and others, and everybody was satisfied with the hospitality. After the function was over, all the kings left one by one, while Krishna remained until the end. He engaged himself with the assembled sages, discussing various matters and clearing their doubts.

Finally, the time for Krishna's departure arrived. When Krishna announced his plans to return to Dwaraka after spending a considerable period in Hastinapur, Pandavas felt a deep sense of loss.

Srikrishna had done everything in his power to support them, giving them moral support right from the day he met them during Draupadi swayamvara. He guided them in building their capital city in Indraprastha and strategised their Rajasuya mission. He even physically bore the injuries caused by the opposing side in the Kurukshetra war and endured them. He saved their lineage by reviving Parikshit to life. All this for a reward of a curse from Gandhari that his Yadava clan, including himself and his brother, would all die thirty-six years later, just as the Kuru race was decimated. A curse Krishna has accepted and told Gandhari that it would happen accordingly.

Pandavas were deeply saddened to allow Srikrishna to leave for Dwaraka despite his spending a considerable time with them. Yudhishthira, in a gesture of utmost respect and gratitude, asked Daruka, Krishna's charioteer, to step down, and he took the reins by himself. His brothers held the Chatra (umbrella) and Chamara(hand fans) to Krishna, symbolising their high respect and deep gratitude.

It was as if they had a premonition that it was, perhaps, one of Krishna's last visits to Hastinapur. After a few miles, the escorting party returned with heavy hearts while Krishna asked Daruka to speed up.

Chapter 21

Master's Ashram Trifurcated

Naimisha

Much water had flown in the river Gomati ever since Master and his group had returned to Naimisha with Little Master's ashes. None of the Ashramites used to call the Little Master by his name when he lived. He was known to have an earlier name, Animish, which was still used by his close associate Asareer and referred to like that, maybe by very senior people in their private conversations. He was known as Charvaka in the royal circles with whom he was in regular touch. He was not addressed as such by the inmates, and he was called Little Master by all of them to perpetuate the notion that the Ashram still belonged to the Master. Little Master wanted it that way.

The sudden and tragic death of Little Master and the manner in which it occurred sent shockwaves through the ashramites. The ashramites struggled to come to terms with the fact that the vibrant figure they had seen just two days ago was now reduced to mere ashes and bones. The pain was particularly acute for those members who had witnessed Little Master's body consumed by flames, uncared for and uncried by the surrounding crowd, a sight that still haunted their memories.

The ashramites were not just in shock; they were seething with anger and frustration. They directed their fury towards Yudhishthira and the Brahmins who had participated in the elimination of their beloved Little Master. 'Is expressing an opinion against the King an offence requiring death punishment?' they questioned, their voices filled with righteous indignation. The act of a crowd of Brahmins taking justice into their own hands and burning a living being in front of the King himself was a bitter pill to swallow. 'Such being the case, who could freely express an opinion?' they lamented collectively.

The ashramites were vocal in their views and, more so, the younger ones who had joined the Ashram after Little Master had taken over from the Master. They were encouraged and got accustomed to participating in active debates and advocating their views publicly. Society allowed it, and free thought, which was part of the ancient culture, was respected by all. After all, they were not proposing anything new. Whatever they were saying was already told by well-respected sages of the past. Anvesh, who acted as the deputy of Little Master, had become the central figure for these inmates, who were offended at the burning of their Little Master.

Some of the seniors, however, felt that the Little Master had crossed his limits in daring Yudhishthira in the open court. They also found fault with him for falsely claiming that he represented all the assembled Brahmins, which was not the case and, in fact, mischievous. That certainly must have pricked the ego or self-esteem of the assembled Brahmins, who were, in general, passive and moderate in their action. Little Master could indeed have an opinion, but it doesn't mean he can express it anywhere and in any manner. Actually, whatever he uttered in that call was the very same guilty pangs Yudhishthira himself felt, which delayed his taking up the crown and needed a lot of persuasion to make him accept the crown. Accusing such a man in front of people, who were all sympathetic to him, was a folly. Little Master was probably expecting a royal execution, but not the mob fury. Little Master, they opined, had clearly misjudged the situation and went on his suicidal mission.

Master had decided to return to his Himalayan ashram to spend the rest of his life there and continue the pursuit of Sankhya doctrine. He had no interest in running the affairs of the Ashram any more and could see that the deputy was groomed for the post and was rearing to assume the leadership. Before leaving the Ashram, Master formally blessed Anvesh to be the successor of Little Master and advised him to be cautious.

The death of Animish, whom he loved like a son, had shaken Master to the core. What actually baffled him was why Animish had taken such an extreme step. He should have known the consequences. He later deciphered Animish's motive from the discussions he had with Asareer. Master analysed what would have transpired that made Anaimish take the extreme step.

Anaimish had developed a deep friendship with Duryodhana, which propelled him to meet the grievously injured dying prince in his last moments. Duryodhana expressed his wish that Yudhishthira's duplicity be exposed to the public as Yudhishthira had staked innumerable Kshatriyas, including his sons, into the war for the sake of the Kingdom and was able to win it only by following unfair methods. Anaimish had promised Duryodhana that he would do so and hence proceeded in that fashion. Whatever might be the faults of Duryodhana, he had a commanding personality, and people did his bidding. "If a deeply learned man like Ashwatthama could indulge in that night carnage without a second thought for consequences, why should one be surprised at Anaimish's self-suicidal mission?" Master thought.

Anaimish must have had a premonition that he would not return to Ashram again. That could be the reason he sought my final blessings, in an unusual way of touching my feet, before he went out on his mission. He became known for his fearless expression of his thoughts in a lucid manner, a quality which had endeared him to many people. "Finally, his fearlessness had killed him," Master thought.

As Master embarked on his journey to the Himalayas, a few inmates expressed their interest in going with him and were taken along. Asareer did not go with them but preferred to stay put in Ashram for a few more years as he wanted to visit the places connected with Krishna and meet the people there. He did not wish to go as far as the Himalayas and miss the chance to view Krishna a few more times during his lifetime.

The two Sankya experts whom Master had brought from the Himalayas to impart the knowledge of Sankhya to the inmates volunteered to stay back and continue their work as more inmates started to show interest in this. Many heard that Krishna had propounded the importance of Sankhya Yoga while conversing with Arjuna before the Kurukshetra war had begun, which kindled a new interest in this subject all of a sudden.

Master and the group that joined him were seen off by all the ashramites till the river point, where the boats would take them on their journey. Master was leaving Naimisha permanently, and this was the last time Naimisha would see him.

Asareer differed from Animish in many ways, but he admired his friend for certain things; honesty, steadfast convictions, the pursuit of truth and his action orientation. Some new revelations about Animish, which he heard, disturbed him. Disciples of Vaishampayana said that Charvaka was a rakshasa and had spent many years in Badarika Ashram. They also attributed this statement to none other than Krishna. Asareer met Animish at quite a young age. They never bothered about enquiring about each other's varna or antecedents. Animish went to the Himalayas quite often to meet Master and spent some years there, and sometimes he went alone. His being seen in Badarika forest could not be ruled out. He was known to have picked up arguments with many on the philosophical theories and propounded contrary theories. None of these assertions were wrong. But Asareer couldn't believe that his friend was a rakshasa. Anybody inimical to the accepted order and even Brahmins who did not follow the stipulated rules were derided as rakshasas, as a matter of practice. Asareer reconciled that his friend was called so because of his controversial speech on the occasion of the coronation of Yudhishthira and his contrarian views on many philosophical concepts aired publicly. His friend had falsely claimed that he was representing the entire Brahmin community, though he was not, and hence, Brahmins had given him a name and burnt him.

Asareer observed that his friend confined himself to criticising Yudhishthira but spoke not a word against Krishna or Vedas, though he had many views on these subjects. Though he repeated many allegations Duryodhana had made in his speech, he did not repeat Duryodhana's strong accusation that Krishna was behind Pandavas directing their actions. Was his friend getting soft on Krishna after all? Asareer had a smile on his face at this thought as he remembered how Animish used to tease him about his faith in Krishna.

Asareer became more devotional after the death of his friend. He went on pilgrimage along with some other sages to various places that had Krishna connections, like Brindavan, Govardhan, Mathura, and Dwaraka. He came under the spell of Upashloka, the son of Pingala and Srikrishna, while in Mathura. Upashloka had established a separate cult called 'Satwata' where people from different varnas and sub-varnas could join to worship Lord Vishnu. Some of the ashramites, along with Asareer, joined the new religion with a different way of life. The new way of life became quickly popular in and around Mathura. The followers of this sect had given less importance to rituals. They devoted more time to praising the miracles and teachings of Lord Krishna, reciting his stories and doing everything in the name of Lord Krishna. They also believed that there was no use of Yagas and such rituals, which would be ineffective in the soon-coming Kaliyuga, and the only way to salvation was the adoption of Bhakti Marga. Asareer had adopted this way and devoted his life to worshipping Krishna. Some of the ashramites followed Asareer, and a separate group was thus formed around Asareer in the Ashram.

The followers of Charvaka had become more vocal, and the followers of Bhakti Marg, now spearheaded by Asareer, had a different routine as prescribed by Upashloka's new religion. Asareer, who kept a low profile earlier, had asserted himself more after the death of his friend. The inmates who were disenchanted with the Charvaka philosophy under the new regime had found an alternative in Bhakti marg represented by Asareer, and gradually, Asareer had a sizable following, and the devotional fervour towards Krishna had assumed speed.

Anvesh, the deputy of Little Master who became his successor, assumed the title of Charvaka to preserve the memory of their Little Master and the inmates who pledged allegiance to him had decided to take forward the views of Charvaka further with more clarity. His followers started to feel proud in calling themselves Charvakites. They observed that though some of the teachings of Sankhya resonated with them, overall goals and approaches of both schools were different. Whereas Sankhya centred their philosophy on the duality of reality, the followers of the Charvaka system started propagating the irrelevance of rebirth. The Charvakites under the new Charvaka felt that the Sankhya philosophy was too theoretical and was not compatible with their core beliefs, so they decided to avoid it from their curriculum.

Charvakites started openly saying that there was no such thing as karma brought forward from previous birth and that there was no carrying down any karma after death either. They advocated that whatever is there, it is in this life. This radical thinking was against the majority's belief in the infallibility of the theory of karma and the need to follow the prescribed procedures and practices as handed over by the predecessors without any question.

However, by the time the philosophy of Charvaka transformed thus, many inmates had begun seeing the intellectual merit of Sankhya philosophy and opposed its exclusion from the curriculum. This resulted in an inevitable split, and those who started following Sankhya called them Sankhites and formed themselves as a separate group.

Thus, gradually, the inmates split into three different streams: adherents of Krishna devotion, followers of Sankhya, and those who called themselves Charvakites. All three groups, however, believed in one thing; that the philosophy of other groups should not corrupt their members. This has led to the ashram being split into three separate entities so that each of them could practice what they believed to be true.

The huge ashram, which was maintained as one from the times of Master and Little Master, was now divided into three separate ashrams, existing adjacent to each other.

Chapter 22

Fifteen Years After The War

Hastinapur

Fifteen years after the war, Dhritarashtra and Gandhari, the senior couple, expressed their wish to retire to the woods. The loss of a hundred sons and the downward turn of their fortune wheel made a significant impact on their ageing hearts. Despite being well treated by Yudhishthira and the other Pandavas, Bhima's occasional barbs and sarcastic words continued to sting them. As the years passed, Dhritarashtra became more philosophical, losing all interest in worldly matters, and gradually started reducing his food intake to weaken his body. Dhritarashtra had come to terms with the fatal mistakes he had made, which led to the loss of his hundred sons and son-in-law and the destruction of the race. This realisation transformed him into a wholly philosophical and spiritual being. The weight of age and grief had visibly withered him. He prepared himself for the forest life by adopting a frugal diet and sleeping on the bare ground, a transformation unnoticed by Yudhishthira. Gandhari's journey mirrored her husband's.

Yudhishthira was shocked when Dhritarashtra indicated his intentions to retire to the woods for the remainder of their lives. He was pained to see the man who once had the strength to crush the iron statue of Bhima to pieces now look like a bare skeleton. Yudhishthira tried to persuade them to stay back, but Dhritarashtra refused. Vedavyasa advised Yudhishthira to let Dhritarashtra have his way as what he desired was in accordance with the scriptures.

Yudhishthira reluctantly made all the necessary arrangements for the old couple to leave Hastinapur forever. He made enormous amounts of money available to Dhritarashtra for performing ceremonies and giving gifts to Brahmins as his final duty to the departed souls. Dhritarashtra delivered a final farewell speech to the people of Hastinapur, wherein he offered his apologies for the omissions and commissions on his part as well as his son. One of the assembled Brahmins, by the name of Samba, came forward to express the public opinion that they were comfortable in the regime of Dhritarashtra and Duryodhana, and they had nothing to complain about. The formalities having been completed, the contingent proceeded to the Vardhaman gate, to see off the departing people.

When Yudhishthira was bidding farewell to Dhritarashtra and Gandhari and seeking their blessings, Kunti announced her intention to accompany the elder couple. Pandavas were shocked as no one had expected her sudden decision. Despite much persuasion from each one of them, Kunti did not relent. Karna's death had badly shaken her, and perhaps she wanted to atone for her guilt by subjecting herself to the hard life of the woods. She also felt it was her duty to serve both Dhritarashtra and Gandhari, who were visually challenged. Sanjaya, too, thought it was his duty to be with his master, Dhritarashtra. Vidura, too, joined the party. He, too, had no interest left in the affairs of the state and relegated all his duties to Yuyutsu.

After the elders, with whom they had developed deep bonds, left, Pandavas found it increasingly difficult to adjust to their absence. The thought of their mother, Kunti, leaving them to endure the hardships of the woods was a heavy burden to bear.

About a year after the elders' departure, Yudhishthira decided to visit them in the forest. The proposal was met with unanimous approval and joy; many expressed their intention to accompany him.

Yudhishthira led a big group consisting of his brothers, Draupadi and other women. All the wives of Kauravas, too, joined them. Many people interested in greeting the elders once more joined the contingent, which had embarked in the direction of the forest where the elders were staying.

The reunion in the forest was a joyous occasion. Pandavas were overjoyed to see their mother despite their reservations about her living conditions. Dhritarashtra had a heart-to-heart talk with the Pandavas, and all the women, including Draupadi, spent quality time with Gandhari and Kunti. Sages from around the Ashram of Dhritarashtra came to greet the Pandavas, engaging them in enlightening conversations.

Yudhishthira was shocked when he learned that Vidura had left the ashram life and was wandering in the forest only to be spotted occasionally by people. Yudhishthira wanted to find him and ventured deep into the forest in search of him. Yudhishthira's heart sank when he finally spotted a naked Vidura standing at a distance. The sight of Vidura, emaciated and almost skeletal, was a stark contrast to the vibrant man he once knew.

Yudhishthira approached him and addressed him to open up a dialogue. Vidura's staring eyes had no expression in them but were brightly lit when Yudhishthira's glance fell upon them. At that very moment, Vidura just leaned back on a tree, and his body became lifeless to the utter shock of Yudhishthira. It was as if Vidura was holding to life only to have his last glimpse of Yudhishthira, whom he loved and nurtured like his son.

Yudhishthira returned to the Ashram and broke the news. While he prepared himself to perform the funeral rites to the body of Vidura, the sages prevented him from doing so, stating that the body of a sanyasi should not be treated as that of a householder, and no rituals ought to be performed.

Vedavyasa, too, arrived and spent a few days together with them. He led the whole contingent one evening to the river Ganga and made them undergo an out-of-the-world experience by invoking his yogic powers. All the dead warriors of the Kurukshetra war emerged from the river as if, by magic, to spend that night with them, and they vanished early in the morning, just as they came. Though everyone knew that experience wouldn't last, it gave them immense pleasure to once meet their dear departed ones. They all cherished the experience and thanked the sage for that blissful experience.

After some days, Dhritarashtra suggested Pandavas plan their departure soon, as their continued presence, though pleasant to him, would disturb the serene atmosphere that sages preferred. Moreover, the absence of the king from Hastinapur for a longer duration was not desirable.

Pandavas and Draupadi took leave of Dhritarashtra, Gandhari and Kunti and went back to Hastinapur with heavy hearts. They wondered how long the three seniors might hold on to life. The old trio had only Sanjaya for company, the one who continued to serve his old king with the same devotion. Pandavas bid an emotional farewell to their loved ones, sages and the forest and moved to Hastinapur with heavy hearts.

The city of Hastinapur stood tall among all these events. The road leading the way out of the capital city, known as Vardhaman Marg, witnessed Yudhishthira leaving the palace with all his brothers and women folk and others. All had returned except the wives of Kauravas.

The people who accompanied the contingent of Yudhishthira had a poignant story to explain. All the wives of Kauravas who had been widowed sixteen years back had now decided to part with their lives and drowned in the river of Ganga to unite with their departed husbands, utilising the opportunity provided by Vedavyasa and under his guidance.

People wondered at the revelation that Vedavyasa had brought to life all the dead souls one night, and there were strange meetings of living people with people who were dead in front of everybody in flesh and blood. They were curious for more details. The Brahmins, who accompanied the contingent, provided information that amazed the listeners. The news percolated downwards to all who cared to know.

'Who all came like that from the river Ganga?' a person asked.

'They say every king who fought in the war and had a living relative there had come and met their loved ones. They especially mentioned Drupada, Virata, Karna, Abhimanyu and many others. The hundred sons of Dhritarashtra had come, and he was able to see them with the grace of Vedavyasa. They had spent a happy time together for one full night. Kunti had specially requested for Karna and was happy to see him in the company of his five brothers. She was delighted. Uttara was happy to see Abhimanyu, and also all others were delighted to find Abhimanyu.'

'Then what happened? Why didn't the wives of Kauravas return?'

'Vedavyasa offered them that if they wished, they could go to the heavenly worlds along with their husbands, and they willingly accepted the offer. All of them had immersed themselves in the river of Ganga. When it was morning, Vedavyasa withdrew his spell, and all the dead people vanished into the river just as they had come.' The people of Hastinapur were amazed at the powers of Vedavyasa and remembered the story for a long time.

After two years, sage Narada arrived in the city of Hastinapur. Pandavas enquired about the well-being of Dhritarashtra and his companions.

Narada told them, 'My purpose for the visit is to inform you precisely of the recent developments. Your father, Dhritarashtra and your mothers, Gandhari and Kunti, had left their mortal bodies and were consumed in a forest fire. Do not mourn for them, and do not feel bad about it. It was time they had to leave this world. The forest fire was, in fact, triggered by the fire left out by Dhritarashtra himself after his morning prayers. Hence, it may be presumed that it was auspicious.'

Pandavas plunged into deep grief on hearing this news.

'I saw Sanjaya on the shores of Ganga, and he told me that he was advised by Dhritarashtra not to try to rescue them, which would be futile, but to leave at once to save himself and spend the rest of his life. Sanjaya had to leave his master with a heavy heart. He proceeded to the Himalayas, and he is meditating in an ashram set up in Badarika.'

Hastinapur witnessed no significant activity in the next eighteen years, except the just rule of Yudhishthira. After the deaths of seniors, Yudhishthira lost interest in ruling the empire but continued to fulfil the responsibilities dutifully. With the support of his brothers, he continued to provide the best rule for Hastinapur. Parikshit grew to be an ideal heir to take over and was well-trained under Kripacharya. Yuyutsu gave the crown prince the best support to make him ready to assume the crown in due course.

Yudhishthira's rule has completed thirty-five years since the war, and the thirty-sixth year was running.

Chapter 23

Countdown For The End of An Era

Dwaraka

Krishna was on his way from Hastinapur to Dwaraka after Pandavas, with heavy hearts, bade him a respectful farewell after Ashvamedha Yaga. When he saw the wandering sage Uttanka on the way, he asked for the chariot to stop. Uttanka was unaware of the happenings of the Kurukshetra war, except that Krishna had gone to Hastinapur for peace talks. He assumed that Krishna would have successfully brokered peace between the cousins. Uttanka was shocked to learn about the subsequent catastrophe when Krishna shared the latest information on the subject. He did not believe that Krishna could not broker peace between the warring groups. He assumed that Krishna did not do it despite being capable, which led to war and heavy bloodshed. Krishna's inaction infuriated Uttanka, and he was about to curse Krishna.

Krishna explained that the war was necessary to establish Dharma and rid the earth of unrighteous rulers, and he performed the role as per the grand design. Krishna had a hard time convincing Uttanka that destiny had pre-decided what was going to happen, and even God could not change it. Uttanka realised the Godhood of Krishna and the rationale for the war. He sought and received Krishna's forgiveness. Krishna, having satisfactorily resolved Uttanka's doubts, continued his passage.

Krishna held no malice towards Uttanka as he understood Uttanka's mindset when posing that question. In fact, the quest ons, "If Krishna is a God, why could he not stop the war, despite going on a peace mission?" or "As Krishna is God and hence is capable of stopping the war, why didn't he?" were raised by many, though very few had guts to confront Krishna with those questions. Uttanka dared and got the answer.

Daruka, Krishna's charioteer, who was privy to this conversation, remembered another incident when Gandhari had a similar confrontation with Srikrishna.

She, too, had questioned Krishna's role in the war.

After the war, Krishna accompanied Pandavas to Dhritarashtra and Gandhari to get their formal blessings. Though Yudhishthira had won the battle, Pandavas had no malice toward the grieving parents, still viewing Dhritarashtra as a father figure. However, the encounter was fraught with anguish.

Though the old couple knew that Pandavas were faultless, Dhritarashtra and Gandhari were unable to control their emotions when they met the killers of their sons for the first time after the war. Dhritarashtra, overcome with emotion, wept as he embraced Yudhishthira, blessing him. But when it was Bhima's turn, the memories of his sons' deaths, especially the brutal slaying of Dusshasana and Duryodhana, overwhelmed the old king. Unable to suppress his fury, he attempted to crush Bhima's bones in his iron grip. Anticipating this, Krishna swiftly replaced Bhima with an iron statue, which was smashed to dust under the pressure of Dhritarashtra's mighty grip. That was the same statue which was specially prepared for Duryodhana's mace practice and, hence, was readily available there. Dhritarashtra later lamented for his hasty act but expressed happiness that Bhima was not harmed. His wrath subsided, and he reconciled with the Pandavas, offering them his blessings.

Pandavas had more mortifying time seeking Gandhari's blessings. Gandhari's grief was more intense. Yudhishthira felt that a toe of his foot burnt with the heat of Gandhari's glance from beneath her blindfold and immediately moved afar.

Gandhari ventilated her ire at Bhima, accusing him of inhuman acts. 'Could you not have spared even one of my sons?' she asked bitterly. 'How could you stoop as low as to drink Dusshasana's blood, being a Kshatriya? And why did you have to resort to deceit to kill Duryodhana?'

Bhima, prepared for her anger, replied humbly. 'Mother Gandhari, your son was an unmatched warrior. He was about to strike my head when he galloped in the air, and my mace found his thighs to be the target. It was me or him at that point, and I had no choice. He would have killed me had I not struck his thighs in self-defence. Who could kill your son in a fair fight? As for Dusshasana's blood, Mother, I did not swallow though it was taken into my mouth; I spat it out after taking it into my mouth in a moment of rage. My actions, however harsh, were driven by my oath and the circumstances of war. I beg your forgiveness.'

Bhima's humble answer and his admission of her son's valour diminished Gandhari's anger towards him. Though still heartbroken, she let her anger subside and blessed the Pandavas, one by one.

Gandhari's simmering anger has then shifted from Pandavas to Krishna, whom her son accused of being behind all the indiscretions the war had witnessed from Pandavas' side. She sincerely believed in the Godhood of Krishna and thought Krishna had it in his power to stop the war but did not. Moreover, she reasoned, he contrived to keep the Yadava contingent out of the equation while allowing others to bear the brunt of the destruction, Kuru clans being the major casualty.

She uttered aloud, 'Krishna! You were capable of stopping the war, but you did not. You could have prevented the disaster had you chosen. Yet you chose not to. You only thought of saving your clan from this catastrophe and allowed other royals to kill one another.'

Overwhelmed by grief and anger, Gandhari cursed Krishna. 'Just as we had helplessly witnessed the destruction of our sons and decimation of clans, you too shall witness the destruction of your Yadava clan. And the death of your sons and grandsons. They will turn on each other, and you will be powerless to stop it. May the Yadava women cry on the dead bodies of their near and dear as the Kuru women are mourning now. My curse will take effect in thirty-six years.'

'So be it, then', Krishna replied.

The chariot reached Dwaraka, and Daruka brought it to a halt at Krishna's palace, and Krishna alighted.

Naimisha, Shamyaprasa

The news of Gandhari's curse was discussed in various ashrams of Naimisha. His disciples asked Vyshampayana about the propriety of Gandhari's curse and Krishna's response. Vyshampayana had already discussed this matter with Vedavyasa and was ready with his answers.

Most of them felt that Gandhari's accusation was unfair. Krishna had taken it upon himself to broker peace between cousins and tried his best to convince Dhritarashtra in the court of Hastinapur. He even foretold what disaster awaited if peace was not accepted. It was Duryodhana who precipitated the issue, and it was Dhritarashtra who mindlessly followed his son. How could Krishna be blamed?

'Gandhari's cursing Krishna and Yadavas looks totally out of context. How could she accuse Krishna of the war?' Some others asked.

Vaishampayana answered, 'Gandhari truly believed in the Godhood of Krishna and thought that Krishna could have averted the war if he had willed. That was the anguish of a mother who lost her hundred sons in just eighteen war days.'

'Understandable, but why did she set a timeline of thirty-six years after the war?'

That was a question uppermost in everybody's mind. The timeline made no sense; if Gandhari was angry, why not immediately? Or in the next few years? During her lifetime?

'Vaishampayana replied,' Only Gandhari can answer that question correctly, and others have to surmise. It could be approximately equivalent to the years of tension Dhritarashtra and Gandhari faced about the impending conflict between their sons and Pandavas. Apparently, she gave a timeline long enough for Yadavas, who are genuinely a united bunch, to divide among themselves and start fighting. However, there is a secret behind this number, which probably Gandhari knew. Dwapara Yuga comes to an end precisely thirty-six years from now. And it was time for Krishna and Balarama to depart from the earth. What Gandhari really cursed is about the clan.'

'Why did Krishna agree to it? He could have negated it. Isn't it?

'He agreed because it was his plan, too. Many devas had taken birth as Yadavas to assist Krishna, and once Krishna departed, they had no business staying here. Do you think Krishna would be affected by the death of his sons or grandsons? He is too philosophical for that. The curse had the least effect on his equanimity. He took the curse in his stride.'

'How do you think Yadavas will fight among themselves?'

'We do not know, as yet. There is a long time before that happens. There will be some divine design for that, too.'

They have to wait for thirty-six years to find the answer.

Dwaraka, a Few Years Later

Years rolled on, and Krishna was acclaimed as the supreme Yogi by the learned sages after the Kurukshetra war, and he came to be recognised and hailed as Yogeeshwar or Yogi Maharaj. Many prominent sages such as Vishvamitra, Durvasa, Brighu, Angirasa, Kashyapa, Atri, Vashishta, Vamadeva, Narada, Ashita and Valikhyas used to visit Dwaraka, along with their disciples, to have a glimpse of him and indulge in discussions with him. There were many other sages, too. Krishna, who established himself as the greatest warrior of the times, had also been the most acclaimed Yogi, something that was unique.

However, Yadavas in Dwaraka became complacent in their comfort zones. Nobody dared attack Dwaraka as in earlier years, as they became invincible under Krishna. They were wealthy and had plenty of resources. As the years rolled on, Yadavas, by and large, started indulging in frivolous activities like drinking and merry-making. They have also become less respectful towards sages, as the sages have become Dwaraka's frequent visitors.

One day, a key contingent of sages, including Durvasa and Vishvamitra, had a halt in a place called Pindaraka, where they were resting. They were met by a group of gopalaks, who had a pregnant woman among them. They requested the sages to predict whether the lady, the wife of Bhabru, would deliver a boy or a girl. It was nothing but a practical joke to challenge the power of those venerated sages. The sages saw through the prank played against them. They could see that there was no pregnancy, and the woman was not a woman at all. It was Samba, the son of Krishna and Jambavati, in the pregnant woman's robes. The fun-loving Samba and his mischievous friends dared to play a practical joke on the sages and were caught. Sages were peeved at their audacity. The enraged sages cursed that the lady so presented to them would certainly deliver, but it would be neither a boy nor a girl. It would be an iron pestle (*a mousala*) that would be the cause for the decimation of their race.

Samba and his friends were shocked to find the next day that Samba had undergone labour pains and delivered an iron pestle, just as the sages had told. Frightened, they rushed to the court, where all the elders were present, and surrendered the 'pestle of curse', informing the whole incident and the curse. Ugrasena commanded that the pestle be pulverised into powder and thrown into the sea to avert the possible danger. They did likewise, but despite breaking and grinding, some tiny pieces were left out.

They mixed the entire powder into the sea and heaved a sigh that they might have averted an attempt on their lives and nullified the curse.

The sages later met Krishna and apologised to him for cursing the Yadava community in a fit of rage. Krishna did not mind their curse, as it was in the course of a divine plan. He indulged in talks with them for which they had come as if nothing had happened. Sages left Dwaraka, having accomplished the task that destiny prescribed for them.

Unknown to everyone, the finely ground iron powder poured into the sea had flown back and got deposited on the shores of Prabhasa. The grass that was grown there was uncharacteristically sturdy and strong. A small iron piece of that cursed pestle fell into the hands of a hunter, who fixed it to one of his arrows.

The killer grass was growing in Prabhasa in size and number, and the time was rolling. The thirty-sixth year after the Kurukshetra war was yet to commence.

Chapter 24

Thirty-Six Years After The War - The End of an Era

Hastinapur

One day, Krishna's charioteer, Daruka, arrived to meet Arjuna. Arjuna was shocked to hear what he said.

'Entire clan of Yadava warriors had fought amongst themselves and perished. My Lord, Krishna, your beloved friend, wanted me to fetch you immediately. He expects to die soon and he foretold Dwaraka would be submerged in the sea seven days after his death.'

Daruka's words struck Arjuna like a thunderbolt, for Krishna was not just a cousin, a friend, and a brother-in-law, but a guide, philosopher and mentor who guided them throughout their lives. He was, in fact, their God.

'Death to Srikrishna, the God of all! Are you in your senses, Daruka? Who was born on the earth that could kill him? Give me the full details. How are Satyaki and Pradyumna?'

'Both of them were killed by the followers of Kritavarma.'

'And what of Kritavarma?'

'He was killed by Satyaki in the first place, supported by Pradyumna.'

'What had triggered the fight?'

'They were all camping on the seashore at Prabhasa, consuming drinks and making merry. Everybody was in a joyous mood, and there was no indication of the impending catastrophe. It all started when the conversation drifted into the improprieties committed in the Kurukshetra War, as to which side did more unrighteous things in the war. Satyaki accused Kritavarma of assisting Ashwatthama in murdering warriors and burning the Pandava camp. An enraged Kritavarma retaliated by pointing out Satyaki's act of killing Bhurishravas, who stopped fighting and sat in a state of Yoga. Arguments escalated, and even Pradyumna joined in supporting Satyaki. Looking at Krishna and Satyabhama, Satyaki recalled Kritavarma's role in the murder of Satrajit in his own house during the night. On remembering the nightmare of her father's murder, Satyabhama broke into sobbing. An impetuous Satyaki put Kritavarma to the sword and attacked his followers. They retaliated by killing both Satyaki and Pradyumna by beating them with the vessels they were holding to drink wine.'

'Did Krishna not try to stop the killings?' Arjuna's voice was full of surprise.'

'It all happened in his presence. He tried initially to reason with them, but the people were in such a mad rage that they did not care for Krishna. They started killing one another with the grass that was grown on the seashore, as they didn't carry any weapons with them. Surprisingly, the blades of grass, when plucked from the ground, looked like iron pestles. They were sharper than swords and stronger than maces and killed those who were hit instantly. One by one, all of Krishna's brothers, sons and grandsons, like Gada, Samba, and Aniruddha, started falling. Krishna himself grew angry and smashed the rest of the Yadavas with the same seashore grass, bashing them left and right. His share in the killing was highest.'

Daruka continued as a perplexed Arjuna absorbed the details in great pain.

'A dejected Balarama left the scene as soon as the drunken brawl escalated into a fight and went far away. When the fight ended, with the last person falling, Krishna went on Balarama's trial to find him. Only Bhabru and I were with him. Soon, we found Balarama sitting below a tree, deep in thought. Krishna advised Bhabru to escort the women to Dwaraka safely and immediately. Krishna, then bade me to fetch you to Dwaraka immediately. He told me that Dwaraka would be submerged in the sea within seven days of his death. He wanted you to take care of his aged parents, women, and children in Dwaraka. We need to hurry.'

Arjuna took no time to accompany Daruka to Dwaraka after quickly briefing his brothers.

Hastinapur later saw a forlorn and sad Arjuna return to the city, bringing with him the women folk and children of the Dwaraka and a few of Krishna's staff who survived the ordeal. He wore the face of a defeated man, and he looked aged. People perceived that the loss of Krishna was most unbearable to Arjuna.

'Did you see how sad he looks?' people whispered.

'He used to wear Gandiva very lightly on his shoulders. Now it looks like a burden.'

'Who is that young boy among the children?'

'He is Vajranabha, great-grandson of Krishna, the son of Aniruddha. He is the sole survivor of the Yadava dynasty, and he is their future king.'

'Dwaraka submerged in waters?' some of them are full of surprise.

'Except for the palace of Srikrishna, everything else was submerged. Entire Dwaraka is now deep under the sea.'

'Never even thought the great Dwaraka would meet such a fate. We in Hastinapur should consider ourselves fortunate to have darshan of Balarama and Krishna many times, though we would not see them ever again.'

The people of Hastinapur loved Krishna a lot. Most of them were his devotees. People of all varnas were united in their devotion to Krishna. They all shared the grief of the Pandava brothers.

Arjuna explained to his brothers, in private, whatever had happened.

'As per Srikrishna's wish, I immediately proceeded to Dwaraka and reported to Vasudeva. Our uncle was a totally devastated man, and he narrated what he had learnt from Krishna. After Daruka left to fetch me, Bhabru was hit by a stray arrow from somewhere, and he collapsed. So, Krishna asked Balarama to wait for his return, and he proceeded to escort the women folk back to Dwaraka. He briefed his father on whatever happened, asked him to wait for me, and told him that I would do what was needed. Then, he took his father's blessings and went out to meet his brother, Balarama, never to return.

Vasudeva, his wives, and all others were in deep shock. I met Krishna's wives to console their great loss. I could not control myself, and I broke down while talking to them, and they, in turn, had to console me. They all told how much Krishna loved them and how much they loved Krishna. I stayed in Krishna's palace to spend a sleepless night.

The following morning, Vasudeva breathed his last. I performed his funeral rites. Four of his wives, Devaki, Rohini, Bhadra and Madira, had performed Sati with him. I visited Prabhasa with Daruka, ministers, and other support staff. Lakhs of Yadava warriors lay dead on the seashore. We went ahead and found Balarama, who left his mortal body in a state of Yoga. We found Krishna in a seemingly sleeping position, his face serene and a smile on his lips. He looked as if he was full of life, but he was not. An arrow pierced his foot, and there was a pool of blood at his feet.'

Arjuna stopped here, overwhelmed by emotions recollecting the scene. The listeners, too, experienced similar emotional turmoil. It was difficult for them to believe that Krishna was no longer there.

'Who hit him, and how a small injury like that could kill Krishna?'

'I examined the arrow. It was fitted with a sharpened part of that cursed pestle, as identified by my accompanying persons. While we were discussing, a hunter presented himself and confessed that it was indeed him who shot that arrow. He said he saw Krishna's moving foot, partly hidden in the bushes, from a distance, mistook it to be that of a deer's neck and aimed it. When he reached to fetch his target, he saw it was not a deer, but Krishna, whom he hit.'

' What an irony! Krishna, who withstood many sharp arrows all over his body for eighteen long days in the Kurukshetra war, succumbing to a hunter's arrow!'

'Yes, unbelievable, but unfortunately, also true. The tiny part of the cursed pestle, which escaped grinding and was thrown into the sea, found its way to the hunter's arrow and then to Krishna's body.'

Arjuna continued after a pause.

The hunter said that in a moment of shock, he momentarily thought that he was looking at Visnu with four hands as described in the scriptures but quickly realised that the person was none other than Krishna. He begged for Krishna's mercy, admitting his folly. Krishna excused him, saying that the hunter was not at fault as his action was pre-ordained.'

Arjuna continued, 'Daruka and others identified the hunter as one named Jara, a man from the Yadava lineage, a cousin of Krishna, but took to hunting. He was the last man to have seen Krishna and got his blessings.'

Arjuna continued. 'I had to believe that our friend, advisor, and God is no longer in this world to guide us. Gandhari's curse materialised in full. And to think we are the reason for the curse bothers me, though Veda Vyasa assuaged me later that it was a predestined outcome. Having performed funeral rights to all those dead, I alerted the people to get prepared for a long journey to Hastinapur, as Dwaraka would be submerged in water seven days after Krishna's demise. Four of Krishna's wives, including Rukmini and Jambavati, had sacrificed themselves to the God of fire. Other wives led by Satyabhama decided to take to Tapasya for the rest of their lives. I left them in suitable places during my journey to Hastinapur.'

Arjuna paused here to take a breath, recollected the saddest part of his journey, and then proceeded.

'What I am going to tell you now might surprise you. Keeping in view the last warning of Krishna, who never ever erred, I had to ensure that the vacation of the grand city of Dwaraka was to be completed fast. As planned, all the old survivors, children and women folk were ready to start by the seventh day morning. They had carried with them all their precious jewels and diamonds. The able-bodied men were limited, primarily staffers, but women and children were lakhs. I asked Vajra to lead the contingent from the front, and I was guarding from the rear.

The moment I stepped out, sea waters came gushing to reclaim the land I vacated, and every forward step of mine made the sea advance to that extent. Everybody wondered to witness this strange spectacle. When we crossed the boundaries of Dwaraka, the sea stopped following us. When we looked back, we saw that the ocean had submerged everything in Dwaraka except Srikrishna's palace.'

Yudhishthira intervened. 'That land belonged to the sea, and it was made available to Srikrishna for building his capital. When he was not there, the sea reclaimed it. Seven days were allowed for you to complete the last rituals and prepare the Dwarakites to vacate the land. What a pity! Most of them would have been born there, and it was the only place they ever knew!'

Everybody nodded in agreement, and Arjuna continued. 'As I told you, the women folk and children numbered in lakhs, and the men were few. Suddenly, Abhiras, the notorious bandits, attacked us from all sides with sticks, and there was a panic in the crowd when the women started running to escape from the thugs. I warned these thugs that they were dealing with the Pandava prince Arjuna, but they did not care about my words. I decided to stall them by using astras and lifted Gandiva. To my utter shock. I did not feel strong enough to lift the mighty bow, and I could not remember a single astra.'

The brothers were shocked. To think that Gandiva becoming heavier for Arjuna was unthinkable.

Arjuna's face assumed a grave expression, and it was as if he was reliving the situation he was narrating.

'At last, I lifted the bow and shot many arrows and killed a great many. But they were thousands in number, did not care for their lives and kept on advancing towards the women and the boxes of gold. And more surprisingly, my quiver, which always supplied me with an unlimited number of arrows, has become empty for once. I had no arrows to use and warded them off with the bow itself, and they just fled away into the forests in all directions, having grabbed whatever they could. Many women, along with gold, gems and precious jewels, were found missing. Some were forcibly taken by them, and some seemed to have gone on their own, probably thinking it was so destined. Abhiras could not touch the major queens and notable ladies who were near me, but those who were on the other end were less fortunate. I had no energy left to pursue these robbers who went in different directions to rescue the stolen women as I was apprehending another surprise attack on the remaining contingent if I left the guard.

We proceeded further, and when we reached Murthikavata, the land of Bhojas, I had left Kritavarma's son in the care of our regent, duly anointing the lad as its future king. Again, when we reached the Saraswati river, I made similar arrangements for Youyudhana, Satyaki's son. The sixteen thousand wives of Krishna merged themselves into that holy river.

The women folk, along with their children relating to the Bhoja and Vrishni races, were settled in these two places. The remaining women, old men and children belonging to Andhaka, Kukuru and other clans were settled in Indraprastha, and I made Vajranabha its king. In due course, he will also take over Mathura, the original kingdom of Yadavas.'

'Great job done by you!' said Yudhishthira. Pandavas' bondage with Yadavas was so intense that they appreciated Arjuna's effort to restore

Yadava's pride. They were dear relatives to Pandavas from their mother's side, all Krishna's people.

Bhima sensed Arjuna's sadness and comforted him. 'You were in a deep shock after losing Krishna and in a disturbed mind at the time when Abhiras attacked. Or there could be some other explanation for the debacle, which we might discover later. Very sad indeed, but you had done the best under the circumstances. Do not take it to heart, my brother.'

Arjuna thanked Bhima for his sentiments and said, ' Yes, there was an explanation. I went to Vyasa's ashram to express my grief and take his advice to restore my peace of mind. I explained everything to him and poured my feelings, expressing that there was no point in living in this world anymore after Krishna's death. Vedavyasa heard the news unperturbed and said everything had happened as destined. He told me that my inability to lift Gandiva, forgetting of astras and emptying of quivers happened to allow the curse of Ashtavakra on Yadava women to happen. They were cursed to be abducted by thieves. Again, the destruction of Yadavas by killing one another with seashore grass was also due to a curse by sages when Krishna's son Samba played a prank on them. Balarama and Krishna were none other than Sesh Nag and Bhagavan Vishnu, and they were eagerly awaited in their abode, Vaikhunta. Even before the Prabhasa debacle, Krishna's chariot with horses and their weapons, including Sudarshan Chakra, returned to their original places, awaiting their Lord to join. Balarama sat in Yoga, and from out of his mouth, a giant Nag was released and merged into the sea, signifying Balarama's departure. Krishna, after his return from Dwaraka and bidding his farewell, found that Balarama had left this world and realised his time had come, too. He slept under a tree, contemplating when he was hit by the arrow, which caused his bleeding. What Jara has experienced was not an illusion, but Krishna had indeed shown him his true form. He was being watched by all the celestial beings waiting to welcome his return to his abode.'

'Vedavyasa further said that Krishna had left the earth at a time he decided, after performing all his duties and leaving his unforgettable legacy. It was foolish to mourn for him. Krishna knew the outcome of

Prabhasa, where a deadly seashore grass grew out of the cursed iron powder awaited them. He had, in fact, led them there. It was thirty-six years after the Kurukshetra war, the time prescribed by Gandhari for the decimation of the Yadava race. Srikrishna had taken it upon himself to ensure both curses are respected.'

Pandavas wondered at destiny's divine plan over which men had little control.

Arjuna continued, 'Vedavyasa further said that though Krishna left this earth, his story would be sung in all corners of the earth forever. He suggested that it is time for us to decide about our future course of action, too. What we have to think about is our future course of action.'

The death of Krishna had a devastating effect on not only Arjuna but all other Pandavas as well.

Yudhishthira looked at his brothers and said, 'Arjuna! Time will conquer everyone on the earth. I am going to surrender to the time. You think and give your views on this.'

Arjuna accepted his elder brother's words and replied, 'Yes, time is time.'

Bhima, Nakula, and Sahadeva also accepted that it was time for them to surrender to time and leave the earth, having fulfilled their roles.

Hastinapur

Yudhishthira chalked out a plan for Mahaprasthana, the grand final journey of life seeking heavenly worlds by walking towards the north, without taking food and keeping the body and mind in yogic state. They decided to circumnavigate Bharatavarsha, their empire, before finally marching northwards. They would first start towards the east, then proceed to the south, and then turn towards the west. They would take one final glimpse at submerged Dwaraka, and finally, they would go towards the northern direction and then to the Himalayas and beyond. They would visit all the holy places of worship during this sojourn.

Yudhishthira called Yuyutsu and entrusted him with the responsibility of guiding the king Parikshit, whom he crowned. He specially advised Subhadra that her grandson had now become king of Hastinapur and Krishna's grandson had become king of Indraprastha and asked her to protect both of them and follow Dharma. Probably, he was apprehensive about the repetition of past feuds between the two mighty kingdoms. He asked Kripa to continue to guide Parikshit as his Guru and lead him on the path of Dharma. He then announced to the people his intent to relinquish the empire and proceed on a journey never to return, along with his brothers and Draupadi, who wished to accompany him.

Hastinapur was shocked to hear this announcement. People knew it was futile to try to stop them. They all understood what Yudhishthira said. Pandavas had played their part in a certain period in the history that was given to them. That time was over. Now, they have to give in to the time.

Hastinapur watched Yudhishthira leaving with his brothers and Draupadi one after another. They were escorted up to the end of the city to pass through the historic Vardhaman gate. Ulupi merged into the sea, and Chitrangada left for her son's Manipura kingdom.

Parikshit, Kripa, Yuyutsu, all the ministers and staff, Subhadra, Uttara and their entourages stood transfixed in shock after bidding Pandavas a final goodbye at the city gates, watching them leave the gates one behind the other. They would return to the palace, perform their respective roles and endeavour their best to continue the legacy left by the illustrious Pandavas. But for the present, they felt a deep void in their hearts. The people who gathered there in large numbers resorted to collective sobbing to ease their hearts' burden.

Hastinapur watched helplessly and bade its final farewell as the brothers crossed the gate. First, it was Yudhishthira who left the gate. He was followed by Bhima, Arjuna, Nakula, Sahadeva and Draupadi in that order. All of them were on foot. They had no escorts. That was the last Hastinapur had seen them. They were lost to time as far as the city was concerned.

Chapter 25

Mystery of Pandavas Unravelled

Naimisha, Shamyaprasa

Vedavyasa speeded up the reciting of Mahabharata after Arjuna went back after meeting him on his way from Dwaraka to Hastinapur, quickly followed by Pandavas' embarking on their final voyage into the unknown, coronating Parikshit and Vajranabha as kings of Hastinapur and Indraprastha respectively.

Vaishampayana would be the first to hear this from Vyasa, and he, in turn, would recite them to his disciples and clear their doubts. Those evening discourses of Vaishampayana were attended by inmates of other ashrams as well, in view of the enormous interest among Naimishites in the subject. While some of the recitals were already known to most of the inmates, some new revelations startled them. Asareer used to avail the opportunity every day.

On this particular day, Vaishampayana was narrating the fate of Pandavas after they departed from Hastinapur. The audience was brimming with curiosity, eager to unravel the destiny of these noble brothers who had renounced their wealth and power and disappeared out of sight. Vaishampayana began his narration, and the audience was captivated.

'The five brothers and Draupadi had embarked on Mahaprasthana, never to return. They had travelled in all three directions before they finally turned to the North and went all the way beyond Meru.

They first travelled to the east and south, had a darshan of the great eastern and southern seas, and offered prayers. Arjuna had parted with his most precious possession, Gandiva, at Agnidev's suggestion by throwing it into the Eastern Sea. He wielded that revered bow ever since he was gifted the same by Agni and for a period close to eighty-five years. He didn't need it anymore.

They had then turned westwards and prayed on the banks of the western sea. They had, at Prabhasa Teertha, a glimpse of submerged Dwaraka, and they paid their final respects to Krishna. They turned towards the North and reached the Himalayas.

Unknown to them, a dog was walking behind them. They noticed it, and they thought that it would leave them somewhere on the way. However, it followed them like a shadow. More about the dog later.

They reached the Himalayas, crossed the great Himagiri Hill, and entered the sea of snow. They had crossed it and reached the mountain of Meru.

When they moved forward like this, Draupadi, who was walking behind all Pandavas and just behind Sahadeva, had fallen, dropping dead. Pandavas, except Yudhishthira, were shocked and saddened to see their companion for years, thus resting on the ground, bereft of life.

Bhima asked his elder brother, who was aware of the fall of Draupadi but didn't slow his pace nor look backwards. *"Why did Draupadi, who had never committed any adharma, fall like this?"*

Yudhishthira replied- *"Bhima! Draupadi was partial in her love towards Arjuna. She reaped the result of that now."*

'The next to fall was Sahadeva. Bhima asked Yudhishthira, *"This brother of ours served us all faithfully and lived without ego. Why did he fall?"*

"Sahadeva never considered any of us, or anybody else for that matter, to be as intelligent and wise as himself, and that's the reason for his fall."

Soon Nakula fell, following Sahadeva. *"This brother Nakula never crossed the path of Dharma and never disobeyed us. Why did he fall?"* Bhima asked.

Replied Yudhishthira, *"Nakula always felt that there was nobody more handsome than him. Don't worry about others, and just follow me. Everybody has to reap the fruits of Karma."*

Vyshampayana continued with his narration, 'Then Arjuna fell.'

As the journey's narration continued, the audience's sympathy for the Pandavas deepened with each fall. First Draupadi, then Sahadeva, followed by Nakula, and now Arjuna. Each fall was not just a physical event but a blow to the audience's understanding of justice and righteousness. It fostered a profound sense of empathy and connection with the characters, and it also raised profound philosophical questions about the nature of Dharma and Karma. They were trying to absorb the wisdom of Yudhishthira, just as Bhima must be undergoing at that point in time.

"Arjuna never said a lie, even for the sake of fun, as far as I remember. How did such a noble soul like him fall like this?" asked Bhima.

"Arjuna said he would kill all the opponents in one day, but he did not do it. Moreover, he belittled all the other archers, which he should not have done. That's why Arjuna, who believed he was the greatest archer, had fallen."

Sooner, it was Bhima's turn to fall. *"Brother, I, too, am falling. Pray tell me, the dearest of your brothers, why do I fall?"*

Yudhishthira did not look back, did not slow his pace as usual, and replied, *"You eat a lot. You never care for others. You boast based on your mighty strength. That led to your downfall."*

Yudhishthira continued his journey forward, accompanied only by the dog that had kept pace with him all along.

When Yudhishthira thus walked, keeping himself in Yoga, a distance that no other human had travelled so far, Devendra himself descended in his chariot and invited him to enter it.

Yudhishthira informed that his brothers and wife had fallen, and he would not consider going to heaven alone. Indra assured him that they had already left their bodies and reached the heavens. Only Yudhishthira was entitled to reach heaven in his mortal body.

Yudhishthira said that he wanted the dog, which had followed them for a long time and had not fallen on its way to accompany him. Upon refusal of his request on the grounds that dogs had no permission to enter heaven in physical bodies, Yudhishthira declined Indra's offer to join him in the chariot alone himself.

The dog was no ordinary dog; it was Lord Yama himself, and he appeared in his divine form when Yudhishthira stood his ground and was ready to forfeit the most incredible opportunity to enter heaven in mortal form for the sake of a principle, which he considered Dharma. Indra and Yama told Yudhishthira that he passed the final test and qualified himself as the best man to enter heaven in a mortal body. Thereupon, Yudhishthira ascended to heaven in Indra's chariot to the welcome salutations of devas and sages.'

As the evening's narration concluded, the audience returned to their respective places, each filled with a mix of emotions. The profound journey of the Pandavas had left them reflective and contemplative, and it would take time for them to fully absorb and appreciate the underlying messages.

Charvaka's Ashram

The next day, in the ashram of Charvaka, as it was being called now, there was a heated deliberation on the recital of Mahaprasthana of Pandavas. The inmates, each with their own philosophical beliefs, discussed and debated the narrative at length, raising thought-provoking questions.

'The narration of Vedavyasa was simply incredulous. How come any person reaches heaven in his mortal body? Even Rama and Krishna, who were supposed to be avatars of Lord Vishnu, were not accorded that privilege.'

'Assuming heavens are there' - another inmate reminded.

'Yes, assuming heavens exist and people would go to either hell or heaven once they die. My wonderment was not on this existing debatable assumption, but how did Yudhishthira deserve such a privilege? He played dice and staked his wife, made his brothers and wife suffer on account of that, and even uttered a lie to bring down his preceptor, Dronacharya. In a way, he was responsible along with Duryodhana for a disastrous war that resulted in killing so many people, and how can he be accorded the rare honour of going to heaven in his human body!'

The audience was deeply engaged, questioning the validity of such a narrative.

'I particularly disliked the reported way Yudhishthira had gone on commenting about the conduct of Draupadi and his brothers after their complete obedience to him, even in adversity. Draupadi was utmost faithful to him despite her suffering from his reckless act of staking her in the game of dice. Still, Yudhishthira said she loved Arjuna more!'

'I do not see what's wrong if she loved Arjuna more? Can we say Yudhishthira loved both Draupadi and Devika in the same way? Asking her to wed five brothers when she was won by one of them in the contest and finally finding fault that she loved one of them more than others is simply unfair, I believe!'

'Yudhishthira was perhaps not blaming Draupadi, but it was only a statement of his perception in reply to Bhima's question. There is a need for some reason why she had fallen, isn't it?' someone opined.

'One and the same; it tantamounts to blaming Draupadi, whether anyone would agree or not,' thundered another inmate, and many seemed to agree as the topic diverted to Arjuna.

'Yudhishthira was critical of Arjuna, too, who was instrumental in all his victories. Arjuna was acknowledged as the best archer of both sides. What if he belittled other archers? Was it not a war strategy and a way of motivating oneself? When did Arjuna say that he would kill the entire

Kaurava army in one day, and in what context? How did Yudhishthira expect Arjuna to kill all the eleven akshauhinis in one day? I think the accusation was unfair.'

'Nor does his interpretation of the failings of Bhima, Nakula and Sahadeva. They were all quite faithful to their elder brother. Bhima needed a large quantity of food because of his bodily requirements. He never stepped back in the war. It was his strong body that had endured the war, and he accounted for many through his sheer physical strength. Were it not mainly the efforts of Bhima and Arjuna that won the war?"

'Kauravas often heckled Bhima for his huge appetite, which Bhima never relished. To hear a similar comment as a verdict for his fall would have certainly broken his heart had he heard it before his fall,' someone quipped.

'The twins never disobeyed their elder brothers. They never prided themselves on their being intelligent or handsome as far as anybody knew. All the interpretations of Yudhishthira seem like figments of his imagination, unsupported by facts.'

'We have no other source to verify the facts, whether Yudhishthira actually said those things, whether Indra had really descended from the heavens to pick up Yudhishthira and whether a dog had accompanied them all the way up to the Meru mountain and then manifested as Lord Yama. Except for the words of Vedavyasa.'

'What else should the people believe? People saw the Pandavas and Draupadi leaving, but they did not come back. There is no alternative version as to what happened to them. Some people saw them walking towards the Himalayas. Nobody survives in that inclement weather for long. They certainly breathed their last in those mountains.'

'That need not be doubted, and possibly they collapsed on the mountains, and that was what they wished, too. If what is now being told is true, what happened to Yudhishthira after he ascended the chariot of

Indra? The story of Pandavas would only be complete after knowing what happened to him!'

'What happens to anybody when he dies? Anyway, you may have to wait for what Vaishampayana will reveal in his next recital to know that version.'

⟶·⊶·❀❀❀·⊷·⟵

Asareer's Ashram

The recitals of Vedavyasa regarding what happened in Mahaprasthana, the final sojourn of Pandavas and Draupadi into oblivion, were also discussed in Asareer's ashram a few days later.

The audience seemed thrilled to learn the final passage of Pandavas and what happened to them after that. Different inmates voiced their feelings and thoughts.

'It was a fitting climax to the story of Pandavas. Yudhishthira being escorted in his mortal body to heaven is a rare event, and it symbolises the victory of a man of Dharma. Gods favour a virtuous man.'

'Even the other Pandavas and Draupadi were near flawless. They had endured a long journey in Yogic stance and had just fallen short of the final victory post only by a few yards. But still, their places were assured in heaven as confirmed by Indra.'

'I was surprised when I first heard that Yudhishthira was told that Draupadi, Pandavas and Karna were suffering in hell, whereas Duryodhana and others were enjoying heaven. Only later was it revealed that it was an illusion created, and Yudhishthira was shown the Narak loka because of his half-truth, in which he told his guru Drona that Ashwatthama was killed.'

'Not necessarily because of that. It was later clarified that every king needs to visit hell at least momentarily because, knowingly or unknowingly, a man in power would tend to commit sins,' supplemented another.

'They all met finally in heaven in their original forms. Draupadi was none other than Swarga Lakshmi!

'Did he see Krishna, Arjuna and other Pandavas?'

'He saw Krishna in his majestic form as Narayana in the company of Arjuna, and they both talked to him.'

'He had seen Bhima in his majestic form in the company of Marudganas by the side of Vayudeva. He also saw Nakula and Sahadeva brightly shining in the company of Ashwins.'

'Did he see Karna too?'

'Indra had shown Yudhishthira all the people he was intending to see. Yudhishthira saw Karna in the company of Adityas. Dhritarashtra was none other than a Gandharva by the same name. Abhimanyu was in the company of Lord Chandra. We did hear earlier that he was a son of Soma and was sent to take human form for a limited period, which explained the early death of Abhimanyu. Bhishma was in the company of Vasus, and Drona was in the company of Brihaspati. Upapandavas, who were Vishvadevas, were in the company of Gandharvas.

Devas had shown him both Naraka loka and Swargaloka. As someone had already pointed out, every king is bound to visit Naraka at least temporarily. All these dead warriors, heroes or villains on the earth alike, spend their time in both of these worlds based on their Karmas, and when they reap the result of both good and bad Karma, they get back to their original form.

Yudhishthira was initially reported to have expressed malice towards Duryodhana, who was seen as being respected in heaven. However, after Yudhishthira bathed in Akasha Ganga and left his mortal body, he got a divine body and all his being was filled with peace. There was no anxiety, no restlessness and no malice towards anybody.

Finally, Yudhishthira was visited by Panduraja along with Kunti and Madri, who came in a 'Vimana' to meet this worthy son. There ends the story of Yudhishthira.

We are fortunate to hear this divine climax of the story of Pandavas, through the grace of sage Vedavyasa, who could see past, present, and future as well as what's happening anywhere in all other worlds. He is none other than another avatar of Vishnu.'

Everybody seemed satisfied after discussing the final recitation of Vedavyasa on the story of Pandavas. The session was coming to a close on an optimised note, in quite a contrast to what happened a few days ago in Charvaka's ashram on the same subject.

One of the new inmates had hesitantly asked as if he doubted he was asking an inappropriate question at an inappropriate time.

'Whatever Yudhishthira said explaining the reasons for the fall of Draupadi and his brothers seems to be rather unfair. This morning, an inmate of Charvaka ashram posed this question, and I had to answer and agree with him that Yudhishthira probably told his opinion, which he believes to be true, but not true in actuality.'

There were murmurs in the audience as they comprehended the question and its impact on the character of Yudhishthira.

Asareer looked at the inmate who posed this question and asked.

'What were your conversations with that Charvaka friend of yours? Come up one by one so that I may answer!'

"It is impossible to love equally all your wives or husbands when you are in a situation of polygamy. Was it a great sin that she loved Arjuna slightly more, that she had to fall?"

The inmate repeated the question posed to him by his friend.

'Draupadi was always faithful to each brother, as much as a wife of a single husband could be, and never had given a room for complaint. There was never an expression of complaint by any of the five brothers in this regard. She performed her role as the wife of all five Pandavas with great skill. However, even unknown to her, she could have loved Arjuna more. Nothing wrong with that or blameworthy. Even other Pandavas would have noticed it but never envied Arjuna for that. In fact, Arjuna was loved more, not only by Draupadi but also by everybody else, including his brothers.

Draupadi could cover a considerable distance and was almost near the final point. All Pandavas, too, kept pace with Yudhishthira almost to the end. The faults were only minor, and from a general point of view, they were not even faults. However, even the tiniest faults count to reach heaven in a mortal body in yogic Dharma. All of them knew the challenge and accepted it fully, confident that they were faultless. They knew they would fall even for the slightest fault of theirs, and you can observe from the questions of Bhima that they were curious to learn the reason rather than being shocked at such a fall. What else were the questions?'

The inmate who raised the point seemed happy at the elaborate answer, which explained that Draupadi was not at fault, and neither was Yudhishthira, in interpreting the reason for her fall. The last lap to reach the final destination required a total embodiment of Dharma in thought, word and action, which only the best of the best could have.

'Nakula and Sahadeva prided themselves on their being handsome and wise. What was wrong with that? They never boasted about their superior qualities with others. They served their elder brother faithfully.'

'Some people were born handsome, and some are not. Some are extremely handsome, just like Nakula. Is there any virtue in being handsome or beautiful? Would it make you a better man or woman? However, people attribute an unnecessary premium to looks, even stating that it is a divine quality. However, the person himself should not pride himself on such possession. A huge pride in one's physical features would ruin one. In Nakula's case, it was not a huge pride, but who does not feel a little proud to have been handsome? Even that slightest pride in physical beauty was cause enough for his fall from the Yogic stance. Yudhishthira had no malice in stating so; it must be the truth.'

There were murmurs of approval in the explanation.

Asareer added, 'Is there anyone who was, who is and who will be more handsome than Krishna?'

There were huge roars of approval supporting the statement from the audience at this pronouncement. Asareer continued.

'Sahadeva was very wise and intelligent. He was a student of Brihaspati, and Drona took special care in teaching him all those arts, noticing his special aptitude and capacity to absorb them. Everybody acknowledged it. However, do you think intelligence is a virtue in itself? Can an intelligent and wise person look down upon others who are less endowed? How does one get such superior intelligence or wisdom unless blessed by God? Hence, a wise person acquires knowledge and becomes intelligent by diligent study and devotion to gurus. One's knowledge should not be considered a privilege but a responsibility bestowed upon one to guide others. Being proud of one's wisdom or intelligence causes one's downfall.

In the case of Sahadeva, he was a virtuous man but could have nurtured a little pride that naturally comes with the knowledge that he was better endowed than the others. This feeling of superiority, though not expressive, was the reason for his fall. Yudhishthira had no malice towards his brothers; he knows every one of them better than they themselves knew, and what he stated must be an absolute truth.'

He did not waste much time to add, 'Who was, is or will be wiser and more intelligent than Krishna?' The audience erupted into loud cheers.

Asareer looked at the inmate who raised the question and said, without waiting to be asked. 'Arjuna did state that he would destroy the entire Kaurava army in a single day, but it had a rider, as that would require the use of Pashupatastra, whereas it can not be used on mere mortals. The war lasted for eighteen days, and even Pandavas suffered high casualties. Arjuna must have assured his elder brother many times in the past that he would destroy the Kaurava army easily. Though whatever Arjuna stated could be true based on his capacities, those statements had a tinge of boastfulness since the Kaurava army had formidable and well-known warriors like Bhishma, Drona, Karna and Ashwatthama, who were not pushovers. Belittling the opponents and disregarding their capacities was considered Arjuna's slightest flaw. Yudhishthira had no malice towards his war-winning brother, but he had to speak the truth and state the reason why Arjuna had fallen from the yogic stance.'

'The greatest warrior ever was, is and will be Krishna.' Somebody shouted from behind, which produced a smile on Asareer's lips and loud claps of approval from the audience.

Asareer continued, 'As far as Bhima was concerned, he had fallen because of his pride in being a strong person and his habit of overeating. I think nobody would question this reasoning as Bhima's habits and traits are well-known to everyone. Physical strength is certainly an asset, but one who is blessed to possess it should not be proud of it and behave boastfully. Eating to the extent required to keep the body strong is acceptable, but eating for the sake of pleasure impedes yogic practice. What Yudhishthira told was the truth.'

'Who was, is and will be known as the strongest person in the world?' somebody shouted from the audience, and there were shouts of "Krishna" and "Krishna" from all around.

Asareer concluded, 'The answers given by Yudhishthira are for universal application, and should not be narrowly interpreted and found fault with. One should shun the qualities of pride based on one's strength, valour, physical beauty, intelligence or any unique quality for that matter. People who possess such attributes may consider themselves fortunate but should not look down upon others who have those qualities less than them. When even such a slight pride in the mighty Pandavas, unobserved by any, could stop them from the highest achievement, we can understand how people with normal abilities, developing great egos, will be judged. As far as loving people is concerned, one should not differentiate between one's siblings or children and, in fact, develop a way of showing love towards everyone, the universal love, the Srikrishna way.

Do not brood over Yudhishthira's comments on your favourite heroes, whom Yudhishthira loved more than any of us, but understand the underlying message of "Dharma." The last message of Yudhishthira, the embodiment of Dharma, whom even Srikrishna respected.'

There were loud shouts of approval all around. The person who raised the question was filled with ecstasy and joined the shouts. The meeting ended with their regular prayer praising Krishna before they retired to sleep.

Naimisha– Shamyaprasa

Vaishampayana respectfully and admiringly complimented sage Vedavyasa, 'It is indeed a great work, revered Acharya. You had succinctly encapsulated the entire story in 24,000 shlokas with remarkable clarity and depth. How would you like this work to be known?

'I would like to call this "Jaya Samhita" as this is ultimately about the victory of Pandavas over Kauravas in the Kurukshetra war and is a triumph of Dharma over Adharma. In this composition, I have chronicled the saga of the Pandavas and Kauravas, capturing all essential details.'

'Quite apt, and the name sounds auspicious too. The descendants of Pandavas, the lineage of Parikshit, would certainly be interested in knowing the true story of their glorious ancestors, and they would benefit a lot from this work.'

'You, Vaishampayana, shall be the one I choose to propagate this knowledge. Recite this to your disciples and let them spread its teachings far and wide. Let the message of Dharma reach all people. Even if Dharma suffers momentary setbacks, one must never waver from its path. In the end, victory will belong to those who uphold it.'

'I would abide by your wise orders,' accepted Vaishampayana with humility.

Vedavyasa's works were monumental. He was not content with merely creating those works but ensured their propagation so that all could benefit. He had entrusted the dissemination of Vedas, which he had meticulously classified, to four of his disciples. Rigveda to Paila, Samaveda to Jaimini, Yajurveda to Vaishampayana and Atharva Veda to Sumantha, who all started teaching these Vedas to vast numbers of disciples, setting separate ashrams.

For the propagation of eighteen Puranas comprising a staggering 409,500 shlokas, Vedavyasa appointed Romaharshana. Romaharshana diligently imparted this knowledge to his disciples, including his son Ugrasravas, until his untimely demise at the hands of Balarama in a moment of unfortunate misunderstanding just before the end of the Mahabharata war. However, the Puranas survived because Romaharshana had already taught all these Puranas to his disciples much earlier, and Ugrasravas had taken over the responsibility.

Sage Suka, Vedavyasa's son, was among the foremost recipients of his father's wisdom and was well-versed in the creations of Vedavyasa.

Now, Vyshampayana was entrusted with the propagation of "Jaya Samhita," or shortly "Jaya" as it was referred to in Naimisha circles, in addition to his responsibility to impart Yajurveda.

Even though the epic "Jaya" with 24,000 shlokas is as big or bigger than some of his eighteen Puranas, he envisioned an even greater impact by expanding the text by incorporating additional narratives and principles of righteous conduct, offering guidance to not only kings but also people in general. He aspired to create a work so comprehensive that it would serve as a compendium of all essential knowledge—a timeless reference beyond a mere historical epic.

Vedavyasa immersed himself in deep meditation, contemplating how he would go about creating such a work.

Chapter 26

Asareer Embarks to Badarika

Asareer's Ashram

There is one place Asareer always wanted to visit before he breathed his last. In fact, it was, perhaps, the place where he wished to breathe his last, and that place was Badarika. Badarika is a sacred place where Nara and Narayana, the divine sages, are believed to reside perpetually. Though they are not visible to ordinary mortals, their spiritual presence is felt throughout the serene surroundings. Unlike Naimisha, where there was always a flurry of activity, Badarika was a calm place, with many sages scattered around the vast territory.

Master had been living there for several years in an ashram he set up. Asareer came to know that Master had now become totally engrossed in his studies and had a number of disciples cutting across various schools of thought. Asareer wanted to meet Master for one last time while both were living, and Asareer mused that not much time was left. He knew he was welcome at any time in Master's ashram for the sake of old times.

Asareer also learned from the disciples of Vaishampayana that both Sanjaya and Uddhava were still living in Badarika in ashrams they set for themselves. Asareer's determination to visit this place and meet these revered persons only strengthened over the years. They were the last links to the history of Mahabharata and Krishna apart from Vedavyasa. Asareer wanted to meet them before he breathed his last.

Asareer felt that his mission at the Naimisha ashram was complete, and Goswami, his able deputy, was quite capable of carrying forward the legacy. Asareer knew that his years were numbered. He believed that if he was still living, it was with the grace of Krishna. If he had to fulfil his ambition to visit Badarika and also test his chances of meeting those whom he wished to meet, it was his last chance. 'Now or never,' Asareer told himself, and he decided that it was now.

Asareer made a momentous announcement to his ashram mates -his decision to depart from Naimisha for good and his selection of a worthy successor.

The choice of a successor posed no difficulty as Roop Goswami, a devout disciple of Asareer, had earned his position through his total faith in the Krishna consciousness and his propensity to compose and sing melodious devotional songs praising Krishna, which had become very popular in the ashram. He was not just a talented musician but also a young, energetic, and passionate follower of the Bhakti cult, making him the ideal candidate to carry forward Asareer's legacy.

Inmates of various ashrams of Naimisha, who knew Asareer, started visiting him. Being one of the longstanding residents of Naimisha and friendly to all, Asareer was a popular person, cutting across multiple ideologies.

However, the current Charvaka was notably absent, having embarked on a tour with some of his disciples a few days earlier. Asareer recalled their last meeting, where he was surprised to note the new vehemence of the new Charvaka.

The man, who was now carrying the name of his friend and insisted all that he be addressed as such, asked him, 'Asareer! You are propagating the devotion to Krishna as the be-all and end-all for every person. Don't you realise the damage you are causing to society?'

Asareer was stunned by this statement. It was nothing but a direct accusation.

'Charvaka, I know you do not believe in devotion, but I do not see how devotion can damage society. The people find peace within themselves by being involved in these devotional activities. What harm do they do to society?'

'Your people are being led into a delusion. They have left rational thinking. They are relying too much on Krishna, and they are forgetting their individual worth and strength. They expect the Lord to do all things for them. It is particularly detrimental to the progress of young children. Devotion may be harmless when you are past your productive age and have nothing else to do but to accept it as the way of life is, cutting the reason and thought process at the very start. That is detrimental to society.'

Asareer did not react. He said in a calm voice. 'It is not the first time I heard this line of argument. Don't forget that my journey started with the process of rational thinking along with your Little Master, whose name you now bear as a title. I had been restless all those years. When I found Krishna, I discovered the peace within. I do not subscribe to the notion that devotion to Krishna when one is young hampers rational thinking in matters which require such kind of thinking. Anyway, I won't enter into an argument with you as the planes we stand on are not the same. I would only say I wish you well, and may the Lord's blessings be on you, and you may realise the truth for yourself one day or the other.'

Charvaka's frustration with these words was evident in the way he got up from his seat and the tone of his voice.

'I know you would not change and would not accept what I say. But, I thought I would tell you once again and keep telling others from your school of thought whenever I have an occasion. I am told that you are planning to leave for the Himalayas in the near future. I may not come back before you leave as I plan to undertake a tour in a week or so. That's why I visited you to bid farewell. I wish you all good, my friend.'

It was the last Asareer had seen Charvaka.

Roop Goswami asked him after Charvaka left. 'Why didn't you refute his argument? He appeared rude the way he had spoken to you. What does he know about God-realisation and the power of prayers? How does it harm children? Is it not instilling in them a discipline and a purpose of life? I thought of replying to every word he uttered but didn't do so because you may not like my interference.'

Asareer's peaceful face displayed a smile. 'Never do such a thing! You do not need to explain to anybody why you are devout. Never argue with people who do not have faith in what you believe. That will corrupt your thoughts. You may win arguments, but the process may sow seeds of doubt in your heart. The best way to face such situations is to be as silent as possible, and it will pass away. That is what I did. Always keep yourself in the company of like-minded people and think about godly ways. That is called Satsang. No point in trying to convince the inconvincibles through arguments.'

Goswami bowed his head. He realised the correctness of Asareer's line of thinking. 'I would forever remember these wise words and make it a point to make all our inmates realise this and adopt it.'

'I am not against free thought and exchange of ideas, but I find that the Sadhakas in the devotional line have no time to indulge in pointless arguments, especially with Charvakites. I get reports, and you also know very well, that the followers of Charvaka are becoming too materialistic, and a few of them even started saying that since there is no afterlife, no punishments and rewards for man's deeds, one should enjoy life as they have only one life. Such a line of thinking would corrupt the minds of Sadhakas. I don't mind their meeting Sankhites for the limited purpose of learning Yoga and meditation, but not beyond that. Learning and using some jargon of Samkhya without understanding their deeper meanings is a waste of time. This self-control would be for their own good.'

Goswami said, 'I agree absolutely. The Sadhakas who went back to their normal lives after completing their tenure here are leading peaceful lives and advocating the Krishna doctrine amongst their friends and relatives. They are well received and well respected by the people.'

'I do not doubt that. I also do not doubt your ability to lead the inmates, protecting them from untoward temptations.'

Asareer remembered all these conversations when he was about to address the inmates for one last time.

He had given his final message to the audience. He opened up and told them about his life experience and how he realised God. He suggested they keep Krishna in mind in whatever activities they engage in and be helpful to the society they live in.

He then answered their queries and took leave of them. The audience was moved by his recital of blissful experiences, particularly those involving Krishna. He was one of the very few who had the darshan of Lord Krishna in action many times, and the audience touched his feet and sought his blessings one last time.

Asareer proceeded the next day. He was to carry as little luggage as possible, and the miniature statue of Krishna was one of the things he packed on purpose.

Asareer had strolled around the ashram that evening, absorbed in memories of the long years he spent there, for one last time. The following day, when he embarked on his journey, everybody's hearts were saddened. Asareer was leaving for good and was never to return. The inmates had waved at him. He waved back and proceeded.

He was accompanied by two young inmates who would travel with him up to the Himalayas to assist him on the way. It was a long journey, and Asareer was too old to undertake the journey alone. The final journey of Asareer had started.

Chapter 27

Asareer's Quest in Badarika

Badarika

Asareer was delighted to meet Master in the Himalayan Ashram, and Master, too, was happy to receive Asareer after a long time. Master was surprised to find new energy displayed by Asareer, who looked more energetic than earlier, though aged. Asareer, in turn, observed that the Master was agile and radiant, defying his advanced years. He was surprised and even amused to see that Master had mellowed and was more available to clarify the doubts of disciples in evening meetings. He was being addressed as Brihaspati by his disciples instead of the impersonal title of Master, a distinct departure from Naimisha days. Asareer later learnt that it was the only name by which Master was known from the earliest times he set foot in Badarika.

Their shared memories of Animish surfaced when they met. It had been years since Animish passed away, but he was fresh in both their minds. He was a shared connection. Master told Asareer, 'Anaimish had wronged in his taking on Yudhishthira. Anaimish was in the pursuit of knowledge, and instead of confining himself to that, he befriended Duryodhana, but that led to his downfall. Yudhishthira was successful because of his Sattva Guna, whereas Duryodhana's Rajo Guna caused his downfall.'

Asareer expressed that it was his opinion, too. He briefed the Master about the developments of his erstwhile Ashram, the split and the three different schools thriving there. Master said his apprehensions about the inmates turning materialistic sadly proved true. He said such a deterioration would actually stunt the growth of philosophical enquiry. Master noted that it was a reason he did not complete and popularise his treatise on which he worked meticulously. Asareer understood Master's apprehension. Whatever reputation the present set of 'Charvakites' builds under present 'Charvaka,' people at large would attribute it to Charvaka and, to some extent, his mentor. Asareer mused, Master may not like his name to be associated with the materialism of Charvakites, which was not his doing, but can he escape from being remembered as the propounder of Charvakism?

Master had by now gone deep into the study of Sankhya and had assimilated what the exponents of the subject, such as Kapila, Asuri, and Panchasikha, had extolled. Master was interacting with the fresh inmates one evening, and Asareer attended the session as an observer. It was really a master class on Sankhya philosophy, and Asareer found it a fantastic experience. Though Asareer was familiar with Sankhya's basic premises and framework, hearing from an expert personally was a different experience altogether.

As Master commenced his talk, there was a pin-drop silence among the audience. That day, Master was expected to explain the basic concepts, and each idea would be elaborately studied in later classes. Asareer thought he was fortunate to have been there on that day. Master proceeded.

'There are only two independent realities from which everything was evolved. One is Purusha (Consciousness), and the other is Prakriti (Matter). Fusion between Purusha and Prakriti leads to the emergence of Buddhi/ Mahat (Intellect) and Ahamkara [Ego].

Prakriti contains Twenty-Three components, including Buddhi/Mahat (Intellect), Ahamkara (Ego) and Manas (Mind). These three components form unconscious matter. The unconscious mind receives illumination from Purusha and creates thought structures that appear to be conscious.

There are twenty other components. Five organs of sense (eyes, ears, nose, tongue, and skin), Five organs of action (voice, legs, arms, reproductive organs, and evacuating organs), Five sub-elements(sound, touch, sight, taste, and smell) called Panchamatra, and Five elements (fire, air, water, earth and space/sky) called Panchabhoota, total up to Twenty. Together with the three elements, Buddhi, Ahamkara and Manas, they are counted as Twenty-Three. Adding the main elements Purusha and Prakriti, they count up to twenty-five.

The subject Sankhya derives its name from the use of numbers,

(Sankhyas), to explain the concept. There are differences between Sankhite scholars regarding the number of these attributes, but it does not matter. The primary thing one should understand is the duality of the reality, Purusha and Prakriti, and how these interact. Purusha, the pure consciousness, attracts Prakriti, the matter, to itself, just like a magnet attracts iron particles, and the creative process commences. This interaction gives rise to Buddhi, the spiritual awareness, and Ahamkara, the ego, which causes ignorance.

There are three Gunas, namely Tamas, Rajas and Sattva, and each Guna represents a set of characteristic traits.

Tamas stands for darkness, ignorance, and inertia or indifference.

Rajas stand for passion, emotion, energy, and expansiveness.

Sattva denotes goodness, enlightenment, and knowledge.

I need not explain what these are, and we all have this in plenty if we introspect our nature sincerely. The point to note is that Sadhakas shall strive to improve their Sattva Guna component and reduce the other two Gunas substantially.

One of the inmates asked. 'How does the liberation come?'

'Only when the Purusha within recognises that it is different from Prakriti and wishes to remove itself from its confines can the being attain Moksha or liberation.'

'How does the Purusha within recognise that it is different from Prakriti?' Another inmate asked.

'I already told you about the three Gunas and the need for Sadhakas to practice improving Sattva guna and reducing the other two gunas. Once Sattva Guna improves beyond a point, and the Sadhaka continues to practice, the realisation that the soul is different from the body occurs.'

'But how is meditation useful in increasing Sattva Guna?'

'The system of Yoga is complementary to a Sadhaka. There is no wisdom like Sankhya and no power like Yoga. Meditation (Dhyana) itself will not improve Sattva Guna, but Yama and Niyama, the steps preceding meditation, will be helpful. You all know the eight limbs of Yoga are Yama, Niyama, Asana, Pranayama, Pratyahara, Dharana, Dhyana, and Samadhi. Following this laid down path, Sadhaka's mind and body will be more attuned to receive and assimilate spiritual knowledge.'

Another inmate asked. 'How long may it take to obtain Moksha ?'

'Depends on the person and the devotion with which he commits to the goal. There is no surety that every Sadhaka will attain it in this birth itself. But that pursuit is the only way to live and die. Acquiring Jnana and getting rid of ignorance is a continuous process of evolving and moving forward towards the goal. No other path without realising this through Jnana is genuine.'

'Many elders follow the methods prescribed in scriptures, traditionally handed over, such as the rituals, homa, yaga and such. Is it not incumbent on people to follow the karmas prescribed for their Varna?'

'It is a good question, and in fact, Sankhya does not proscribe Karmas, but it is of secondary importance. I believe that these Karmas are meant to keep Grihasts (Householders) on a righteous path and discipline them so that they would acquire Satvik qualities once they take up Vanaprastha; these Karmas are not at all relevant if they fail to create and improve the Sattva guna of Jiva. Even suffering the body by doing righteous tapasya does not yield any result on its own. The prayers and yagas that people do to fulfil their worldly desires will not take them near to salvation.

Becoming Satvik, more Satvik, and much more Satvik is the only way.'

The inmates didn't ask further questions, and the class was dismissed.

Asareer, who was keenly watching, still had some questions left. He asked Master in a private conversation, 'How about Brahman here?'

Master said, 'It is the beauty of the system. The concept of Brahman is not relevant here. Everything evolves out of fusion between Purusha and Prakriti, without a need for interference by Brahman. There is no need for Brahman in Sankhya philosophy.'

Asareer hesitated, but it was his last chance to learn about Master's mind. He asked, 'How about Srikrishna? Was he not the avatar of God? If everybody has to obtain salvation by following the path of Jnana, why do we require Krishna?'

Master knew Asareer's devotion to Krishna. It was a sensitive question. He did not want to offend Asareer, but he had to reveal the truth, as he believed.

'Krishna was a highly evolved soul. He had shunned the Rajasa and Tamasa qualities since the beginning and highly developed his Sattva Guna. Yoga came to him naturally. Such of those are rarely born, and people see God in them. One may emulate his methods and follow in the path of Jnana. However, merely praying to Krishna and expecting Krishna to give salvation just does not happen. At best, it may help Sadhakas stick to a routine and have peace of mind, provided he develops Sattva Guna and subjugates the six deadly vices. Devotion without knowledge does not help.'

Asareer did not argue. He joined Master and others in meditation. He spent quite a few days in the ashram following their routine and spent time in the evenings with Master to speak to him personally and share his thoughts. He took part in the meditation by the inmates and listened to the discourse of Master and other experts on more advanced topics of Sankhya every day. He understood the teachings of Sankhya much more clearly now, but the non-significance of God in the whole process did not appeal to him.

After spending a few more days there, he decided to pursue his journey to the other desired destinations and took leave of Master. He touched Master's feet to take his blessings. Master had fondly embraced him and muttered his good luck wishes. Both of them knew they were not going to see each other again.

Chapter 28

Asareer Meets Sanjaya

Sanjaya's Ashram

Asareer had no difficulty in finding Sanjaya's ashram in Badarika, where he took shelter. These ashrams never denied hosting the guests who visited them on the way for as many days as they wished.

Asareer introduced himself to Sanjaya, and Sanjaya liked him at first glance, spotting in Asareer a sincere enquirer of spiritual truths. Asareer had spent a few days in the ashram, availing the opportunity to spend time with Sanjaya. Asareer had many conversations with Sanjaya and was able to quench his inquisitiveness.

Sanjaya explained how he had come to the Himalayas and set up the ashram. When the forest fire caught Dhritarashtra, Gandhari, and Kunti, Sanjaya was with Dhritarashtra and tried to rescue him. However, Dhritarashtra persuaded Sanjaya to leave them, stating that the rescue efforts would not be successful. He further informed Sanjaya that he wanted to be consumed by fire and breathe his last, and no effort be made to save him. Sanjaya understood his perspective and advised Dhritarashtra to keep his body in a Yoga stance and bear the inevitable. Dhritarashtra did accordingly and breathed his last.

Sanjaya had spent some time on the banks of the Ganga, where he met Narada and informed him of the fate of Dhritarashtra, Gandhari, and Kunti. Later, he reached the Himalayas and set up his ashram. Mostly, he spends his time in meditation. Asareer requested Sanjaya to explain the spiritual knowledge that transpired between Krishna and Arjuna in the field of Kurukshetra, which is being cited by various rishis as the Bhagavad Gita. Sanjaya, having heard Krishna deliver it to Arjuna, was the best person to understand the context and the purpose. As Sanjaya agreed to do so, many inmates, too, joined to hear and get benefitted.

Sanjaya recalled the text for a few minutes and delivered the salient portions of the text, with explanations wherever he thought necessary. Asareer had experienced great joy in hearing the entire text as well as the commentary given by Sanjaya and wished his Master was also there with him to share the experience.

One of the inmates asked, 'So, are we to understand that Lord Krishna had told Karma was not to be ignored, but one has to do the duties incumbent on him?'

'Yes, Karma Yoga can not be undermined, while Krishna had explained other methods like Sankhya, Yoga and the path of devotion. Mind you, the very purpose Krishna initiated his message was to dispel Arjuna's ignorance and make him see the broader purpose of his duty. The other philosophical truths Srikrishna revealed were to answer Arjuna's doubts and clear his confusion.

However, the karmas done with a desire to get something as a reward are called Kamya karmas, and the people who indulge in such karmas will never be peaceful. What Krishna advocated was 'Nishkama Karma.' The prescribed duties need to be performed without expecting a return. We should not perform 'karma' in anticipation of reward, nor stop performing what is to be performed for the fear of not getting a reward. We must perform and leave the results in the hands of God. In fact, it was this clarification that propelled Arjuna to realise that his duty was to fight the opposition even though they were kith and kin.'

'Is it true that Krishna declared that he was the only God and one shall shun all dharmas and come under his rescue?'

'Of course, yes, it was a great piece of advice. There was no ambiguity.

Krishna could say that because he was God. However, what Krishna implied when he said "I" was not his then-present physical form of Krishna. Nor the Vishnu, whose avatar he was believed to be. That "I" is the supreme Brahman from which the entire creation happened. However, there was nothing wrong, even if one understood that it was Krishna himself in his physical form, representing the whole universe, which he really is. God is by definition formless, and Sadhakas can worship any image they can identify with God.'

Sanjaya continued. 'Krishna did not even say praying to other forms of God is wrong. What he said was that all prayers offered to any God would ultimately reach him. Krishna is nothing but the universe personified. He is present everywhere. But why does one need to go to other gods when Krishna is there? Why do you need to dig a well if you reside on the banks of a perennial river?'

'Why did Lord Krishna suggest various methods instead of only one method to be followed by all?'

'All men are not of the same nature and can not follow the same path. One should choose a path most agreeable to his nature. One should not leave the path of Karma and take Sanyas ashram before the time for that ripens, as he may still be bound by the desires as well as duties of Grihasta ashram. He should keep performing the prescribed karmas, but slowly, he should stop expecting results to be gained from such Karma. That is how he would put himself on the path of Nishkama karma. From there, he can turn to Jnanayoga and attain salvation at this very birth by cultivating Sattva Guna and controlling Tamas and Rajas gunas. Such an emancipation requires escape from the subjugation of six vices- Kama(Desire), Krodha(Anger), Lobha(Avarice), Moha(Delusion), Mada(Insolence), and Matsarya(Envy). Through the continuous practice of shedding these vices only, Sattva Guna can be improved, which is necessary whether a Sadhaka continues on the path of Jnana or embraces the path of Bhakti.'

'Can one say man does not need to follow the prescribed rituals of Vedas if he follows the path of Jnana?'

'Krishna suggested no denial of Vedas. What he said was that the ignorant praise many rites and rituals that lead to pleasure and wealth. Attaining heaven should not be one's objective in performing rituals. However, he also said sacrifices, austerities, and donations are not to be relinquished, as such actions would purify the performer. Thus, one should be aware of the purpose of one's actions. You should not go on saying that these rituals are not necessary. One should not disturb or despise the condition of the ignorant as it may spoil him both ways and make him "Ubhaya Brashta." Just observe Krishna. He regularly meditated and prayed. He respected Brahmins and sages. Was it necessary for him? He did it because people would emulate him, and his not offering prayers will render others reluctant to worship.'

'Very well said! Which is the best Dharma to be followed as there are different ways to worship?' another questioned.

'Yudhishthira asked Bhishma the same question when the latter was on his bed of arrows but still imparted knowledge to Yudhishthira. Whichever Dharma you may follow, it ultimately leads to the one God. Bhishma advised Yudhishthira not to be confused among various dharmas but to be devoted to Lord Vishnu. Krishna himself told Arjuna to leave all doubts and find shelter in him. Following Dharma is the ultimate goal and the only way also.'

The questions continued, and Sanjaya answered them duly, explaining Gita's purpose.

One of the inmates had raised a question. 'Can you please enlighten us precisely on how to distinguish between Dharma and adharma, how to follow the path of Dharma, and how to reach the goal of Dharma?'

Sanjaya replied to the question in detail and explained what he meant by Dharma. 'You all know the society is divided into four varnas, and there are four ashramas a man has to pass. The dharmas for each Varna and ashrama were clearly defined and specified. There are common dharmas for all varnas. Let me mention some of the fundamental principles of Dharma. Not having anger, being truthful, being faithful to your spouse, cleanliness, sharing, and not being crooked are some of them. Similarly, Manu had told many dharmas such as courage, perseverance, control over sense organs, not stealing others' money, knowledge, truthfulness, shunning anger, the pursuit of studies and so on. In addition, there are dharmas based on Varna. Dharmas for Kings are distinct, which are necessary to keep all other dharmas in balance. A king should act like a pregnant lady in that she shuns to consume as per her liking, being mindful of the possible adverse effects on the child in her womb. Similarly, a King shall do what is useful to his people and not what pleases him. Ashram dharmas are prescribed only for Brahmins. However, the people of other varnas can also undertake these ashrams if they so desire, provided they qualify themselves by following the dharmas prescribed above. Some karmas were proscribed because they were undesirable. A clear path of life was prescribed for all varnas. Brahmins are responsible for guiding all others on the righteous path and making them perform their duties. All varnas emanated from Brahman only, and this shall not be forgotten. The King shall ensure that these dharmas are maintained, crime is punished, and the common men are protected. Giving danas to the desired and needy, treating the guest as equal to God, and respecting the elders and scholars are dharmas to be followed. All these dharmas are prescribed to maintain the order in society and allow the people of all varnas to better their lots.'

Asareer asked, 'How could Krishna tell that Brahman was supreme if he advocated Sankhya philosophy as well since it was irrelevant in the context of Sankhya philosophy? Is it not contradictory?'

'Good question. The Sankhya Yoga enunciated by Krishna is not the same as the Sankhya philosophy in circulation attributed to sage Kapila. As per wisdom passed over generations, it was God himself who was born as sage Kapila and preached Sankhya Yoga. Kapila was known as an amsha-avatar of Vishnu.

However, the philosophy got modified under various other sages over time, but it still carried the name of Sage Kapila. Here, Krishna clarified that the two main basic phenomena under Sankhya philosophy," Prakriti" and "Purusha", did not exist by themselves alone, but Brahman created them. One should not get confused that Krishna had endorsed Sankhya in the present corrupted form, where there is no place for Brahman, but realise that he had given a new meaning to the whole philosophy, which is, in fact, its original intent.'

The discourse was complete, and the inmates commenced meditation, duly joined by Asareer. After spending some more days, Asareer took leave of Sanjaya and proceeded deep into Badarika Vana.

Chapter 29

Srikrishna's Last Sermon

Uddhava's Ashram

Uddhava set up his ashram deep in the forest of Badarika to meditate on Krishna, and he engaged himself in that activity most of the time. He had many inmates, too, to whom he preached Krishna's philosophy. Asareer had known Uddhava a long time ago when both were young in Naimisha, but he was not sure whether Uddhava would even remember him after all these years. However, Uddhava did not take much time to recognise him. He welcomed Asareer to stay with him as long as he wished. Asareer had become an inmate, and the routine suited him very well. It is most similar to what he had adopted in his ashram in Naimisha. He felt that he benefited from various discourses Uddhava was giving to his inmates.

Uddhava informed Asareer one day how painful it was for him to part with Srikrishna's company, with whom he had spent many years in close association. When Krishna was preparing everybody to go to Prabhasa, Uddhava guessed that Srikrishna was preparing for the materialising of Sages' curses and clearing his way to leave his mortal body.

'He confirmed that my hunch was correct and his exit was imminent. I could not control my emotions on his confirmation, and tears flowed down my face. I beseeched him to take me along with him, but he said I should live on the earth for some more years. He advised me to dissociate myself from the bonds of my relatives and friends and leave Dwaraka at once and go to Badarika and do tapasya,' said Uddhava, reflecting on the past.

'What was his final message to you, if any?' asked Asareer.

'It was a lengthy discussion, some of which you had already heard in my discourses in the past few days. Krishna cleared me of all my doubts and set me on this path. He told me that within seven days after he left the earth, Kaliyuga would enter and cautioned me to lead a life without getting trapped in the Kamya karmas.'

'Did he tell you how this Kaliyuga would be different from Dwapara Yuga?'

'Certainly! He had indicated to me what all the sages were foretelling about the Kaliyuga. Sages have been forewarning about the deteriorating characteristics of Dharma in Kaliyuga. Being in the last phase of Dwapara Yuga for most of our life, where the characters of Kali Yuga had already set in, it is not difficult for us to realise how things are going to take shape. I would mention a few forebodings; in the Kaliyuga, the system of Varna would be breached. Kshatriya would lose their right to rule, and Brahmins would abandon the duties cast on them. Varna and Ashrama laws, which were sacrosanct in earlier yugas, would lose relevance. The world will be prevailed by untruth and deceit. Charity gets a back seat. The rich will be respected even if they earn money by improper means. The strong will harass the weak. Poor will not get justice. Life spans will be considerably reduced, and people will not be as strong as they are now. The power to rule will be obtained by the strongest of the brutes. The business will divorce ethics. Feeding the family itself becomes the topmost priority.

People with half knowledge will masquerade as pundits and preach things which they, themselves, do not believe. Brahmins and sanyasis exhibit external attire to claim their status without being pure in hearts. People do pious activities only to get fame. More and more people stop believing in God.'

'Does it continue like that forever, a total deterioration in all aspects?'

'Of course not. At the fag end of Kaliyuga, Vishnu would take birth as Kalki and restore order and bring about the Kritayuga once again. Both Surya Vamsha King Sage Maru and Chandra Vamsha King Sage Devapi would come to rule and usher in the new order. Till that time, the people would suffer the effects of Kali invariably because of the domination of Rajasa and Tamasa qualities.'

One of the inmates asked, 'It is being said that in Kaliyuga, Dharma will run on only one leg. What does it mean? Can this be explained?'

Uddhava explained. 'It is not like Dharma would have only one leg in Kaliyuga and four legs in Krita Yuga. It was only a thumb rule to remember. Dharma's four legs are Satyam (Truthfulness), Daya (Compassion), Tapasya(Meditation), and Dana(Charity). These will gradually come down in each Yuga by a fourth portion. Thus, these four qualities, which would be fully present in Treta yuga, which is also called Satya Yuga because of that reason, will be almost one-fourth in Kaliyuga. So, in general parlance, four one-fourths being one, people say Dharma runs on one leg in Kaliyuga. These four qualities of Dharma will be replaced with four other characteristics - untruth, violence, dissatisfaction, and dispute. The number of legs remains to be four, but the quality of legs becomes very low in Kaliyuga.'

One of the inmates asked, 'Is there any way a man can still keep himself away from the ill effects of Kaliyuga and liberate himself.'

Uddhava answered, 'The irony is that it is easier to get liberation in Kaliyuga than in other Yugas. However, people do not realise this, are influenced by Maya, and run after material comforts. In Krita Yuga, a hard tapasya was needed; in Treta Yuga, it was yajnas and yagas, and in Dwapara Yuga, it was regular archana, Yoga, dhyana and dana were the ways to liberation. What was to be achieved by mastering Vedas and shastras, performing Yagas and Yajnas, visiting holy Kshetras and tirthas, performing yagas and danas in earlier yugas is obtainable in Kaliyuga by singing God's praise and immersing in his stories and enjoying them.

Bhakti marg is the only way to salvation in Kaliyuga. Unfortunately, most people won't realise its significance. The influence of Charvaka aided by the onset of Kaliyuga is going to speed up the process of deterioration of Dharma in Kaliyuga.'

Asareer felt a bit uneasy hearing the last sentence as Uddhava looked at him, smiling. Uddhava added, looking at Asareer, 'There is no blaming of Charvaka. He was necessary in Kaliyuga just like Duryodhana was a Kalipurusha meant to usher in Kaliyuga. These persons are products of destiny and were needed to act as catalysts for Kaliyuga.'

The discourse ended for that day.

In another evening discourse, Uddhava delivered some more insights into his conversation with Srikrishna in his final meeting. 'While Srikrishna sent me to Badarika, advising me to leave all relationships, realising that they are all perishable things, he also asked me to look for Him in every object and know that the whole universe is Him. Then I asked him to advise me how I, being a prisoner of "Maya," might be able to do that.

Uddhava took a break and continued. 'This is what Srikrishna had told me in response. I may not be able to tell you the entire conversation word for word, but I will summarise the vital essence. Now, hear the words of Srikrishna, the Lord of the universe.'

Uddhava spoke as if he were Krishna, and his face became radiant as each word was spoken. The tone was confident.

"Uddhava! Every man has to follow the dharmas of Varna and ashrama and shun away the worries dictated by physical desires. One should follow Yama and Niyama and follow the destined karmas. However, Karmas, done with a desire, Kamya karmas, will only lead to misery. Only Nishkama Karma needs to be done. People who are slaves to Rajas and Tamas Gunas will not reach me, and devotees with Sattva Gunas will only reach me. Such people invariably possess the following qualities. Please note the essential traits of a satpurush are compassion for the entire creation in the world, nonviolence, equanimity in

good and bad phases of life, truthfulness, absence of hatred and jealousy, lack of desires, being kind and friendly to all, and control of sense organs. One should perform the duties enjoined on oneself to the best of one's abilities without expecting any returns in exchange. Most important is keeping the company of good people who have the above qualities, and not to fall into bad company. By constantly praying to me and singing my songs, hearing my stories, and serving in temples, one can slowly develop in the path of Bhakti. It is challenging for people to attain true Bhakti, but those who take this path can achieve it by practice. By being close to the people who have already reached a higher status, one will be keeping away from wasteful pursuits and practices."

'At this stage, I asked him about the other paths like Jnana and Karma, which he explained in detail. I asked him to clarify whether the correct number of tattvas is 7,9,25, or 28 in view of the various versions prevailing. Hear what he said in his own words.'

"Uddhava! All the numbers you quoted are correct, as stated by different sages. Some people count ten indriyas and add 'manas"; they reckon it as 11. All the ten organs, five matras, five elements," manas"," buddhi"," chitta", and "ahamkara" put together, there exist, in all, 24 tatvas. Some add Jlva and Eswara and count 26. Some add "kala" (Time) and count as 27. Those who treat Jiva and Eswara as one reduce it to 25. I added Purusha, Prakriti, Mahat and Aham to the 24 and reckoned it as 28. These differences arose due to different logic adopted by deep-thinking Sankhites. The number is not that important. Whatever the arguments, one has to firmly believe that the body and the Jivatma residing in it are different. Realising this is liberation. Death is only to the body but not to the jiva dwelling in it."

Uddhava continued after a pause, 'He further clarified the need for three different ways to liberation suggested. Men are made of Satvik, Rajas and Tamas gunas, and everyone has different proportions of these gunas; hence, every path is not suitable for anybody. Therefore, one has to choose the path that is most suitable for one. People who are doing Karma for material benefit and heaven can adopt Karma marga. But gradually, the sadhaka may shift to nishkama karma. For those who are not interested in material life and realise that the world is temporary, Jnana Marga is suitable. The followers of karma yoga, after some time, either take up Jnana Yoga or Bhakti Yoga, which appealed to them.'

As the audience sat in rapt attention, as if Krishna himself was speaking to them, Uddhava concluded the session with the following message.

Let me tell you why I prefer Bhakti over other paths. If you observe keenly, the paths of devotion and Jnana are not significantly different. In both ways, a Sadhaka needs to increase the proportion of Sattva guna and control the vices. Knowledge, when finally matured, realises God and merges into Bhakti, whereas a devotee on the path of Bhakti sees God everywhere and in everything. The path of Bhakti is most accessible for everyone and is most suitable for Kaliyuga.'

As the meeting ended, the inmates retired to evening prayers filled with wonderment, happily joined by Asareer.

Asareer spent a few more days wholly immersed in understanding Uddhava Geeta. Uddhava patiently explained to Asareer the intricacies of Kriya Yoga, Hamsa Gita, Bikshu Gita, and various other aspects he gleaned from Krishna and also from his profound knowledge in multiple sessions, each session, adding immense joy to Asareer and clarifying his vague doubts.

He realised that his Master's philosophical quest for truth was reconciled so beautifully with the concept of God by Krishna by placing Eswara above Purusha and Prakriti, the two fundamental elements recognised by Sankhya. In a way, it looked like the quest for knowledge was also a quest for God. Asareer was fully convinced that Bhakti, the path of devotion, was the authentic way to the liberation of the soul within this life. There may be other paths, but for him, the path of Bhakti was most appealing.

Asareer took leave of Uddhava and felt that his purpose in visiting Badarika was fulfilled. He began his return journey alone; the lack of companions did not bother Asareer. He was not even sure where he wanted to go. He kept on walking, thinking, ruminating on what he heard, learnt, internalised, and realised in the past few months during his stay in Badarika. His mind was full of the truths he had absorbed.

He personally believed Krishna to be God, but even if people think that Krishna was only an evolved soul, as his Master chose to classify him, it didn't matter to him. Krishna, for future generations, could just be a symbol like the many that already exist, like Shiva, Rama, Shakti and the like. One may pray to any image; the ultimate prayer will reach God. What is essential is not just to believe that someone is God, though it helps, but to realise the distinction between the physical body and the indwelling Jiva, the indestructible spark of God.

The best way to keep oneself away from worldly attraction is to feel the presence of Srikrishna everywhere in the universe, become a devotee and see Him in every being. Asareer wanted to tell everybody and anybody who would listen.

He was not sure whether he would ever reach Naimisha and meet his inmates, but it didn't bother him. He was cleared of all his doubts, and his mind was filled with Krishna. He knew his days were numbered, and this awareness exhilarated him instead of causing dread. He felt liberated.

His body may fall somewhere in the Himalayas itself, or it may travel up to the plains. He might step into his Alma Mater for one last time and address all his inmates. Or, he might breathe his last in the meantime. It did not matter to him any more.

He was not that body, *the sareer*. He was *asareer*, the Jiva, which is one of Krishna's images. He will be one with Krishna sooner, with a smile gracing his lips.

Asareer moved and moved.

Chapter 30

Epilogue

Naimisha, Shamyaprasa

Vedavyasa continued to work on the epic "Jaya Samhita" and made it much broader to suit detailed narration by weaving intricate Upakhyanas and philosophical insights from Vedas and Upanishads. From the vast body of shlokas thus compiled, he culled out about one lakh shlokas to be recited on the Earth. Vedavyasa had planned to present a much larger version to Sage Narada and Sage Devala for their propagation elsewhere.

Vyshampayana, who Vedavyasa advised to disseminate this new work of one lakh shlokas instead of "Jaya Samhita," was surprised to find the sheer volume of the expanded version. It contained eighteen parts, called "parvas." The final version was the most voluminous single work by Vedavyasa and surpassed any existing Purana in size. It was longer than the two large Puranas: Padma Purana, which had 55,000 shlokas, and Skanda Purana, which had 81,100 shlokas. Vaishampayana sought guidance on its recitation.

'Begin,' Vedavyasa advised, 'by capturing the attention of the audience with a concise summary of one hundred and fifty verses, which I provided in the beginning, then unfold the complete narrative, depending on who wants to listen. No need to recite the whole work in one go, and it can be spread over a number of days. Tailor your recitation to the audience's inquisitiveness and needs. You may answer whatever questions the inquisitive listeners pose to you midway through the narration, and you will find those answers in the text itself. I would leave it to your best judgement what exactly you would like to narrate without disturbing the main storyline.'

Vaishampayana understood and began imparting this work to his disciples, who would carry the epic's legacy forward.

This work became famously known as "Bharata Samhita" or more commonly "Bharata" because it contained the story of Bharatavamshi kings and began to be respectfully called "Maha Bharata" in scholarly circles because of its sheer volume and its intrinsic merit.

Later, Vedavyasa also recited the story of Krishna's clan to act as a supplement to the magnificent Mahabharata, and he called it "Harivamsha." This work was later hailed as "Khil Parva" as if it was a part of Mahabharata. These epics, being 'itihasas', could be further extended in time to capture the subsequent history.

As Kaliyuga, the age of discord and decay, had already dawned, its effects were becoming increasingly evident. Vedavyasa watched with growing concern as people struggled to grasp the path of Dharma, the cornerstone of a harmonious life. He lamented people's pursuit of Artha and Kama, blind to Dharma's vital role. He lamented, reflecting on the way people were behaving, without realising the importance of Dharma in pursuing Ardha and Kama.

He expected that his Mahabharata would act as a moral document, a deterrent to adharma, and a guide to the conduct of future kings and people in general. However, he was distraught that the message of Dharma he so sincerely upheld in Mahabharata was not being received well by the people who were still defending and criticising various kings who took part in the war and died, instead of grasping the dharmic essence he had interwoven in the epic. He was pained to observe the deteriorating quality of Dharma despite knowing that Dharma would come down by one more notch in Kaliyuga. Vyasa's mind continued to be restless. He openly lamented,

"I am crying aloud with both my hands raised. Why doesn't anybody hear my word? Guided by Dharma alone, one shall attain Artha and Kama beneficially. Why don't you follow Dharma?"

"Why don't you understand that one should not leave the path of Dharma because of desire, fear, avarice or even for self-protection? Dharma is permanent. Pleasure and pain are temporary. Jiva is permanent, but the bonds to life are impermanent."

When Vedavyasa was in such a state of mind, his ashram was visited by sage Narada. Sensing Vedavyasa's sorrow, Narada explained the reason for Vyasa's restlessness.

He addressed Vedavyasa thus, 'You have crafted a masterpiece, the Mahabharata, celebrating Dharma's triumph. It is being hailed as the Fifth Veda in the circle of sages. Sages hailed it to the extent of saying that whatever is there to learn is available in Mahabharata, and whatever is not there in Mahabharata does not exist anywhere,' he paused, ' but how about your portrayal of Krishna in the epic? His divine nature was understated, as the glorious and miraculous acts of his past were mentioned only through indirect references. Those divine acts were merely alluded to but not described in detail.

Your Mahabharata is a glorious story of your grandsons, Pandavas and Kauravas, and Srikrishna plays a significant role in the victory of Pandavas, upholding Dharma. Srkrishna comes out as a great warrior and a great philosopher because he taught the Gita to Arjuna. Still, his Godhood, despite the Vishwaroopa, remains ambiguous. While many praise him and treat him as God, some question his divinity. Your epic lacks an unequivocal declaration of Krishna's Godhood.

Do you remember what you told Arjuna when he paid his last visit to you? Didn't you say to him that Krishna's story will be sung in all corners of the earth forever? Deep within you, you are aware you haven't presented that whole story of Krishna to be sung with devotional fervour. Not even in Harivamsha, and you feel guilty about it. This feeling of guilt is the source of your unease.'

Wisdom dawned on Vedavyasa as he realised the truth in Sage Narada's judgement. He understood the root cause of his restlessness. He looked forward to the solution from the divine sage.

Narada continued. 'Your concern for Dharma is valid, but in the Kali Yuga, devotion is the best path to Dharma. Artha and Kama should be rooted in Dharma, no doubt, but devotion is needed to sustain Dharma. Works devoid of devotional fervour bring no true bliss. Your epic focused on Dharma, neglecting Bhakti.

I advise you to create a work extolling Krishna's divinity from birth till he departs. Illuminate his divine deeds, impossible for mortals. Visualise what Krishna did in Brindavan and the miraculous activities he performed, many unobserved by the people around and ununderstood but which were watched by celestials in wonderment. By glorifying Krishna's deeds, your sorrow will be replaced with pure joy. Such a work would calm all the turbulences of your mind. Mark my words, your blissful satisfaction on completion of such work will far outweigh the sense of fulfilment that you felt on any of your previous works, whether it was the classification of Vedas, working on Brahma Sutras, Upanishads, Ashtadasa Puranas, Hari Vamsha or the great epic Mahabharata. Once you unload your heart by praising the Lord's deeds and extolling the merits of Bhakti, your misery will turn into unblemished joy.'

Vedavyasa realised the wisdom of sage Narada's words and the value of his direction and thanked him for the timely advice. Sage Narada blessed Vedavyasa and went on his way, having said what he intended to.

Vedavyasa sat in meditation to contemplate the story of Srikrishna from the beginning. He would write it in such a way that it would be "God's own story" and would leave no one in doubt about Krishna's Godhood, and people who hear the story would dance with joy.

His son Suka, a sage and a learned disciple, saw his father in deep meditation, visualising the story of Krishna, which would be a part of Bhagavata Purana. He knew intuitively that the new creation would be a great work of devotion, and he would be the one to disseminate it to the world.

The dense forest of Naimisha witnessed Vedavyasa in deep meditation. The stage was set for the creation of another great work, and Naimisha prided herself on it. "Men may come, and Men may go, but I live on forever," Naimisha seemed to whisper. Yugas may come and pass, but Naimisha would provide the links with the immortal past through the great records of history that Vyasa and his disciples created. A history so resplendent with unbelievable action that it ranks to be classified as mythology.

Naimisha was vibrant. Vedavyasa was immersed in deep meditation. Gomati murmured in anticipation, expecting to hear the new song of God—a song for all generations, which would not stop being listened to by all future generations.

Another epic work, God's Own Story, was in the making.

What Happened Afterwards?

Readers might be interested to know what happened thereafter to Parikshit and the Chandravamsha dynasty. While reading the original Mahabharata is the best solution, let me give you a brief flavour of what you will find.

In fact, the whole Mahabharata story was told as a flashback. After Pandavas left on Mahaprasthana, Parikshit ruled Hastinapur, guided and helped by Kripacharya and Yuyutsu, and Indraprastha was ruled by Vajranabha. Watched by Subhadra, the respectful mother figure, both kingdoms flourished.

Vedavyasa completes Srimadbhagavatam, extolling the Godhood of Srikrishna, as advised by Sage Narada.

As fate would have it, Parikshit once goes hunting in the forest and loses track of a deer, which leads him to Rishi Shamika's ashram, where he finds the sage meditating. An exhausted and thirsty Parikshit feels insulted when the sage doesn't respond to his greetings. In a fit of frustrated anger, Parikshit picks up a dead snake and throws it around the sage's neck. When Shringi, his son, returns and finds out, he curses Parikshit to be bitten by Takshaka in seven days. Takshaka, the father of Ashwasena, who Arjuna killed in the Kurukshetra war, takes it upon himself to deliver that curse.

While Parikshit, after his return, broods over his uncharacteristic indiscretion committed to a venerable sage, the sage himself disapproves of the curse of his son on a king as just as Parikshit. Though the curse can not be reversed, the sage alerts Parikshit about the curse.

Parikshit knows that his death is imminent and resigns to his fate. He places himself in a palace. That is when Sage Suka enters and, at the request of Parikshit, recites Srimadbhagavatam, which gives Parikshit immense joy and prepares him to face the eventuality. Detached from all bonds and worries after hearing Srimadbhagavatam, Parikshit was ready to meet Takshaka.

On the seventh day, when the time set for the curse almost neared, Takshaka sneaks his way to emerge in the form of a tiny insect from a fruit bitten by Parikshit. Assuming his ferocious form, Takshaka delivers his venomous bite, that burns the entire building itself.

Parikshit could have been saved by one Sage Kashyapa, who had the antidote to Takshaka's venom, but Takshaka lures him away with enormous gold. That was an interesting side story.

Janamejaya, his son, yet a child, becomes a king, and when he knows later how his father met his death, he decides to punish the whole Naga race. For that, he performs a "Sarpa Yaga," a sacrificial ritual involving the burning of serpents. Many serpents come flying and fall into the fire. However, before Takshaka's turn came, Janamejaya was made to stop the ritual by sage Astika, the son of Jaratkaru, who was born for this very purpose. The story of Jaratkaru and Astika is another fascinating tale.

The Sarpa Yaga was destined on account of a curse by Kadruva, the mother of serpents, who had cursed the Nagas to be burnt in a sacrificial fire. All the happenings were as per Brahma's script. This mindboggling revelation connects the happenings of Dwapara Yuga and Kaliyuga to that of Krita Yuga and shows the intricate role of destiny in human life.

During this, Sarpa Yaga, sage Vyshampayana, a disciple of Vedavyasa, arrives and recites the story of Mahabharata to Janamejaya, clearing his doubts. Suta, son of Romaharshana, another disciple of Vedavyasa, who hears this narration retells this story to Saunaka and his disciples in Naimisharanya, after which it becomes popular all over.

The story of Mahabharata, whether one may call it history, mythology, Itihasa or Purana, has become a tremendous literary source that continues to inspire generations. Its immense, timeless charm continues to attract new readerships generation after generation.

Story Prior to The End Game

This book is the third part of the series, which may be called the Naimisha Trilogy. However, since it is only a continuous story, divided into three parts because of its sheer size, it can even be categorised as a Sri Krishna Triple Decker. This is the third and final deck.

Readers who knew Mahabharata and Srimadbhagavatam would indeed find this third part easy to follow, even if they haven't read the first two. However, readers may note that the characters Animish and Asareer are fictional, and they represent two different and opposite thought processes and beliefs. Readers can learn about them through their interactions.

In the first book, Krishna was born in the captivity of his uncle Kamsa but escapes to grow up in the care of Yashoda and Nandagopa along with Balarama, overcoming all the attempts on his life by destroying the demons sent by his uncle, Kamsa. Finally, he fulfills Akash Vani's prophecy and kills Kams, and unites with his biological parents, Vasudeva and Devaki. However, he still has a bigger problem on hand: dealing with Jarasandha, Kamsa's father-in-law.

Parallelly, Pandavas and Kauravas complete their education and exhibit their prowess in a public graduation ceremony, where Karna presents himself and challenges Arjuna. Though the duel does not materialise, the polarisation becomes complete, with Karna being befriended by Duryodhana.

Animish, who attends the ceremony along with Asareer, thinks that things are going to be terrible between the cousins and the situation is like a game of chess where opening moves are played and a long tussle is awaited. This book is, "The Beginning," the opening phase of a Chess game.

In the second book, Krishna and Balarama keep on defeating Jarasandha's regularly mounted attacks on Mathura and, in a strategic move, shift their capital to a safer place, Dwaraka. There, they marry and settle in Dwaraka, avoiding the menace of Jarasandha. Krishna unites with Pandavas and gets Jarasandha killed through Bhima. By the end of the second book, Krishna gets rid of many of his enemies and begins to be hailed as Vishnu's incarnation.

Yudhishthira becomes a crown prince, but Pandavas face conspiratorial attempts on their lives. They escape to live incognito, faking death in a fire accident. They resurface after the five brothers marry Draupadi and forge ties with the powerful Panchala. Hastinapur gets bifurcated, Pandavas build Indraprastha, perform Rajasuya, and Yudhishthira becomes an emperor. Thereafter, Yudhishthira loses to Shakuni twice in a dice game, and Pandavas undergo exile of thirteen years, including one year of incognito exile. Pandavas, by the end of the second book, complete their Ajnatavasa and get ready to face Kauravas in a war if their kingdom is not returned. This second book is "The Middle Game-Moves& Countermoves," the mid phase of a Chess game.

Now read the third and the last book, "The End Game- Check, Check & Mate," where all the characters meet their trysts with destiny. Do not miss reading the first two books to enjoy the fictional narrative of Animish and Asareer and how these characters evolve over the three books.

Author's Note

While the first book, '*The Beginning*' of this series, titled *Naimisha-God's Own Story*, gave me the joy of becoming a published author, the third and final book, '*The End Game*', fills me with immense satisfaction that the project is now complete.

What began as a story written for my own enjoyment turned into a much larger endeavour when the temptation to publish it for circulation got the better of me. The desire to share it with a broader audience, once triggered, was both exciting and daunting. I faced the enormity of the task ahead of me on one hand and my inadequacies on the other. Nonetheless, like a lone soldier who does not back out, even when the enemy is formidable, I continued my battle with whatever weapons and skills I had. That this third and final part of this book is in your hands greatly relieves me, and I share my emotions and happiness with you.

I express my respectful gratitude to Vedavyasa, whose epics— *Srimadbhagavatam*, *Mahabharata*, and *Harivamsha*—have inspired generations and continue to cast their magic on us today. Most of my story and details, as you will observe, are based on these epics. I tried to be as near to the authentic versions as possible while narrating these events and took liberty while dealing with my fictional storyline.

As I mentioned in my previous books, I remain indebted to the countless known and unknown authors of books, various websites, and editing tools of Grammarly, which helped me in bringing out all the three volumes.

Though I said my fight was solitary, help and encouragement came on the way, primarily from my immediate family members, to whom I owe a big thanks. I also thank my relatives, friends, erstwhile colleagues, co-Quorans, and fellow authors I have met on this journey. Their encouragement, interest, and support have meant a great deal to me.

The subtitle Check, Check & Mate was suggested by my son Ravi Teja, who is an avid lover of chess. I also thank him for helping me finalise the book cover and proofread it. My thanks to my beloved wife, Maani, for her constant encouragement, so also to my son and my daughter, Jahnavi Samira, and their spouses, Bhargavi Bala and Sai Madhav, who supported me in completing the series of three volumes of this series.

I particularly thank my readers who encouraged the first two books and even took the time to share their reviews. I hope this third and final book, too, meets their expectations and generates a fresh readership.

I thank the Team Notion Press for bringing this book to life and into your hands.

Happy reading!

Thank You
M.C.R.Sesha
mcrsesha@gmail.com

About The Author

This is Sesha's third and final book of the series .This trilogy is about Krishna's story ,which is culled from both Srimadbhagavatam and Mahabharata .This trilogy is also about Pandavas and Kauravas ,as detailed in Mahabharata .Not many books attempted to combine these two connected epics that happened at the same time with matching timelines. The author has also added an interesting spin of fiction to this storyline, turning it into a unique experiment .The Naimisha Trilogy thus offers a new perspective to the known stories and makes this series an interesting read for enthusiastic readers .As the story covers a vast canvas ,it is spread over three books.

The author has explained in detail in the first book the idea and background for writing this story and has come up with the second and third books in successive years, meeting his promise to the readers and himself.

The author, a former Public sector banking executive who worked in top management, took to writing in his second innings. He is deeply interested in literature, epics in particular. He and his wife, Maani, reside in Hyderabad, indulging in literary pursuits, travelling and cherishing their shared moments with their grandchildren Shrinika, Rishika Tanvi, Rohit Karthikeya, and Samyukta, the author's ardent fans, though not necessarily of his books.